THE M. D.

THE
M.D.
A HORROR STORY

THOMAS M. DISCH

Alfred A. Knopf
NEW YORK
1991

THIS IS A BORZOI BOOK
PUBLISHED BY ALFRED A. KNOPF, INC.

Copyright © 1991 by Thomas M. Disch

ISBN 0-394-58662-X
LC 90-53564

Manufactured in the United States of America

FIRST EDITION

For Phil and Betsy Pochoda

The young murderer doesn't come from a typical American family. The average American parent doesn't need to fear being murdered.

—*Dr. Elissa P. Benedek,*
as quoted in "Children Who Kill,"
New York Times, Oct. 11, 1983

BOOK ONE

1

On the Friday before Christmas vacation Sister Mary Symphorosa informed the kindergarten class at Our Lady of Mercy School that there was no Santa Claus, that the presents you found beside the Christmas tree on Christmas morning were from your parents, and that it was pagan and impious nonsense and a sin against the First Commandment to think otherwise. She made the same announcement every year, and at least one of the children could always be counted on to have a temper tantrum or otherwise show defiance. This year it was Billy Michaels, generally such a quiet child, who threw himself on the floor and lay on his back screaming and thrashing about and generally calling attention to himself.

Sister Symphorosa looked on, fingering the large wooden crucifix that anchored her rosary beads to her full skirts. She was not particularly alarmed. She even took a professional satisfaction in the boy's hysterical behavior, as an exorcist might in having driven out a devil. She considered this annual ritual of disillusionment a duty imposed upon her as a defender of the faith. Children ought not to be brought up to believe in something they will necessarily discover to be untrue, an experience that can only blight the budding leaves of a true religious faith. The myth of Santa Claus was, as she had just explained to the children, a pagan practice, and therefore sinful, all the more because it had attached itself to a Christian holy day. She walked decisively to the back of the room, hauled the boy up by his shirt collar, and plopped him down into his seat. He let out a final yelp of protest, and she slapped his face soundly. "Enough of that."

He caught his breath and glared at her.

Before he could renew his foolishness, Sister Symphorosa turned her back on him and continued talking to the children as though nothing unusual had happened. "Now, who can tell me what the First Commandment instructs us to do?"

No hands went up. Sister Symphorosa had shifted gears too fast for them. Everything that she had told them in the last two weeks about

Moses and the Golden Calf and the Ten Commandments had vanished from their erratic memories. Hints were of no help.

"The First Commandment," Sister Symphorosa announced, in the tones of another Moses reproaching the tribes of Israel, "is 'I am the Lord thy God; thou shalt have no strange gods before thee.' And what is this Santa Claus but a strange god? He can fly all about the world in a magic sleigh with flying reindeer. He is supposed to know if you're good or bad—"

Billy Michaels produced an audible gurgling sound, as though he were being strangled—or getting ready to throw another tantrum.

"Billy Michaels, be quiet and sit still. Only *God*, who is omniscient, knows that. Only God knows the secrets we each have in our hearts. God knows that, because God knows everything, but Santa Claus can't know anything, because Santa Claus does not exist, and never did, though there was a St. Nicholas once. But he did not live at the North Pole. No one lives there, it is much too cold. The real St. Nicholas lived in a town called Myra, where he was a bishop like our own dear Bishop Fitzgerald, and his feast day is the sixth of December."

There was a long silence. Sister Symphorosa surveyed the rows and files of wide-eyed faces, searching them for signs of defiance or inattention. They all seemed satisfactorily subdued.

"St. Nicholas," she resumed in a cheerier tone, "is the patron saint of children and of storekeepers, and that must be how the legends of Santa Claus got started." She broke off as she did not want to take the children out of their depth. Enough to smash the idol; she did not need to write its history.

"When you go home from school today, children, I want you to tell your parents that you understand that there is no Santa Claus. Tell them that and then *thank* them for all the lovely presents they gave you when they were pretending to be Santa. And tell them they don't have to pretend anymore. And if you have any little brothers or sisters who believe in Santa Claus you must tell them too, because it is a sin against the First Commandment to worship gods that don't exist. Do you all understand?"

Some children nodded, and there were a few whispery *Yes, Sisters*. But Billy Michaels didn't move a muscle.

"Billy," Sister Symphorosa insisted, "do you understand?"

The boy gave no sign that he had heard her.

"Billy," she said in a tone of patient instruction such as one might use in teaching a parrot speech, "I am talking to you. I asked you a question."

Reluctantly, the boy's eyes turned toward her. There was fear in his look, but defiance still smoldered in his contumacious little heart. She felt an impulse to strike him again, but checked it. An obstinate spirit demands correction, but she must be more judicious in the administration of corporal punishment, since she had twice already been called to task by Sister Fidelis, the principal of OLM, for what the younger nun regarded as excessive severity. Sister Fidelis was too easily cowed by interfering parents. But she was the principal, and Sister Symphorosa was bound by her vow of obedience. Unless the boy offered provocation, she must deal with him tenderly.

"And you understand now, don't you, Billy, that there is no Santa Claus?"

"I saw him," Billy said.

"You saw a *picture* of him," Sister Symphorosa said.

"No, he was alive. And he looked just like he does in his pictures. He was fat and he had a red suit and a bag full of presents."

"Then you saw someone dressed up to *look* like Santa Claus. Many businesses pay money to bums they find on the streets so they will *pretend* to be Santa Claus. But they are only old bums. And that's what you saw."

"No," said Billy, "I saw him come down the chimney. He wasn't the Santa's helper at Dayton's, I've seen him too. This was the real Santa Claus."

There was a giggle from the front of the classroom. Many of the children already understood that there was no Santa. Indeed, Sister Symphorosa sometimes speculated that the deceit of Santa Claus was one that children practiced on their parents rather than the other way round, that they all understood the practical impossibility of flying reindeer and of Santa's simultaneous appearance on a global basis, but that they knew they'd get more presents if they went along with the whole charade. This was a possibility she found extremely angering.

"William," she said quite sternly, "you must not tell lies."

"I'm not lying."

Sister Symphorosa bit her lip. In the face of such obstinacy the only proper course was to administer corporal punishment. But since the boy was now behaving sedately she must restrain herself. Let Sister Fidelis solve the problem, if she could, with her liberal principles!

Sister Symphorosa wrote out a note to Sister Fidelis, folded it, and handed it to the Michaels boy. "I want you to take this note to the principal. Do you know where her office is?"

The boy nodded.

"You tell Sister Fidelis what you told me, and if she agrees that you saw Santa Claus come down the chimney, then she will give you a note to me saying that you are not a liar. But if she does not, then you will have to apologize to me and to the entire class for wasting our time with such ridiculous nonsense. And you will not be allowed back into my class without either that note or an apology. Because I cannot tolerate liars."

When he was out of the room, Sister Symphorosa, as a kind of reward to the rest of the class, told them the true story of St. Nicholas, bishop of Myra, how he'd miraculously brought back to life three rich youths whom a wicked innkeeper had murdered, dismembered, and hidden in a salting tub.

"And that," Sister Symphorosa said, rounding off the wonderful tale with a lesson, "is why St. Nicholas is the patron saint of children, and why we still pray to him to be protected from robbers and thieves. But he is *not* Santa Claus. I hope that is clear. Now, are there any questions?"

The Burdon girl raised her hand.

"Yes, Sally?"

"Sister, what is a salting tub?"

"A salting tub, Sally, is what butchers used to use in the olden days to keep meat from turning bad. When meat isn't properly preserved, it rots and gets worms in it. But if we put meat into a tub of salty water, it won't go bad. Of course, that was in the days before refrigerators and deep freezes. If St. Nicholas had lived today, he would very likely have found the bodies of the three rich youths in a deep freeze. Are there any other questions?"

There were no more questions, so Sister Symphorosa used the rest of the afternoon to teach the children to sing Christmas carols. They sang "O Come All Ye Faithful" and then "Adeste Fideles," "Silent Night," and "We Three Kings of Orient Are." Then she let them make requests. One of them asked for "Jingle Bells," but no one suggested a song about Santa Claus.

She dismissed the class with a sense that she had done a good day's work.

Then she remembered the Michaels boy. He had not yet returned from the principal's office. It would not do to go running after him. That would only make him feel more self-important. She took her rosary from the drawer of her desk, kissed the silver crucifix, and made the sign of the cross: "In the name of the Father, and of the Son, and of the Holy Ghost. Amen."

Then she pondered the first Joyful Mystery, which is the Annunciation.

2

At a little after four o'clock, just as "General Hospital" had come to its suspenseful Friday afternoon climax, the smoke alarm in the kitchen went off, and then, before old Mrs. Obstschmecker had quite figured out what was happening, the phone started ringing. She picked up the phone, said "Hello?" and only then realized that the alarm was still ringing and that there was black smoke coming out of the doorway to the kitchen. "I'm sorry," she said. "I can't talk now. Something is burning." She set the receiver down on a stack of clothes to be ironed on the dining room table and hurried into the kitchen, where, as she'd already guessed, the percolator on the back coil was giving off a steady stream of smoke. It was also producing a stench of burning Bakelite, but old Mrs. Obstschmecker had a poor sense of smell, which is how the burning coffeepot had gone so long undetected.

"Oh dear," she fretted aloud, as she plunged the semimolten bottom of the pot into a pan of rinse water, to spectacular effect, "Madge is going to be furious." For a variety of reasons, real and imagined, Mrs. Obstschmecker lived in terror of her daughter Madge and did not want to give her cause for anger or even complaint. Madge was sure to interpret the ruined coffeepot as another sign of her mother's slipping memory, and Mrs. Obstschmecker was certain that all such signs were being set down in some mental ledger book Madge kept against the day that Mrs. Obstschmecker was to be shipped off to some nursing home. Madge had worked at nursing homes and she knew what they were like, and even so she was beginning to throw out hints. A nursing home! Mrs. Obstschmecker would as soon have gone to prison!

Open the windows, that's what she must do. Open the windows and air out the room. She got two of the kitchen windows open, but the third stuck. All the while, the smoke alarm went on ringing, making it impossible to concentrate on anything else. Mrs. Obstschmecker did not want to risk standing on a chair, so she took up a copy of the *Pioneer Press* from the kitchen table and used it as a fan to fan away the smoke from around the alarm. As her arms rose and fell, the dewlaps pendant from her upper arms waggled and her well-buoyed bosom heaved. "Stop it," she commanded the alarm. "Stop it right now."

And it did. The very instant she told it to, the alarm stopped ringing. "Well," she said, "thank goodness."

She noticed the back coil of the stove still glowing red and realized she hadn't turned it off. She did that now. There were blobs and dribbles of the melted coffeepot sticking to the red-hot coil. It was going to be impossible to clean the coffeepot. She would have to buy a new one and hope Madge wouldn't notice. Ned could go out and buy it for her when he got home from school. Which he should be already. Both children were *always* home by the end of "General Hospital." Unless Ned had to stay for choir practice, and on the last day before Christmas vacation that was possible. But Billy should have got home by now.

"Billy?" she called out. She went into the dining room and called again, and then again at the foot of the stairs. Mrs. Obstschmecker felt more exasperated than worried. The child knew his way home from school, and if he'd stopped at a friend's house after school to watch the cartoons he was forbidden to watch here at home (they seemed to give him nightmares, at least according to Madge), so much the better. It meant that he had such a thing as a friend.

Such an impossible child! Mrs. Obstschmecker hadn't been at all surprised when the sister had called up a month ago to complain to Madge that the boy refused to take a nap at the prescribed kindergarten naptime of two o'clock. "I believe," the sister had said, "that this boy is possessed by a devil!" Madge didn't know, and had not thought to ask, whether she'd meant it literally or just as a way of talking. Madge wasn't very religious. Mrs. Obstschmecker believed that too much religion was bad for teaching discipline, since when children started thinking too much about what was right and what was wrong, they tended to get rebellious and to question the rules their parents laid down for them. Now, though, she had to wonder whether it might not have been a better idea to bring Madge up a really solid Catholic, like Mrs. Wolfgren's daughter Karen, who was such a model of devotion to her poor bedridden mother. You couldn't help envying someone with a daughter like Karen.

Mrs. Obstschmecker returned to the kitchen to see if the air had cleared enough to close the windows. The second window proved balky, and before she could get it unstuck, the doorbell rang. As she passed through the dining room to answer it, she noticed the phone receiver lying on the ironing. She picked it up and said, "I'm sorry, I can't talk to you now," and returned it to its cradle. The doorbell rang again. "I'm coming, I'm coming. Hold your horses."

She tugged the heavy wooden door open, and, seeing the visitor to be a woman, unlatched the storm door of aluminum and hazily transparent plastic. She opened the outer door, and gaped. "Sondra," she said with belated recognition.

"Is Billy home?" Sondra asked. Sondra was now Sondra Winckelmeyer, but once she'd been Sondra Michaels. She was Billy's mother.

"What? No. Not yet."

"Has the school called?"

"What? No. No one's called."

"I tried to call," Sondra said, pushing her way past Mrs. Obstschmecker into the hall, "but the line's been busy for the last half hour."

"I've been here," Mrs. Obstschmecker said defensively, "every minute." She noticed, closing the door, that there was a fine dusting of new snow on the steps up to the porch and on the sidewalk beyond. It was so nearly dark that the streetlights were on, those gruesome yellow phosphorous lights that had replaced the nice old-fashioned kind up and down the entire length of Calumet.

"Do you know where Billy is?" Sondra insisted. She'd already taken off her coat and thrown it over the platform rocker. The collar of the coat was silver fox.

"No. But he must be on his way home by now."

"And Edward?"

"Edward? Oh, you mean Ned. He's probably at choir practice. He'll be singing a solo in the Nativity Pageant this year. Is there something wrong?"

"That's what I'm here to find out. If your phone is working, I'd like to call the school and find out if they've found him yet."

"Why are you so sure that he's lost? Children often dawdle on the way home from school. He might have stopped at a friend's. Or gone into a store."

"What the principal told me," Sondra explained, "is that he was sent down to her office with a note, but that he never went there, and he's nowhere in the school building, though his coat is still in the cloakroom. They tried calling here, but your line was busy, so then they called me."

"You mean Billy is out in this weather without a coat?"

"Apparently. Where is the phone?"

Mrs. Obstschmecker, feeling resentful of the invasion but with no grounds for protest, showed Sondra to the phone, and Sondra dialed the school's number, which was busy. Then she dialed her own home in Willowville, and her stepdaughter Judith answered and said there'd been no new phone calls.

"Where is Madge? When will she be home?" Sondra wanted to know.

"She should be here any minute now."

"Meaning? An hour? Half an hour?"

"Meaning any minute now."

"What smells so funny?" Sondra asked, turning her head from side to side and sniffing. Her brown hair was frosted a silver gray to match the collar of her coat, and her clothes—a skirt of heavy brown wool and a bulky pumpkin-colored sweater with a velvety surface—looked like they'd cost a bundle.

"The coffeepot probably. It . . . boiled over. But you don't mean to say that Billy's out in this weather without a coat? It's starting to snow. It's freezing out."

"That is why the principal is concerned, obviously."

"Why would Billy do such a thing?"

"Apparently his kindergarten teacher, who has some ridiculous name I can never remember—"

"Symphorosa."

"That one, yes. She told her kindergarten class that there is no Santa Claus, and Billy got upset. The principal didn't go into any more details than that."

There was a sound of footsteps on the wooden porch, then a louder tromping sound, which Mrs. Obstschmecker knew to be her son-in-law cleaning off his shoes on the doormat.

"Sondra," Henry said, coming into the house.

"Henry, do you know where Billy is?" Talking to Mrs. Obst-schmecker, Sondra had spoken brusquely, her voice pitched low like someone in charge. Speaking to her ex-husband, her voice rose to a whine.

"Goddamn it, you mean he's still not home? They called me at the hotel, and I kept trying to call here, but the line was always busy." He looked accusingly at Mrs. Obstschmecker.

"I haven't talked to anyone all afternoon," Mrs. Obstschmecker said half truthfully.

"Has anyone thought to look upstairs?" Sondra suggested. "Perhaps he came home and went to his room without saying anything."

"Why would he do a thing like that?" Mrs. Obstschmecker demanded indignantly.

"Afraid of being punished, perhaps. Anyhow, you should look."

"You're right," said Henry.

"Meanwhile," Sondra said, "I've got my car outside, so I'll drive around the neighborhood. Do you have any idea where he's likely to have gone? Where would he usually go to be by himself?"

"He wouldn't," said Mrs. Obstschmecker.

"All children have somewhere to go, a hiding place, a tree house, somewhere private."

"I'll check out the attic and the basement," Henry said.

"Oh, he wouldn't go into the attic," said Mrs. Obstschmecker. "He's afraid of it."

"Do you have another jacket I can bring with me, in case I do find him?" Sondra asked.

"We got him a new jacket for Christmas, but it's wrapped up as a present."

"Well, unwrap it."

"Right."

While Henry looked through the upstairs rooms, Sondra phoned the school again. This time the line wasn't busy, but the nun she talked to had nothing more to tell her about Billy.

Henry came downstairs with one of Ned's old winter jackets and gave it to Sondra, who set off to look for Billy in her car, while Henry went on foot along Calumet, looking into the various stores.

Collapsing into the platform rocker, Mrs. Obstschmecker felt a brief flickering of friendship for her daughter's stepson, who, by running off this way, would deflect attention from the melted coffeepot. But it was only a flicker and soon was replaced by Mrs. Obstschmecker's inveterate dislike, a dislike based not just on the natural resentment anyone would feel who had to treat a stranger as a member of her own family but also on the undeniable fact that the boy was peculiar. While the light in the old house thickened to night, she rocked in the creaking platform rocker and thought of punishments and disciplines that she might suggest to Madge when Madge found out what had happened and started to fume.

3

Just as it started to get dark, the snow began to fall. Every time he saw a car go by beyond the stone fence enclosing Brosner Park, Billy would scrunch down inside his sweater like a turtle trying to disappear inside its shell. It was so cold that for a while he'd been crying from the sheer misery of it, but now except for his fingers, which were so stiff inside his pants pockets that he couldn't move them, the cold didn't bother him much at all.

This part of the park—Nabisco Hill—was almost always deserted except when there was enough snow for sledding. Sometimes a dog, off its leash, would come zigzagging up to the top of the hill, snuffling at the dry grass, but the dogs' owners usually didn't follow them here. In the whole neighborhood Nabisco Hill was the best place to come to be by yourself.

But it *was* cold. There wasn't even a tree trunk to lean against to keep out of the wind. Last summer they'd cut down lots of the trees when they got Dutch elm disease. Trees could get sick the same as people, but when they did, they were cut down. Of course, you couldn't very well send a tree to the hospital. That was a funny idea, a hospital for trees, the sort of idea his brother would have liked—or else made fun of Billy for having. Billy could never tell which way Ned would swing. Sometimes he was as nice as the people on TV, but other times he was so mean that Billy would have liked to bash him over the head, like Cain in the story of Cain and Abel. In fact, it wasn't Cain who got bashed, it was Cain who did the bashing. But he *should* have got bashed, and Billy's memory had a way of remembering things the way they should have been.

It wasn't really lying. He *had* seen Santa Claus, only it was a different way of seeing. Billy could only see things this other way when it was night and there were no lights on close by and he was by himself. He could have done it now if he'd wanted to, just by looking at the snow, and then *into* the snow, using his eyes like little drill bits digging into wood. At first the snow wasn't any color in particular. Not white like people always said, but not like any other ordinary color that you could find in a box of Crayolas. At night, when you looked into it, the snow came to have all kinds of swirls and speckles like the TV when it wasn't working, and the deeper you looked the brighter everything got, and the more details there were, until the dots made a real picture. They were doing that now in the little doily of snow spread on a big rock. The colors whirled in a melty way and then got hard until they made a definite shape, a shining ball like a Christmas tree bulb. The glitter in the snow became icicles, and then slowly a whole Christmas tree took shape, with tiny bright winking lights. It was as clear as a picture on TV. The one funny thing about it was it didn't have any size. It was both big and little at the same time, and Billy felt the same himself, dimensionless. But the tree was real, as real as the snow it was inside of. Billy was not pretending. He could see it.

Sometimes, though not as often, you could hear things too. A squeaky sound like someone whistling, only not very well. Ned whistled the same way. But you could only hear that when everything else was completely quiet. Here on the hill there was another sound that got in the way, a sort of low *whoosh* like a ceiling fan that never stopped, as though the whole city were one big car running on neutral.

And then, above that *whoosh*, he could hear it, a faraway high-pitched wailing like an ambulance in another part of town, but coming nearer. The lights on the tree started to blink faster and then there was a kind of purple flash and there was Santa, there in the snow, looking at Billy and smiling. His beard, instead of being pure white, was the same fizzy pink and purple as the snow but otherwise he looked just the way he should.

—*Hi there, Billy,* he said, in a rumbly voice. *What are you doing out so late? You must be cold.*

"I am."

—*Well then, maybe it's time you headed for home. I'll bet your mother is worried.*

"Sister Symphorosa—" Billy began, feeling he had to explain everything from the beginning for Santa's benefit.

But Santa waved away his explanations, and the smoke from the pipe in his hand made long snaky S's in the air.—*Never mind Sister Symphorosa. That's no reason for you to freeze to death in the park.*

"Then you're not angry with me?"

—*Oh-ho! You're worried about your Christmas presents, are you?*

He shook his head. "She said that you . . ." He couldn't put it into words.

Santa smiled. The smoke from his pipe made a kind of halo around his head.—*She said that I'm not real, I suppose.*

"And she tried to make me say so, too. She said you were like a pagan god."

—*Well, I suppose I am in many ways. They had their good points, some of them.*

"She said that no one can live at the North Pole because it's too cold."

—*That shows how little she knows about the North Pole. The best thing to do with people like that is just ignore them.*

"I tried. But she wrote out a note to the principal and sent me to her office. And the note said I couldn't come back to her class, even after the Christmas holiday, unless I said . . ." Billy's voice trailed off desolately. It didn't seem worth trying to explain things, even to Santa.

—*That I don't exist? Well, you should have just lied and said what she wanted you to say.*

"But lying's wrong."

—*Not to someone like Sister Symphorosa. Lying is only wrong with someone you trust. If you lied to me, that would be wrong. But enough of this talk, you've got to get home, or you'll get an even worse cold than you've got already.*

"I'd rather be here. With you."

—You can't always get what you want. But don't worry about Christmas. I've already got you most of what you asked for.

"If I go home now, will you come and talk to me again, later?"

—No bargains, Billy. Maybe I will, maybe I won't, it all depends. I like you, you know that.

"I'll probably get a spanking if I go home now."

Santa Claus looked at his wristwatch.—*No,* he said, *I don't think so. It's too late, they're worried. But when you do go home, you mustn't tell them about talking with me. They won't like that, you know, and telling them would only cause more trouble.*

"No bargains," said Billy with a sly smile.

Santa laughed, and his stomach, inside the tight-fitting red snowsuit, actually did shake like a bowl of Jell-O just the way it said on the record.—*I'll tell you what. You keep our talk a secret, and later I'll tell you a better secret. How's that?*

"What better secret?" Billy demanded.

—I'll tell you where your brother has hidden his poison stick.

"Promise?"

—Promise. And our secret?

"I won't tell anyone. But that doesn't mean I have to say what Sister Symphorosa says I have to say."

—Oh, I don't care what you do with her. So now you'll go home?

"Okay."

—Then close your eyes.

Billy closed his eyes, and when he opened them again, Santa was gone, and the snow was just ordinary cold blank snow. The ground was entirely covered, and it was coming down harder than ever. He stood up and rubbed at his cold cheeks with his cold fingers. Then he set off down Nabisco Hill in the direction of Calumet, slipping and sliding on the snow-slicked grass. It was terribly cold, and he had a ten-block walk home, but that scarcely seemed to matter compared to the secret that glowed, like a charcoal briquet, in his heart.

4

Sondra Winckelmeyer stood at the foot of Nabisco Hill in Brosner Park, feeling a bittersweet affection for the worn-out old neighborhood. She'd grown up only five blocks from here, and the duplex they'd lived in when Billy was a baby wasn't much farther off. She'd wheeled the old dinosaur of a baby buggy back and forth between these wooden benches and the duplex practically every day during the summer of 1967. She wondered if the park had been this run down back then, or if it was just seeing it at this time of year that made it look so drab and awful, the trees bare and the grass dead and the trash barrels overflowing with cans and bottles and newspapers. Affection curdled to loathing, not just for Brosner Park but the whole blighted neighborhood. It had become a slum, there was no other word for it, and poor Billy had to grow up here and go to a school that was more than half colored, and wear his stepbrother's old clothes, and eat fat Mrs. Obstschmecker's dreadful cooking. It was as though he'd been kidnapped, only there was no way to pay a ransom to the kidnappers. And Sondra had only herself to blame, since if she'd played her cards right, she'd still have Billy and everything would be squared away.

"Billy!" she shouted into the darkness of the park. "Billy, if you're hiding somewhere, come out. Billy?"

There was no answer.

From the foot of the hill it was possible to see only a small section of the park, but from the top she'd be able to see pretty well all of it. It didn't seem likely that Billy would be in the park with a snowstorm starting and having no warm clothes, but having come this far, she might as well be thorough. Using the jacket she'd brought for Billy as a muff, she trudged up the path to the top of the hill. Whatever had that nun done to make Billy run off in such weather? They would probably never get a straight answer to that question. On the last school day before Christmas to be telling the children there was no Santa Claus! Children still in kindergarten. Sondra couldn't fathom it.

"Billy!" she called out as she got near the top of the hill. She stopped to catch her breath and called again, feeling futile and ridiculous making such a commotion in the empty park. The jacket wrapped about her hands came undone, and the wind slipped through its armholes and made the arms billow out like wind socks.

Sondra concentrated on her footing, and so, as she reached the top of the hill, she noticed a large rock. Sondra was not ordinarily one to pay attention to the details of natural landscapes. Rocks and trees and even flowers were all generic entities to her uninquiring eye. And yet something in the conformation of this particular rock made her bend down and look at it closely. There was no snow on it, that was the odd thing about it. Instead a thin sheet of crackly ice covered the irregular convexities of its surface like a crystalline pie crust, and for a moment she was quite certain she could make out, in the swirls and crackles of the ice, the smiling face of Santa Claus. She blinked, but the face was still there in the ice, almost as clear as if it had been printed on a greeting card, smiling and seeming to wink at her, and yet not really friendly but somehow threatening. She touched the ice with one gloved finger and at once the icy mirage disintegrated. A shudder passed through her, as though the cold of the snowy hill had invaded every tissue of her body. *Talk about the power of suggestion*, she thought, making a deliberate effort to regard the apparition as a joke and so dismiss it.

Sondra returned to where she'd parked the Buick by the entrance to the park. The vinyl seat was already stiff from the cold as she got behind the wheel. It suddenly got to her: this was serious. The kid could freeze to death. But no, really, that was impossible. Someone would see him out in the cold and take him home and call the police. This wasn't the damned wilderness, this was the city of St. Paul, Minnesota, and children didn't get lost in blizzards on the city streets and die of exposure, for Christ's sake.

Reassured by her denial of such a possibility, Sondra started up the engine and headed back to 1350 Calumet. Coming to the first traffic light, she stopped and scanned the sidewalk and shop fronts hopefully. A gigantic full-color head of Santa Claus had been scotch-taped to the window of the Rexall drugstore on the corner. His eyes seemed to glint with malicious pleasure. *Jesus*, she thought, *I am cracking up.*

5

After spending most of the early afternoon with an elderly parishioner dying of cancer, Father Windakiewiczowa returned to the parish church of Our Lady of Mercy to hear the confessions of forty-two third- and fourth-graders. To hear them whispering their little sins through the screen of the confessional was almost as restorative as a cold bottle of beer. Or better yet, given the state of the weather, a shot of peppermint schnapps. By the time the last penance of ten Our Fathers and ten Hail Marys had been meted out, Father Windakiewiczowa felt ready to face even Joan Zerby's deathbed repinings and recriminations. Though what he was more likely to have to face was a frozen tuna noodle casserole, since Mrs. Hickey, the rectory's housekeeper, had taken off for the week before Christmas to visit her sister in St. Cloud, leaving a freezer full of neatly labeled and mingily portioned dinners.

No sooner had he got back to the rectory and hung his overcoat on the hook in the hallway than the phone rang. He waited four rings, hoping Father Youngermann would be on hand to answer it. Then, with the certain conviction that he was letting himself in for more trouble, he picked up the receiver and said, "Our Lady of Mercy."

"Could I speak to Father Windakiewiczowa, please," a woman's voice demanded.

"Speaking."

"Father, this is Madge Michaels."

Father Windakiewiczowa flipped through the Rolodex of his memory. "Ah, Mrs. Michaels, yes. Your husband has been helping run our Bingo Nights. What can I do for you?"

Mrs. Michaels had a very clear idea of what he could do for her, an idea that Father Windakiewiczowa regarded with blank disbelief.

"Mrs. Michaels," he protested, when she'd finished laying out her demands, "I couldn't possibly undertake to do what you ask. For one thing, Sister Symphorosa is entitled to conduct her class in whatever way she thinks fit."

"Even if that means driving my child out into a snowstorm without his winter clothes? And slapping him in the face when he was already in a state near hysteria?"

"Sister Symphorosa is an experienced teacher, and I'm sure she wouldn't have—"

"I am an experienced nurse, Father, and my son may have to be hospitalized because of that woman."

"I sympathize with your distress, Mrs. Michaels, but—"

"I sympathize with your distress, Father, when the story is published in the newspaper."

"Now, Mrs. Michaels, that would be . . . entirely unnecessary."

"I hope so, Father. And if Billy hears from Sister Symphorosa by his bedtime, which is eight o'clock, you have my word that I won't make any waves—no matter how sick the boy may get. *And* I would also like to have someone bring Billy's coat home."

"I'll see that is done this evening, Mrs. Michaels. But as to being able to persuade Sister—"

The line went dead. He had been hung up on.

Obviously he was going to have to try to mollify Mrs. Michaels. He had no doubt at all as to the essential accuracy of what the woman had told him. Sister Symphorosa's enmity to Santa Claus had more than once aroused parental indignation, and while she could scarcely be blamed for the boy's running off half-dressed into the snowstorm, it undoubtedly did look bad. The *Pioneer Press* was generally well disposed toward the Church, but in this case the attraction of the "human interest" might prove too great. He would have to pull rank.

But not before he had his allotted before-dinner two ounces of schnapps, which he drank directly from the glass measuring cup, by way of avoiding extra dishwashing. He rinsed and dried the measuring cup and returned it to its place on the second cupboard shelf. Then he bundled into his overcoat and walked the two blocks to the convent through the thick-falling snow. The cold and glitter of the winter night seemed to mingle with the lingering bite of the schnapps to produce a sensation of briskness and vigor. By the time he'd reached the convent door he was almost looking forward to confronting Sister Symphorosa, since it was a conflict from which in its nature he must emerge as victor. Nuns, finally, must do as they're told.

6

When Billy got home there was no one there but Grandma Obst-schmecker, who wasn't his grandmother but had to be called Grandma Obstschmecker anyway, and his brother Ned, who was actually his step-brother. As soon as he saw Billy, red-faced and shivering, Ned said, "Boy, are *you* in trouble!" Then he ran out of the house to look for Billy's parents. That left Billy by himself with Grandma Obstschmecker, who didn't seem at all angry, even when she found out he'd gone to the bath-room in his pants. She promised to put his pants in the washing machine in the basement and wash and dry them herself and not tell Madge. Billy was more worried about the disgrace of messing up his pants than about anything else. Grandma O. made him promise to take a hot bath right away, which he did, and which started him shivering worse than he'd been shivering when he first came in the house. He was out of the bathtub and in his pajamas by the time Ned got back with his father. His father came tromping up the stairs so loud that Grandma Obstschmecker had to shout out "Henry! Please!" Then the two of them whispered outside the door to the bedroom, and while they were whispering, Madge came home, and so Billy was left for the time being to himself while the grown-ups argued in the living room. Billy could have heard the whole argument by going out to the heat transom in the upstairs hallway, but he was feel-ing strange and wanted nothing but just to lie there under the two extra blankets Grandma Obstschmecker had spread over him and drift off to sleep. But for some reason he wasn't able to now. It was probably too long before bedtime. Or else it was part of the pneumonia that Grandma Obst-schmecker said he would get when she was drying him off after his bath. He'd been sick for a long time when he was five, and one of the things he still remembered about it was lying in the bed and not being able to sleep. That was when he'd learned how to see things on the ceiling when it was dark. The argument downstairs ended, and his mother came up to sit beside him for a while, and that was nice, even if he couldn't smell her hair the way he usually could, and then Madge came up with the ther-mometer. While Billy warmed the thermometer under his tongue, Madge said, "Well, I talked to him," and Billy's mother said, "What did he say?" and Madge said there was no telling, they'd just have to wait.

A while later, after his mother had kissed him good-bye and gone back to Willowville, the phone rang. Billy knew right away that this was what Madge had said they'd have to wait for, and sure enough a little later Ned came upstairs to tell him to come down, there was a phone call for him. "From who?" Billy wanted to know. "You'll find out," Ned told him ominously.

When he went to the phone, which had been placed at the end of the dining room table, where Grandma Obstschmecker usually sat, the whole family was hovering round just the way they would have been for an important TV program, only instead of the TV it was Billy they were watching. Madge was in the doorway to the kitchen with rubber scouring gloves on, and Ned was sitting at the other end of the table, pretending to do his homework. Grandma Obstschmecker was in her platform rocker, which had been turned from facing the TV to face into the dining room instead. Billy's father was sitting in the bay window with all the potted geraniums, fingering a copy of *TV Guide*. Billy looked at the phone mistrustfully, and then at Madge, who pursed her lips in a grim, thin smile. "It's for you, Billy. It's Sister Symphorosa."

His heart sank, but he picked up the receiver and said, "Hello."

"Good evening, Billy. This is Sister Symphorosa."

He nodded.

There was a long pause, and then she said, "We've all been very concerned for you here at the convent, Billy. Quite a few of the sisters have been out looking for you, as far off as McCarron's Boulevard."

Billy didn't know where McCarron's Boulevard was, but just from the sound of Sister Symphorosa's voice he knew it must have been quite a ways. Her voice had the sort of trembling sound it got just before she exploded and hit someone. He was glad she was on the phone and not in the same room, since he didn't know what he was supposed to say to her. He said he was sorry. That was usually a safe bet with grown-ups.

"Well," said the sister, in the same trembly voice, "we'll deal with all that when school resumes again, after the holidays. But tonight I just wanted to say that I was . . . mistaken . . . in telling you there is no Santa Claus. Father Windakiewiczowa has come to the convent this evening— he is here with me right now—to inform me that there *is* a Santa Claus. And that he is—how did you put it, Father?" There was a short pause filled with a mumbling sound, and the sister resumed, in a tone of barely restrained fury: "He is the spirit of love incarnate. So, I hope you find that information reassuring."

Billy didn't know what to say, and said nothing.

"Do you have any *questions* about Santa Claus, Billy?"

Billy almost didn't have the nerve—but finally did ask: "Does he really come down chimneys?"

"Just a moment, I'll ask Father Windakiewiczowa. He's the expert here on Santa Claus. Father, Billy wants to know if Santa Claus really comes down chimneys." Another pause. "Yes, Billy, he really does. Any other questions?"

Billy shook his head.

"If you have no more questions, I should like to remind you—with Father Windakiewiczowa's permission—that we also celebrate the birth of the Christ Child at Christmas. I hope you remember some of what I told your classmates about how Jesus came to be born in Bethlehem?"

"Yes, Sister."

"He was born so that we might be saved from our sins!"

She really sounded like she would explode any moment. Billy was glad he wasn't Father Windakiewiczowa, though of course being a priest (and a grown-up) meant that Sister Symphorosa wouldn't explode at him.

She would wait till Billy was back at school and then get him.

"Billy, are you listening to me?"

"Yes, Sister."

"I wonder if you could tell me—tell all of us—where you *went* when I sent you down to the principal's office."

Billy could feel his face and hands starting to sweat. He stared at the little holes drilled into the telephone mouthpiece as hard as he could, so he wouldn't have to meet the collective gaze of his family, who were all looking at him and straining to hear the other end of the conversation. Then a strange thing happened. Without his trying, he was able to *see* Sister Symphorosa. Her pale blue eyes had a funny glow inside them, like the glow of the night lamp that burned all night inside the bathroom, and there were beads of sweat all over her forehead (just as there were, he realized, on his own forehead), and her hands were gripping the phone receiver like the handle of an ax. She was furious—with him and with Father Windakiewiczowa and even, Billy realized, with Santa Claus. At first he thought she'd been lying to him, that she didn't believe in Santa Claus but was only saying it because she had to. But *seeing* her like this he knew that she really did believe in Santa Claus. You can't hate something the way she hated Santa if you don't believe in it.

Billy's long silence, though not intended as simple obstinacy, finally accomplished the same purpose. Sister Symphorosa finally retreated to a more easily answered question. "How are you feeling?"

"Okay," he said noncommittally.

"Mrs. Michaels was worried that you might come down with a bad cold as a result of your going out with no snowsuit."

Billy looked at the tiny face in the mouthpiece of the telephone, squinting and blinking to try to make it go away. He knew from the way she was biting her lip and from the way the blue wormy thing wiggled on the back of her hand (which was, Billy knew, one of the veins that squirt the blood to every part of the body) that what she really wanted to say was that she hoped he *would* get a bad cold.

"I'm fine," he insisted. And thought: *And I hope you get the cold instead of me. I hope you get pneumonia!*

"Well, good night, Billy," she said in a softer voice, as though she'd suddenly given up being angry. "Have a Merry Christmas."

"Good night, Sister."

She held on to the phone a little while longer, as though she were waiting to see if he'd wish her a Merry Christmas in return, but he wouldn't, and finally she hung up. When she did, he stopped being able to see her face in the mouthpiece of the phone.

"Well?" Grandma Obstschmecker demanded. "What did she have to say?"

"She said . . ." Something funny was happening to the light in the dining room, as though little by little it were leaking out into the snowy night. He tilted his head back to see if that would make things better. "She said there really is a Santa Claus." He smiled triumphantly, and then his eyes rolled up and his knees caved in and the lights went out completely.

"What a little actor he is," Grandma Obstschmecker commented acidly.

Madge bent down over her stepson and felt his forehead and his pulse and made a professional *tsk* of concern. "He isn't acting, Mother. He's fainted." She grasped Billy under his armpits and lifted him into a seated position. "Henry," she ordered her husband, "help me carry him up to the bedroom."

7

It was Sunday night, the night before the night before Christmas, and the kids had been put to bed. Madge had gone off to work (she'd been on the night shift for the past three months; it paid more), and Henry Michaels and his mother-in-law were sitting at the dining room table wrapping Christmas presents. Or rather, Henry was. Mrs. Obstschmecker, having been unable to find proper to-and-from cards in the box of last year's left-over wrapping supplies, had taken on the more congenial tasks of supervision and advice. Henry's style of wrapping presents was inventive but not very neat, and this gave Mrs. Obstschmecker plenty of opportunity for constructive criticism. Henry nodded at each of her suggestions and then went right on wrapping the presents his way.

Mrs. Obstschmecker turned to politics. "I can't *believe* that they are seriously talking about impeaching the president. The president!"

Henry, who had been enjoying every minute of Watergate, smiled. "Who else could they impeach, Grandma Obstschmecker? Impeachments are reserved specially for presidents. Ordinary people just go to jail."

"I wish you wouldn't call me Grandma, Henry. I'm Ned's Grandma, but I don't think I'm old enough to be yours."

"Sure, whatever you say. But you see my point about impeachment, don't you? That's the only way they've got to nail him."

"He is not a criminal. Nothing's been *proven*. Aren't people supposed to be innocent until proven guilty?" This was an argument she had employed several times in discussions of Watergate, and she'd never known it not to produce at least grudging assent. But Henry just went on as though she hadn't said anything worth considering, without even looking up from his wrapping.

"Nothing's been proven," Henry said, " 'cause he's sitting on those tapes and won't budge."

"The tapes are full of national security secrets," Mrs. Obstschmecker pleaded.

"Yes, and then some," said Henry.

"You're as bad as all the rest. You just want to *drive* him out of office, and you don't care how you do it. I think it's a sin, the way that poor man is being made to suffer."

Mrs. Obstschmecker regarded her son-in-law balefully. She didn't understand how he could be so disagreeable all the time without ever actually quarreling. Whenever she had disagreed with Mr. Obstschmecker, dead now these past three years, they'd ending up screaming and yelling. They didn't just make a lot of nasty little jokes the way Henry Michaels did. She would never understand why her daughter had wanted to marry the man. Unless it was the way he looked.

He looked like JFK. Except that his hair was more reddish than JFK's, and his body more spindly, and his ears, despite his haircut, stuck out from his head, and there were dark crescents in the loose flesh under his eyes as a result (he claimed) of his job (which he'd just lost) as assistant manager of the Leif Ericson Hotel—aside from those details he looked (in his mother-in-law's eyes) exactly the same.

While to many people such a resemblance, if they had seen it, would have counted in his favor, to Mrs. Obstschmecker it represented everything intolerable in her son-in-law: long hair, a lot of holier-than-thou liberal ideas (he was *against* the war and in favor of sex education), and a general sense that he was laughing up his sleeve at ordinary people such as herself.

"Pass me the scissors," he said. Not "*Please* pass me the scissors"; just "Pass me the scissors." Typical.

"They're right in front of you," she said.

Henry sliced off a section of blue-and-silver Christmas bells wrapping large enough for the recording of comedian Poppy Mueller narrating *Fairy Tales the World Over*.

"Well, *I* still believe in him," Mrs. Obstschmecker declared.

Henry looked up with the sly grin he used to sweeten his insults. "That makes two of you."

"What?" She narrowed her eyes, trying to figure out his remark. "If you mean to say no one else believes in the president but me and the president himself, you're quite wrong. Billy Graham was on the news just tonight saying that he has every confidence in the president's integrity. And that's a quote. He said he may have made some errors of judgment but that he's a man of integrity. And Billy Graham wouldn't say that if he didn't believe in the president."

"That's very loyal of Billy Graham, but it's not what I meant."

"What did you mean then?"

"I meant we've got two true believers right here in the family—you believing in Nixon and Billy upstairs believing in Santa Claus."

Mrs. Obstschmecker emitted a little sneeze of laughter, but she felt no better for it. Laughing at Henry's jokes was like being tricked into agreeing with him.

She changed the subject to something certain to be unwelcome. "What's happening at the hotel?"

"Today they closed down the coffee shop."

"And that beautiful restaurant, with the big chandelier?"

"That was closed down the day they made the announcement, two weeks ago."

"I just can't understand it. Such a fine old building. Where will people *stay* when they come to St. Paul if there's no hotel?"

"They won't come here. They don't already—that was the problem, that's why we're closing. The downtown is a ghost town after dark."

"I still remember when Mr. Obstschmecker's cousin Gladys had her marriage reception in that ballroom. That was almost thirty years ago. Mr. Obstschmecker was still wearing his uniform. My goodness, it doesn't *seem* that long ago."

Henry had finished scotch-taping the Poppy Mueller LP's wrappings and was measuring a cellophane package of underpants against a remnant of glossy red paper salvaged from last Christmas. There was just barely enough, which gave Henry a ping of mathematical satisfaction.

Mrs. Obstschmecker had begun a reconstruction of her husband's cousin's wedding reception at the Leif Ericson Hotel in 1945, or possibly 1944, when she was interrupted by loud cries that seemed to come from the ceiling directly overhead. She looked up at the heat transom fearfully.

"It's Ned," Henry said matter-of-factly, putting down the package of underpants and getting up from the table. "He's having one of his nightmares."

Henry went up to Ned's bedroom, a huge dark cave with its own private sun porch that faced north and so never received any direct sunlight. He switched on the single 60-watt overhead bulb, summoning dim forms from the darkness. Ned was lying rigid in the middle of a big brass-framed bed (one of the Obstschmecker heirlooms), staring up with blank-eyed terror at the peeling paint on the high ceiling and shouting out over and over, "I didn't see it! I wasn't there!" Sometimes he'd throw in "You've got to believe me, I didn't see anything!"

"I believe you, I believe you," Henry said, shaking the boy's shoulder. "Now come on, wake up."

It was never easy to wake Ned when he was in the grip of his night terrors. Madge had asked a woman doctor in the psychiatric ward about Ned's problem, and the doctor had explained that it was clinically different from ordinary nightmares but nothing to worry about. He would outgrow them.

Henry pulled the boy into a sitting position and shouted at him: "Ned, wake up—it's only a dream."

"I didn't see it!" Ned screamed in reply, twisting his body to break out of Henry's grip. "I wasn't there!" It was as though he were defying a torturer who was trying to get him to confess—but to what crime, imagined or real, Ned would probably not be able to say once he was awakened. For unlike dreams, these night terrors seemed to vanish without a trace at the moment of waking. All Ned had ever been able to say about them was that they involved someone with a squeaky voice and that the scariest thing about them was a feeling of being crushed beneath a slowly moving weight.

The boy shook his head back and forth, whipping his sweat-curled hair from side to side. "I didn't see it!" he shouted one last time—and then awoke. The eyes that had been trapped, open but sightless, in the nightmare regarded Henry with recognition, and the lips still flecked with spittle offered him a tired smile. "Hi. I guess I was dreaming again."

Henry nodded.

"I'm sorry. I hope I didn't wake everyone up. Is it late?"

"It's not even eleven yet."

"Mom's still at work?"

Henry nodded. "And I'm downstairs wrapping presents with Grandma Obstschmecker."

Ned wiped the spittle from his mouth. "What are you doing wrapping presents? I thought they all came from Santa Claus."

"Okay, smart guy, we're not wrapping presents. We're discussing politics. You want to come down and discuss politics with your grandmother?"

"No thanks. I think I'd rather have another nightmare."

"No more nightmares tonight. Doctor's orders." He gave the boy a hug and eased his still tense body back against the damp pillow. "You can read for a while if you want to."

Ned shook his head.

"See you in the morning," Henry said, switching off the light.

There was no response from the darkness.

Henry made sure that Billy was sleeping soundly (for a wonder, the boy hadn't come down with a cold as a penalty for his adventure of two days ago). Then he took a piss in the bathroom sink and returned downstairs to finish wrapping presents.

8

It was the day after the day after Christmas, and Ned had the house all to himself. His mother, who had Thursdays off, and Henry, now officially

unemployed, had gone to an early matinee of a brand-new and suppos-
edly very gross horror movie called *The Exorcist*, while Grandma Obstschmecker had taken Billy to a free puppet-show version of *Snow White
and the Seven Dwarfs*, leaving Ned at liberty to use the phone or plunder
the icebox or play with any of Billy's Christmas presents without Billy's
knowing. Instead, he had spread open his three-ring binder on the dining
room table to do some Extra Credit homework for Miss Brophy's Core
Curriculum class.

The Caduceus

he wrote across the top of a sheet of the wide-lined paper, where the title
was supposed to go, and then, on the next line:

(Symbol of Medical Science)

He skipped two lines, and began:

> Mercury was a diety worshiped by the ancient Romans. He
> was the god of roads and messengers. Statues and pictures of
> Mercury show him wearing winged shoes and a winged cap, sym-
> bols of his speedy delivery of messages.

In the encyclopedia article Ned was copying, from his own edition of
the *Junior Universe of Knowledge Encyclopedia*, the wording was slightly different, and there was some dull stuff about modern words ("commerce,"
"merchandise," and "merchant") that were related to Mercury's name.
Ned didn't bother copying those parts.

> He is also shown holding a winged wand, or staff, called a
> caduceus. His caduceus had two serpents twisted around it to pro-
> tect him as he journeyed through heaven and earth. In later times
> Mercury became the god of magic and science, and so his cadu-
> ceus is now a symbol of the science of medicine. Among the
> Oroonookoo Indians of South America similar winged "witch-
> sticks" are used in ceremonies of healing as well as in rituals of
> black magic.

This was, in fact, a little stronger than what the *Junior Universe* had to
say about the subject. In particular the information about the Oroonookoo Indians had come from a comic-book column "Stranger Than Fic-

tion!" in the February 1972 issue of the *Green Magician*, where there had been a drawing of an Oroonookoo witch-stick that had made a strong impression on Ned, due to the fact that he possessed something that looked almost exactly like what the artist had drawn. However Ned's witch-stick or caduceus or whatever it was hadn't come from South America or ancient Greece. He'd made it himself by tying the dried corpse of some kind of sparrow to the end of a strange twisty doubled-up stick. The way the two pieces of wood had twined around each other really did make them look like a pair of snakes. Ned hadn't had any particular idea in mind when he'd made the thing except that it looked kind of neat in a spooky sort of way.

For a while just after he'd made it Ned had used the crucified dead sparrow to terrorize his little brother. He would hold it out in front of him and wave it back and forth and intone in his solemnest tone of threat, "Watch out—I'm going to touch you with the poison stick. Watch out!" And Billy, who was wonderfully terrorizable, would run off in a state of panic and just about wet his pants from fear of what he imagined the stick would do. It was dumb, but it was fun, and teasing (according to what Father Windakiewiczowa had told Ned in confession) was generally only a venial sin, so long as it didn't involve physical abuse.

"The Roman gods were not like our God," Ned continued down the page.

> They were not always virtuous. Mercury was famed not only as a messenger and a healer but as a thief. Criminals prayed to him as their protector. One of the planets is named for him, as well as the element mercury, which is found in every thermometer. By a strange irony, mercury poisoning is one of the deadliest diseases known to man. Its symptoms include sore mouth and gums, loose teeth, intestinal disorders, and often death. The caduceus of the god Mercury may be a symbol of medical science, but the element mercury is just the opposite!

The page was almost filled, and Ned wrote his name and homeroom number in the corner, and then in the opposite corner "For Extra Credit." He smiled with the satisfaction of closure. The school did not have a copy of the *Junior Universe*, nor did the local library branch, and so even if Miss Brophy suspected that his paper had been copied from a book, there was no way she could prove it. The encyclopedia had come as a present from his real father, Lance Hill, who lived in Canada and sold the *Junior Universe of Knowledge Encyclopedia* for a living. Or at least that's what he'd been doing for a living last year when he'd sent the set to Ned for a Christmas present. Since then Ned's father had dropped out of sight, except for a postcard in July from Whitehorse in the Yukon Territory ("The Northern Lights are really something!") and a letter to Madge a couple of weeks later asking for money. (Ned wasn't supposed to have read the letter, but like the god Mercury, he was sneaky and knew all of his mother's hiding places.) Ned felt sorry for his father, who hated Canada and couldn't find any kind of good job there but had to live there because he was a draft dodger; but he didn't really miss him, since Lance had fled across the border way back in 1967, when the war was just getting into high gear and when Ned was only five. Even before that Lance and Madge had not been living together, and so Ned had few clear memories of "the hippie" (as Grandma Obstschmecker referred to him). The clearest was of a picnic in someone's backyard where there was a horseshoe game. All through a long summer afternoon (as Ned recalled) his father had tried to throw a horseshoe that would go around the stake in the ground and make the wonderful ringing sound that announced to the other picnickers that a point had been scored, but he never did. His throws kept getting wilder and wilder, and there was a fight around the car when it was time to drive home about who would do the driving. Lance lost, and Madge drove. Now what kind of father was that? On the whole Ned felt he was a lot better off with Henry for a father, even if it did mean explaining to everyone he met why his last name was Hill when his parents' last name was Michaels.

Billy and Grandma Obstschmecker got home a little after four, and Ned, who had been mastering the art of taking apart and putting together a puzzle consisting of four bent nails, settled down at the kitchen table with a glass of milk and a wedge of lardy-slice (an Obstschmecker holiday specialty) to listen to Billy's breathless retelling of the story of Snow White. Grandma Obstschmecker, meanwhile, went to take a nap in her room on the first floor.

When Billy reached the high point of the story, the witch's presentation of the poisoned apple, he detoured from strict narrative sequence to ask Ned: "There really aren't witches like that, are there? Grandma said it's all just make-believe, all the stuff about princes and magic and dwarfs."

Ned considered the flakes of lardy-slice sprinkled over the marble-patterned Formica tabletop. "Well, no, I wouldn't say so. I mean, there really are dwarfs, I've seen photographs and I've seen them in movies, and there are princes in England and places like that. And there used to be witches all over the place. And people were so scared of what they could do, they used to burn them alive."

"How?" Billy wanted to know.

"Well, first they'd tie them to a stake, a really big piece of wood, and then they'd build a bonfire around their feet. And people would come and watch it happen."

"Why don't they do it anymore?"

"Not everyone believes in witches anymore. Not here in America anyway. They do in Haiti though. They have voodoo there. And in South America there are the Oroonookoo Indians."

Billy, who had already been informed about the practices and powers of the Oroonookoo Indians, nodded gravely. "They're the ones with the *sticks*. But why don't the people who *believe* in witches burn them anymore?"

"I guess because the government won't let them."

Billy still wasn't satisfied. "But suppose there was a witch who does bad things like kill people, or put them to sleep like the witch did to Snow White, what about that?"

Ned took a judicious sip of milk while he considered the problem, then delivered his verdict. "I guess with witches what you've got to do is fight back with witches. But with *good* witches."

The idea that witches might be good was new to Billy. "What do good witches do?"

Off the top of his head Ned had no answer to that. Then he had a flash of inspiration. "The good witches are like saints. Or priests. Like the priest in the movie Mom and Dad went off to see. *The Exorcist*."

"That's about the kid who gets the devil inside of her and says all the dirty words?" (This had been Grandma Obstschmecker's synopsis of the movie when she'd turned down the opportunity, offered earlier that day, to go downtown and see *The Exorcist* with Madge and Henry.)

Ned nodded. "And do you remember the other night on TV when there was that priest on the talk show explaining that there really are devils that do that, get inside of people and make them act crazy? And what a priest can do is he can drive out the devil, and that's what an exorcist is, someone who does that. So I guess what a good witch would do would be to reverse what the bad witch was doing. Like if the bad witch was making people sick, the good witch could make them better again."

Billy thought that over carefully, and the more he thought about it, the more it seemed to make sense.

Ned, meanwhile, had to fight against the temptation to feel angry because he hadn't been allowed to see *The Exorcist*. He felt he was mature enough to see a movie that had dirty words in it. Things had probably been different in the past, when his parents had grown up. Back then, kids probably never heard those words. But now they *used* them, even at a Catholic school, even at Our Lady of Mercy. Ned had read *The Exorcist* from cover to cover, having snitched it from Henry's mound of coverless paperbacks in a box in the attic. He thought it was a terrific story, and he'd have loved to see all the scary parts done really believably in a movie. But Madge had said no, absolutely not, and Henry had backed her up, and so now Ned would never see the movie, since it was rated R and Ned wouldn't be allowed in the theater without a grown-up with him. It was so unfair, especially considering the fact that Ned had a vocation to the priesthood and that *The Exorcist* was a movie with a priest as the hero, but getting angry about it was a sin—specifically a sin against the Fourth Commandment, Honor thy father and mother.

9

"And how is the king of Bowling Pin Kingdom?" Henry asked, entering his son's bedroom after a pro forma rap on the door.

The bowling pins of the kingdom in question were deployed in various significant combinations throughout the room, some promenading in open sight, others skulking under the bed or peering out from the mouths of V-shaped caverns formed by spread-open books. The larger bowling pins were grown-ups, the smaller were children, but politically the pins were organized into two factions that did not respect the generation gap. These were the Greens, led by Dundor, the large green bowling pin, and his concubine Fluff, the large yellow bowling pin, and the Reds, led by the witch Icksy and her son Reinhardt, the large and small red bowling pins. Icksy had once murdered Dundor's only son, Hans, and Dundor had made a vow to conquer the old Red witch and all her people, who had been forced to retreat, after a long series of battles, to the caverns of Ho Chi Minh Mountain in the darkest corner of the bedroom. The victorious Greens, by contrast, enjoyed a luxurious life among the coleuses and prayer plants that formed the Hanging Gardens of Wyomia in front of the double window and on its sills. Billy looked after these descendants of the downstairs houseplants himself, or rather Dundor's chancellor did, as part of his duty in running the kingdom's vast irrigation project. The chancellor's official name was Cardinal Richloo, but he also had a secret name, known only to himself and to Icksy, the Red witch. It was because she had this power over Dundor's most trusted servant that the Reds had been able to survive so long the invasions of the Greens, but now, as a result of Santa Claus's major Christmas present to Billy, things were getting desperate. Santa had given Billy a toy train that ran on steel tracks, and Dundor had laid the tracks from Wyomia westward to the foothills of Ho Chi Minh Mountain. Once the holiday truce expired, Dundor would move his troops and supplies by train to the heart of his enemies' territory and bomb them back to the Stone Ages. At least that was what he was threatening to do on his nightly television broadcast to his subjects.

Needless to say, Billy could not explain all of this to his father. Not because Henry wouldn't have been interested. He would probably have been too interested, being himself a great teller and welder-together of stories. But the long struggle between the Greens and the Reds was Billy's private property, and he didn't want anyone else coming in and telling any of the bowling pins what to do, not his father, and not Ned, and certainly not Grandma Obstschmecker, who was always asking questions about them in the hope Billy would provide further proof for her contention that his hours with the bowling pins represented an unhealthy interest and therefore should be taken away from him.

Instead of answering his father's question, Billy parried with one of his own. "What time is it?"

"Time for bed."

"You said you'd read me a story tonight."

"That's what I'm here for. Have you picked out a book?"

"I will now."

While Billy went to Ho Chi Minh Mountain to select his bedtime story, Henry sat down on the edge of the large, lumpy bed. Just as though he'd eased into a hot bath, he could feel the tensions in his back and shoulders and neck easing away. He loved the rituals of bedtime as much as Billy did, and even had a theory, which he'd never told anyone, not even Madge, that the time he spent spinning tales for Billy had a therapeutic value equal at least to Tylenol or Ben-Gay.

Billy returned with a picture book called *The Night Before Christmas*. "Read this."

Henry wrinkled his forehead into a question. "This? Are you sure? Tonight is the night after the night after Christmas. Santa Claus is down at the South Pole, taking a vacation."

"I know. But I like the way it sounds: *'Twas the night before Christmas, and all through the* house *not a creature was stirring, not even a* mouse."

"That's called rhyming, when two words make the same sound.

There's lots of other stories that rhyme, not just *The Night Before Christmas*."

"I know, but I like this one."

"Your brother says that you're able to read it by yourself. Has your reading really got that good?"

"But that's not the same as when you read it. You read *better* than I do."

"Well, I'm glad to hear that I'm still employable somewhere. Okay, we'll read *The Night Before Christmas* one more time, but that'll be it with Santa Claus till next year. Okay?"

"Okay," Billy conceded reluctantly.

Billy was lifted up onto his father's lap, and Henry began to read the poem.

Alerted by the warning that this must be his farewell to Santa Claus, Billy gave the words his total attention, and he was able to pose any number of relevant questions by way of drawing out the story. What are sugar plums? Why did they wear hats to bed? How does the snow have a breast? If Santa rides in "a miniature sleigh" and is able to come down through a chimney, what is his actual size? Why was he called an elf? Had he really been the bishop of Myra, like Sister Symphorosa said, or was that someone else?

"Now, Billy, I'm not the world's leading authority on Santa Claus, or Saint Nicholas, or the bishop of Myra. In fact, Billy, we should probably have a serious discussion about this. I promised your mother we would clear up any confusion before you went back to school, so maybe this would be the right moment."

"Aren't you going to finish reading the book?" Billy asked with alarm.

"All right, we'll finish reading it, and *then* we'll have a serious discussion." Henry looked down at the page that showed a close-up of Santa smoking a pipe and winking. "'He was chubby and plump,'" he read for a second time, "'—a right jolly old elf;/ And I laughed, when I saw him, in spite of myself./ A wink of his eye and a twist of his head/ Soon gave me to know I had nothing to dread./ He spoke not a word—'"

"What's 'dread'?"

Henry laughed. "It's the same as being afraid."

"Why should anyone be afraid of Santa Claus?"

"They shouldn't. That's what the poem is saying. When Santa winks at the man in the poem, he knows he has *nothing* to dread."

"But he must have been worried before he saw Santa wink at him, or he wouldn't be thinking that. Would he?"

"I never thought about it before, but that seems to make sense. Well, it must be because Santa's got magical powers. He's got flying reindeer, and he can change his size to get down chimneys, and if he can do things like that, who knows what else he might be able to do, if he wanted."

"Is he like the good witches?"

Henry cocked his head to the side, and checked the beginning of a grin. "What and who are good witches?"

"Like in the movie you went to see today."

"*The Exorcist?* Has Ned been talking to you about that?"

"There was a witch in *Snow White*, so we were talking about witches, and he said there are good witches and bad witches, and the good witches use their magic to make people better."

"Well, Billy, in my experience witches have always been women. When a man uses magic, good or bad, he's called a wizard, or maybe a sorcerer, and I've never heard Santa Claus referred to by either of those terms. The poem calls him an elf, and I think all elves know some magic."

"He looks just like a person though. Except he's fat. But he doesn't have pointy ears."

"Like Mr. Spock?"

"Like elves do," Billy explained impatiently.

"Who's to say exactly what elves look like? It all depends on who's telling the story about them. They may have pointy ears, they may not. They're only make-believe, after all."

"But you said—!"

"What?"

"You said Santa is an elf."

Henry nodded. "Right."

"But Santa isn't make-believe. Sister Symphorosa *telephoned!*"

"Billy, she did that because your mother asked her to. She did it to be nice and so you wouldn't be upset at Christmastime. And there's a way in which it's true to say there is a Santa Claus."

"But what about my train?" Billy demanded, aghast at this unexpected betrayal.

"What about it?"

"Where did it come from?"

"From us."

"From a store?"

Henry nodded. "From K-Mart."

"You just paid money for it?"

"No, actually—we charged it. Someday, hopefully, we'll pay money for it."

Billy looked at the picture book with dismay. He tried to slide down from his father's lap, but Henry scissored his legs together and trapped him.

"Hey, don't you want to hear the end of the poem?"

Billy shook his head, but avoided meeting his father's eye. He tried to press his legs apart, and Henry, feeling sorry for him, let him loose. He stood beside the bed in his pajamas, looking balefully at the toy train that had been bought at K-Mart, mute.

Is he angry with me? Henry asked himself. He wouldn't have blamed him if he was. The kid obviously had a thing about Santa Claus that went beyond the usual simple ploy of believing in Santa so you could ask for more expensive presents than your parents could afford.

"Well, *I* want to hear the rest of it, and you can listen or not listen, just as you like." Henry turned to a new page that showed Santa loading up the stocking hung by the chimney, and read:

> *"He spoke not a word, but went straight to his work,*
> *And filled all the stockings; then turned like a jerk . . ."*

Henry glanced sideways to see if this violation of the familiar text would provoke some protest from Billy, but he just stood there looking stricken.

> *"And laying his finger aside of his nose,*
> *And giving a nod, up the chimney he rose.*
> *He sprang to his sleigh, to his team gave a whistle,*
> *And away they all flew like the down of a thistle;*
> *But I heard him exclaim, ere he drove out of sight . . ."*

Henry paused, as he always did, for Billy to join him in a choral rendition of Santa's farewell cry, but Billy would have none of it.

Henry closed the book with a sigh and got up from the bed. "Listen, Billy, I'm sorry I had to be the one to tell you, but your mother and I decided—"

"She's not my mother," Billy said, in an even, colorless tone.

"We decided," Henry went on, "that as soon as Christmas was past we'd better tell you. Maybe we were wrong. You'd have figured it out yourself as soon as you started thinking about it."

Billy walked over to the light switch beside the door. "I want to go to bed now," he said, with his hand poised over the switch.

"Right," said his father. He put the picture book on top of the chest of drawers. In the doorway he turned round to ask: "What about a good-night kiss?" He hunkered down invitingly.

Billy shook his head, and turned off the light. "I'm too old for that now," he explained, with just a tremble of bitterness in his voice.

He closed the door.

10

That very night Icksy the witch dispatched her raven Karn to the secret Tinker Toy–built office of Cardinal Richloo between the dresser and the closet door. Karn told the aged chancellor that the time had come when he must help Icksy defeat Dundor or else she would reveal his, Richloo's, secret name and coloration (for Cardinal Richloo was actually pink and had been painted over with green fingerpaint at the time he had joined the Green faction, back in September when Dundor's son Hans was murdered and the war began). Richloo was very upset, but he agreed to obey Icksy's command to derail the troop trains bound for Ho Chi Minh Mountain.

Then, as Karn was returning to the Reds' territory, the darkness of the bedroom started to shimmer and the wind of the raven's wings made a strange whistling sound, and Billy caught his breath, knowing that the story was no longer for him to make up, that whatever was going to happen now would happen without Billy's say-so.

Karn flew higher and higher, and Billy felt himself being drawn upward after the powerful raven, like a car at the end of a tow line. Then at a certain height the raven lighted on the branch of a tree, and Billy found himself beneath the tree face to face with a young man in a short white dress of a type to be seen here and there in the pages of his brother's *Junior Universe of Knowledge*. The man's eyes were black as the raven's feathers, and his lips were so red he looked like he'd put on lipstick. Billy felt strange being there under the tree in his pajamas, meeting with such a weird person, but underneath the strangeness there was a new kind of excitement he'd never felt before.

—*Hi there, Billy*, said the red-lipped stranger in a rumbly voice just like the voice of Santa Claus, though clearly he was too young to be Santa Claus. *We meet again.*

"You're not Santa Claus."

The red lips curled in superior, grown-up smile.—*Indeed, I am not Santa Claus.*

"Who are you?"

—*That's for me to know and you to find out.*

"You're a pagan god."

The stranger laughed. It was a warm, good-humored laugh, and Billy remembered the line from the poem: "I laughed when I saw him, in spite of myself."

The stranger winked and twisted his head to the side.—*That's quite warm. But which pagan god, can you guess that?*

Billy shook his head.

—*Have you ever heard of a god called Mercury?*

"Mercury?" Billy echoed. "There's mercury in a thermometer."

—*Yes, and there's a planet called Mercury too. But before those things were, I was a god. The god of thieves and criminals, but also the god of doctors and of businessmen. Surely you knew that though. Didn't you read the paper your brother wrote for Extra Credit in Miss Brophy's class?*

"That's right," said Billy. "I forgot about that."

—*Did you forget—or were you lying? Eh?* The red lips pursed in a smile of mild amusement. *Mind you,* he went on, *there's nothing wrong with lying, so long as you're not caught. But what is wiser than a lie is a partial truth. I received my staff from Jupiter on condition that I never tell a downright lie. Yet some say I received it from my brother Apollo, who is actually my half brother. And I can't remember which is the truth, for I was your age at the time of the transaction.*

"You mean . . . the caduceus?" Billy asked in a whisper.

Mercury nodded.—*You have read your brother's paper, and so you know the secret name of my staff. But you do not know where it is hidden, and you do not know how to use it.*

"Tell me!" Billy insisted.

—*And why should I do that?*

Billy had to think. Then: "Because you promised. You said if I kept our talk a secret, you'd tell me where it was."

The young god ruffled the feathers of his winged helmet, as though deliberating.—*Wasn't it Santa Claus who made that promise?* he countered at last.

Billy shook his head vigorously. "It was you."

—*Why do you think that?*

"Because there isn't any Santa Claus."

—*But I do exist?*

"Yes."

—Again: why do you think that?

"If the poison stick is where you say it is, that's why."

The god began to disappear, not by fading away into the blackness all around but by shrinking into a smaller and smaller size. When he had shrunk almost as small as Billy, Billy remembered something he had said and called out, "Wait!"

—Yes? said Mercury, while he went on shrinking.

"You said you'd teach me how to use it."

—No, what I actually said was that you didn't know how to use it, and so you don't. But I made no promise. I only promised I would help you find it. And I will. It is in the garage.

"Where in the garage?"

—Where Karn might find it, if he looked.

"And when I've got it, will you show me—"

Mercury lifted his hand, and though he was now no taller from head to toe than one of the larger bowling pins, the gesture silenced Billy at once. *—Do what I tell you—and I will tell you what else you want to know.*

"What must I do? Tell me and I'll do it tonight."

—Bomb Dundor's railway. Destroy it utterly. Let the Greens be overwhelmed and the people of Wyomia enslaved. Do this, and all the power of the caduceus will be yours.

"Swear!" Billy insisted.

—By the beard of Jupiter I swear! By the tits of my mother Maia, I swear! And by my staff—suddenly, just as he vanished into a pinpoint of brightness, the caduceus appeared in Mercury's hand, a twisted stick to which were affixed the dessicated wings of a dead bird—*I swear.*

For a long time Billy went on staring at the ceiling of his bedroom. Then, when he was sure that everyone else in the house was asleep, he put on his fuzzy bunny slippers and went downstairs to find the hidden caduceus and to carry out the god's instructions.

11

The note had been put where Henry would have to find it when he sat down for breakfast at a quarter to ten, beside the cereal bowl Madge had set out when she got home from the night shift. It was written, not printed, in pencil on lined paper torn from a spiral notebook, and so at first glance Henry supposed it must have been from Ned. Reading it, he realized it was from Billy, and he didn't know which was more amazing, what the kid had written or the fact that he was writing in script almost as clearly as Ned, who was in sixth grade.

> Dear Dad,
> I am sorry about last night. I was acting like a little kid. Why be angry with you? When you got me such swell presents for Christmas. I should say Thank you very much. You are a wonderful Dad. Here is a big kiss. I hope you get another job soon.
> Your sincere son,
> William Michaels

Henry started crying. Admittedly, he was an easy cry. On Christmas Day when he'd been watching *The Wizard of Oz* for the umpteenth time while the women supervised the turkey and its trimmings and the kids test-drove their toys, Henry had cried at regular intervals from the opening credits all the way to Dorothy's return to Kansas and her family. He'd even been torn up by one or two of the commercials. Anything that smacked of doomed hopes, cheerful suffering, obdurate loyalty, or grand illusions could get to Henry right where he lived and unloose either a trickle or a torrent, depending on the levels of his emotional reservoir.

This morning those levels were low, and the pleasure of crying soon gave way to practical considerations. If the kid had really written the note himself, and not got his brother to do it for him, then he was wasting his time in kindergarten. Henry was already worried about sending Billy back to Sister Symphorosa's classroom.

Henry called Ned downstairs and asked him if he'd written the note. Ned said he hadn't.

"How did he learn to write so well? Have you been helping him?"

"No. But sometimes he stands looking over my shoulder while I do my homework. And yeah, one time, maybe a year ago, he wanted me to show just how I held the pencil in my hand. But I thought that was for drawing. He writes okay, doesn't he? I mean, for being only six."

"Is his reading just as precocious?"

"I don't know. He's sort of secretive about it, I guess 'cause he likes to get read *to*. He probably figures if we knew how well he could read things himself, we wouldn't want to read to him. But he does watch 'Sesame Street' like a hawk. And I've seen him when he didn't think I was watching, reading books that didn't have any pictures, or anyhow not very interesting pictures. Like my encyclopedia."

"Why didn't you tell me before?"

Ned shrugged. "What's there to tell. *I* could read when I was in kindergarten. I couldn't write, but I could read. Lots of kids can, it's nothing special."

It occurred to Henry that his stepson might not be as pleased to discern unusual talents in Billy as he was. Till now Ned had been a real overachiever at school, bringing home report cards with long strings of A's and B+'s even in categories like Conduct and Physical Education. Ned might not enjoy the competition of a brighter younger brother.

"Where is Billy right now?" he asked Ned.

"He went out with his sled. To the park, I suppose."

"By himself?"

"Probably with Ronny Tuttle. I don't know. I'm not my brother's keeper. What I'd like to know is where he got his paper from. *He* doesn't have a three-ring notebook. He must have got it from *my* notebook."

"Oh, Ned, don't be petty. What's a single piece of paper?"

"It's not the paper. It's a matter of privacy. You wouldn't want someone messing around in your desk, would you?"

Henry smiled appreciatively. He was always pleased to see either of the kids score debating points. Each one represented a step onward along the road to law school, which was the ambition he secretly cherished on behalf of both boys. Madge, he knew, wanted Ned to become a doctor.

Ned went off with a sense of having scored a point against Henry, and Henry, who believed in following his impulses without a whole lot of pondering, looked up the number of the rectory of Our Lady of Mercy and telephoned. By a stroke of good luck it was Father Youngermann who answered, not Father Windakiewiczowa. Father Youngermann agreed to see Henry at eleven thirty in the rectory, if he was free to drive over to the rectory. Henry said he was, which was not strictly true, since Henry couldn't drive anywhere legally, his license having been revoked after a bad drunk-driving accident in '69, the same accident that had landed him in the hospital where he'd met Madge and courted her from the inside of a plaster cast.

Henry walked to the rectory and explained the situation to Father Youngermann, who agreed that Henry's idea sounded good but said the decision really belonged in the hands of the school's new principal, Sister Fidelis. Father Youngermann phoned the nun, who agreed to see Henry briefly at the convent of Our Lady of Mercy two blocks away, beyond the school and the parking lot.

Sister Fidelis turned out to be a young woman with a pretty face and a full figure that her habit could not entirely neutralize. She was the kind of nun you saw only in Hollywood movies, played by Ingrid Bergman or Julie Andrews or Sally Field. Henry explained the situation and his concern about Billy's returning to Sister Symphorosa's classroom, and Sister Fidelis nodded and made sympathetic noises all the while and even volunteered some commentary of her own on the subject of Sister Symphorosa. Without Henry's having to make a suggestion, she proposed that if Billy could indeed read and write as well as the note he'd left at the breakfast table indicated, and if he could do simple addition and subtraction besides (or learn to with just a little private tutoring), then he would be bumped ahead to second grade, skipping first grade altogether. Henry was surprised at how little resistance he encountered and said so as he was leaving the convent.

"Oh, we believe in pushing our children to *excel*," Sister Fidelis said, with an earnest smile. "It's all very different now from when we were in school. How old are you, Mr. Michaels—about thirty-five?"

Henry winced. Women usually guessed him to be younger than he was. "Close enough," he said. "Thirty-three."

"Well, when we went to grade school, it was unheard of to let children skip grades, no matter how bright they might have been. The reason usually given was that somehow one would not be properly socialized if one were not in a classroom with one's precise contemporaries. But that's nonsense. The real reason was simply that few teachers were willing to face the challenge they represented. It is easier simply to deny that the gifted have special needs, but I think it only fair that if we expect more from the gifted, then we must be prepared to give them more, especially when they are as young as your son and cannot simply plunder libraries. Oh dear, I'm afraid I've got on my hobbyhorse again. You must excuse me."

"Excuse you!" Henry answered, taking up her style of somewhat breathless candor, as a tenor joining the soprano in a duet will take his tempo from the one she has established. "Everything you've been saying is music to my ears. I really was worried about Billy having to spend hours playing Farmer in the Dell when he could be learning long division. Don't get me wrong, though. I don't want to pressure the kid into becoming another Einstein. But I do want him to be able to move ahead at his own natural pace. It looks like that will be quite fast enough without my pushing."

Sister Fidelis laughed, but in a conspiratorial way. "Now, Mr. Michaels, you must not say anything against Farmer in the Dell. It is a tradition of several centuries, and for anything to last so long there must be a reason. But before I gallop off on a long-winded lecture on the history of ring dances (about which I know virtually nothing), I really must excuse myself. I have *two* piano students waiting for me."

Henry held out his hand and presented his friendliest smile. "Sister, it's been a pleasure."

Sister Fidelis added the pledge of her left hand over their handshake to declare, "I shouldn't say this, Mr. Michaels, but I really hope he is as bright as you say he may be."

"Well, good-bye, Sister."

"Good-bye, Mr. Michaels. Drive carefully, the streets are icy today."

Henry blushed. He'd never felt the shame of his license revocation so intensely.

12

At four o'clock, as it was beginning to get dark, Madge Michaels started the engine of her ponderous red Dodge Monaco, waited until she was sure it wouldn't die on her, and then backed the car out of the garage, crushing the plastic engine of Dundor's troop train to smithereens with its right rear wheel and to further smithereens with the right front wheel. The car radio was tuned to WCCO, and so Madge didn't hear the crunch of breaking plastic; neither, since she had swiveled around for a backward view of the driveway, did she see the wreckage left on the floor of the garage; nor if she had seen it, could she have realized the full implications this "accident" would have for the poor Greens, doomed now to defeat, slavery, and in the particular case of Dundor, impeachment and the ax.

Billy, however, perched in the storage space of the garage, did witness the destruction of the toy train, and seeing its wreckage, he rejoiced. At once, boldly, he called on Mercury to fulfill his promise and teach him to use the caduceus, which he had already ferreted out from behind the stack of defunct screens where Ned had hidden it.

Gods, of course, are not obliged to answer our prayers at our convenience. Many may never be answered at all. But Billy was not upset when no image formed in the latent darkness, for he knew that he had been forcing the issue. It was enough, for now, that he'd found the poison stick just where the god had told him it would be. Now it was his, and he meant to hide it where Ned would never think to look—in the attic, beneath a fleecy layer of insulation. Soon, Billy was confident, Mercury would return and fulfill his promise. Meanwhile, the destruction of the Greens must continue.

He swept up the shatterings of the plastic engine and put them in one of the sealed bags that had already been put out into the garbage can in the alley behind the garage. Then, with the caduceus hidden under the jacket of his snowsuit, he went into the house by the kitchen door and, making certain no one saw him, he went up to the attic. He was supposed to be afraid of the attic, since Ned had told him it was haunted by the ghost of Grandpa Obstschmecker, whom Billy remembered with dim horror as a very fat man who had tried to hook him around the neck with the curvy part of his wooden cane whenever Billy got too near his platform rocker. That was just about all that Billy could remember of the man, but it was enough to have made the attic a place of dread. However, now that he felt himself to be under the protection of Mercury, Billy felt no fear about going into the attic. Indeed, he felt no fear of anything supernatural.

He buried the caduceus under the gray nubbles of insulation that filled the long trough between the joists of the floor at the eastern end of the attic, where no boards had been laid. The roof sloped so close to the floor at this end of the attic that even Billy had to stoop low to keep from scraping his scalp on the nails that stuck out of the musty-smelling planks overhead. With a parting single-fingered caress of the withered wings Billy left his treasure secure within its mound of mineral wool.

And there for many long weeks it lay undisturbed though never unremembered. Heavy drifts of snow blanketed the roof above, and melted, and froze, and were replaced by deeper drifts. Dundor was beheaded (by a miter box saw) and his corpse hung in the Hanging Gardens of Wyomia for all its citizens to shudder at and mourn. Reinhardt was crowned king, and on the very day of his coronation his mother Icksy persuaded him to sign a decree putting to death all who would not worship the god Mercury and offer sacrifices to him of burnt marshmallow. Fortunately for the peace of the realm none of the unhappy Greens—all of them reduced to slavery now—dared to oppose Reinhardt's decree, but even this universal submission did not persuade the god to speak to Billy again. Strain his eyes as he might to see beyond the blackness of the bedroom ceiling, Billy could see nothing but random flickerings of the dimmest hues from which neither face nor sceneries emerged.

Meanwhile in the world of daylight, he had entered the second grade, where already he was at the top of his class, even in arithmetic. His new teacher, Miss Beane, was not a nun but a member of a Third Order. A short, fat, redheaded woman with eyeglasses that looked like a pair of television screens, Miss Beane immediately made Billy her pet and held him up as an example to all those in Room 201 who had not yet memorized the addition and subtraction tables. Billy had done so in three days and then, on his own and without telling anyone, memorized the multiplication and division tables too. Arithmetic came as naturally to Billy as swimming to a trout; he couldn't understand why other kids made such a fuss about it.

Second grade was much more fun than kindergarten. About the only part of it he didn't like was having to listen to the dumber kids trying to read aloud, but even that offered the novel pleasure of a conscious superiority. In kindergarten winning and losing had only been part of a game—and not even a game like checkers that took some thinking but dumb games like Old Maid or Snap. But second grade was the real thing. There were report cards, and you either got good grades or bad grades, passed or failed, and the kids who failed (the black kids, mostly) would end up dropping out of school and turning to drugs and becoming muggers and going to jail, while the kids who did best at school would go on to college eventually and then to success in life. Part of this Billy had figured out for himself, and part of it came from remarks dropped by Miss Beane and conversations with his father and with Ned.

Not that Billy, who wouldn't be seven until April, was all that concerned about that still very distant future in which he'd be accounted either a success or a failure. Right now he was just getting his bearings in, and hugely enjoying, what Miss Beane liked to call the world of books. He had his own library card now, with which he could take out as many as eight books at a time. At first he'd mostly checked out picture books, since you could finish a book that had mostly pictures in it in no time at all. But then one Saturday in the middle of February when he'd asked Madge if she would drive him to the library, Madge pointed out that he'd checked out eight books from the library only the day before yesterday. Billy protested that he'd finished all eight books he'd taken out. Madge had agreed to take him back to the library but only on condition that he start checking out real books that were meant to be read, instead of picture books. The real books turned out to be much more fun, since Billy's imagination could usually supply better images than most of the ones in the picture books, which were scribbly or blurry, while the pictures that Billy could see just by closing his eyes were as clear and detailed as a Technicolor movie.

The one subject that Billy did not naturally excel in was religion. He could recite the answers to catechism questions well enough when he was called on to do so, but he didn't like a lot of the things he was supposed to *do* in order to be a good Catholic. One Friday afternoon there was to be a class play about Blessed Father Martin Lugger, an Austrian priest of the nineteenth century responsible for developing devotion to Our Lady of Mercy. Billy was to play the part of Father Lugger's companion, Father Kreuzer, and for that role he was to wear one of the cassocks worn by the altar boys when they served Mass. But Billy insisted the cassock was a dress and wouldn't wear it. Even when Father Youngermann, wearing a cassock himself, came over from the rectory to remonstrate, Billy remained fierce in his resistance, and finally the part of Father Kreuzer was given to Jules Johnson, and Billy was stigmatized with a minus sign in the category of Shows a Cooperative Attitude on his report card.

The next to last day in February was Ash Wednesday, the first day of Lent and the day when Catholics go to Mass and have ashes smooshed on their foreheads. The entire student body of Our Lady of Mercy had to be at that Mass and wait while the grown-ups got their foreheads smooshed, and then it was the kids' turn, pew after pew after pew. Even with three priests doing the job as fast as possible, saying the words that went with the ashes like tongue twisters perfectly mastered ("Remembermanthatthouartdustanduntodustthoushaltreturn! Remembermanthatthouartdustanduntodustthoushaltreturn!"), the process took more than half an hour. Billy got Father Windakiewiczowa and a great glob of ashes that covered half his forehead and then fell in black sprinkles over his nose and his cheeks. Billy didn't realize what a bonus of ashes he'd gotten till recess, when he caught a look at himself in the mirror in the boys' lavatory. He looked ridiculous, but there was no way, with the lavatory full of other kids, to wash the stuff off. Anyhow, everybody else was smeared the same way. The ashes only became a problem when he had to walk home after school. Usually he and Ned went home together, but Ned was taking Lent seriously and had begun a novena that was going to keep him on after school for an extra half hour till Lent was over. Billy refused to join Ned in making the novena (morning Mass was already more church than he had appetite for), and since it was too cold to wait in the playground, Billy headed home by himself.

The way he was supposed to walk home was along Coughlin Avenue to Ludens, then west on Ludens to Calumet. These streets had the most stores and the most traffic. But it was dull always to walk home the same way, and if he went over to Calumet along Lind Street and then turned north, he would go through Brosner Park. Or if he walked north on Kuhn

Avenue, he would go by the duplex where he'd lived before his parents got divorced. Ned would never take the Kuhn Avenue route, since it went past the Weyerhauser Junior High School, which was about half black and regarded as an enemy of Our Lady of Mercy. But Billy had never had problems on the way to and from school, being still so small that bigger kids didn't think he was worth bothering. So on the afternoon of Ash Wednesday, being on his own, Billy decided to go home by way of Kuhn Avenue.

Kuhn Avenue wasn't really that much different from Calumet, except that the houses were squeezed a little closer together, and a few had cardboard nailed up over windows that had been broken, and the cars in the driveways were sometimes just wrecks, but otherwise Kuhn Avenue was like anywhere else, with front yards full of trampled snow or nontrampled snow, depending on whether or not there were kids in the houses, and lots of young pine trees not much bigger than Christmas trees that had been planted to replace the dying elms. Most of the sidewalks had been kept well shoveled all through the winter and so didn't have a buildup of ice, the way the sidewalks along Calumet Avenue generally did.

1633 Kuhn Avenue, where Billy used to live, was a house of cream-colored stucco with brown wood trim. The Michaelses had lived in the upstairs part of the house, and a family called the Cornings lived downstairs. There were only three Cornings, Marion, Orville, and Bubby. Bubby was handicapped and sat in the downstairs front window of 1633 Kuhn Avenue from morning to night, looking at the traffic go by and rocking his body back and forth in the wheelchair that he was strapped into. Bubby had made a strong impression on Billy when they'd been neighbors. In summers, when Bubby's wheelchair would be parked in the backyard, Billy would use Bubby for an audience to the ever-ongoing adventures of Ronald Rabbit (those were the days before the bowling pin kingdom had come into being), and though Marion Corning had at first disapproved and tried to get Billy to keep away from her son, who was then ten years old, Bubby had made it clear, by various gurglings and thrashings about, that he enjoyed these private theatricals and wanted them to continue.

He was there today, as usual, in the downstairs window, and he seemed to Billy to have grown almost to adult size since the last time he'd seen him. His head lolled to one side, and his eyes wouldn't focus on anything. Even when Billy threw a very soft snowball at the window to get his attention, even then Bubby just sat there. Like (Billy remembered his father saying this of him) a vegetable. Children like Bubby never went to school, or got married, or worked, or did anything at all. They just got fed and grew. Billy found the whole thing fascinating.

Even so, Billy didn't linger long in the front yard of 1633. The weather was too cold, and Bubby too unresponsive. He continued on his way along Kuhn Avenue till he came to the corner of Pillsbury and the cyclone-fenced playground of Weyerhauser Junior High School. He didn't even see the kids who beat him up until they ran up from where they'd been hiding behind a parked truck and caught hold of his arms. They took his books and threw them on the other side of the fence. They made fun of the ashes on his forehead and washed them off with snow. They looked in all his pockets to see if he had any money, and when they were sure he didn't, they lifted him up by his arms and legs and swung him back and forth and then let go, so that he cannonballed into a big heap of snow that a snowplow had piled up in the gutter. By the time he'd got to his feet and blinked the snow out of his eyes, they were gone, but he remembered their faces and he knew their names, and he was so sure he would get even with them that he didn't even bother crying.

At home Grandma Obstschmecker bawled him out for not waiting for Ned and for walking on Kuhn Avenue, and all the while she was bawling him out he smiled to himself and thought that he would get even with her too. And just that thought seemed to do the trick because right in the middle of her tirade she got one of her headaches and had to go lie down in her room. When Ned got home he made a big fuss about Billy's having washed the ashes off his forehead before Billy could tell him how it had happened. So Billy didn't bother trying to explain, he just included Ned on his enemies list and took a book up to his room and read till it was time for dinner, which tonight was a frozen pizza, since neither Madge nor Henry was home to declare otherwise and Grandma O. loved frozen pizzas as much as they did.

Lately Billy's official bedtime had been extended from nine to ten o'clock, but tonight he went to bed at eight thirty. He turned off the lights and looked up at the ceiling, as certain that Mercury would know his need and come to him as someone waiting at a bus stop is certain that a bus will come, probably in the next fifteen or twenty minutes.

First there was a kind of bubbling, as though the bedroom had become a giant percolator filled with boiling black coffee, and then the god appeared, without any clothes except the winged sandals and helmet he was shown wearing in the grown-ups' encyclopedia at the library. The caduceus he carried was exactly like the one hidden under the insulation in the attic.

Billy spoke first. "I did what you said."

—*Yes. I know.*

Something in the way he said it made Billy think of Santa Claus, and of the song:

> *He knows if you are sleeping;*
> *He knows if you're awake;*
> *He knows if you've been bad or good . . .*

—*Oh no*, Mercury said lightly. *I don't concern myself with "bad" and "good."*

"How can you tell what I'm thinking?"

—*A god knows that first of all. I also know that you want to be able to use your new talent, and I'm here to explain. But you must listen carefully, I won't repeat myself.*

His new talent? "No," Billy said carefully, "I want to know how to use the stick. The poison stick that makes people sick."

Mercury tapped the winged tip of the caduceus on his bright-red lips.—*Already, Billy, even as you say that, you are doing one of the things you must do to make the caduceus effective. You're rhyming. Do you understand how words rhyme?*

"When one of them sounds like the other, like house and mouse?"

—*Exactly. When you would curse someone with the power of the caduceus, the curse must rhyme. So until you have become quite handy at rhyming you'd do well to work out your curses ahead of time so that they'll be accurate. That is the first thing to know. The second is that you cannot use the caduceus to undo what it has done. You can use it for healing, but not to remove its own curse. The third thing to bear in mind is that the caduceus you have is weak from lack of use. Think of it as a flashlight with its battery almost dead. It will grow stronger as you use it, and you will be able to transfer its power to other, less conspicuous agents: a spoon, for instance, or a cigarette. But for now only its direct touch can work harm. One final caution: It will not kill. Not directly. It may engender afflictions that will lead to death, and you may easily learn, by study, what afflictions those may be, and how cruel or blunted their pathology. But death as such is in the hands of . . . other gods. I believe that covers it. Do you have any questions?*

"How long will it last?"

—*It comes with a lifetime guarantee.*

"Does it work on animals?"

—*Surely. On anything that grows; plants as well.*

Billy chuckled, thinking of what he'd be able to do to various dogs in various backyards that he had to pass on his way to school.

Mercury smiled.—*Now, Billy, you must kneel and worship me.*

"What?"

—*Power is never free. It must be paid for, and spiritual power is paid for by worship. Just place your hand on the end of the caduceus.*

Mercury extended his wand with the winged tip foremost. Billy put his hand on it. To his surprise it seemed warm and pliant. A smell filled the room, like the smell of hamburgers charring on an outdoor grill.

—*Repeat after me: Thou, Mercury, art my god. I place my being in thy care.*

"Thou, Mercury, art my god. I place my being in thy care."

—*Now I lay my soul in pawn.*

"Now I lay my soul in pawn."

—*This upon thy staff I swear.*

"This upon thy staff I swear."

Billy felt a brief itching sensation in the palm of his hand. Then the caduceus vanished, and the god as well, and Billy found himself alone in the darkness, covered in sweat and trembling with the amazement of having such power.

13

Because Henry Michaels was divorced from his true wife, Sondra, and Ned's mother was divorced from her true husband, Lance, they were both of them eternally damned to hell so long as they went on living together as man and wife (or so long as Sondra Winckelmeyer and Lance Hill were both still alive). This had been a source of a general, low-grade feeling of distress to Ned ever since his mother had sat him down and explained that, despite the teachings of the Church, she and Henry were getting married and snotty little Billy Michaels was going to be his stepbrother. Now, however, the likelihood of their damnation had become Ned's despair and daily obsession.

Ned's concern had become urgent when, in the third week of Lent, an African missionary had come to Our Lady of Mercy to conduct a retreat for the upper grades. In the course of this retreat the priest, Father Borghese, had described the suffering of the souls in hell, souls of those who had died while living in a bad marriage (like that of his mother to Henry Michaels), or in the course of an abortion, or in an automobile accident shortly after committing secret sins of impurity. Father Borghese had described the pains of hell and its sickening stench, and he spoke of the terrible sorrow of the damned, forever denied the sight of God. Then, in a voice as beautiful as a singer singing, he had asked *Why? Why* did people do it? *Why* did they risk an eternity of happiness for a few fleeting instants of sensual satisfaction? Again and again, the missionary priest's *Why*'s resounded through the nave of Our Lady of Mercy, and there was nowhere to turn, no way to hide from the certain doom the priest had pronounced against his mother and Henry, whose resurrected flesh would be covered with open, suppurating sores, whose mouths would be filled with the slime and slither of undying worms and scorpions, who would weep for mercy and receive none. There could be no mercy for those who had refused God's love in their lifetime. His fatherly love would be denied them throughout eternity, and the souls of the blessed would look down from their heavenly glory and be made glad by the terrors and sorrows of the damned.

Ned had found this so-much-more-vivid certainty of his mother's and Henry's damnation upsetting in a wholly new way. It seemed only a matter of days or weeks until they would go to their terrible reward. He began to have worse nightmares than ever, from which he would awake trembling and sweating. Once he wet his bed. Madge began to hint that he might be taken to visit a psychiatrist, Dr. Helbron, in the Foshay Tower. How could he explain that the problem wasn't his, it was *theirs*, the adulterous pair's?

On Wednesday of Holy Week Ned went to confession with Father Windakiewiczowa and demanded to know what he personally must do to lead the two sinners from their lives of sin. Must he reproach Madge and Henry for living in adultery? Must he remind them of the terrible dangers they faced each day that went by without repentance? Should he, as other protesters have done, go on a hunger strike until they had agreed to submit to the Church's holy authority?

No, Father Windakiewiczowa had advised, on no account was he to say a word to either of them. Ned must confine his efforts on their behalf to prayer and perhaps some moderate fasting, such as giving up desserts. It was the job of their confessors to stir Madge's and Henry's sluggish consciences.

Would Father Windakiewiczowa do that, then? Ned then implored. Would he phone Madge and Henry, and arrange a visit, and urge them to repent and turn from their sins? Father Windakiewiczowa became rather brusque at this point and told Ned, in effect, to mind his own business. Ned was meted out an unusually stiff penance (though he'd had virtually nothing to confess on his own account except his unwilling involvement in his mother's illicit cohabitation with Henry) and dismissed from the confessional.

Like the man in the gospel story, Ned's last state was worse than his first. He walked through the bright early-April weather like a prisoner heading to his execution. How was he to go on living with them? How could he sit down at the same table, knowing that soon it would be their flesh singed and seared and not some sirloin steak? And to be forbidden even to talk about it!

But that wasn't exactly what the priest had made him promise. He couldn't talk about it with his mother or Henry, but nothing had been said about Billy. Billy was only just turned seven, but he was preparing for his First Communion, and he was brighter than most seven-year-olds, and they shared the same dilemma. Maybe *together* they could do something to save their parents from hell. In any case, they could *talk* about it.

But when Ned got home Billy was not in his room, or anywhere downstairs, and his outdoor jacket and galoshes were in the hallway by the back door, which meant that he had to be somewhere in the house. Grandma Obstschmecker was alone in her own room, drowsing in front of a game show. There was no sign of Billy in the basement, or in the other bedrooms upstairs, or on the sun porch.

Only one possibility remained.

Ned opened the door to the attic and peered up the steep stairs at the dark-raftered underside of the house's roof. "Billy?" he called out. "Are you up there?" In reply there was a kind of rustling sound. "Billy?" he called out again.

This time Billy answered: "I'm up here, stay out."

Ned went up the stairs. The air was colder up here than it was out of doors, and very damp. He began to feel a stirring of resentment toward Billy. The attic had never been officially declared to be Ned's private domain, but he considered it such. Billy was supposed to be afraid to come up here, afraid of Grandpa Obstschmecker's ghost.

At the top of the stairs Ned looked about and saw Billy squatting down at the far end of the attic, where no floorboards had been laid. A long slanting ray of the setting sun entered at the west dormer window and lanced through the space as though on purpose to expose the boy's trespassing presence.

"What are you doing up here?" Ned demanded.

"None of your business."

"I thought you were afraid to come in the attic by yourself?"

"Why should I be afraid? Are you?"

Ned said, "No," and then he thought about it and realized that maybe he was. He had made up the story about Grandpa Obstschmecker's ghost himself in order to throw a little scare into Billy, and he knew that ghosts were not supposed to be real. But people's souls did live on somewhere or other, and long-dead saints often returned in visions, and what was the difference really between a ghost and a vision?

Billy got a mean smile on his face. "You are so, I can see it, you're afraid."

Ned shook his head. "Why are you up here?"

Billy shrugged. "To play."

"But it's cold." Ned could already feel goose bumps developing on his arms and across his chest as the damp air penetrated the thin cotton/polyester of his shirt.

"I've got a sweater on."

Ned noticed that there were wads of the insulating wool all over Billy's brown sweater and his corduroy pants, as though he'd been rolling around in the stuff. He walked nearer to where Billy was hunkered down. The cold floorboards creaked.

Billy backed away. "What do you *want?*" he whined. "Can't you see I'm busy?"

"Busy?"

"Just leave me *alone!*"

Ned knew now for certain that Billy was doing something wrong, but he couldn't imagine what. Billy was too young by many years to be committing a sin of impurity. But what other kind of sin could you commit in an attic all by yourself?

Without forming a conscious strategy, Ned decided that the best course was to be straightforward and bring up the matter of their parents' imperiled souls. "I was just at confession," he began.

At first Billy couldn't figure what Ned was getting at. He kept expecting Ned to tell about some sin he'd committed, but instead it was all stuff about his father and Madge going to hell because they weren't married.

"But they are married," Billy insisted. "They've got the photograph in their bedroom."

"Not in the eyes of the Church. Only their first marriages count—your dad's to Sondra, and my mom's to Lance. That's who they're really married to."

"Well, I think it's a dumb idea."

"But if they die they'll go to hell. Automatically. You can't just ignore that."

"That's what *you* say. But Dad goes to communion. He couldn't do that if he had a mortal sin."

"That just adds to the sins. If you go to communion when you're in a state of mortal sin, it makes it worse."

"Why talk to *me* about it?" Billy reasoned. "You should talk to them."

Ned shook his head sorrowfully. "I can't."

"If they do go to hell, it's their own fault, but *I* don't think they'd go to hell for changing their minds about who they should be married to. My mother says she's a lot happier now with Mr. Winckelmeyer, so what can my dad do? He can't go and live with the Winckelmeyers. And *your* dad—" Billy broke off diplomatically. It was an unwritten rule that nobody ever talked about Lance Hill.

"What about my dad?" Ned insisted, feeling aggrieved.

Billy smiled condescendingly, a carbon copy of the smile he'd seen his father use at the mention of Lance Hill.

"What about my dad?"

Billy sighed and repeated the epithet he'd heard Madge use, drunk in the kitchen talking with Henry. "He's a cocksucker."

Billy was unaware of the force of the tabooed word and the precautions governing its use, so he was not prepared for Ned's reaction. Ned scrambled forward and grabbed at Billy but didn't get a good hold. Billy skittered sideways on his knees, crouching low to duck beneath the rafters as they slanted down to the floor. Ned struck at him but his hand hit a rafter, and a protruding nail incised a long red line down the back of his fist. He screamed out "Jesus Christ!" before he could stop himself, then had to wonder if he'd just committed a mortal sin. The possibility made him even angrier. "I'm going to *kill* you," he told Billy.

"It wasn't me that said so," Billy defended himself. "It was your mother, she said so. I just heard her talking with Dad."

Ned knew Billy was telling the truth, but that didn't make it any easier to stomach.

The blood was running down his hand and dripping from the tips of his fingers. The red drops turned black when they fell on the fleece of insulating wool. And there, as though his blood were pointing to it, was the dessicated wingtip of the caduceus. He pushed aside the little mound of insulation that covered the stick to which the wings were secured. "You *stole* this! That's what you were doing up here. You stole it, and you came up here to hide it."

"Don't touch it!" Billy warned, waving his hands at Ned as he might shoo away a bird that had lighted on the lawn.

"Don't touch it!" Ned repeated. "You're telling *me* not to touch it? Oh, that is rich! Do you know what this is? Do you know what I can *do* with it?" The stories he'd told Billy about the powers of the poison stick came back to him, and he decided he would teach his brother a lesson.

"It's dangerous," Billy said, backing away.

"You bet your ass it's dangerous. It's so dangerous it's going to—" He did not finish his threat, for he had taken the caduceus into his bleeding hand and at once a tremor passed through his body, like a wind moving through him, an electric wind that tore at the tissues of his body, twisting and reordering atom and molecule, shattering the crystal lattices of the DNA as a greater wind might shatter the windows of a house, and ever, as it moved through the lymph and in the muscles and along the veins and arteries, gathering new force, wreaking new destruction, inflicting new pain, pain so unimaginable that simply from the wonder of it Ned could not have spoken. He tried to let go of the caduceus, but his hand was welded to it as though it were a high voltage line that he had grasped, which in a way it was. The vibration had spread to every part of his body: in his ears, so that he heard a kind of howling, the sound of the twisting and wrenching of bone and ligament; in his throat, so that he could not speak or draw breath; in his ankles and his knees, so that his legs grew weak and he fell, striking a floor joist with his hip and landing face down in the insulation. Its fibers scratched at his eyes, and he had not even the self-command to keep his eyelids pressed shut.

"I told you," Billy said in a low, reproachful voice. "But you wouldn't listen." He got a grip on Ned's arm and pulled him over on his side.

Ned began to choke. His eyes rolled back to show their whites, and his eyelids began fluttering arrhythmically. Then, from having been tense and trembling, his body went limp, and the caduceus fell from his fingers.

Billy bent down and picked it up. A residue of the power that had passed through made Billy's hand tingle with a strange pleasure that vanished almost as soon as it was felt. It left behind a feeling of sadness, but of great calm too. He knew just what he must do to avoid being blamed for what had happened. There was no reason he should be blamed; what had happened to Ned was an accident. Billy had never meant for the curse he'd placed on the caduceus to light on his stepbrother.

> *Filthy dirty grimy grubby*
> *When I touch you, be like Bubby!*

"I'm sorry," Billy said calmly. "I really am sorry. But I'd already said the words. And I can't change them. I was going to use it on the guys who beat me up. I would never have used it on you." There was a tear in his eye; he was telling the truth. It *had* been an accident.

Ned's body began to rock back and forth slowly, as though in a cradle. Saliva flowed out of his slack mouth and down round his left cheek to drip into the insulation.

Billy bent down and looked closely at his face. "Can you understand me?"

Ned made a rhythmic mewling sound, just like Bubby Corning when he'd first known him, back on Kuhn, before he became a total vegetable.

Billy hid the caduceus under the insulation in another part of the attic. Then he went down to the bathroom (leaving the attic door open, so that when his father went to look for Ned at dinnertime, he'd know right away where to go) and systematically picked off each and every fleck of insulation from his sweater and pants. He knew there would be questions as soon as Ned was discovered, so by way of accounting for his own whereabouts after school, he inveigled his grandmother into a game of checkers. She was a terrible checkers player—never able to think ahead beyond the next move and therefore always astonished and resentful when she lost. Billy deliberately let her win the first game so she was amenable to a rematch. Toward the end of that game, Henry and Madge got home with a Chinese takeout dinner.

It was Madge who found Ned in the attic and who drove him to the hospital in the Dodge. The hospital couldn't do anything for him, of course. For most of the next month Ned was tested, and Billy had to go through a lot of tests too, but nothing helped. Ned's condition remained the same as when Madge had found him. The doctors didn't have an explanation. Sometimes, they said, these things happen. Sometimes there is no explanation.

BOOK TWO

14

The elm in the backyard that had been dying from Dutch elm disease was alive again, not just on the mend but actually flourishing, and Ned seemed to be in communion with it in some strange way, his mind coming to awareness as the light of the dawn stirred in its leaves and easing into sleep only as the last glow of dusk left the sky. He could *feel* the juices bubbling up through the trunk of the tree, the shifting pressures of its different membranes, the thirsts of the roots, the lower leaves' greedy twistings up for the light that the shadow of the house denied them; he could feel them in his own flesh, like a tune that's always on the radio, filling you with its beat even when you're not thinking of it.

Not that Ned felt any better himself as a result of this awareness of the born-again elm. His own body remained inert and benumbed, a mere anchor of living meat tethering his ever-conscious mind to the daybed on the north-facing, elm-shaded sun porch behind his bedroom. It had been Henry's idea to let him spend the warmer months of the year out here, where he could watch whatever might be happening in the alley and the backyard. In effect it meant that he could watch the leaves of the elm turn this way and that way as the breezes determined. Yet even this random flickering yielded a kind of comfort, a smoothing-over of the prevailing ache of his own vegetative existence, the torment of being unable by so much as the blinking of an eye to indicate to those who tended the needs of his body—feeding him, diapering him, clipping his nails—that he was still a human being, that he could think, though not always very clearly, and that it was Billy who was responsible for his being this way, little goddamned Billy whose voice and footsteps and daily visits to the sun porch were like flames licking up from the coals of hell, searing Ned with a hatred that was still as intense as in the first weeks in the hospital when he'd slowly come to realize what had happened and now would always go on happening just the same, this living death, this *eternal* torment.

Eternity. The African missionary, Father Borghese, had talked to them at the retreat about eternity, how no living person could ever understand what it was like, what it meant that something should just go on and on and on, a pain that never changes, with no hope that it can ever be relieved. Father Borghese had even made the comparison of how a sick person lying in bed will shift from one side to another, or cough up phlegm, or put a washcloth on his forehead, but that in the eternity of hell even such small comforts are denied the damned. "We cannot imagine that," the priest had said, in a low, moaning voice, "we can't begin to understand." But Ned understood. Ned could have given Father Borghese lessons in the meaning of eternity and hell and the torments of the damned, the worst of which, according to the priest, was the despair of being denied, forever, the sight of God. But on that score he'd been wrong. After only a little while in hell the damned stop believing in God, supposing that they ever had. Or they came to believe in a very different kind of god, not the kindly creator of heaven and earth but the cruel architect of the inferno the damned inhabited, one who could look down, gloating, from his power and glory and take satisfaction in their suffering.

Such a god as Billy Michaels.

Not that Billy could be said to gloat. Almost the opposite was true. He was the ideal kid brother and faithful companion, always ready to help out with the messy job of feeding him, and never giving up on the unverifiable idea that Ned had a living mind trapped inside the inert hulk of his body, an idea that both Henry and Grandma Obstschmecker had long since given up on, though for Madge's sake they maintained a half-hearted fiction. But Billy seemed to have no doubt at all. Early in the morning and again as soon as he was home from school, he would come to Ned's bedside to read aloud from the comic strips in the *Star Tribune*, holding up the paper before Ned's face and pointing to each of the characters in turn, to Lucy in "Peanuts," to Dagwood, to Dennis the Menace, and Mark Trail, reading the words in the speech balloons, and then, if there was a joke, explaining it. Or he would tell Ned about the day's events at school or in the neighborhood, who'd flunked social studies, who'd been sent to detention for fighting on the playground, whose car had got its fender mashed on the thruway. Often when he had homework to do he would bring it into Ned's bedroom and work at the table beside the window, while Ned, weighted down by the chains of his paralysis, would lie in bed, staring at the ceiling or at the wall, according as his impotent carcass had last been positioned, and have to listen to the droning remarks of his tormentor. He must hear Billy's homework assignments read aloud, long catechism lessons recited until they'd been got down pat, biographies of Daniel Boone and the first astronauts in space. Even in summer Billy persisted in tormenting Ned with his damned brotherly love. Eventually it had become a source of concern to Henry that his son was spending too much time with the invalid, that there might be something morbid in this vigilant concern. Ned had heard Henry discussing it with Madge when they'd been sitting in the backyard drinking beers while they waited for ribs to be barbecued.

"I don't see what possible harm there can be in it," Madge said. "It's kindness, that's all it is. If someone learns to be kind at age eight, maybe they'll grow up to be kind adults."

"It's not his being kind I worry about. It's the *time* he spends up there. Talking to him. It's like those bowling pins he used to play with."

"You never objected to those."

"He was younger then."

"You're saying that Ned is like a bowling pin?"

"No, Madge, you know that isn't what I meant."

"And he's up there now in the sun porch, listening to every word we say."

Henry had no reply to that, and a few minutes later Ned heard the bang of the screen door to the kitchen.

The leaves flickered. From far off there was the sound of a lawn mower. A robin lighted on a branch of the elm and flew off. Eternity continued.

15

"When I was your age," Henry reminisced, resting his rake against the trunk of the elm tree and digging into the pocket of his shirt for a crumpled package of Kents, "there was none of this nonsense about bagging leaves, and nobody talked about composting then, either. We just burned them. Either in a trash barrel or in a big pile in the back alley. That was one of the nice things about this time of year, the smell of bonfires everywhere you went. It's a nice smell." He lit a cigarette, considered the flame until it got too close to his finger, then flicked it out.

"Could we make a bonfire?" Billy asked hopefully. He had the job of going through the piles of raked leaves and taking out any sticks large enough to puncture the leaf bags. His sweatshirt and pants were covered with shreds and crumbles of dead elm leaves, and the stuff had got down inside the neck of his sweatshirt and was making him itch like crazy.

"Sorry, pal, but if a cop car drove by and saw it, I could get fined two hundred dollars, and that's a pretty high price to pay for the pleasure of burning leaves."

"Why rake them up at all? Why not just leave them where they are?"

"Because the lawn wouldn't grow in the spring. If you ever go into a real forest you won't find a lot of grass underfoot. So if you want a nice lawn you've got to rake the leaves."

Henry took up the rake with a sigh and started making a new leaf pile. The wire teeth of the fan-shaped rake snagged in the rank grass beneath the littering leaves, grass Henry had not mowed since early in September. The process reminded him of his hog-bristle hairbrush on the bathroom ledge with its steadily accumulating tangle of lost hair. A bald spot was definitely starting to be visible at the back of his head. "It's not only the trees that are losing their thatch," he commented ruefully.

Billy looked up, waiting for the "but also" that would round off Henry's meaning. When it didn't come, he asked, "What's thatch?"

"It's what people in England used to use to cover the roofs of their houses before asphalt shingles were invented."

Billy looked up at the roof of the Obstschmecker house. The green trim had flaked away around all the second story windows and on the attic's gable, and the drainpipe had got disconnected from the gutter, but the shingles all seemed to be in good shape.

"It's an expression for hair," Henry explained. "I was thinking how I'm losing my hair just the way the trees are losing their leaves. It happens to some men when they get older, but I wasn't expecting it to happen to me, not for a while yet."

"What makes men get bald?"

"Billy, if I could answer that question, I'd be a millionaire. Some men still have a full head of hair at eighty, others start going bald while they're in college, and no one knows why. It's something in the genes—and don't ask me what genes are, because all I can tell you about them is that they're the smallest part of every person, so small you can only see them in a microscope, and only doctors at universities know anything about them."

Billy nodded knowingly. "We've studied about genes in Science. They're what kids get from their parents. I got half my genes from you and the other half from Mom, and you both got your genes from your dads and moms and so on all the way back to Adam and Eve."

"Well, you're more of an expert on the subject than I am."

Billy extracted a longish windfallen branch from the leaf pile and snapped it into three manageable pieces. "When you were my age, did you put on costumes and go trick-or-treating on Halloween?"

Henry smiled, and nodded. "Sure, up to a certain age."

"What age?"

"Ten or eleven. Maybe twelve. I was a shortie till high school, so I could keep on trick-or-treating longer than most kids."

"How'd you dress up?"

"As a ghost, when I was little. Then one year I was a pirate with a black patch over my eye, and another time I was a bum. And one time I must have worn a mask from the dime store because I can remember the mouth of the mask getting soggy and shapeless after I'd eaten a piece of apple pie without taking it off. Can't remember what it was a mask *of*, though."

Billy sprang his trap. "So why can't *I* go trick-or-treating?"

"We've been through all that, pardner. You know why."

"Other kids get to. There's no law against it like against burning leaves."

"But your school doesn't like the idea, and they're having a nice party on Halloween where you'll get just as much candy as if you went around from house to house asking for it. And no one's parents will have to worry about the chance of someone playing nasty tricks."

"You mean, putting razor blades inside of apples and like that?"

"Right, it's been known to happen."

"But I won't go to places like old Mrs. Wirtz's. I'll just go to places that have a jack-o'-lantern in the window. That's what Ralph says to do. He gets to go trick-or-treating and he's only in second grade."

"But he goes to the public school, right? And they're not throwing a party for their kids to go to."

"But I don't want to go to the stupid party. I know what it'll be like. We'll have to sit in the auditorium and watch old movies. And the older kids will take all the best candy for themselves and just leave popcorn and apples and that stuff for the little kids. That's what happened last year."

Henry sighed. He was in total sympathy with his son's feelings in the matter. A school-sponsored party couldn't begin to compare with the excitement of going trick-or-treating, and as for the danger of razors in apples, he figured that was in the same class of risk as being highjacked when you take an airplane or getting hit by lightning. The real reason for the ban on trick-or-treating, which was not even hinted at in the letter from Sister Fidelis that had been sent home with all the students at Our Lady of Mercy, was that the neighborhood was now at least one-third colored, and having troops of grade-school kids parading around after dark with sacks of candy was an open invitation to disaster. But naturally you didn't want to spell that out in a way that would be obvious to the kids. It would sound too much like prejudice.

Hoping to shift ground, Henry asked, "What are you going to wear for your costume?" The unstated assumption was that the costume in question was the one Billy would wear to the school party.

At first Billy was silent, sensing that any answer would represent his surrender to the idea of the school party. But then, almost as though he'd been following the drift of Henry's unspoken thoughts, he announced, "I'm going as a colored person."

"What?" Henry reacted with sincere dismay. "No, that would not be a good idea, Billy."

"Why not? I'll put charcoal on my hands and face like I did last summer by accident when we had the picnic. You said then I looked just like Little Black Sambo. And Mom laughed."

"Billy, there are kids at your school who are colored, and for them the color of their skin is a sensitive matter. They would think you were making fun of them."

"But it's just a costume. If I have to go to that dumb party that's what I want to wear."

Once again Henry had to admire his son's skill as a negotiator.

"Tell you what, Billy, let's leave it up to your mother. If Madge says it's okay for you to go to your Halloween party in blackface, you can. Okay?"

"Okay," said Billy. "And otherwise I can go out trick-or-treating?"

"No," said Henry judiciously. "That's out of the question. Now let's finish stuffing these leaf bags, what do you say?"

Billy said nothing but trudged, with seeming obedience, over to the separate pile of twigs and branches, to deposit the latest pickings from the mound of raked leaves.

Called, he thought. *Crawled. Walled.*

He stared into the woodpile as intently as if it were ablaze.

Falled. But "falled" was not a word. And neither was "talled." He started going through the alphabet systematically, trying to find a word that would rhyme with "bald." *Scald?* That was a real word, but he couldn't think of any way to fit it into a curse that would work. He'd learned, over the last year and a half, that only real words would work. If you used nonsense words, the curse either didn't work at all or was very, very weak.

He tackled the problem from the other direction:

Touch the handle of this *rake* . . .

But he didn't want to give Henry a stomachache, or any other kind of ache either: he wanted him to go bald.

Then all at once he realized that the answer was staring him in the face. He reached down and took one of the largest and most jaggedy twigs from the woodpile. Twig in hand, he headed for the back door.

"Hey, we've got a lot more bags to stuff," Henry said.

"I've got to go to the toilet," Billy lied.

All the way up to the stairs of the attic, and all the while he rubbed the twig and the caduceus together, transferring the power of the one piece of wood to the other, he continued to mutter, and improve on, the curse that the twig would carry:

> *One touch of this leafless twig*
> *Will make you bald as Porky Pig.*

When he returned to the backyard he dropped the twig on a part of the lawn his father had not yet got round to raking. Then, with an impish grin, he volunteered to take over the job of stuffing the leaves into the plastic bags.

Henry was happy to be done with the stooping and the bending. Before he started raking again, he lit another cigarette—but then, before he could start raking, Grandma O. came to the back door to announce a phone call from the Snelling Employment Service.

"Hey!" said Henry. "That could be it. Cross your fingers for me, kid." He dashed into the house, and Billy felt a sudden rush of relief. Almost from the moment he'd dropped his twig on the lawn, like a mine ready to explode, he'd wished he hadn't done it. His dad really didn't deserve anything so awful to happen (and for his dad, Billy knew, being bald really would be awful).

He broke the twig in two, and then broke each of those pieces in two. But he wasn't sure, even so, that being broken would have removed the curse from it. Burning seemed safer. He went to where Henry had left his flannel shirt hanging on the wooden railing of the back stairs and took a book of Hunt's Tomato Catsup matches from the shirt's pocket.

With the first match the pieces of the twig lighted easily, but they wouldn't stay lit. They fell out of the tepee shape in which Billy had positioned them and lay smoldering on the square of concrete that served as the bottom step of the wooden staircase.

The wind blew out the next match he tried to light.

The third seemed to take. Billy watched, mesmerized, as an orange flame wriggled up the smooth gray bole of one twig like a living creature. The flame-creature crawled from one twig to another. It grew, and shrank, and grew again, as Billy would hold one twig at an angle to another, the way you light candles from wick to wick.

"Good heavens! William! What on *earth* do you think you're doing?" Grandma Obstschmecker was down the steps before Billy could think what to do. She grabbed the burning pieces of the twig from his hand, and threw them to the ground, and stamped on them till the flames were out.

"You know better than to play with matches. Whatever possessed you to do a thing like that? And right by these old steps. You could have set the whole house on fire. William, why are you *smiling?*"

"I'm sorry, Grandma." But it was really impossible not to smile at the idea of Grandma O. with her head as bald as Porky Pig. He tried to think about how he was probably going to be punished for starting the fire, but then he'd think of Grandma O. bald as an egg and the grin would come back, he couldn't help it.

"What do you think is so funny, William? Tell me."

"Nothing, Grandma."

Maybe, he thought, the fire would have already done away with the curse. Maybe she wouldn't go bald. It would be interesting to find out. Thinking about it like that, scientifically, it was possible to stop smirking.

Grandma O. regarded him quizzically, and then delivered her final verdict. "You are the strange one," she said, "and no doubt about it." Then she went back into the house.

For just a moment Billy had the feeling he used to have when he was smaller and had been able to see to the inside of things, to where there were faces and bodies and buildings and animals. It was a feeling of being at the same time very large and very small. Taller than the tallest grown-up and smaller than the smallest gene. The light in the backyard seemed to flicker, as though a cloud had passed across the sun, and a gust of wind sprang up to lift some of the raked leaves from their mounds and piles and scatter them back across the raked part of the lawn. Then the feeling was gone and everything was the way it had been before.

16

"Hey, listen to this, this is interesting." Billy aimed the beam of the little plastic tensor lamp at the column of text in the *Junior Universe of Knowledge* under the heading of **Halloween** and read aloud:

> "**Halloween** is one of the oldest holidays that we celebrate. It comes on the 31st of October. The word Halloween is a contraction for "All Hallows Eve," that is, the night before the Christian festival of All Saints' Day. But Halloween and the customs associated with it go back long before the Christian era. It goes back to the time of the ancient Druids, who lived in England and northern Europe when those lands were still one vast forest, where wolves stalked through the night and men lived in fear. The Druids reckoned that the new year began at Halloween and not on January 1st, so that for them Halloween was also New Year's Eve!
>
> "The Druid name for Halloween was Oidhche Shamhna, that is, the Vigil of Saman. Saman was the Druid god of Death, and on his feast night, it was believed, Lord Saman would summon the souls of all the wicked who had died in the last year and who had been living since their deaths in the bodies of animals."

"Hey," Billy commented, "this is really creepy stuff, isn't it?"

Ned, who had been propped into a sitting position in his bed, listened, as mute and powerless as any minion of Lord Saman.

Billy continued reading from the *Junior Universe:*

> "In Christian times many people continued to believe that All Hallows Eve was the one night of the year when ghosts and witches were most likely to wander abroad. They also continued the Druid custom of building great bonfires in thanksgiving for the year's harvest. Stones would be placed in these bonfires, one for each member of the family. In the morning the ashes of the fire would be sifted to look for the stones, and if any were missing or

had been damaged, it was believed that the person represented by that stone would die within the year.

"Though we no longer credit such superstitions in modern times, Halloween is still associated, in many minds, with the uncanny and the supernatural. The jack-o'-lanterns glowing in the windows of our homes are a reminder of the Druids' ancient bonfires and their forest-world of witches and ghost-haunted wild animals. For us, too, Halloween is a fit time for giving thanks and for sharing the pleasures and benefits of civilized life. And the candy too!"

Billy closed the thick volume for letters *G* through *I* and returned it to its own little bookcase at the side of Ned's bed. He felt Ned's diaper to be sure it was dry, and then he sat down on the edge of the mattress. The only light on in the room was the tensor lamp at the table where Billy had been reading, and this far away it gave Ned's pale, slack features a weird look that would have been scary to someone who wasn't as used to it as Billy. Once, when he'd had the house to himself except for Grandma O., who was taking a nap, Billy had brought his friend Ralph Johnson up to Ned's bedroom and let Ralph see Ned laid out on the bed with just his diaper on and drooling. He'd shown Ralph how you could tell Ned was alive by holding a mirror up in front of his mouth and had dared Ralph to hold the mirror himself, but Ralph wouldn't come that close to the bed. Any time after that that Billy wanted to play Parcheesi or Sorry with Ralph, they had to play in the dining room or the living room. Ralph refused to go to any of the upstairs rooms because of Ned's being upstairs.

Even without Ned in it his bedroom would have struck an outsider as creepy because of the small jungle of houseplants standing in pots and hanging in baskets in front of the three windows that looked out onto the sun porch. Some were the original coleuses and prayer plants from the Hanging Gardens of Wyomia (banished from Billy's own room by the decree of the victorious young bowling pin king, Reinhardt), and others were their descendants. There was also enough glacial ivy sprawling out of pots and baskets to have supplied a small florist shop. Despite the lack of direct sunlight in the room, and despite the minimal attention they received, all the plants were thriving with thick twisty stems and fat, rather yellowish leaves. The reason for this unnatural vitality was that Billy had used the positive powers of the caduceus on them to ensure their health, just the way he had saved the elm tree in the backyard from the common fate of the other elms in the neighborhood, which had all had to be cut down because of Dutch elm disease.

At first Billy had been reluctant to use the caduceus for such a big undertaking. The elm was huge, almost twice as high as the Obstschmecker house, and it seemed to be in the first stage of infestation. Billy didn't have to be reminded that the power in the caduceus was the same as in an electric battery: if you didn't recharge it, it went dead. When he had the caduceus in his hand and he closed his eyes and concentrated, he could even feel the charge from the caduceus inside his own body. It was like the trembling you can feel when you're walking on a bridge and a truck drives across at the same time. Or like the tuning fork that Sister Catherine had struck during a science demonstration on the subject of sound waves. But in the end, seeing how much the old tree seemed to mean to Madge and to Grandma O., and just because it was so tremendously big, Billy had used the caduceus to make the elm better.

Strangely, curing the elm, instead of draining power from the caduceus, had given it incredibly more. Not a tuning fork now, but an electric drill or a live snake wriggling in his hands. Finally Billy figured out the reason: it was because Dutch elm disease was transmitted by beetles that burrow under a tree's bark, and what the caduceus did was to make all those hundreds and thousands, maybe millions, of beetles get sick and die. Making the tree healthy again may have used some of the caduceus's positive power, but not as much as the caduceus had gained from what it had done to the beetles. Once Billy realized this he'd made sure to take the caduceus outdoors every so often (hidden from sight in his KISS knapsack) to get it charged up and coincidentally to save one of the elms in Brosner Park.

He was proud of the power he possessed and of his secret good deeds on behalf of Brosner Park, but he was never tempted to take credit or brag, not to other kids and certainly not to grown-ups. Partly it was a matter of not having that many friends, but more it was from a feeling, hazy but strong, that the power of the caduceus could only diminish by being known—and doubted. Grown-ups didn't believe in anything that wasn't a part of their everyday world. They said they did, some of them, and the nuns and priests would talk about the power of prayer, but they didn't really, and their not believing was contagious the way a disease was contagious. It had happened to him once already with Santa Claus, and he didn't want it to happen again, and so even when he went to confession with Father Windakiewiczowa he hadn't explained what he'd done to Ned. He'd confessed to having "hurt" his brother but insisted that it had been an accident. Father Windakiewiczowa hadn't wanted any more details, he'd just given him a penance of ten Our Fathers and ten Hail Marys, and Billy was back to his basic state of grace.

There was one more reason Billy was never tempted to speak of the caduceus and its powers. He had the perfect person to share his secrets with right at home. Ned might not be able to do much else at all, but he could listen. And things became clearer as a result of spelling them out for Ned's benefit. Like the way that Sister Catherine had kept the whole class from going on a field trip to the Como Zoo because of five boys' coming back late from recess. Billy had blamed Sister Catherine, but in talking about it to Ned, he realized she was probably right, she probably couldn't trust those five boys to stay together with the class and not go off on their own, and so really she didn't have any choice, and the fault was the fault of the five boys, not hers.

They were all five of them black, but that was something you weren't supposed to pay any attention to, since prejudice was a mortal sin.

"I don't care all that much about the field trip," Billy explained to his brother, whose head had tipped sideways again so that his eyes seemed fixed on the highest-hung basket of coleus. "I've been to the zoo lots of times. But it isn't fair. They do things wrong and we all get blamed, and if you tell on them, like Geraldine McKune did when Lyman Sinclair wrote 'fuck' at the bottom of the vocabulary list on the blackboard, they'll beat you up. Geraldine's a girl, so they didn't beat *her* up, but they did pour ink down the arms of her white coat when it was hanging in the cloakroom. There was no way to prove it was Lyman. But everyone, including Sister, knows that if it wasn't Lyman it was one of the other four, everyone knows. And it isn't fair."

Billy looked to Ned for confirmation, saw that his head was lolling to the side, and readjusted head and pillow to their standard relation.

"Well, look at that," said Madge from the doorway. "The little orderly is on the job around the clock."

Even without turning round, Billy could tell that Madge had been drinking. Sober, she never had much to say except "That's nice," or "That's interesting," or "I'm busy now, go bother your father," but when she drank there was a sarcastic streak to everything she said, or maybe the difference was just that there was a point to it. Billy usually liked her better when she was drunk. Indeed, most people did, including Henry, though it was Henry who kept arguing that she had to do something about her problem before it became serious.

"He's dry," said Billy, backing away from the bed.

Madge nodded, and clawed with a blunt fingernail at the black scarf knotted under her chin. More and more she'd taken to wearing black clothes when she didn't have to be in her nurse's uniform. They were more practical. Henry said they made her look like an old woman and had given her a red dress for her birthday, which she almost never wore. Billy thought the black clothes made her look witchy and liked them for that reason, though he'd have never said so to her, supposing she'd ever have asked his opinion. There was an understanding between the two of them that they would get in each other's way as little as possible.

Without thinking through the psychological equation, Billy understood that Madge's apparent coldness toward him was a side effect of her having to go on living with Ned the way he was now, feeling a love for him that could never be returned but could never be buried and mourned and forgotten either. So Billy didn't blame her, but he did feel sad for a while, as he stood outside the bedroom door and listened to Madge, when she thought she was alone with Ned, as she began to talk to him in a low, singsongy voice, like one of the old women at the back of Our Lady of Mercy murmuring their prayers. He wished there were something he could do to help, some medicine that would make her feel better than the fifth of vodka in the freezer compartment of the icebox behind the half-gallon brick of Sealtest, not to hide it from anyone, since they all knew it was there, but just to keep it politely out of sight.

And right then, since his mind was already on the caduceus, because of what had happened earlier with Grandma O. in the backyard, Billy had an inspiration. There *was* a medicine he could give her. Hadn't he heard his father say, when he was arguing with Madge about her drinking, that her alcoholism was a disease? If that was so, then Billy could cure her of it with the caduceus!

Alcoholism—what in the world would rhyme with that? Nothing at all. In which case the thing to do was turn the words around so that the hard one didn't have to come last. For instance: "You're not an alcoholic now."

What rhymed with "now"?

17

Old age is full of tribulations, whoever you are, but for a mean-spirited or sour-tempered person—and Mrs. Obstschmecker was both of those things—old age is more full of tribulations than for most. You find out then who your real friends are, or you find you don't have any. About the only person left she could honestly count as a friend was Mrs. Wolfgren, but a month ago Mrs. Wolfgren had been taken off to a "home" by her ungrateful daughter Karen. St. Jude's Residence. St. Judas's came closer to the truth. Now even on the days Madge had off from work and was free to drive her mother somewhere, Mrs. Obstschmecker had no desire to see Mrs. Wolfgren, not in the dismal little room that she had to share with another woman who was practically dead from some kind of cancer. It was too awful. And in any case Mrs. Wolfgren was no longer much fun to visit. She had nothing to talk about but her bowel movements and how she had slept, and she didn't have the concentration for a single hand of rummy, much less an entire game, and nothing Mrs. Obstschmecker had to say to her seemed to register any more than if she'd been talking to Ned. Awful, just awful.

But she couldn't let herself become a complete stay-at-home or she would gradually end up like Mrs. Wolfgren herself. She had to keep active, do things. Her doctor said so, and Madge agreed. But what? Gardening was the ideal solution, but now at the end of October (this was the morning of Halloween), there was precious little gardening to be done, except to look after the houseplants, which were all in thriving condition anyhow and needed no looking after. Walking was good exercise, but Mrs. Obstschmecker no longer felt safe walking in her own neighborhood, and in any case a long walk usually made her hip act up. She could take the bus downtown, but downtown St. Paul had changed so much over the last so many years that it was almost like visiting a city in some other state, Chicago or Denver, and to get to downtown Minneapolis required a transfer at Coughlin and Larpenter, where she might have to wait half an hour or longer, and she didn't feel up to that, especially with the weather looking so uncertain.

"I know," she said aloud, as she stood facing the full-length mirror on the door of the hallway closet, undecided whether or not to take out her coat, "I'll have my hair done."

She didn't, if truth be told, actually require a perm, since she'd got her last perm just a week before Labor Day. A shampoo would do the job, then a little set to the curls in front while Sonia did her nails. At once she felt more cheerful.

She put on her brown coat and a trim little toque in almost the same shade of brown and set off for the bus stop. The bus arrived without too long a wait, and for the length of the ride Mrs. Obstschmecker was the only passenger. At the corner of Ludens and Coughlin she thanked the driver politely (he was a colored man who'd been driving that route as long as Mrs. Obstschmecker could remember), and he said she was welcome.

And there, between the corner drugstore and a new laundromat that had been just an empty shell for years, was Ludens Beauty Salon. Poster-sized advertisements for hair preparations adorned the windows and served to screen the intimate work that went on within from the view of casual passersby (of which at this hour on a Friday morning there were few).

"Mrs. Obstschmecker!" Sonia declared, a tart smile puckering her vivid lips into a cupid's bow. "What a nice surprise. Come in!"

"I should have called," said Mrs. Obstschmecker, allowing Sonia to remove her coat. "But I was out walking and I saw the bus and I had this sudden impulse. I hope you can squeeze me in. I just want a wash and a light set. And my nails, of course." She handed Sonia her hat.

Mrs. Obstschmecker settled her large body into the shampooing chair with a feeling mildly apprehensive and mildly adventurous, much as (in earlier years) she would have felt having been coaxed onto one of the tamer rides at the State Fair. Sonia tucked a towel about the unbuttoned neck of Mrs. Obstschmecker's dress and then, ever so gradually, lowered the back of the chair until Mrs. Obstschmecker's head rested against the chill molded porcelain of the shampooing basin.

"Now just relax, dear," said Sonia.

Mrs. Obstschmecker smiled up at the twin bars of the fluorescent fixtures, and did, to a degree, relax. She listened to the gentle *whoosh* of warm water from the rubber tube connected to the faucet of the basin and then, as she felt the first soothing warmth of the spray, she closed her eyes and exhaled the breath that she'd held clenched in her chest since the first lowering of the chair.

There was a spluttering sound as Sonia squirted a glob of the shampoo into her hand. Then Sonia's soft, soap-lubricated hands began to press and prod and palpate Mrs. Obstschmecker's scalp. There was a tingling feeling that became a tickling sensation. The usual even tempo of Sonia's soothing hands became irregular, then stopped entirely.

"Mrs. Obstschmecker," she said, in a tone that seemed almost threatening, "what have you been *doing* to your hair?"

"What do you mean?"

"Have you been using some kind of dye? You know at your age, the hair is very delicate. It can't sustain harsh chemical treatment."

Mrs. Obstschmecker tried to open her eyes but at once they started to sting from the shampoo. And her scalp was all pins and needles. "I haven't done *anything* to my hair," she protested weakly. "What's the matter? Why does it feel so . . ."

"I'll tell you *this*, lady," Sonia said, in a voice that was almost unrecognizable. "*I* am not going to be held responsible. This is pure *baby* shampoo, there is nothing in it that could possibly account for . . . something like this."

Mrs. Obstschmecker struggled to lift herself into a sitting position with no success. Her eyes stung. Her scalp felt like it was on fire.

"Lie back," Sonia said sternly. "I'll rinse out the shampoo. But I *won't* take responsibility."

The warm water sluiced through the rubber tube and across Mrs. Obstschmecker's forehead, affording an almost instantaneous relief as it flowed downward across her tingling scalp. But that relief was cut short by Sonia's sincerely horror-stricken whisper, "Jesus."

Mrs. Obstschmecker struggled to sit up, this time with real determination, but Sonia pushed her back roughly into the shampooing chair. "No," she said. "Let me wrap a towel around your head first. And then I want you to leave."

Without bothering to dry her hair, Sonia wrapped a large white towel around Mrs. Obstschmecker's head, and then she levered the chair back into a sitting position.

"I don't understand," Mrs. Obstschmecker said, almost whimpering. "Why are you behaving like this? You owe me some kind of explanation."

Sonia folded her arms across her water-splotched blouse. "You want an explanation? Look in the sink."

Mrs. Obstschmecker got up out of the chair and went to stand over the shampoo basin. As she tilted her head to look down at the mass of foam-whitened hair clogging the drain, the towel about her head came loose and fell to her shoulders.

"It's not my fault," Sonia insisted stonily.

For the first time since her earliest childhood (for as a girl she had been quite sedate and not given to tantrums and displays) Mrs. Obstschmecker screamed. She lifted her hands to touch the sides of her head, as though touch might contradict the evidence of sight. Not a curl of hair remained on her head. She was as bald as Porky Pig.

18

By the time Henry got home, all smiles, with a Red Owl shopping bag bulging with a good-sized pumpkin and several bags of candy, Madge was seething. She'd spent most of the last four hours trying to comfort or at least to quiet her hysterical mother. Finally it was only by the professional expedient of giving Mrs. Obstschmecker a placebo that she was told was a powerful barbiturate and tranquilizer that Madge had been able to get a minute to herself. Time enough to mix a screwdriver and then to call the lawyer whose name Dr. Allard of chemotherapy had given her. Alex Grossbart had offices in the Foshay Tower and specialized in products liability law. She called the office and managed to talk her way past the receptionist and get Grossbart's advice as to the immediate steps to be taken. Then she just sat and stewed.

"Hey," said Henry, setting down the shopping bag, "what's wrong? Why are you home from the hospital so early? Is something the matter with Ned?"

"Why are *you* home so late?"

He held up his arms in mock surrender to her anger. "Hey, I'm inno-cent. Just following the instructions you gave me this morning. Remem-ber?" He reached down into the shopping bag with both hands, took out the pumpkin, and held it up as a peace offering. "I got this, and the candy for Billy to take to his party, and other candy for the trick-or-treaters who come round here. They had a special on miniature Heath bars. You want one?"

Madge grimaced. "Not with orange juice."

Henry looked at the almost empty glass in Madge's hand. He knew her well enough to know that except at breakfast she didn't drink orange juice unless she was having a screwdriver, but he made no comment. "Something must be wrong. You look shell-shocked."

"It's Mother," Madge said, letting her shoulders slump. "She's had an accident. And I don't understand it. It makes no sense."

"Goddamn. She didn't fall again, did she?"

Madge shook her head woefully. "She's lost her hair."

Henry crinkled his eyebrows into an expression of puzzlement and sat in the chair across the kitchen table from his wife. "Run that one by again."

Madge took a deep breath and launched into the account that she'd already, waiting for Henry, recited in her imagination a dozen times—how Grandma O. had called the hospital in a state of upset bordering on incoherence, how she'd tried to get *him* to go fetch the poor woman from the beauty parlor on Ludens Street but couldn't get hold of him ("But you know, Madge, that I'm *usually* not here at that time of day"—a protest that won him only a baleful glance), how she'd driven to the beauty parlor and found Grandma O. in a state of near collapse and was screamed at by the woman who ran the place. "As though what had happened were Mother's fault! Poor Mother just sat there with her hands trembling and almost out of her mind, and really I couldn't blame her. It looks so dreadful. But you musn't say anything to her, Henry. She's *very* touchy about it, anyone would be."

"Let me get this straight. She went into a beauty parlor and started getting a *shampoo*, and the shampoo took off *all* her hair?"

"Well, obviously, it wasn't shampoo. There must have been a mistake in the packaging, or else this Sonia is lying, but she swears it was just ordinary baby shampoo that she'd bought at a drugstore. I did have the presence of mind to take the shampoo bottle she used so it can be analyzed. I told her if she didn't let me take it with me I would call the police in then and there. She's almost as upset as Mother, of course. Something like that could ruin her business. It's only a hole-in-the-wall operation. And she's not insured against this sort of thing happening."

Henry tried to envision his mother-in-law bald.

"Henry, this isn't funny. This is serious. Mother's in a state. Imagine if the same thing had happened to you."

"No, you're right, of course. But I don't see there's much that can be done. Will it grow out again?"

Madge scowled. "Now how would I know that? God, I hope so. Mother's certain she has cancer. She must have heard of baldness being a side effect of chemotherapy and confused cause and effect. She's in such a state, but the lawyer says you have to take a picture of her. As soon as possible. Is there film in the camera?"

"The lawyer? This is the first I've heard of a lawyer."

"Dr. Allard in chemotherapy gave me his name. He specializes in cases like this."

"Dr. Allard or the lawyer?"

"Henry, please, this is nothing to joke about. I went to chemotherapy in the first place because I had the harebrained idea—"

"*Hare*brained? Now who's cracking wise?"

"Henry! I went there because I thought they might have an extra woman's wig on hand. Sometimes when they're counseling women who face chemotherapy and the prospect of massive hair loss—"

"Oof, that sounds worse than going bald."

Madge finished the screwdriver with a gulp and a grimace. "Anyhow, they didn't have one, but in the process of my asking, Dr. Allard suggested I get in touch with this lawyer Alex Grossbart in the Foshay Tower. So I called him, and he said that what we had to do right away is take photographs of . . . the accident. In profile and looking straight ahead. In case we do end up suing the manufacturer, it will be necessary as evidence in the court. So if the camera doesn't have film in it, maybe you could get some?"

"Sure. But does it have to be this minute? The drugstore stays open till nine."

"Whenever."

"It's too bad there's no positive role models for bald women. If you're a man, there's Kojak, and Yul Brynner, and, um, Mr. Clean. But not much for women."

Before Madge could decide whether he was being sarcastic or sincere, the front door slammed shut loudly and a moment later Billy appeared in the kitchen to announce, with tears running down his face and a general air of tragic loss: "I'm not going to the Halloween party!"

"Billy-boy, what's the problem? Did you get in a fight at school?" Henry patted his lap. "Come, sit down, tell us what happened."

Billy shook his head and wiped at the tears on his cheek with the cuffs of his flannel shirt, but he did not move any closer to his father. "I wasn't in a fight. I didn't do anything wrong. I just went to the blackboard to do a division problem and everyone started laughing. Sister told them to stop, and they stopped for a while, and I explained the problem, which was how many times does six go into ninety-five."

"You've got me," said Henry. "How many times?"

But Billy was not to be humored so easily. He frowned down at the kitchen floor and fresh tears formed at the corners of his eyes. Henry felt the sudden familiar ache of parental helplessness and got down on his knees beside Billy and hugged him till the boy's body surrendered to the force of his love and Billy returned the hug and began to cry in earnest.

"I didn't do *anything*," he sobbed. "But they were all laughing, and then Sister saw what it was and she took it off my back and tore it up. But she wouldn't say what it said. She made everyone stay in class an extra fifteen minutes, because no one would say who'd put it on my back. It wasn't Janet Daly, who has the desk behind me, 'cause she was out sick today. And all the time during the detention period they kept laughing, all of them. I waited out on the playground till they were let out, but no one would tell me what was on the paper, not even my best friends. They said they couldn't read it. But they were laughing."

"Maybe it was funny—did you ever think of that?"

Billy's body stiffened at the betrayal represented by Henry's suggestion.

"I know what it probably said," said Madge in her cool Nurse-Michaels tone of voice. "It probably said 'Kick me.'"

"Probably," Henry agreed, grateful for Madge's quick teamwork.

"Kick me?" Billy repeated.

"That's what kids used to stick on other kids' backs back when I was in school," Madge said, nodding. "They usually didn't do it in the classroom, though, they did it at recess. It was a very common practical joke in those days. But you shouldn't take it so seriously. No one means any real harm by it."

Billy looked baleful but he'd stopped crying. "And if you have that on your back on the playground and someone reads it, then do they kick you?"

"That's the joke," said Henry. "Of course, it's never a joke to really hurt someone, but that's not usually the result. Anyhow I don't think you should miss the Halloween party on account of a practical joke that everyone else has probably forgotten by now. Tell you what, you go up to your room and think it over, and in a couple minutes I'll bring up that pumpkin there on the table and we can carve it into a jack-o'-lantern. Okay?"

Billy brightened. Carving the jack-o'-lantern was the best part of Halloween. "Why can't we do it now?"

"Because," said Madge, "your father and I have to talk about something. Grandma O. has had . . . an accident. And she's feeling very upset. And for the time being we should all try to just . . . stay out of her way."

"What kind of accident?"

Madge hesitated and then, seeing no way round having to tell him, she said, "An accident at the beauty parlor she went to."

"All her hair came off when she got shampooed," said Henry, trying but still not quite managing to keep a straight face.

"All of it?" Billy asked.

"Yes," said Madge, "but we must all try to act as though there's nothing . . . strange about the way she looks. It's been very upsetting for her. Think what you felt like at school when everyone was laughing and then just imagine what Grandma must feel."

"So we shouldn't stare at her," Henry elaborated, "or make any remarks that she might hear. Now, you scoot on upstairs."

Reluctantly, with his grievance against his classmates still gnawing at his pride like the fox the famous Spartan boy concealed beneath his shirt, Billy went upstairs. He paused at the door of Ned's bedroom. Telling his parents what had happened at school hadn't made him feel that much better, and he wasn't inclined to go over it all again with Ned. It would just give him something to gloat about. As for what had happened to Grandma O.'s hair, Billy had gathered, from his father's amused reaction, that that didn't represent any serious harm, but was more in the nature of a practical joke. But at the moment his own misery loomed too large for him to take much pleasure in the joke.

In his own room, he came upon a fresh reminder of his dilemma. There on the hook on the inside of the open closet door were the white jacket, white pants, and broken stethoscope that were the costume he and his parents had finally agreed he would go to the party in, instead of blacking his face with charcoal and coming as Little Black Sambo, an idea that Billy had been persuaded would be unwise.

It had been an easy costume to put together. The pants were from his First Communion the year before, and the jacket was one his mother had got from the very smallest nurse's aide at the hospital. There was also, atop the dresser, a headband with one of the funny flashlights on it that doctors use to look down people's throats, plus a supply of wooden sticks for holding down their tongues. A doctor's costume, clearly, but not just any doctor. Billy had been planning to go to the party as the hero of his favorite movie, which he'd seen twice when it came out the year before, *Young Frankenstein*.

What most people don't realize about Frankenstein is that he isn't the monster, he's the doctor. So really this was the perfect costume for Halloween, and Billy, though he'd complained so much about having to attend the school party instead of going treat-or-treating, had been looking forward intensely to wearing his Frankenstein costume to the party and repeating some of the jokes from the movie and using the sticks to depress people's tongues and generally showing off and having fun. But now, because of what had happened in class, he would have to stay home. The unfairness of the situation rankled, but what could he do, what could he do?

19

Pumpkins are always tougher than you remember, and as Henry was sawing down from the corner of the jack-o'-lantern's grinning mouth, the knife blade slipped and almost took off his finger. It did take off the jack-o'-lantern's single central tooth. "This is one jack-o'-lantern," Henry quipped, by way of an apology for the thing's bland toothlessness, "that's eaten too much candy."

Billy frowned, not immediately making the connection.

"He's lost all his teeth," Henry explained, rotating the jack-o'-lantern so that its minimalist face—triangle eyes, a triangle nose, and a simple crescent for a mouth—confronted Billy head on. "Because he eats too much candy and never brushes his teeth. Didn't you know that candy rots teeth?"

Billy giggled and gave his seal of approval. "Neat."

Henry next fit the white hurricane candle into the pumpkin's hollowed core, another process less easily accomplished than memory gave warning of. Ten minutes and two books of matches later, however, the candle stood stable on its base, and when the lid was put in place and the light in the room turned off, the effect was undeniably eerie. *What a weird thing for people to do*, he thought. *Wonder how it ever got started*.

The lighting of the jack-o'-lantern must have brought similar thoughts to Billy's mind, for he asked his father: "Dad, when was the first jack-o'-lantern?"

Henry relished the challenge of improvising plausible answers to Billy's dicier questions, and he proceeded to explain that in early times people had believed that ghosts, being naturally attracted to candle flames, as moths are, could be trapped inside a pumpkin shell and then made to tell their secrets, such as where they'd hidden their money before they died. He was even able to offer as supporting evidence the nursery rhyme about Peter, the pumpkin eater, who put his wife (his dead wife, in Peter's case) into a pumpkin shell.

Before Billy could begin to cross-examine him on this bit of instant folklore, there was a summons from downstairs. Madge had got back from the drugstore with a roll of film and wanted Henry to put it in the camera.

Henry rolled up the heap of seeds and pulp inside the newspapers spread out on the floor of Billy's room, but he left the jack-o'-lantern, all aglow and giving off a vivid stink of burnt pumpkin, on the top of the dresser, making Billy promise that if it started smoking more than it was already that he would blow out the candle. On the way downstairs he checked his watch. Six forty-five. Less than half an hour to jolly Grandma O. into modeling her new trouble-free hairdo and then Madge would have to drive Billy to his party. Really they ought to wait till morning when, as a rule, Grandma O. was in a better humor than just after dinner (if you could call Swanson's Chicken Pies and canned peas a dinner). But Madge had got the bee in her bonnet that the pictures had to be taken tonight, so what the hell.

Madge was in the kitchen. The camera and the roll of film were on the table. "You load the film, will you, Henry, while I go talk to Mother again. She's still so upset, and the idea of taking photos of what's happened is naturally not very appealing, but I pointed out that if she wants to be able to sue the manufacturer she'll need the evidence, and that seemed to bring her round."

"Hey," said Henry, poker-faced. "That's what I call strength of character."

Henry loaded the camera, and then, feeling antsy, took the wrappings and the contents of an ashtray over to the plastic garbage pail under the sink. He opened the pail with the foot lever and saw, on top of the crunched-up Swanson's Chicken Pie boxes, the emptied fifth of vodka from the freezer. On a hunch he checked the freezer. There was now a full quart of vodka peeking out from behind the brick of Sealtest. That explained why Madge had been so willing to make the trip out of the house to get the film. Under the circumstances Henry could hardly blame her.

He helped himself to a swig from the still-warm lip of the bottle and returned it to the freezer just as Madge gave the all-clear to come to Grandma O.'s bedroom.

She was sitting in the platform rocker which had been moved to the middle of the room directly under the brass lighting fixture where the light was brightest for taking a picture. The camera did have a flash attachment, but they knew from experience that it wasn't that dependable. She was wearing her pink quilted housecoat and, incongruously, Madge's cold-weather cap with the fake fur earflaps that could be (and were now) tied under the chin. The cap was bulky enough in itself that it would have looked much the same on any head that it fit, however bald or hirsute. But it also looked ludicrous, and Henry had to restrain an impulse to smile.

"Hello, Grandma O.," he said in a soft, placating tone, such as one might adopt toward a dog known to be ill-tempered. "I was sorry to hear about your accident. It's a terrible thing to happen."

Mrs. Obstschmecker pressed her lips together tightly and agreed to this proposition with an almost imperceptible nod.

"Mother," Madge said, in the same tone of voice as Henry, "you'll have to take your cap off now. So Henry can take the pictures."

Mrs. Obstschmecker glared at the camera in Henry's hand and then, still glaring, undid the knotted strings of the cap. The task proved unexpectedly difficult, for the knot had been made very tight, and the loose, crepey flesh of her underchin prevented ready access. Finally it was Madge who got the knot undone, and Madge who, when Grandma O. remained stock-still, took off the cap to expose the hairless pink ovoid of her head.

Henry snorted.

It was a minuscule snort, as snorts go, but it might as well have been a full-scale guffaw. Mrs. Obstschmecker's glare became a laser beam.

Henry tried to look away, he tried to control his breath, but it was too late. He could feel the first tremors of laughter shaking his chest. He lowered his gaze to the camera in his hand, hoping to hide the smile he could not restrain. And then, irresistible now, it welled out of him. First a chuckle. Then the long inhalation of surrender, and at last the fatal, fated laughter.

Mrs. Obstschmecker rose in fury from the platform rocker and grabbed the camera from his hands. "Get out of my room!" she screamed at him. "Get out!"

"Mother!" Madge pleaded.

"Get out of my *house!*" She hurled the camera at her retreating son-in-law. It struck a framed photograph of the late Mr. Obstschmecker that hung beside the door, then ricocheted to knock a small ceramic poodle off its perch on a knickknack shelf. The glass of the frame and the poodle shattered, and Mrs. Obstschmecker began to choke, and then to gasp, from sheer incapacity to express by words or gestures the extent of her rage. Her face—and scalp—had darkened from their natural rosy pink to a pale, mottled magenta.

"Mother, please. Henry certainly didn't mean to—"

"He meant to, all right," Mrs. Obstschmecker declared, all of a tremble. "And I meant what I said. He's leaving."

"Mother, the best thing for you to do now is sit down and calm yourself. You're overwrought. And that's dangerous. We can discuss this again in the morning."

"There's nothing to discuss."

The doorbell rang. A separate buzzer had been wired from the front doorbell to Mrs. Obstschmecker's bedroom so that she would be able to hear the ringing of the bell even here. The force of the old woman's fury was converted at once to abject fear. "Madge, who can that be? At this hour? Oh dear God, I can't let anyone see me like this. Where is that hat? Madge? Madge, what's wrong?"

Something was indeed very wrong with Madge if Mrs. Obstschmecker, in such extremity, should have been aware of it. But Madge, who was as little inclined as her mother to be seen to suffer, only shook her head vehemently and tried to make it to the bathroom in time, walking doubled-over in quick short steps. She still held the cap with the furry earlaps she'd helped Mrs. Obstschmecker remove, and when the first spasms of vomiting began, halfway to the bathroom, her unthinking impulse was to hold it up to her mouth to catch the vomitus. Even as the vomiting went on, Madge continued, slowly, to head toward the bathroom and so managed to reach the toilet without having soiled either her own clothes or the carpet. She emptied the pea-speckled contents of the ruined cap into the bowl of the toilet and then knelt down beside it to await the next spasm, which came at once.

Mrs. Obstschmecker, while Madge went on vomiting, stood outside the bathroom door momentarily forgetful of her own distress. "Madge," she called through the door (for she would never violate the sanctity of an occupied bathroom), "Madge, what is it?"

Madge made no reply, except further retching sounds, but at the other door there was a light tap, and Henry said, "Don't mind the doorbell, it was just the first kids coming for tricks or treats." There was a pause, and he said, "Grandma O., I'm sorry about my laughing. I didn't mean to. It just burst out, I couldn't help it. But I truly am sorry."

"Go away," said Mrs. Obstschmecker, unrelenting. "Just go away and leave me alone."

Turning away from the bathroom door, Mrs. Obstschmecker saw, framed in the night mirror of an uncurtained window, her own transmogrified image and held her hands up before her eyes to blot out the sight. The image of her own skull laid bare by a surgeon's scalpel could not have been more horrible. We can all imagine death more easily than we can live with shame.

The doorbell rang again.

20

When his father had left the room, which was illumined only by the toothless jack-o'-lantern's glow, Billy did not turn on the lights but plunked himself down cross-legged in the middle of his bed and regarded the newly carved face with the disinterested patience of a well-fed cat surveying a mouse hole, not really expecting anything to happen but ready if it should and meanwhile pleased to contemplate a sight innately beautiful.

The flickering light of the candle flame diffused through the pierced rind of the fruit and gave a faint, jiggly sort of life to things about the room, especially to the jointed cardboard skeleton that Billy had paid $1.95 for from his own money and that now hung on the wall beside the bed just opposite the jack-o'-lantern. Until this very moment Billy had felt that he'd pretty much wasted his money buying the skeleton, it hadn't seemed that spooky. But now, by jack-o'-lantern light, it was thoroughly spooky. Death, Billy realized with a sudden flash of insight, was something that was finally going to happen to everyone, and that was why people celebrated Halloween and All Saints' Day the next day, to remind themselves of that fact, and that's why you hung up skeletons and jack-o'-lanterns. A jack-o'-lantern is a kind of skull, a skull that's got a candle stuck in it, and someday your own skull is going to have all its mushy brains scooped out of it, or probably just rotted down to black glop the way a compost heap ends up, and it'll be as empty as the inside of a pumpkin, and you'll be dead.

"Dead and gone," people said, as if they knew for sure where you went after you died. But did they? Didn't Billy already know more than anyone else could about heaven or hell or whatever it was than any of the priests and nuns at school who only told you stories they'd been told themselves, who didn't know, the way that Billy did, what it was like to talk with a supernatural being, face to face, and to receive power from that source?

He smiled at the jack-o'-lantern. Tonight he was going to *use* that power. Why not? Why not show the kids who thought it was so funny to laugh at him what it was like to be laughed at. He could do something really mean to them, like give them all diarrhea. He only had to figure out a way to do it.

—*Good evening, Billy,* said a voice from quite nearby. It was a raspier, older voice than Billy remembered from before, but he knew whom it had to belong to.

Reverently Billy replied: "Hi."

—*I see you have already begun to celebrate my solemnities. I am pleased.*

Billy saw a black snake, segmented like a worm, ooze out of the light-flooded eye socket of the jack-o'-lantern, which was now not just a jack-o'-lantern but a skull at the same time. Strands of seedy pulp hung down from the skull's gap-toothed jaw and waggled about as the skull spoke to him and the jaw was jerked about. The last bit of the snake squeezed out of the eye socket and dropped with a plop to the hardwood floor.

—*I am altogether pleased. You have wielded great powers without incurring harm to yourself. That in itself is unusual and worthy of praise. But worthier is the way you have made that power increase. Now tell me—and quickly, for this is a busy night for Saman, Lord of Death—*"

"I thought you said you were—"

The snake that had been crawling across the floor with a slow undulant motion reared up and hissed loudly, just as a monitor would hiss for silence in a classroom.

—*I have many names, as you do. Sometimes you are William, sometimes Billy, sometimes Bill. And so it is with me. Tonight, on All Hallows Eve, I am Saman, lord of Death, and I would have you tell me now, at once, why you have summoned me to you?*

"Did I?" Billy asked, but the question was put more to himself than to the skull, which now was no longer a skull entirely but halfway to being a jack-o'-lantern again.

Saman made no reply, but waited in a dignified way for Billy to answer his question. As he waited, a late-surviving moth perched itself upon the smiling mouth of the jack-o'-lantern and peeked into its flaming interior.

"Okay," Billy said, "maybe you can help me think of a way that I can take care of those kids in my class. Especially Lyman Sinclair and those friends of his."

Skull-faced Saman grinned.—*Why yes, I know just the thing. It's something your father mentioned, don't you remember? He said, "Didn't you know that candy rots teeth?" Those were his words exactly.*

Billy nodded. He knew what Saman had in mind, and it was nastier than diarrhea. "How can I do it?"

The moth crawled into the jack-o'-lantern's mouth and a moment later there was a sharp popping sound and a flash of light.

—*See where my familiar Rottencore has found a nest to sleep.*

Billy looked and could just make out, at the base of the closet door, the broken stethoscope where it had fallen to the floor. Intertwined with its rubber tubing, the black wormlike snake had coiled itself so that tubes and snake were tangled into a single snarl, like the extension cords that were kept in the lowest drawer of the pantry cabinet.

—*Go to him*, Saman commanded, *and take him in your hands.*

Slowly, as though he were indeed a cat stalking some careless prey, Billy got up from the bed and crossed the room to the closet door. He stooped and inched his hand toward the motionless snake.

—*Take him in both hands, Billy*, the voice of Saman bade, *with a firm grasp. Do you think young Dr. Frankenstein would hesitate to touch any shape of mortal flesh? You must be fearless.*

Fearlessly Billy took the snake up in both his hands. It was soft and wet and cold, but though the coils of its black body stirred in the bowl of his joined hands, and though its head lifted to issue a lazy hiss, it did not seem to resist.

Billy turned, snake in hand, to face his god.

And there he stood revealed in his entire being, a naked man. But somehow colorless, bleached as sometimes on TV the color switches to black and white. A dead body it seemed, but alive. He was Saman, lord of the Dead, and Mercury, the god of magic and science.

The god smiled down on his worshiper, and spoke:—*Bravely done, young Frankenstein, bravely done. Now, do you know what more you must do?*

Billy knew, but just to be sure he said, "Tell me."

—*Take Rottencore to the attic. Lend him the power of the caduceus and feed him the candies you would curse. The curse is yours to give: I cannot speak it. Trust Rottencore and trust yourself. Be strong, and be careful. Increase of power brings increase of risk. And Billy?*

"Yes?"

The god had vanished. Only the glowing jack-o'-lantern remained, grinning its toothless grin.—*Happy Halloween.*

21

The trick-or-treaters were coming to the door at a regular rate. Every five minutes or so there would be another little pack of them, in costumes of all degrees of imaginative design, from the perfunctory (one boy, who was large enough to have been a teenager, appeared all by himself with no disguise but a paper bag with eyeholes in it and "BOO" crayoned across the forehead) to the perfectionist (matching three-foot-tall ballerinas in tutus and toe shoes). Henry tended to favor homemade ghosts and witches with extra rations of licorice and candy corn and to scant the Dr. Spocks and Batmen who'd been put together at the five and dime or by K-Mart, but even for those he favored there were no Heath bars. The Heath bars had vanished from the kitchen table before Henry had been able to pocket a single one for himself, which was a source of real regret since, though they were his favorite candy bar, he hadn't tasted one in years. He wasn't generally much of a candy eater, but with a whole $2.79 bag of them in the house . . .

He thought of calling upstairs for Billy, but so long as Madge was holed up with her hysterical mother there was no point in having Billy under his feet. It seemed strange that Billy wasn't already in his costume and pestering Madge to drive him to Our Lady of Mercy, and Henry wondered if the boy had had another mood swing and decided he didn't want to go to the school party after all. In any case, until Madge was ready, Billy might as well stay upstairs. Seeing the steady procession of trick-or-treaters coming to the house would only make him fretful that he couldn't be doing the same thing.

Madge didn't come out of Grandma O.'s room till almost a quarter past seven, at which point she announced that she would not be able to drive Billy to his party. She was too sick.

Henry began to object, thinking this was her way to punish him for pushing Grandma O. over the edge. But then he caught a whiff of the vomit on her breath and took a second look and realized that she wasn't putting him on. "Jesus, you *are* sick. What's wrong?"

"I don't know, I just started throwing up and there was no stopping. Food poisoning, I thought, but Grandma O. says her stomach feels fine. One small blessing is that my getting sick seems to have calmed her down a little, though she's still threatening you with eviction, as of noon tomorrow. That was a dumb thing to do, Henry."

"I couldn't help myself. It's just like throwing up. Once a laugh starts to come, there's no stopping it. But that's not important. You look terrible: if it's not food poisoning . . . ?"

"It's probably just all the hours of stress, and then that last scene in Mother's room triggered it. While it lasted it was so violent. I don't remember ever, ever being sick in just that way. But I feel all right now. My stomach must be totally empty. It was awful."

"Hey, I'm sorry." Henry pulled her close to him for a kiss, and then crinkled his nose with mock disgust. "Phew! you better go brush your teeth."

"My comforter," Madge said sarcastically, but with a grateful smile even so.

"Can you handle the trick-or-treaters, if I walk Billy to his party?"

"Sure, I'll just put buckets either side of the door. But you don't have to do that. When he came home, he said he didn't *want* to go."

"I know, but it's Halloween. And Halloween is like . . . I don't know, it's a kind of national Be Kind to Children Day, right? If he can walk to his damned school and back five times a week, I guess I can do it one night of the year."

"You're a noble, self-sacrificing man, Henry Michaels, and as soon as I brush my teeth I'll give you an award as Father of the Year."

"Give it to me now," he said, nuzzling his nose against her cheek. "I think I could get into vomit. As long as it's yours."

"Don't be disgusting," she said, turning her head aside.

Before Henry could advance his conjugal flirtation further, the doorbell rang again. "Saved by the bell," he said, taking up the divided serving dish in which he'd put the two kinds of candy and heading for the door.

He was greeted by a lighted jack-o'-lantern of heroic proportions that was held up mask-wise by a child robed in dirty brown burlap. "Trick or treat!" a girl's voice declared from behind the mammoth pumpkin.

"Madge, come and look at this," said Henry, genuinely impressed. Then to the girl bearing the jack-o'-lantern, "You are definitely this year's winner for most original costume. How in the world do you get that pumpkin from house to house? It must weigh twenty pounds."

"Surprise!" said a grown-up standing in the shadows beyond the reach of the porch light.

The jack-o'-lantern was lowered to chest level, revealing the familiar features (for all that they'd been whitened with powder) of Judith Winckelmeyer. "Happy Halloween, Mr. Michaels," she said in a thin but still musical voice that seemed all of a piece with her physical appearance, the prim lips and chiseled nose, the dark eyes and hair, the elfin face so well suited to the present occasion. There was nothing in Judith's appearance (or, so far as Henry knew, in her character) that seemed to stem from the genes of her father, plump, prosperous Ben Winckelmeyer. "And you too, Mrs. Michaels, Happy Halloween."

"Judy. Sondra. This *is* a surprise," Henry said. "Come in the house."

"Please." Madge echoed the invitation hollowly. "Do."

Sondra stepped forward into the porch light. She was wearing a knee-length coat of tawny orange suede and carried a large layer cake with frosting in exactly the same shade of orange. A jack-o'-lantern face had been painted with black icing on top of the cake.

Sondra smiled her smile that said, *Let's forget about everything in the past and just try and be nice.* "Is Billy still home?" she asked, pausing at the base of the porch steps. "Or has he already gone to his school party?"

"He's somewhere upstairs," Henry said. "Getting into his costume." He stared at his ex-wife with the same kind of respectful and purely theoretical hunger he felt for the cake she was carrying. When she'd been married to *him*, she'd never looked so foxy. It was all packaging, all icing on the cake, all the effect of Ben Winckelmeyer's money.

"I brought a cake," Sondra said, with the same placatory smile.

"I see," said Madge, regarding the layer cake with a hunger anything but theoretical. Her emptied stomach rumbled its longing, and her mouth lusted for a slice. "It looks scrumptious."

Sondra mounted the steps carefully. Henry noted the boots she wore: calf-high, semi-western boots in the same suede as the coat. There was no telling what the whole outfit must have cost. She handed the cake to

Madge and followed her stepdaughter through the door that Henry was holding open.

Madge and Henry followed them inside. Room for the jack-o'-lantern was made on the mantel over the fireplace, and magazines and ashtrays were cleared from the coffee table in front of the couch so that the cake could be properly admired.

"Judith made it all herself," Sondra said, wriggling out of the sleeves of her coat to reveal a black silk blouse decorated with a pearl pin, which, if the pearls were real, must have cost even more than the outer, suede layer of her outfit.

"It's *fun* to cook," Judith said. She'd seated herself cross-legged on the rug just to the side of the coffee table. "I'm just starting to learn, but I like it, it's like doing chemistry. And it's pretty to look at, too."

"Now," said Sondra with a nervous laugh, "if she'd only learn that the result is meant to be eaten!"

"Mother is always after me to eat more. If I ate *everything* you said I should in a single day, Mother, I'd soon be as fat as Winky."

"Who's Winky?" Madge asked. "And how fat is she?"

"Winky was his family's nickname for Ben when he was a little boy, and ever since Judith found that out from her aunt she's insisted on calling her father Winky. He hates it."

"He does not hate it, Mother, he just thinks it's silly. That's what a nickname is for, isn't it, to make you feel dumb? If he'd stop calling me Judy, I'd stop calling him Winky, I've told him that a thousand times."

Henry smiled, recognizing in the last phrase from Judith's mouth an expression he'd heard endless times from Sondra's lips: "Henry, we've gone through that a thousand times," or "Henry, if I've told you once I've told you a thousand times." Without either of them knowing it, Sondra was having a real influence over Ben Winckelmeyer's daughter—despite the girl's insistence on maintaining a skeptical distance from her step-mother.

Madge caught Henry's smile and by the smallest wrinkling of her forehead gave him to know that it was not good manners to be eliciting these revealing details about the Winckelmeyers' household from the guileless Judith. Madge turned to the girl with a polite, cheery smile (the one she flashed on children at the hospital whenever she came into their ward) and asked her the question it is always safe to ask of any child. "How old are you now, Judith?"

"Eleven and two-thirds. How old are you?"

"Judith, really!" Sondra scolded. "Can't you be nice?"

"There's nothing not nice about her question," said Madge, who was ten years older than Sondra but didn't in fact give a hoot about it. For Madge the question wasn't how old you were but how well you stacked up compared to other people the same age. Despite the smoking and despite the booze, Madge felt herself to be in good shape, relative to Henry's ex. "I'm thirty-nine," she lied. She wouldn't be thirty-nine till January.

"That's some witch costume you got on," Henry said, and that was a lie too, or at least insincere. If the compliment had been paid to Sondra it would have been true enough, but the outfit Judith was wearing made her look more like a miniature derelict than a witch. "It's spooky."

Judith giggled.

"She's not a witch, Henry," said Sondra. "She's St. Clare."

Henry looked puzzled. "St. Clair, Minnesota?"

"St. Clare the saint," Sondra explained, with a little grimace of disapproval.

"St. Clare was the sister of St. Francis," Judith elaborated. "She founded the order of Poor Clares almost five hundred years ago."

"Isn't that unusual," Madge said. Then, as that seemed more of a criticism of the costume than a simple observation, she added: "I mean, isn't it unusual to dress up as a saint on Halloween?"

"If I stay up past midnight, it will be All Saints' Day."

"I hope you don't intend to go to Mass as St. Clare," Sondra said lightly. "Your father wouldn't appreciate that."

"Of course not, Mother, don't be silly." This time it was Judith's turn to change the subject. "Where is William?"

Henry sprang up from the couch. "Good question. I'll go upstairs and get him now. Billy's been getting into his costume. Wait'll you see it, it's a humdinger."

Henry left the three women to carry on the sparring match by themselves and went up the stairs and down the hall to Billy's room, but even before he opened the door he knew Billy wasn't there.

A faint, uncanny flicker of nameless feeling touched Henry's heart as he looked about the empty room. It was like the poem that all the girls in junior year at Alexander Ramsey High School had memorized and recited time and again. "Little Boy Blue," by Eugene Field. He couldn't remember the poem itself, only the groan that had gone up from the boys in the class each time the old tearjerker got put through its paces. There were Billy's toys and his books. There, in the corner, were the two sets of bowling pins, arranged now in conventional ten-pin triangles. And there, still, on the closet door, was his doctor costume.

But the jack-o'-lantern, where was that?

"Billy?" he called aloud. "Billy, where are you?"

There was no answer.

Somehow Henry hadn't expected one. He went back out into the hall and saw that the door to Ned's room was ajar, letting the dim glow of the night-light beside his bed spill out into the dark hallway. *Of course*, he thought, *that's where Billy would be*. He'd taken the jack-o'-lantern to show it to Ned.

But Ned's room was empty, too—or so to Henry's blindered sight it appeared. He steadfastly refused to treat Ned's comatose body as though the boy's mind and spirit were still alive within its husk of flesh. Henry returned to the hallway without sparing a glance for the body in the bed.

"*Billy!*" he called again more loudly. "Billy, your mother is here!"

This time there was a muffled reply and a muted clattering sound. But from where? The doors to the other rooms stood open, and they were dark within—all but the door to the attic, and surely Billy would not be there.

But when he opened the door to the attic, Henry could see a faint wavering of candlelight on the bare rafters, and when he began to mount the stairs, Billy's voice issued clearly from the darkness: "I *said* I'll be right down, Dad!"

"What are you doing up here?" Henry asked of the darkness.

"I just brought the jack-o'-lantern up here to see it where it's really dark, that's all."

Henry had reached the head of the stairs, and now he could see Billy at the far end of cavernous space kneeling in front of the jack-o'-lantern and hastily stuffing something that was scattered across the floorboards into his KISS knapsack.

"Your mother's downstairs, with Judith. If you hurry, they can give you a ride with them to your party. Madge's not feeling well, so I was meaning to walk you over there, but as long as they're here with a car—" Henry broke off. He was close enough to Billy now to see that what he'd been stuffing into his knapsack was the missing Heath bars.

"Okay," Billy said. "I'm hurrying. I'm done. I'll put on my costume right away." He buckled the knapsack closed and put his arms through the straps. Then, taking up the jack-o'-lantern in both hands, he got to his feet. The candle flame wavered as Billy turned round, and the jack-o'-lantern seemed for a moment to be a sentient, living thing.

"It does look spookier up here, doesn't it, Dad?"

"Yes," Henry agreed, "it does. Now give me the jack-o'-lantern. I don't want you tripping on the stairs and setting the whole house on fire. Go get into your costume. Pronto."

Billy handed the jack-o'-lantern to his father and reluctantly headed for the stairs. Halfway there he turned around. "Aren't you coming down, too?"

"In a bit."

Alone, Henry placed the pumpkin on the floor and swept his hand about in the dark spaces overhead, trying to find the string for the light, only to discover, when his hand had grasped it, that the bulb had burnt out. Then, using the pumpkin as a flashlight, he examined the area of the attic where he'd found Billy, feeling a little foolish to be playing detective this way, with no idea of what he might be looking for, but feeling also a strange uneasiness. Surely, it was just the contagion of the boy's Halloween high spirits. Kids have this hunger for blood and gore because . . . well, because they're human. Grown-ups, after all, have pretty much the same hunger. Henry had almost persuaded himself to give up scanning the bare floorboards, when he saw, with a start of genuine fear, a black wriggling motion that some ancient deep-rooted instinct interpreted as "Snake!" But that was absurd; the thing he saw, at the farthest reach of the jack-o'-lantern's light, just where the floorboards gave way to a seeming carpet of insulating wool, was not in motion and not, certainly, a snake. It was (he squatted, set down the jack-o'-lantern, and picked the thing up) the broken stethoscope Madge had brought home for Billy's costume.

And beside it was the explanation for Billy's being up here: an empty Heath wrapper. Of course. He'd come up to the attic to make sure he got his share of the best candy while there was still a chance. Candy eaten in secret is always sweeter than candy that comes with your parents' seal of approval.

A good theory, but in fact when he picked up the wrapper, it wasn't empty. Henry let himself be tempted briefly. He did like Heath bars, but the hard crunchy part was hell on his teeth. There was a gap between two of his back left lower molars that no amount of brushing ever got clean when stuff got impacted there.

Giving himself a mental pat on the back for resisting the temptation, Henry pocketed the little candy bar, took up the jack-o'-lantern with its toothless grin, and headed back down to the lamplit living room and the social sparring and (thinking more positively) the strong possibility, once his ex had taken Billy off to the school party, of having a piece of *his* favorite candy.

22

"Did she drink her Mickey Finn?" Henry asked, when Madge returned to the kitchen with the tray and the dishes she'd brought in to her mother for her evening snack.

"Down to the last drop. She gobbled the cake, drank the Sanka, and popped right off. Older people are like that with Amytal, it hits them harder. The camera's wrecked, by the way."

She put the dishes in the sink and returned the tray to its appointed place on the pantry shelf. Then she rejoined Henry at the kitchen table, accepting a cigarette from the pack he held out to her.

"How's your stomach now?" he asked.

"No problem. Judith's cake was a bit sweeter than I like—"

"It was like drowning in marshmallow syrup," Henry commented.

"That didn't stop you, I see, from having a second slice while I was with Mother." She lit the cigarette and waved out the match. "Isn't that Judith a pill, though?"

Henry grinned. "It's hard to gauge with her dressed up in that gunny-sack, but I thought she was sort of cute. In a year or so she'll be a regular little Lolita."

"You," Madge said, smiling. "You've got a one-track mind."

"Tonight I do."

"Well, just hold your horses. There'll be kids ringing the doorbell for a while yet, and you're not going to want to deal with soaped windows tomorrow. After I'm back from picking up Billy there'll be time enough for ess ee ex."

"You're sure you're feeling up to the drive? I wouldn't mind the walk. It'd do me good."

"I'm feeling fine. Whatever it was, it's out of my system. And what I'd like right now is a drink. How about you?"

"Sure, name your poison."

"There's nothing but orange juice for a mixer."

"Let me do it."

Henry got up from the table and started making screwdrivers, talking while he popped ice cubes from the tray and mixed the contents of bottle and carton. "Didn't Billy get into a state about those Heath bars? He's not usually like that. Here they bring over that damned five-buck pumpkin and a whole cake, and he won't let 'em have one miserable piece of candy."

"It's the holidays. Kids go crazy at the holidays. Anyhow Sondra says that Judith doesn't touch candy of any kind. She's the ultimate finicky eater. Remember two years ago—she wouldn't eat *anything* but peanut butter and banana sandwiches. Now it's health food. At dinner she eats vegetables and salad but won't touch meat. I told Sondra if she doesn't watch out she's going to have an anorexic on her hands."

The screwdrivers were fixed. Henry handed one to Madge and said, "Want to go in the living room? Maybe there's something on TV."

"Sure." She stubbed out the cigarette in the ashtray and took a long ice-tinkling swallow from the drink.

The doorbell rang.

"Damn," said Henry. He took up the serving dish with the candy in it and went to the front door.

It was Billy's friend Ralph Johnson and, looking on from the base of the porch steps, his father, a guy about Henry's age but already paunchy from his job at some downtown bank. Ralph was dressed as an Indian, with stripes of lipstick war paint on his cheeks and a homemade headdress of brightly dyed chicken feathers. "Trick or treat!" he shouted, holding up his shopping bag.

"Kee-wah-wah-yu-a-nah," said Henry.

Ralph Johnson screwed up his face and said, "What?"

"Kee-wah-wah-yu-a-nah," Henry repeated. "That's Indian talk for 'What is your tribe, young warrior?'"

Ralph looked blank, and his father said, "He's an Apache, I think." His speech seemed oddly slurred. Henry took a closer look, and the man smiled in reply, exposing a nightmarish mouthful of long, snaggly, discolored teeth.

Henry freaked. The sight of Johnson's hideous teeth registered as a personal, direct threat to the soundness of his own dental condition. Only when Johnson burst into laughter and popped the trick teeth from his mouth did Henry realize he'd been taken in.

"Jesus," he said, with a feeble laugh. "I really thought for a moment there—"

"Yeah, they fool most people," Johnson said.

"Well, here's some treats for the young Apache here." Henry scooped candy corn and licorice from the serving dish into the boy's shopping bag. "And here's a little something for Old Sabertooth." He dug into his pocket and produced the miniature Heath bar he'd picked up from the floor of the attic. He tossed it to Johnson, who caught it neatly. "Now remember, brush your teeth after you eat that. Or you'll regret it."

"Right, dental hygiene, very important." Johnson slipped the trick teeth back in his mouth and gave Henry a parting grin. Even knowing the teeth were fake, it was disconcerting.

"You should have seen the Johnson kid's dad," Henry said, returning to the kitchen. "He was wearing—oh, no."

Madge was on her knees beside the sink, retching convulsively into the yellow plastic dishpan from the sink. The onset of the vomiting had evidently caught her by surprise, for most of the vomit—still essentially recognizable as cake—had been spewed across the floor.

Henry got down on his knees beside her. She tried to wriggle away from his consoling hug. There were tears in her eyes.

"Madge, what in hell is wrong?"

She wiped her mouth with the back of her hand and coughed to clear her throat. She tried to answer him, though her only answer would have been to say she didn't know, but the peristaltic convulsions began again.

They continued, off and on, for another half an hour, and by the time they'd stopped there could be no thought of her driving anywhere in the car. Henry wanted to take her to the hospital, but she refused to consider it.

"I'll be going there tomorrow in any case. And all I want now is some sleep."

There was no point in trying to argue with Madge when she was sick, since she could pull rank and insist that as a nurse she knew best what had to be done. So Henry didn't try to override her veto. Instead he bustled about, cleaning up the mess in the kitchen and seeing that she had a supply of pails and pans beside the bed. Then it was time to set off for Our Lady of Mercy.

A block from the house he had to turn back and get his raincoat and an umbrella. *So tell me, God,* he prayed, partly in jest and partly in earnest, as he stepped down from the front porch a second time into the drizzle that was thickening into a regular downpour, *what have I done to deserve this?*

23

All through *Frankenstein* Billy kept thinking of the candy he'd put in the big bowl back in his homeroom, the bowl into which all Sister Catherine's fourth graders had poured their various contributions and from which, when they went home, they would be taking their separate portions. In previous years a school-wide distribution of Halloween goodies had taken place here in the gymnasium, but as the principal, Sister Fidelis, had announced at the afternoon assembly, due to incidents of older children misappropriating the candy of the younger children, now only the games and horror movie and costume awards would take place in the gym, and candy would be doled out in their separate homerooms.

Which made what Billy was doing much more fair, since only the kids who had laughed at him and then refused to say why, only those kids would have their teeth rot.

More fair, yes, but wasn't there something basically unfair about the whole idea? Didn't he always resent it when the whole class got detention for something that just one or two people had done wrong? And wasn't that what he was doing now, only worse? Meanwhile the story on the screen (which Billy knew well from the times he'd seen it on TV) had got to the point where Boris Karloff has met the little girl he will soon throw into the stream, a crime he commits not because he's mean but just because he's so incredibly stupid. He had this dumb uncomprehending look on his face that was scarier than if he'd been deliberately nasty and snarly like a vampire. Some of the small girls in the front rows were already squealing with anticipation.

Billy got up from his folding chair and made his way to the aisle, bumping knees and stepping on feet. Clumsily, Karloff picked up the little girl, and there was a general hubbub of screams and cheering as he heaved her into the water.

Sister Symphorosa was standing guard at the exit. At first she pretended not to notice Billy and continued to scowl reproachfully at the figures on the screen. He tugged more insistently at the loosely knit gray wool of her cardigan.

She directed her scowl toward him. "Yes?"

"Sister, excuse me, I have to go to the toilet."

"Can't you wait till the movie's over?"

"But it won't be over for a long time yet. There's a whole lot of stuff that happens first. He kills a woman who's getting married, and they chase after him, and there's a fight inside a place where there's this thing spinning around. And I really do have to go to the toilet—*badly.*"

It was his correct use of the adverbial "badly" that tipped the balance. Sister Symphorosa handed him a hallway pass and let him slip out the exit.

To the left was the nearest boys' lavatory, but there was another close by his homeroom, which was to the right past the main stairway and then down the corridor and around to the right again, the floor plan of the school being in the shape of a square with a small hunk taken out of it so that you couldn't get back to corner A (the gymnasium) from corner D (his homeroom). Wherever the walls of the hallway weren't given over to metal lockers they'd been decorated with Halloween decorations in as many styles and media as there were classrooms along the hallway. Sister Terence's third-graders had produced a three-foot-high and ten-foot-long mural on a scroll of paper showing different rooms inside a haunted house with a wide variety of witches and monsters, none (to Billy's mind) very persuasive. Miss Beane's second-graders had produced, as usual, a much livelier display, a giant checkerboard with jack-o'-lanterns cut from orange paper pasted on the black squares alternating with black skulls on the white squares. Everyone who'd ever had Miss Beane for second grade agreed that her art classes were the most fun of any teacher in the school's, even though she always made you do things exactly her way.

Billy slowed as he approached the main stairwell, since this was where he was most liable to encounter a monitor, if there was one. He'd already thought up his excuse for going to the farther-off lavatory (namely, that the three stalls in the other lav were all occupied), but the best thing would be to get to his destination without being noticed at all. It might take time to weed out all the Heath bars in the bowl, more time than anyone was likely to spend on the toilet.

He could hear a voice, two voices, a man's saying "Mm-hm" and "Uh-huh" and the voice of Sister Fidelis, fluent and flutelike. They were standing next to the double doors of the main entrance, down half a flight of stairs from the hallway. Only Sister Fidelis was clearly in view, for the man had taken a position partly inside and partly outside the double doors so as not to be officially smoking inside the school building. Even so, the smell of his cigarette cut through the usual school smells of polish and chalk dust with the force of sacrilege, like a rock and roll radio station being turned on in church.

Billy took a deep breath, got his pass ready to show, and started walk-ing along the hall, hoping the school principal would be too caught up in her conversation to notice him. And indeed it wasn't Sister Fidelis who called out "Billy, hey! Billy, come down here."

It was his father.

Billy walked down the half flight of stairs toward Henry with the lightness of knowing he was no longer responsible for anything that might happen. He had been stopped, it was out of his hands. "Hi, Dad. Hello, Sister." He held up his hallway pass, and Sister Fidelis nodded without looking at it.

"So, how is the Halloween party going?" his father asked. "And what are you doing out here in the hall?"

"They're showing *Frankenstein*, but I had to leave to go to the bath-room."

Henry smiled. "It didn't get too scary for you, did it?" He flicked his cigarette outside into the drizzling darkness and got down to business. "Well, you hurry up with your business in the bathroom. I'm going to have to take you home a little ahead of schedule. Your mother got sick again, so I'm afraid there's no chauffeur service tonight."

"I'm sorry to hear that," Sister Fidelis said politely. "I hope it's nothing serious."

"It's some kind of flu, she says."

Sister Fidelis sighed. "Yes, it's getting to be that season. In any case, Billy mustn't go home without a share of the Halloween treats. So, Billy, when you've washed your hands, you can take your father to your home-room and help yourself to some of the candy from the bowl. I'm sorry you won't be able to see the end of the movie, but your father tells me you're already an expert in the matter of Frankenstein."

Billy nodded. "I've seen this movie before, and another one that was basically the same but in color, and then last year I saw *Young Frankenstein*. That one was my favorite. It's funnier than this one. But it's scarier too."

Sister Fidelis offered her hand to Henry. "It was nice, having this chance to talk, and I shall pray for Mrs. Michael's quick recovery—and for your unfortunate mother-in-law, as well. Such a strange thing to hap-pen. Well, duty calls, I really must patrol the halls. All that candy could tempt the saints themselves. Good night, and Happy Halloween." Half-way up the stairs she turned around and addressed Billy. "And I expect to see you at the eight o'clock High Mass tomorrow, William. All Saints' Day is a holy day of obligation."

"I know, Sister."

Henry insisted on accompanying Billy to the bathroom, but didn't go in with him. Billy entered a stall, waited a suitable amount of time, flushed the toilet, and returned to his father. Then there was no help for it: Billy led the way to his homeroom.

And there on the main blackboard in huge white letters made with the chalk turned on its side was the dirtiest word in the English language and then the school's initials—OLM.

And there was the bowl of candy, but now by some miracle emptied of its contents, all but a few worm-eaten apples.

Billy felt an immense elation. Even before he'd figured out logically what had happened, he knew he didn't have to feel worried anymore, or guilty, or afraid. He understood the meaning of being "saved."

"Is this where the candy was?" Henry asked, tipping the bowl so that the mottled windfalls rolled about in it.

Billy nodded. "It was full almost to the top."

"What a damned rotten trick. Who in hell would have . . ."

"Probably kids from Weyerhauser."

Henry had thought as much himself, but hadn't wanted to say so to Billy. He nodded gravely but noncommittally. "We'd better go tell Sister Fidelis. But first"—he went to the blackboard and picked up an eraser—"we'd better erase this."

"Maybe you shouldn't," said Billy. "It could be evidence."

"If they ever need anyone to testify in court as to what was written on the blackboard, we can both be witnesses, okay? Meanwhile—" He erased the giant obscenity, but even erased the letters left ghosts of themselves and FUCK OLM remained legible if you concentrated.

"Write something else on the blackboard, Dad, like 'Happy Halloween,' and no one will notice what's underneath."

"Right," said Henry.

That done, they returned to tell Sister Fidelis about their discovery. Her main concern was whether there had also been vandalism, and learning that there had not, she said, "That's a blessing. Of course, it's a terrible thing, but if it's only a matter of candy being taken, that can be remedied easily enough."

"How do you suppose they got in?" Henry asked.

"A school isn't a fortress, Mr. Michaels. Anyone able to climb the fence about the playground can get onto the window ledge of that room. We try to keep the windows latched shut for that reason, but sometimes—" She lifted her hands in a gesture of resignation. "I realize that you're anxious to get home, Mr. Michaels, but I'd appreciate it if you would take my place here at the door for a short time, say five minutes, while I go about and restock the bowl for Billy's classroom from the bowls in the other rooms. The children never need know what happened if I do it now."

"Of course, Sister. I'd be happy to."

"Billy, you come help me."

Billy followed Sister Fidelis back to his homeroom, and then, with Billy carrying the gradually weightier bowl, they went from one school-room to the next, taking larger portions where the supplies were more abundant. The first and second grade classrooms were definitely the best supplied. By the time they had reached the seventh grade classroom up-stairs there was more candy in the bowl Billy was carrying than in the classroom's bowl, and Sister Fidelis decided that they had gathered enough. They took the filled bowl back to his homeroom, where Billy would have forgotten to take any candy at all for himself if Sister Fidelis hadn't told him to. "Oh go on, don't be shy—take more than that. But do me a favor, will you, William?"

"Sister?"

"Don't mention to the other children about what you and your father discovered. Of course, if anyone were to *ask* you about it directly, you would have to tell the truth. Lying is always a sin. But if no one asks you . . ."

Billy nodded. "Yes, Sister, I'll keep it a secret."

"Good," she said, and rewarded him with a final handful of candy from the bowl.

As they approached the stairwell, they could hear an argument going on between Billy's father and some people insisting they be let in to the school. Henry was saying, rather angrily, that they would have to wait until Sister Fidelis was back and could identify them as students, and they were insisting on coming in right away.

Sister Fidelis quickened her pace so that Billy almost had to run to keep up with her. As Billy and Sister Fidelis came to the stairs leading down to the doors and could see them, the boys who had been trying to push past Henry suddenly reversed course and backed out onto the side-walk.

Sister Fidelis went right out the door after them and demanded to know what they wanted. There was no immediate reply.

Billy pressed his face up against the lowest glass panel of one of the doors to see what was happening. There were four older boys, seventh- or eighth-graders probably, and all four were wearing identical Richard Nixon rubber masks. You couldn't tell if they were black or white, even by looking at their hands, because they were all wearing gloves. But they had talked the way that colored kids talked when they'd been arguing with Henry. "Hey, man, you can't do that!" and "Who you anyhow says we can't come in here?"

"Take off those masks and let me see who you are," Sister Fidelis demanded.

"I'm Richard Nixon," one of the boys said in a tone of loud defiance, and the other three laughed and chorused his claim. "Yeah, that's who I am, I'm Richard Nixon." They held their hands up with fingers spread out to make V's.

"Yeah," said the first boy, "I'm Richard Nixon, and I ain't no crook." This time their laughter sounded less forced.

"Well, Richard Nixon, I'm afraid you'll have to find somewhere else to celebrate Halloween. The party here is only for students at OLM. I'm sorry, but that's the rule."

Having made their defiance, the four scale-model Richard Nixons headed away from the school and out into the street. Reaching the opposite sidewalk, they turned around and shouted aloud the same obscene message that had been written on the blackboard in Billy's homeroom. Then they turned and ran off into the darkness.

"You know, Sister," Henry said, as Sister Fidelis returned indoors, "I'll bet those were the same kids who made off with the candy from Billy's classroom."

"Returning to the scene of the crime? That would be bold of them, but I suppose we'll never know. Thank you for service beyond the call of duty."

"I'd say it was exactly what my duty called for, Sister, and I'm glad I was able to be some help. Will you be all right here by yourself?"

"They were just children acting up. It is Halloween, after all." She laughed lightly. "This isn't the blackboard jungle, yet. And I've already kept you too long from your poor wife. So thank you again, and good night to you both."

Henry stepped out the door, opened up his umbrella, and waited for Billy to crowd in under it with him. They set off home at a carefully measured pace, so as both to keep out of the rain as much as possible. As they walked they ate candy from Billy's knapsack, and Henry spun more tall tales about the origins of Halloween and Billy told him what he'd read on that subject in the *Junior Universe of Knowledge*. They agreed that the ancient Druids must have been interesting people.

24

Henry couldn't sleep. He'd lain in bed an hour listening to Madge's irregular snoring (she'd taken one of her blue angels from the bottle she kept hidden in her stocking drawer), and he was still as wide awake as ever. *I'll read a book*, he thought, *and raid the icebox*. In pajama tops and bathrobe he went out into the hall and, after checking to see that Billy was sleeping well, down the stairs. The house had developed a deep-rooted chilliness, the funereal cold of a stone church or some other building where the furnace doesn't regularly operate. His feet cringed at each step and his bare legs began to get goose bumps. November already. Heating bills. And this old Victorian mastodon ate up oil almost as fast as you could pump it into the tank. Combine that with the taxes, and the monthly bite was nearly as much as an average family paid for rent. Maybe he should finally do what he was always threatening to and set up a wood-burning stove in the living room. The chimney and flue for the fireplace seemed to be in good enough shape. But without a steady supply of firewood, would it really represent a saving?

As so often, Henry's daydream of a heroic undertaking had led him to recognize what it was he wanted in the way of instant gratification. A fire in the fireplace! There was just enough wood stacked beside the fireplace to get a cozy blaze going. Before fixing himself a snack, he formed a little tepee of kindling under the three slenderest logs from the stack and set it blazing. By the time he was back with a drink and a sandwich of cheese and catsup on toasted rye, the logs had caught and the flames were having their own Halloween celebration, leaping and crackling.

There is something primordial about fire, something almost religious. Henry only had to sit watching a fire for ten or fifteen minutes and his mind was off in another dimension. It was hard not to believe that a fire wasn't alive, that the flames weren't more than excited gases. Hadn't one of the Old Testament characters seen God inside a burning tree? And there was something else, something he'd just heard about lately, what was it? Ah yes, the thing Billy had told him about the Druids (the kid had a memory like a steel trap, nothing got away), how they set special bonfires on Halloween and put the stones in them, one for each member of the family.

Henry was not superstitious as a general rule. He didn't worry about walking under ladders or doing things on Friday the thirteenth. He treated black cats exactly the same as white cats, and he had no lucky coins or key rings or such as that. But sometimes things did happen that were hard to explain, such as the time a friend had got him to ask a question to the *I Ching* and the question he'd asked was whether or not to get a Honda 650 he'd seen advertised and the *I Ching*'s answer had been "The Prince shall receive a gift of many horses." That certainly had to be more than blind chance. Henry had a similar respect for the messages in fortune cookies, but only when he felt an inner prompting that said this particular fortune cookie was one to be heeded.

And he had that feeling now. He didn't act on it at once, since he was just starting to enjoy the glow of the fire, but he couldn't get rid of the idea about the Druids and the stones they put in their Halloween bonfires. But even after he'd returned from the kitchen with a second drink, he didn't seriously consider going out into the alley with a flashlight to find four appropriate stones. Five, with Ned.

Then it dawned on him that, thanks to Ned, there was a good supply of stones all over the house. Ned had been a collector of "interesting" sticks and stones and had always been bringing home weeds with pretty flowers or an odd-looking rock. The flowers would get stuck in a waterglass and die in a day or two and get thrown out, but the rocks had been deposited, like so many never-to-be-hatched eggs, in the pots of the various houseplants. After Ned's accident these nests of rocks had become so many little domestic shrines, commemorating the Ned of that earlier, happier time.

He went into the dining room, turned the light on, and began to collect rocks from among the potted houseplants: three largish stones for the three grown-ups, and smaller ones to represent Ned and Billy. The largest, smooth and slightly pink, would represent Grandma O., as symbolizing her baldness. The black stone (basalt?) would stand for Madge, and the one flecked with what looked like bits of mica would be his own. Ned's stone looked like a small gray potato, and Billy's was a chalky white shard of what might be marble.

He placed all five stones on the hearth and used the fire shovel to push them back so they were dead center under the blazing logs. Then he laid two more logs slantwise across the fire, hiding the stones from sight. The new logs began to hiss and crackle, and Henry soon had to push the chair farther back from the fire to keep the hair on his shins from getting singed. He sipped his screwdriver and watched the flames and enjoyed the fire's heat and felt the tension draining out of his muscles like water from a tub.

What a day. But it was over. He didn't even need a third drink to go to sleep. He just put down the empty glass on the floor, drew up his legs into a fetal position so that his bathrobe would cover them, and conked out.

He woke at 5 a.m. to the muted chiming of the grandfather clock from Mrs. Obstschmecker's bedroom. He knew a moment of confusion as to why he should be waking in a chair in the living room and freezing his ass off. Then it all came back, and he looked at the fireplace where the logs—all but one charred stump—had been reduced to a smooth mound of gray ashes.

This is stupid, he thought, dipping his hands into the mound of ashes and feeling about for the stones. He found Grandma O.'s stone first, and then Ned's. Neither had been affected by the fire. Madge's stone had got knocked to the back of the fireplace, probably by the falling of a log from the andirons, but it too was intact. His own, however, had split right down the middle. Weighing the sundered halves in his hands, he wished he'd never started his little experiment. You didn't have to be a Druid priest to know that this had to be accounted an ill omen. *Enough of this shit*, he thought. *I'll make breakfast.*

But by that point it was too late to stop. He had to find the fifth stone and to make sure that no similar harm had come to it. He continued feeling around in the ashes, but all his fingers could discover were small charred knobs and knots of wood undevoured by the flames. He became more systematic. He spread a newspaper beside the fireplace and began to sift the ashes through his fingers, shovelful by shovelful. Billy's stone seemed to have vanished, and that simply wasn't possible.

When Madge came down the stairs to make breakfast an hour later, he was still on his hands and knees by the fireplace, sifting the ashes, for a second time, through the largest of the kitchen sieves.

"Henry," she said sleepily, "what's wrong?"

"Nothing," he said. "Nothing's wrong. I made a fire last night and I was just taking out the ashes. Go back to bed."

"But I have to get ready for work. What *are* you doing? You're filthy."

"I'm looking for Billy," he said, as the tears returned in force. "I'm looking for my son Billy."

"Have you spent the whole night sitting down here *drinking?*" Madge demanded.

Henry shook his head and wiped at his tears with the soot-blackened cuffs of his pajamas. But there was nothing he could say, no way possible to explain.

She sighed. "Well, I can't really say I blame you. After what we all went through yesterday. Go get cleaned up and I'll make some coffee. God, what a madhouse." She turned her back dismissively and went into the kitchen.

Henry, admitting defeat, went to the upstairs bathroom, washed his hands and face, and began to shave. But all the while he shaved the tears would keep trickling down into the shaving foam. Something terrible was going to happen and there was nothing he could do to prevent it. He knew it sure as hell.

25

"Your great-grandfather Olaf Hagerup," his mother said brightly, after Billy had been strapped into his seat with the seat belt, "which is to say, my mother's father, had to be the stubbornest-minded man there ever was. One time the whole family went to a circus that had come to Brain-ard, just a little circus of course, nothing on the order of what we'll see today." She turned on the ignition, and the factory-fresh Electra's V-8 engine came on like a light bulb. "But it was big enough to have basic circus animals like lions and tigers and I suppose an elephant." She backed the car with a crunching sound into a waist-high mound of snow the plows had built up all along Calumet, then lurched forward into the street, spinning the back tires in the snow. "Olaf sat there through the whole performance, and afterward when he was home, he *insisted* that the animals he'd seen were just people dressed up in costumes! In my grandfather's universe there simply wasn't room for lions and tigers. Isn't that amazing, he could see them with his own eyes, but he refused to admit they were real."

Billy nodded. Half his mind was on his mother's story, but the other half was worried about her driving. His father was always making remarks about what a bad driver Sondra had been, and after a two-day thaw followed by a medium-sized blizzard, the streets were at their most treacherous. Henry had tried to argue them into taking a bus downtown, but Sondra had laughed and said Henry was suffering from sour grapes, meaning that it was only because *he* couldn't drive that he was in favor of the bus. In fact, though he didn't bother correcting her, Henry could drive again. His license had been restored just after the new year, and he and Madge had celebrated by driving all the way to Mankato and back to go to the funeral of a cousin of Henry's whom Henry hadn't seen since he was fifteen and the cousin was twelve.

"Penny for your thoughts," Sondra said, glancing sideways. At the same moment the back end of the Electra fishtailed turning off Calumet onto Johnson at the corner of Brosner Park.

Billy held his breath till the car had corrected course. Then he said, "I was thinking you must not know Dad's got his driving license back."

"Has he? That's nice. It should certainly make your lives a lot easier. Personally, I can't imagine getting along without a car. Not living in Willowville. But I'm not surprised Henry didn't say anything. He's become so . . . private lately. I hope he's been feeling all right."

"He's fine, Mom. Everyone is fine."

Sondra made a grimace of skepticism, and Billy took a deep breath and braced himself for the interrogation he could see coming. Each time his mother managed to get him to herself she would start in with the questions. It was almost as though she'd written them down on a list, like groceries: "How is poor old Mrs. Obstschmecker?" and "Is Henry still working at the bar on Lake Street?"

"How is poor old Mrs. Obstschmecker?" Sondra asked.

"She's fine."

"And her hair? Has it started to grow back?"

"No, not yet."

"Well, it's been how long? Almost four months. The last couple times I stopped by at the house I haven't seen her. That's why I asked if she was well."

"She doesn't come out of her room much anymore. I guess she feels funny being bald."

"Does she come to meals? Does she watch TV?"

"She's got her own TV in her room, and Madge brings her her meals on a tray."

Sondra digested this information till they'd reached Snelling, where she had to stop for the traffic light.

"Madge has been having some problems too, I understand."

"She's okay now. She found out that when she drinks alcohol it makes her throw up. It's some kind of allergy. I'm not even supposed to know about it, so don't say I told you."

"My lips are sealed."

Now, Billy thought, she was going to ask him about Henry's bartending job on the weekends. But instead she said: "It seems your school has been in the news."

"Really? On TV?"

"No. Just a small notice in the Minneapolis newspaper. Ben pointed it out to me yesterday. It seems there's some kind of 'dental emergency' at your school and another public school nearby."

"Oh, there were only two kids from OLM that had that happen. The other kids are all at Weyerhauser. They sent us home with pink cards that we had to take to the dentist to show we'd had him look at our teeth. And mine are all okay except for one little cavity that was in a baby tooth that's loose anyhow."

"You wouldn't know any of the children involved, would you?"

"One's in our class," Billy confirmed, smiling at the thought of the goofy way Lyman Sinclair looked since the Heath bars had done their job on him. Either Lyman had managed to pocket some candy from the bowl before heading for the movie in the gym or else he was a friend of the kids from Weyerhauser and had shared some of what they'd stolen.

"A friend of yours?" Sondra asked.

"No, he's a colored kid. All the kids that happened to were colored. It's probably because they don't brush their teeth the right way. You have to move the brush in a circle. Like this." Billy imitated the movements of the ideal toothbrusher, as seen in the long dull film about dental hygiene that everyone in the school had had to sit through on the day the pink cards had been distributed.

Sondra smiled. The pantomime of toothbrushing was somehow reassuring. But she felt obliged to say, "The fact that the boy is colored doesn't mean he couldn't be your friend. I had a colored friend in high school, and that was back when there were many fewer colored people in the area."

"Yeah, but Lyman Sinclair is a real bully. He's older than most of the other kids, and bigger, and Sister Catherine has told him in front of the whole class that he's probably going to end up in reform school if he keeps on acting like he does."

"Still," Sondra said, with a virtuous tightening of her hands on the steering wheel, "it's a terrible thing for anyone at any age to lose all their teeth all at once."

"Oh, for sure," Billy agreed. But he couldn't resist adding, "But it does make him look funny, and he can't talk the same way he used to either. There must have been something wrong with the false teeth he had. And then he got in a fight, like he always does, and his teeth got broken."

Sondra shook her head. "The poor boy."

Billy grinned. "And then, last week, *someone* wrote this math problem on the blackboard. It said, 'Lyman Sinclair had thirty-two teeth. On Halloween he ate five candy bars and all his teeth rotted and fell out. If the tooth fairy pays twenty-five cents for each tooth that Lyman leaves under his pillow, how much money must she pay Lyman?'"

Sondra smiled. "And you wouldn't know who the someone was who wrote that on the blackboard, would you?"

Billy shook his head, all innocence. "It had to be someone who came back to the classroom during lunch hour. But they never found out who. Sister Catherine was pretty mad about it."

"Well, whoever it was, I expect he's sorry now. That boy must have gone through terrible suffering and—"

"Mom!" Billy warned. "Watch out for the—"

Too late. The Mercury Comet sedan she'd pulled out alongside of at last decided to pass the pickup that had been dawdling along ahead of it. As the Comet moved left into Sondra's lane its left back fender slammed into the side of the Electra, sending it spinning across the ice-slicked surface of the street.

Sondra closed her eyes and gripped the steering wheel reflexively, not with any thought of controlling the spin but talismanlike in the hope it would protect her.

Billy, as he'd been told to do if he was ever in an accident, curled forward as far as the seat belt let him and covered his head with his arms. He didn't look up until the car had come to a full stop, having slid into the snowbank on the opposite side of Snelling, facing in the opposite direction to which they'd been driving.

"Oh God Jesus, Billy—are you all right?"

Billy uncovered his head. "I'm okay, Mom. Are you?"

Sondra began to cry. Then, as far as both their seat belts allowed it, she hugged him. A city bus lumbered to a stop beside the Electra, and the driver got out and knocked on the window and asked Sondra if she was all right. "Yes," she shouted through her tears. "I'm fine! Thank you!" The driver got back in his bus and drove away. Across the street there was no sign of the Mercury that had slammed into them.

"It's a miracle," said Sondra. "A miracle we're both alive. That idiot, pulling out without even looking. And there's no sign of him now, and Lord knows what he did to the car."

She tried to move the car ahead, but they were solidly lodged in the snowdrift. The back tires had no purchase and spun about futilely. Sondra sighed. "I'm going to have to call for a tow, Billy. You can come with me or stay in the car, whichever you like."

"I'll stay here. If a policeman comes, I can tell him what happened. It really wasn't your fault, Mom, I could see that."

"Thank you, darling." She gave him a kiss and went to find a pay phone.

During the ten minutes she was gone, Billy's mind was a tennis match of panicky decisions to do one thing and then to do the opposite. He'd acted so calmly right after the accident, but now alone in the car it was as though the accident were still happening, the car still spinning around in the middle of Snelling out of control and the only way to stop it was to tell his mother everything. Why Grandma O. had gone bald. Why Madge couldn't drink any kind of liquor anymore without throwing up. Why all those kids—and Ralph Johnson's father, too—had lost their teeth.

But then there was Ned, lying upstairs in his endless coma, and if he began to explain about those other things, he'd have to explain about that too. And he couldn't do that, not ever.

And he didn't want to give up the caduceus, especially now that it was so charged up. Ever since Halloween it was like grabbing hold of a live electric wire. If he could only think of the right way to use all that power, a way to help his father and mother, and Madge too, all the people he really loved, and to help them in a way that wouldn't backfire like what he'd done for Madge had backfired. Because Madge did not seem at all happier as a result of not being an alcoholic anymore. Sometimes she got gloomy in a way she never used to, and she was cranky more often, and she seemed to have a fight with Henry almost every night about something or other. So the next time he did anyone a favor, he had to be sure of what he was doing.

Sondra returned to the car with a paper bag from which she produced two Styrofoam cups, one leaking milky coffee, the other leaking watery cocoa. There was also a box of candy-coated popcorn called Scrunchies, which promised, like their more famous competitor, Cracker Jacks, "A Free Gift in Every Box!"

It was when Billy had dug halfway down into the candied popcorn and discovered the free gift that he realized that nothing that had happened that day had been an accident—because it had all been leading to this. His problem was solved, and it was as easy as looking up the right answer in the back of the teacher's special copy of the arithmetic workbook.

The free gift came wrapped inside an inch-square envelope of translucent paper. It was a single shiny new penny wedged into a slotted piece of cardboard. Above the penny it said, "Official Lucky Loafer Penny." Under it there was a little poem:

With this you'll be no **wealthy** man
But be as **healthy** as you can!

"Gee thanks, Mom!" Billy said, leaning across the seat to kiss his mother. "You sure picked the right box. This is a super prize."

Sondra thought he was overdoing it, but she was touched by what seemed to be his deliberate effort to make her feel better about the accident and the likelihood of their missing the first half of the circus. It broke her heart, it really did, that she could only have him a few hours at a time on weekends and holidays. He was such a sweet kid. She wanted a bigger share of him. Really, she wanted him all.

26

He could tell, after he'd touched it to the third penny, that all the caduceus's power had been used up. In a way he was pleased. Though it meant he would have to wait a while before he could do for Sondra what he was doing for Henry and Madge, he reasoned that the benefit he was conferring must be great, since before he'd used it on the three pennies the caduceus had had such a lot of energy in it and now it was empty.

The first penny went to Henry. "Hey, Dad," he said, just after Henry had got up from the sofa at the end of the Nightly News, "this change dropped out of your pocket." He pretended to pick up four coins from where Henry had been sprawled and then went over to him and put them in his hand—first the original bright new penny that had come as a prize with the candy and then, just because it seemed more convincing, two dimes and a quarter. Henry smiled and said thank you and pocketed the change, marveling a little at Billy's honesty. He was certain that when he'd been his age he'd have acted on the philosophy that finders are keepers.

The second penny went to Madge. Billy waited till Saturday, which was her cleaning day, and when she'd started mopping the kitchen linoleum with the O'Cedar sponge mop, he went into the bathroom and put the penny on the floor beside the toilet. She always mopped the bathroom right after the kitchen. And sure enough, when the bathroom floor was dry enough for Billy to be allowed to go back in, the penny was gone from the floor. He knew she'd taken it because she was the one who always repeated "See a penny, pick it up, and all that day you'll have good luck" whenever she saw a penny lying on the ground.

Getting the third penny to connect with Grandma O. was more of a problem. Because he couldn't be sure if this penny had the same *full* zap of health that the first two did, he hadn't wanted to give it to his mother. There'd be time, later on, when the caduceus was charged up again, to do it right. But he figured that Grandma O., being as old as she was, wouldn't have the same long-term health requirements: he'd heard his father and Madge discussing the old woman's potential for longevity and Madge had said five years with luck. Indeed, if Billy hadn't had misgivings about the full effectiveness of the third penny, he probably wouldn't have thought to do Grandma O. a good turn at all. If there'd been a pet in the house he'd more likely have blessed that hypothetical dog or cat with whatever power the third penny had. But there wasn't a pet, and he did feel a little guilty about what had happened to Grandma O.'s hair, and finally he simply was curious as to what being "as healthy as you can" would represent in Grandma O.'s case. Would her memory improve? Would she be less cranky? Would she be able to move around more easily? He considered it an interesting scientific experiment.

The problem was, since Grandma O. almost never left the house anymore and so had very little practical use for money, how could he get her to touch the penny? If she saw a penny on the floor, she certainly wouldn't stoop to pick it up. And he couldn't say, "Hey, Grandma, isn't this your penny?" because she'd just say no, it wasn't, and give him one of her suspicious looks. But finally he figured out a way to do it. He put the third penny into the slotted square of cardboard that the original Official Lucky Loafer Penny had come in, and one afternoon when he was home from school and both Madge and his father were out of the house, he knocked on the door of Grandma O.'s room. Only after a second knock did Grandma O. say, "Yes, what is it?" Billy said he had a question he wanted to ask her. By then she'd come to stand on the other side of the door. "What is the question?" she asked.

Billy said, "I can't ask you till I show you what it is I want to ask you about first."

Reluctantly Grandma O. took the hook out of its eyelet and opened the door. She was wearing a wig that looked more or less like the hair she used to have, but she still didn't believe it fooled anyone. When people looked at her, she felt that they could see through the wig with X-ray vision and were secretly laughing at the spectacle of her baldness. "Well, what is it?" she demanded, standing in the doorway to keep Billy from coming into her room, as though he were a salesman or a Jehovah's Witness.

"What's *this* supposed to mean?" He handed her the square of cardboard with the penny in it.

She held it up in front of her nose and squinted at it. "The print's too small," she said, "I can't read it." She tried to hand it back to him, but he'd put his hands in his pockets.

"What it *says*," he explained, "is 'Official Lucky Loafer Penny.' But what does that *mean?*"

A smile of genuine if fleeting pleasure wrinkled Mrs. Obstschmecker's lips. Rarely was her larger experience of the world appealed to as a source of wisdom or information. "A loafer was a kind of shoe people used to wear, young people mostly. That was before everyone started wearing tennis shoes all the time. And every loafer had a kind of I don't know what you call it. A slit. And it was just big enough to fit a penny inside of."

She ran her fingertip back and forth across the penny.

"Did *you* wear loafers?"

"Goodness no! But Madge did, I remember now. Penny loafers, that was the word for them. Isn't that strange, I can remember her loafers on her feet with the white bobby socks as plain as if it were yesterday! Brown penny loafers. But she had nickels in the slits, not pennies. Maybe inflation had already started by then, that's always the hardest thing to remember, what a particular thing would cost in a particular year. There used to be candy you could buy for just one penny. But not anymore."

She handed the Official Lucky Loafer Penny back to Billy, who accepted it now with a glow of conscious benevolence. He had to fight against telling her the favor he'd just done for her, or even hinting at it. Grandma O. had a nose for secrets. But he couldn't resist reading aloud the little poem printed beneath the penny: "Listen to what else it says here:

> 'With this you'll be no wealthy man
> But be as healthy as you can.'

Do you think that that's really true, Grandma? Can one penny really be luckier for someone than any other penny?"

"No, no, that isn't very likely, is it?" Again she smiled. "But I remember how your grandfather, that's to say my poor late husband Mr. Obstschmecker, he had a silver dollar that he would never part with. It's hard to believe he's been dead six years already. It seems like only yesterday. He was buried with that silver dollar."

Good health is not a condition like baldness that is immediately recognizable, and so Billy had no sure way of knowing whether the three pennies were having their intended effect. Some weeks went by, and no one in the house came down with a cold or the flu, but who could say that that was his doing?

27

His kite had mounted so high that he'd almost run out of string. It was so high you could barely make out what color it was, but that was also because it was pale blue, about the blue you'd get if you poured a little milk into the blue of the sky and mixed them together. It was beautiful, but it was hard to say why. It wasn't just that it was so high up. Planes fly higher, but you're not connected to a plane by a length of string. The string felt alive, the way it tugged at you, like a bird on a long long leash, asking to be unreeled to some even more incredible height, or the way it would suddenly take a nosedive and the string would go slack and you'd have to wind it in as fast as you could when suddenly, bing, it would snap tight again.

Because it was Ascension Day and a holy day of obligation, OLM had the day off but the kids at the public school didn't, and so Billy had Brosner Park virtually to himself. His was the only kite in the sky. He felt as though he were the center of all St. Paul, the one link connecting sky and city, heaven and earth. He wondered for how many blocks around the park it was possible to see his kite, how many people were looking at it at this very moment and marveling.

While Billy had been gazing up at his kite, one of his classmates from OLM had come up the path, unnoticed, from the direction of Coughlin Avenue.

"Howza brain," Lyman Sinclair said to Billy by way of greeting when he stepped within his field of vision. He smiled a gummy smile at him, which, in combination with his dark sunglasses, did not register as friendly. Ever since he'd broken his first set of dentures, Lyman had taken to pocketing his prosthesis whenever he wasn't indoors.

"Hi, Lyman." Billy tried not to sound afraid. He glanced back over his shoulder to see if Lyman had come up the hill by himself. He had. There was not another person to be seen, not so much as a passing car.

"Fleyn a cut uhyuh?"

Billy couldn't understand a word Lyman had said, only that it had taken the form of a question. Even at school, with his dentures in and making an effort to speak the classroom English Sister Catherine insisted on, it was usually difficult to understand what Lyman was saying. The words all slid together into a mush.

"I'm flying a kite," Billy said. It was a dumb thing to say, because obviously that's what he was doing, but talking to Lyman was like talking to someone who speaks another language. You felt you had to say things as simply as possible.

"Lemme have it." Lyman held out his hand. This time there was no difficulty understanding him. He wanted Billy's kite.

Billy experienced a moment of genuine doubt. Was Lyman asking to have the kite as his own? Or only to feel it tugging at him from the sky? To feel that tug and then to give it back? Then he realized it didn't really matter what Lyman wanted: *he* didn't want Lyman touching his kite. Period. He shook his head and took a few short steps backwards, away from the pull of the wind. He realized that he was trapped by the kite in the same way the kite was trapped by him. He couldn't run away from Lyman without surrendering the kite to him. And Billy was not a surrenderer.

"Juzz fah amminuh," Lyman said, in a reasonable tone of voice but tilting his sunglass-visored face at an angle that said *or else*.

"No," said Billy quietly, concentrating his attention on the kite string as he began to rewind it around its wooden spool. "I have to get going home."

"Gotta do your homewurg, huh?" Lyman said. "Gotta figger how mudge a toof fairy gonna pay fer ma *tee?*" He was speaking as clearly as he was able, and with a force of rancor that made Billy look up, despite himself, to regard Lyman's toothless smile and then the nightmarish, slow opening of a pocketknife. Lyman reached up to catch the tense kite string, then quickly backed away from Billy with the kite in his control. He held the knife blade to the string of the kite as to the throat of a hostage. "It wuz you, wuznit? It wuz you wrode thad shit onna blagboar?"

Billy shook his head.

"Uh-huh." Lyman's lips curled into an expression that would have been a snarl if he'd been wearing his dentures. "It wuz you. Uhnue alla-tom it wuz you." He took a tight grip on the kite string and cut the string, but then, just as Billy was about to admit defeat and run away, Lyman, instead of enjoying the spoils of his victory, offered the tense, severed kite string back to Billy.

High up in the sky and far to the northwest the kite canted sideways and began to dip. Billy took the string in his left hand and, dropping the useless spool, began with his right hand to wind the string as fast as he could about knuckles and palm of his left hand. The string was growing slack faster than he could wind it but then there a gust that pulled it taut again, forming a sudden painful tourniquet about his hand. Billy made a cry of pain, and Lyman an appreciative "Huh!"

Lyman snatched up the spool with its remnant of string from where Billy had dropped it when he'd been given the kite string. He snapped it in two across his knee and flung the pieces as far as he could. "Seeyuh, brain," he said, and ran down the hill in the direction he'd come from.

Billy had no choice, if he was to save the kite, but to keep winding the string about his hand. It was a constant fight against the wind, which wanted to keep the kite aloft. Every new burst pulled the thickening reel of string tighter. Hoping to relieve the pressure on his left hand, he pulled the string back with his right hand to keep it slack, and soon his right hand was bleeding from a dozen thin nicks and slices. Finally the pain in both hands was too much and he decided to give up the fight and let the kite go free.

But the string had knotted itself into an inextricable tangle about his left hand and he couldn't get it off. He tried to break the string but that was just as impossible without a sharp edge to bring to bear against it.

The wind picked up. He felt as a fish must feel that's been hooked and is being reeled in to its death. If only the kite would plummet to the ground, but it was flying perfectly. He got his right foot on the string to create more slack and tried again with both hands to snap it in two, but the string was too strong. It was, in fact, a thin nylon fishline that an article about kites in a magazine in the school library had recommended as being the best compromise between strength and lightness. He'd spent almost four dollars for it, three times as much as the cost of the kite.

A sudden gust caught him unawares and yanked the nylon line from under his shoe. It sliced into the side of his hand like a wire cheese slicer into a hunk of cheddar. Blood flowed down over the back of his hand and dripped from his fingertips. The blood made the kite string slippery, and when he tried to grip it his whole hand seemed on fire with pain. But he managed, with the help of his elbow and a momentary shift of wind, to get some slack back into the line.

Like an animal with its foot in a trap, Billy now tried to gnaw his way to freedom. Lifting his left hand, he was able to bite at the slack length of line between his hands. The first bite had no effect. He bit down harder, and just as the nylon thread slipped like dental floss between his new-grown central incisor and the milktooth beside it, the wind gusted and the line snapped taut, pulling free from his bleeding right hand and yanking out both front incisors with a single deft impulse of energy. The line parted, cut by the very teeth it had extracted, and the kite mounted into a last brief flight of glory before it took its final plunge.

Billy fell to his knees, shocked beyond screaming. Blood gushed from his torn gums and from the right side of his mouth where the kite string had made a deep incision, but all the pain was concentrated in his right hand. The left hand in its tourniquet of kite string was numb, and when he tried to raise that hand to his mouth to staunch the blood spurting onto his shirt and pants, it was as though his whole left arm had turned into a single block of wood unhinged at wrist or elbow.

All the way home, the entire ten blocks' stumbling run along Calumet, spattering the sidewalk with droplets of blood, his thoughts were fixed not on his own pain but on Lyman Sinclair, on how he hated Lyman Sinclair, on the horror of his toothless smile. He didn't know he'd lost two teeth himself. He knew only that his mouth was bleeding, that his hands hurt, that he had to get home. He kept turning round to look behind him as though he were being pursued and fearful his pursuer would overtake him. Once an older woman trimming the hedge on her lawn tried to make him stop, but he ran by, ignoring her calls of "Little boy!" and "Young man!"

He got home just as Henry was pulling up into the driveway with the backseat of the Dodge filled with bags and boxes from his weekly shopping expedition to the Country Club Market at Rice and Wheelock. When he saw Billy covered with blood and lurching up the sidewalk toward the house, Henry slammed on the brakes. The old Dodge bucked to a stop, and Henry sprang out of the car and raced toward Billy, who, seeing his father, stopped where he was and simply waited to be taken up in his arms.

All of Henry's alarms went off at once. He swept up Billy and ran with him out to the street, looking for whoever had been chasing him, trembling with anger. Then, disappointed of any outlet for that anger, he tried to comfort Billy and at the same time to find out what had happened to him. He made him open his mouth and saw where the two teeth had been torn from the gum. "Who did this?" he demanded. But Billy would only shake his head, refusing speech now that tears were possible. Then Henry discovered the hand trapped in the tangle of fishline, its fingers red and swollen with blood, and he remembered Billy setting off for the park with his new blue kite. "Is this the string from your kite, Billy?" he asked, trying not to sound panicky.

Billy nodded.

Henry made a more secure cradle of his arms and carried Billy to the car, then thought better of it and changed course for the front door. "We'll get you to the hospital right off the bat, Billy, but first I want to cut that string off your hand. Okay?"

Billy nodded.

Be calm, Henry told himself. *Madge does this every day.* But it was hard to be calm when first he couldn't find any scissors but the old blunt scissors in the kitchen drawer, which wouldn't do the job at all. He ended up having to use the sharpest of the paring knives, and twice, in severing the last loops of string, he nicked the boy's hand. When he apologized, Billy said he didn't have any feeling in the hand at all. But when the last of the string was off and the blood rushed back into circulation, Billy started to howl with pain.

"What in the world—" said Mrs. Obstschmecker, appearing in the kitchen doorway.

"Billy had an accident," Henry said, lifting Billy from the kitchen chair. "I can't explain now, and in fact I don't know what happened. He seems to have been in a fight. I have to take him to the emergency room at Ramsay Northwestern. Call Madge, would you? Thank God she left me the car today."

"But what do you want me to *tell* Madge?" Mrs. Obstschmecker whined. But she whined too late, for Henry was already out the door.

She phoned Madge at the hospital and told her what little she knew—how Billy was in such a state and Henry in a worse state than him, and the blood all over both of them and a whole kitchen towel soaked with it.

"But why?" Madge insisted, keeping her voice professionally calm. "What happened? Was he in some kind of accident?"

"No, a fight Henry said. And there's all this string just covered with blood on the kitchen floor. I wish I understood what was going on! But he did say for you to go down to the emergency room, that's where he was taking Billy."

For the next half hour, while she waited for either Henry or Madge to phone back and tell her what was happening, Mrs. Obstschmecker busied herself cleaning up the blood spattered all over the kitchen. Of late Mrs. Obstschmecker had not concerned herself with housekeeping outside of her own two rooms, but it was less upsetting to mop up the blood than to sit by the phone and stare at it. She'd gone through half a roll of paper towels and still hadn't begun to deal with the splotches on the living room and dining room carpets when instead of the phone ringing the doorbell buzzed. Mrs. Obstschmecker no longer dealt with visitors in a day-to-day way. When the doorbell rang, she went to her room and let someone else answer it if there was anyone home, and if there wasn't, she just waited for the visitor to go away. But today, obviously, was not an ordinary day, so she went to the door, which Henry had left standing wide open, and there were two uniformed policemen.

"Mrs. Henry Michaels?" the taller of the policemen said.

"That's my daughter," said Mrs. Obstschmecker.

"Is she here? Could we talk with her?"

"She's at work. But I'm her mother. Is something wrong?"

The policemen exchanged a glance that made it clear that something very definitely was wrong.

"Is the boy *badly* hurt?" she demanded, unable to believe that Billy could have been seriously injured and still have been making such a fuss.

"Has the hospital already—" the first policeman began, but was overridden by his partner saying, reassuringly, "The boy is fine. He's suffered some cuts and abrasions, and he seems to have lost a couple of teeth, but he's going to be fine. It's a good thing he had his seat belt on."

"There was an accident?"

There was an accident. It had happened at Snelling and McGill, outside a Lincoln/Mercury dealership. Henry had been speeding. A bicycle veered out onto Snelling from behind a parked semi. Henry braked and twisted the wheel. The right front tire blew, and the old Dodge went careening into the pole that supported the dealership's revolving sign. The pole was snapped in two by the impact, and Henry, who had failed to secure his seat belt, was thrown headfirst against, and through, the windshield. He went into shock instantly and was declared dead shortly after being admitted to the hospital emergency ward. Which meant, according to Mrs. Obstschmecker, when she would speak of these events in later years, that he'd died a painless death. "And that's a blessing, isn't it?" she would always add. "That is a blessing."

BOOK THREE

28

He was in that in-between state, warmer and more pleasant than any bathtub, of being awake without quite being behind the driver's wheel of consciousness, when he saw the envelope being slipped under his bedroom door, a pale pink rectangle that appeared and then either disappeared or else he drifted back to sleep for a few moments. Then it appeared a second time (or he awoke) and this time was not taken back. *It's from Judith,* he thought. Because only Judith would be using pink envelopes. The duvet suddenly felt much too warm and at the same moment the slanting sunlight spotlighting the dust motes intensified as though he'd taken off a pair of sunglasses. *I've got to get up*, he told himself. The message traveled slowly to whatever part of his mind translated such decisions into muscular contractions. Then, gingerly, with toes and knees he nudged the ungainly duvet sideways, exposing himself to the spring morning air in graduated dosages.

Only when he was sitting up and positioning his flipper in his mouth did it dawn on him what today was. His birthday. He was thirteen years old, an official teenager. He wondered what sort of official birthday presents he would get, but it wasn't a wonder keen enough to accelerate his getting dressed. He didn't think the birthday monster was liable to bring him anything he really ached to have. His mother would buy him a lot of sport clothes with designer labels, and maybe a tennis racket, since she'd been dropping hints about how much fun tennis was and how he ought to get more exercise, and then almost certainly (since at Christmas he'd been given his own "home entertainment center" complete with hi-fi, tape deck, and a twelve-inch TV) a lot of records and tapes. What Winky would give him he couldn't imagine, but he doubted it would be anything he wanted. Maybe just money, and that would be okay. He'd begun to appreciate money.

And from Judith? Last year it had been a novena. And if the pink envelope peeking in under the door was any indication, it looked like this year would be more of the same. He didn't blame her, she was sincere enough about all that stuff, she probably spent a couple of hours a day on her knees, but he couldn't get very excited about it either. It wasn't so much that prayers are cheap. He knew she refused on principle to accept an allowance from her father, so she didn't have money to spend on presents. But surely she knew by now that *he* didn't believe in novenas. It was like someone promising you that he'd spend an hour a day talking to himself and dedicate it to you. Thanks a lot.

As it turned out, Judith must have had some thoughts along the same lines, for her letter, though indeed a birthday offering, was an entirely different proposition. Eight pages of floral-decorated, scallop-edged scented stationery filled on both sides with Judith's supremely legible handwriting. (Four years earlier he'd given her that stationery for a Christmas present, and she, instead of simply throwing it away, had reserved it for letters she wrote to him. She'd never stated that as a policy, and by the time he'd figured out for himself the reason for the stationery's wonderful longevity, he was old enough to appreciate her sense of poetic justice. And every time he got another letter from her and another whiff of that scent, the lesson sank in a little deeper: Never give to others a gift you wouldn't be happy to receive yourself.)

The letter read:

Dear William,

There—you have my birthday present. Do you like it? Do you know what it is? It was given to you once before already almost thirteen years ago—but somewhere along the way it got lost & now I'd like to give it back to you—your own name, your *true* name, William.

You've been a "Billy" for so long that you may not like my idea at all & if that's how you feel I will respect your choice. Or you might like "Bill" instead of "William"—but somehow I don't see you as a Bill, perhaps because the only Bill I know well is Bill Burdon, who was the editor of the *Chronicle* two years ago when I was just starting at St. Tom's & a person I never felt real sympathy for—tho Bill was nice enough in his own way—the Way of the Jock. Anyhow William is a name with *many* positive associations—beginning in 1066 with William the Conqueror & including William Shakespeare. Also William of Ockham, who invented Ockham's Razor (no, that is not off the top of my head, I used the *Britannica*). But not any very important *saints*, unless William Cuffitella (whose feast day is April 4) is important. Somehow I doubt it. All I can find out about William Cuffitella is that he was a Sicilian hermit who died on his knees. "His body was found in that position, and all who touched it were cured of what ailed them." Well, you do say you want to go to medical school!!

It seems strange to me that I can write to you so easily but always have such a hard time talking with you when we're together. Actually it's probably not strange at all—but an ancient truth about older sisters and younger brothers—& younger step-brothers even more so. I know you think I don't have a sense of humor—& you're probably right because Ms. Arnold says the same thing. But I do think many things are funny even tho I don't laugh out loud at them—& I appreciate the spirit you've brought to our "family circle." You've made us all much happier people.

It is now 2 a.m. and I still haven't said the basic thing I wanted to say when I began writing this—which is that *I love you*. And not like some dutiful stepsister & not because my confessor said that would be something I ought to tell you. In fact what made me think to say it is a little embarrassing—it was seeing Mary Tyler Moore in *Ordinary People* and wanting *her* to say that to her son & then wondering whether I was any different. I see you every day & know all your moods, some of which are pretty rotten (some of mine are too) & we argue a lot—but I do respect you & *that* is what my birthday present means if it means anything.

You know Jason Schechner from the Math Honors course and the Computer Club. Back when Jason and I were freshmen, he wrote a paper for English about his bar mitzvah, which is a special kind of birthday party for when a Jewish boy turns thirteen. At a bar mitzvah you have to stand up and make a speech that is always supposed to start: "Today I am a man." So, here you are turning thirteen & I was writing in my Diary "Tomorrow Billy is a man" & it sounded wrong. But when I changed that, in my head, to "Tomorrow *William* is a man," it seemed perfectly natural and quite true.

(By the way Jason's sister Lisa has told me she thinks you're "sort of cute," and since she didn't swear me to secrecy or anything like that, I suppose I should mention it. Maybe that's even what she had in mind!!)

Of course in many ways we're both still children. We *have* to live here in Willowville in our parents' house, we *have* to attend St. Tom's or some other high school, we can't vote or get married, etc. But in the way that counts most we *are* grown-ups—not just because thirteen is some magic number, but because from the moment we decide that we're responsible for what we say and do and how we behave towards each other we are! So if I ever forget what I've been saying in this letter & begin to treat you like a "kid brother" & not like an equal, just stop me. Please.

Today you are a man, William! Congratulations & Happy Birthday!!

Judith

His basic reaction was one long cringe. If becoming Judith's equal meant becoming equally earnest, equally preachy, equally holier-than-thou, then he would rather remain her kid brother forever. But the idea about his name was another matter. William: he liked the sound of it. And she was right that Billy sounded like a youngster. The only grown-up Billys he could think of were baseball players. Or Billy the *Kid*.

William Michaels.

He went into his bathroom and confronted this new being in the mirror over the sink. "Hello," he said, in the voice he used when he answered the phone and wanted someone to think he was a grown-up. "I'm William Michaels."

The figure in the mirror pondered this a moment, then flipped the flipper loose and grinned, revealing the gap made by the missing front teeth. "Bullshit," whispered the kid in the mirror.

William sucked the flipper back into place and scowled—not at the kid in the mirror but at the new pimple that had appeared overnight on his forehead an inch southwest from the part of his hair.

There was a knock on the bedroom door, and he shouted out, "I'm in the bathroom."

"That's all right, there's no rush. But your father wanted you to know that they'll be showing Mount St. Helens on the news in just a couple minutes. He thought you'd want to see it erupt."

"Thanks, Mom. I'll turn on the TV in here."

"And, William?"

It was the first time his mother had ever called him William. Judith had already been at work.

"Yes, Mom?"

"Happy Birthday."

29

Why, Ben Winckelmeyer wondered, not for the first time in his life, are the shells of pistachio nuts dyed red? The fingers and thumb of his right hand still were discolored from the bowl of pistachios he'd shucked and eaten the night before. The plastic casing of the Big Ben by his bed also bore witness to his indulgence. So, too, doubtless, did the pages of the magazines he'd leafed through and the monthly statement for his CMA account. It must be that at some level people actually *like* having red fingertips. Women, after all, paint their nails red.

It had been one of those nights, insomniac, his mind monologuing a mile a minute, ever since, at exactly three fifteen (the hands of the Big Ben were luminous), he'd been awakened by the faint, intermittent creaks of someone slowly descending the stairs. His wife's bedroom and Judith's were ranged like his own along the ground floor gallery of the sprawling split-level. Only Billy inhabited the upstairs, and he was generally a sound sleeper. In any case, he was not a tiptoer. The footsteps continued past his bedroom door and faded to silence. Then the click of a door latching closed. He lay there thinking. Not the hazy thoughts that lead back toward sleep, but crisp, clear, business-oriented thoughts that soon had him looking about for pen and paper. And, since he was already out of bed, a cigarette.

He'd smoked the last of the pack in the bedroom while he was watching the Late News, but he knew there was a carton in his office. So it was his turn to tiptoe *up* the stairs, creak by creak, and past Billy's bedroom, where he had noticed, by the dim light of the ankle-level night-lights recessed into the wall, an envelope wedged in under the door. That resolved the mystery of the midnight prowler, for Judith was wont to bare her soul every so often in letters delivered late at night under the door. Her last such communication to him had been a five-page, well-reasoned, and vigorously written plea for him to quit smoking, or, if he couldn't quit smoking, to stop doing work for ATA, the American Tobacco Alliance. She made it clear that this was not a matter she wished to discuss with him. There was no room for discussion. Working for the cigarette industry was sinful. Period. Ben had honored her insistence not to talk about it and gone on smoking, and MIMA—the Minneapolis Institute of Motivational

Analysis—continued to be funded by ATA, and Judith, ever since, lived under a kind of self-imposed house arrest, refusing to have an allowance, and grimacing in a martyred way whenever he or Sondra lit a cigarette. She had not, however, suggested going off to live with Rhoda in Florida, though Rhoda, who barely scraped along on her alimony and hungered for child support, was always trying to tempt her daughter down there.

Naturally Ben was curious as to what Judith might have to say to Billy that required the urgency of one of her night letters, and having no compunctions about privacy, he slipped it out from under the door and took it into his office to read. Fortunately before he opened it he'd noticed the telltale traces of the pistachio-shell dye on his fingers and washed his hands until (though the skin was still discolored) he could handle the paper without leaving red smudges.

He was pleasantly surprised by both the style and content of his daughter's latest letter. Admittedly, it was bossy of her to presume to decide for her stepbrother what name he should go by, but bossiness wasn't necessarily a bad quality, if it was effective. Then one saluted it as a gift for leadership. He returned the letter to its place under Billy's door and made a mental note to call his stepson William. He made a second mental note to get the boy some kind of birthday present above and beyond the usual envelope of cash. What Judith had said about his making the "family circle" happier was undoubtedly true. Now if Billy—William, that is— would only extend his ameliorative capabilities to include a cure for Judith's anorexia. . . .

Food. That's the direction the tobacco companies had to move in. That's what he'd come up here to write a note about. The primal addiction. They might outlaw smoking, but food? Plus, there was an irrational component in food purchases that made the business a suitable takeover target for the tobacco industry. With all the billions in profits piling up, and no way, really, to expand the market . . .

Then came the deflating awareness that this was the megalomania of 3:30 a.m. He might as well write a note to President Carter about how to deal with the hostage crisis. Think small: that was the proper economic/ ecologic niche for MIMA. Motivational analysis, not investment strategy. Such as, returning to what he'd wondered about earlier, why pistachio nuts are dyed red. The ones that are left their natural color seem to taste the same. Yet one always buys the red nuts, why? People must *like* having their fingers dyed red.

Could it be the same for smokers?

So far as Ben knew, there was nothing in the literature about the subliminal motives surrounding tobacco stains. The assumption seemed to be that this was an embarrassing aspect of smoking better left unexplored. But what if smokers liked having nicotine-stained fingers! ATA would almost certainly agree to fund at least a pilot investigation. The industry ached to be able to sponsor any kind of product-oriented research that wasn't connected to disease and/or the mortality rates of smokers. The idea was good for $200,000, minimum. Dan Turnage would be flying into the Twin Cities from the Baltimore headquarters of ATA this afternoon. He could spring the proposal on him. Turnage, admittedly, was only a figurehead, but he'd be delighted to be treated like a functional executive.

Ben tightened the drawstring of his pajamas, raised the rolltop of his mahogany desk, and started to write up the proposal. It was finished, along with a pack of Pall Malls, by the time the kids had left for school.

30

According to his stepfather, who took a fanatical interest in everything connected to Watergate, the lunch William had put together at the salad bar was the favorite lunch of Richard Nixon: cottage cheese covered with catsup. To which William also added croutons and Baco-Bits. It was no gourmet treat but it went down quick. When he was done, he wiped the Formica tabletop dry with a paper napkin and spread open his German notebook. At St. Tom's there was no official study hall, just this corner of the school cafeteria, or else the library, the idea being that everyone at the school was supposed to be such an overachiever that any extra hour of the day went to some easy elective like art or working in the *Chronicle* office. But in the forty-five minutes he had for lunch William could generally count on getting his German assignment done in the lunchroom and then go to his German class in the next period with the foreign language motor in his head still functioning.

Today's assignment was to write a page-long essay describing one of his earliest memories. William was generally pretty good at German. He could zip down a page filling in the blanks with the right verb forms, pronouns, et cetera, as fast as he could handle his homework for algebra. He was good at remembering all the irrational rules for the sex of nouns. A dream is masculine, cream is feminine, children are neuter. But essay assignments were another matter. Dwayne Nielson, the German teacher, liked to pose questions that were *relevant*, a word that, as used by Nielson, seemed to mean nosy, prying, snoopy. The other seven students in the class appeared not to resent Nielson's giving them the third degree under the guise of an exercise in grammar. But William did—so bitterly in the first couple of weeks of class that he'd almost switched to French (but Judith was studying French, and one of the best reasons for studying any foreign language is to be able to say things that the people you live with can't understand). Then somewhere around Thanksgiving he had realized that the way to deal with the problem was simply to lie. He could still remember the question going round the table until his own turn came and Nielson asked: "*Wilhelm, hast du ein Bruder? Wie alt ist er? Erzähl uns von ihnem.*" How was he supposed to answer that? Yes, I've got a brother. His name is Ned, and he's seventeen years old, and he's spent every day of his life for the past six years or so laid out like a corpse in a dark bedroom staring at nothing, and sometimes there's baby food dried into little green scabs in the stubble of his beard, and he has to wear diapers because he's incontinent. There was no way that William was going to "share" that information with Nielson, his classmates, and, inside of twenty-four hours, with everyone else at St. Tom's. (It was a small school, with fewer than three hundred students in all four grades.) So he lied. It was easy: he wasn't under oath, and no one had any reason to doubt his answer. No, he had said, in halting but grammatically correct German, "I do not have a brother, but I do have a sister, Judith, who is fifteen. She is very active in the battle against—" And then he had to ask Nielson the word for "abortion," which got Nielson flustered because he didn't know it and had to look it up in the dictionary. From that day on William had known he could handle Nielson simply by putting him on the defensive.

But this time Nielson had hit on an assignment that went right to the heart of William's problem. Because it wasn't just that William was *shy* about speaking of the details of his personal life. To a very large degree he simply didn't remember them. Whenever he returned to the so-called scenes of his childhood, on a visit to Grandma O.'s big old house on Calumet or driving past OLM, the parochial school he'd attended up through fourth grade, it was like looking at pictures in some stranger's photo album. His childhood had been erased, like a file deleted from the memory of a computer. A few odds and ends survived: the plots of movies he'd seen, and almost every word of a scratchy record of fairy tales narrated by a dead comedian called Poppy Mueller. But all the important things were gone. What kind of stepbrother Ned had been before he'd got the illness that made him a vegetable. How Sondra and his real father, Henry Michaels, had got on before their divorce, when they'd been living together on Kuhn Avenue. Maybe that was too early in his childhood for him to be expected to remember much of it. But the years he'd gone to OLM were also a blank. And those were just the things he *knew* he didn't remember. There was no telling how many other files might have been deleted in the same way, without his knowing it. Because, if you don't know something happened, how can you be aware that you've forgotten it?

He'd wondered, at times, since he'd become aware of these gaps in his memory, whether they were really that unusual. He was always curious to know what other kids his age could remember about their own childhood, and mostly what they remembered seemed to be times they'd done something wrong and got caught and punished for it, or fights they'd been in, or places they'd gone for vacation with their families. William figured that a lot of that kind of remembering was actually people telling each other the *story* of how something had happened: it was the story they remembered, not what happened. But he didn't have anyone he could hear the stories of his own childhood from, since his father was dead, and his mother hadn't seen that much of him in the years right after the divorce, and Madge and Grandma O., when he would visit them in their creepy old house, showed no inclination to reminisce—not, at least, about *his* childhood. Grandma O. was full of information about growing up in Anoka in the twenties, and Madge would tell things she remembered from when she'd worked at the hospital, but on more personal matters she was as tight-lipped as a POW in a war movie. So William figured there was nothing functionally wrong with his memory that couldn't be accounted for simply by lack of exercise.

Even so, he had tried to keep the extent of his memory loss a private matter, fearing that if it were suspected he would have to return to the psychiatrist in the Foshay Tower to whom he'd been sent immediately after the accident. Dr. Helbron. He'd hated his trips to Helbron's office even more than the sessions at the orthodontist, when he was being fitted for the flipper. Now, however, that he didn't have to deal with Helbron, there was little danger of having his secret discovered, since there was no one else he knew who showed any curiosity about his past—no one but Herr Professor Nielson. And Nielson's attention was usually directed to those students who craved it and actively clamored for it, the hand wavers and brownnoses.

So the thing to do was to avoid being interesting. You had to look ordinary. Bright, but ordinary. Bright was okay at St. Tom's, where the faster you moved up the academic ladder and the higher the scores you racked up on that ultimate video arcade game called the SATs, the better your credit rating. But ordinary was no less important. Ordinary was wearing the school uniform, which was, like the uniform most grown-ups wore, not a specific set of clothes but a style. Expensive but not loud or trendy. Ordinary as in the movie everyone was going to and which was set right here in Minneapolis, *Ordinary People*. It wasn't necessarily that easy (aside from having the right clothes) to achieve genuine ordinariness. You might be too fat, or have the kind of acne that made people cringe when they saw you, or you might have noticeably strange ideas that you couldn't shut up about, such as Judith with all her various crusades. But for his own part William was pretty sure he still qualified as ordinary, and he intended to hang on to that status by whatever means it might take.

So, what would constitute an *ordinary* early memory? What would an ordinary thirteen-year-old remember about his ordinary childhood?

He looked down at the paper plate with its dregs of catsup-dyed whey, and there was the answer: food. He could remember all kinds of food from his childhood that his mother never cooked, foods he felt a genuine nostalgia for when he saw them at the supermarket. Spam. Spam sandwiches with spongy slices of Wonder Bread soaking up the butter the Spam was fried in. Butter was the same word in German as in English, and feminine in gender: *die Butter*. Frozen pizzas, and the choice between the kind with gray nubbles of sausage and little red discs of pepperoni. Pizza in German had to be *Pizza*, but what was its sex? He made it feminine, figuring that Nielson wouldn't know the sex of pizzas any more than he did. What else? Strawberry ice cream, that was a memory that went back to Kuhn Avenue and the ice cream truck that came by in the summertime. In no time at all he'd filled a page with early memories of food, writing in a rush and mixing the German and English together like cottage cheese and catsup. Then he set to work looking up the German for the words he'd left in English, and by the time the bell buzzed to announce the next period, he had every word in place. When he read it aloud in class, there wasn't one of his classmates who didn't think that William wasn't entirely ordinary with ordinary memories of an ordinary childhood.

31

Of the twelve members of the Computer Club at St. Tom's, four had Apples, two had Ataris, one had a Commodore PET, and the others had video game machines, except for William, who didn't have anything, yet.

He'd joined the club to learn BASIC and scrounge time on the club's kit-built Altair, a donation to the Computer Club from its president, Jason Schechner, who'd moved up to an Apple the Christmas before last. The video game machine owners were not considered serious members and had been allowed into the club only to comply with the Student Council's bylaw that required any student organization receiving the use of school facilities to have at least ten members. The video game contingent almost never came to meetings, and when they did it was to try and involve the others in their own ever-continuing game of Dungeon and Dragons.

William probably wouldn't have gone to room 202, where the club was to meet that afternoon, since he knew that Larry Binns had not come to school today and so would not be demonstrating, as scheduled, the version of Space Invaders he'd programmed on his Apple. Plus, four other members of the club were off with the Debate team to Bishop Cretin High School for the last meet of the year. But then in math class Jason Schechner's sister, Lisa, had handed him a note from her brother saying to be sure not to miss the meeting at three o'clock. There was no reason given, but William recognized the note as a command and he was accustomed to deferring to Jason's authority, whenever convenient. Jason was sixteen, and was taking advantage of the University-linked accelerated studies program to get his diploma from St. Tom's in just three years, which he'd been able to do without damaging his reputation as one of St. Tom's leading goof-offs and free spirits. He was using his Apple to design a kind of music-box-cum-guitar that would let its "player" pretend to be playing at virtuoso level. So far it wasn't a marketable commodity, but you could see the promise. That Jason, with all his popularity and advantages, should deign to be William's friend was considered something of a social anomaly by Jason's other friends, who were all seniors or already in college, but it didn't surprise William. Jason was a brain, and William was a brain, and brains have a way of forming a double orbit.

And so, obedient to Jason's note, William had not headed out, after the last bell of the day, to Bus 4, which serviced Willowville, New Hope, and the other north-lying suburbs. Instead he'd gone from his locker directly to room 202. Like most of the second-floor classrooms at St. Tom's, which had yet to grow into all its hand-me-down square footage from its earlier incarnation as an Episcopal seminary, room 202 functioned as an attic. In addition to a supply of old metal filing cabinets and nests of stacking chairs, there were a number of orphaned exhibits from the science fairs of yesteryear, looking a bit enigmatic now that they'd been cannibalized of their reusable elements and had lost, in most cases, their explanatory posters.

In the central panel of the frieze of blackboards at the front of the room someone had left a message:

HAPPY BIRTHDAY!

In smaller script beneath this, "I'll be a few minutes late. Please wait. Jason." For some reason Jason's birthday greeting made William uneasy, and he took the eraser from the narrow ledge at the base of the blackboard and began erasing the chalked letters. No amount of erasing seemed to make the message completely illegible. The uneasiness intensified to a kind of panic, which was stupid, because there was no real need for him to be doing this in the first place. It was as though the letters he had to erase were not the actual ones he could see, ghostlike, glimmering behind the overlapping veils of smeared chalk dust; as though another message were decipherable behind it, which squinting his eyes almost closed he could read:

HAPPY HALLOWEEN

For a moment it was as though he were there again, in the fourth grade classroom at OLM, on the night of the Halloween party, the night the candy had been stolen from the big bowl. He remembered the obscenity the thieves had written on the blackboard, and how it remained there even after his father had erased it, and how he'd suggested writing another message over it—the same he could see now, until he blinked it back to what he knew was there, the words Jason had written there and he'd just now erased: Happy Birthday.

But the memory remained, and he felt like a fisherman who has spent the whole day trolling without once feeling a tug on his line when at last a fish strikes. All the time he'd sat there in the lunchroom trying to dredge up an early memory, racking his brains for a single clear detail from the years he'd been at OLM, and now suddenly he could *see* that old classroom superimposed over the uniform tawny orange of room 202, as though these walls were only a kind of veil through which he could witness that earlier scene: the empty desks, and the damp coats in the cloakroom where his classmates had left them when they'd gone to watch *Frankenstein* in the gym. He could remember getting up during the movie and going to the nun at the door to ask permission to go to the toilet, but that had been a lie: he'd really wanted to go back to the classroom alone. But *why*? And why did that big metal bowl, emptied of all but a few worm-eaten apples, seem in retrospect a *happy* memory? The significance of these recollections remained tantalizingly out of reach, as though he'd been spinning the dial of the TV and caught a single vivid scene from an old movie, but without the sound, without knowing how the story began or where it was going.

"Hey there. Happy Birthday," said a voice from behind him, as though reading the message erased from the blackboard.

He turned around to face his friend. "Jason, hi."

Jason was dressed not in the normative designer-brand sportswear favored by most St. Tom's students but in prefaded jeans, heirloom sneakers, and a black sweatshirt pledging his allegiance to Led Zeppelin. Somehow the effect remained normative. The suntanned, swimming-trimmed body inhabiting these clothes was obviously a product of affluent suburbia and not of that romantic, dangerous inner city that Jason visited two or three nights a month to attend rock concerts or go drinking with a fake ID. "Glad you got my note. And glad to *see* you. Two reasons: Reason number one, I wanted to give you this." He handed William a small package, about the size of a cigarette pack, wrapped in a white paper napkin and held together with two red rubber bands, of the very small kind that Jason used (when he was not at school) to hold his hair together in a ponytail. "Well? Aren't you going to *open* it? You can't thank me properly until you do."

"What's the second reason?" William asked suspiciously. "There isn't going to be some kind of surprise party, is there? I told my mother I didn't want anything like that. And I was serious."

"The second reason has nothing to do with your mother. It may be a surprise, if you let me keep it one, but not a surprise you'll have any objection to. Okay? Now open your present and thank me for it."

He opened the napkin-wrapped birthday present. It was a pack of Camel cigarettes. An open pack, and only partially full.

"Cigarettes? I'm thirteen so suddenly I've got to start smoking *cigarettes?* Jason, what is this—1950?"

Jason smiled knowingly. "Not cigarettes, schmuck. Joints, grown in Jamaica, hand-rolled by yours truly. You see, it's true, what the representative of our Police Department said about the danger of drugs being ever-present in our schools. Here you are now, confronting the danger."

"I've confronted the danger before, thanks. It only made me feel sleepy."

"It could have been you needed to sleep at the time, but you were repressing it. This stuff unleashes all your most stifled longings, all those buried feelings. It's a scientifically proven fact." He smirked, and the separate silken hairs of his incipient mustache twitched like the sentient whiskers of a rabbit. St. Tom's dress code allowed for the growth of any amount of facial hair, but this was a liberty that few of the students either wished or were able to exercise. Jason's mustache, such as it was, was one of only seven in the entire student body. "So, what do you say, shall we drop some dynamite down the old mine shaft, hm?"

William was of two minds. On the one hand, he theoretically disapproved of drugs, or at least felt leery about taking them. On the other hand, he *was* curious. His earlier experiment had been two years ago, after his team had lost a Little League game, and it hadn't amounted to more than a couple of puffs. The results had not been drowsiness (that was a white lie) but a coughing fit. Since then he had mastered the art of inhaling tobacco smoke without going into convulsions. *Why not?* he asked himself, and right away he thought of one good reason.

"Well, I'd like to, but I don't think we should do it here, do you?"

"I'll let you in on a secret. Unless you begin to manifest clinical symptoms of acute psychosis, no one will hassle you for sneaking a joint up here in Orangeville. The janitors do it, the jocks do it, even J. D. McCudahy does it."

J. D. McCudahy was the principal of St. Tom's.

"I don't believe you," said William.

"Believe what you like." Jason helped himself from the Camel pack, then took a red butane lighter from the pocket of his jeans and lighted the joint. "Some people say—" he began, holding the smoke in his lungs. Then exhaled, and continued in his normal voice, "that pot dulls your brain, messes up your thinking. But what *I* think"—he handed the lighted joint to William, who accepted it with studied casualness, an actor in the movie Jason was directing. Jason resumed his train of thought—"is that pot intensifies it. If you're an illiterate *dude* with an attention span limited to a Tom and Jerry cartoon, then pot will intensify your empty-headedness, and eventually you'll progress to a drug that will wipe out consciousness altogether. But"—he reached for the joint, inhaled, handed it back—"if you've already got some kind of mental life going, then the pot will just bring some more zest to it. Calculus is a gas on grass."

William found that hard to believe, but he didn't say so. He'd become fascinated with the blackboard again, where, to his relief, no words were legible now, not "Happy Birthday," not "Happy Halloween."

"Have you ever had hallucinations?" he asked, partly to keep Jason talking, partly out of real curiosity.

"On pot? Are you serious?" Jason squinted good-humoredly at William through the thin helices of smoke.

"Drugs can do that, can't they? And even without drugs. A few minutes ago, right in this room before we were smoking, I had a minor hallucination. I was looking at the blackboard where I'd erased what you'd written and I could swear I could still read the words, but instead of saying 'Happy Birthday," what I saw was 'Happy Halloween.' Now, with the pot, I don't see anything."

"Oh well, at *that* level," Jason said, with the same confident authority that Dr. Helbron had possessed on all matters concerning his professional specialty, the mind, "we all hallucinate. Pot excites the eye's phosphene activity, which also relates to dreaming, and to the fizzle of colors you see after you've been looking at something bright and then close your eyes."

William had pushed the right button, and Jason went on to explain everything he knew about the chemistry of the brain, which led in turn to Jason's hobbyhorse, which was the problem of how to account for miracles. Jason had become a zealous atheist, after a happy childhood as a Reform Jew untroubled by questions of faith. Miracles, according to Jason, when they weren't out-and-out frauds, could also be the result of phosphene activity that had been coordinated by some telepathic means so that a single hallucination could be experienced by a group of people in unison.

"I'll tell you the book you've got to read," Jason said, when his theory had been stated and the joint smoked down to a twist of paper. "No, better than that I'll lend it to you. Aldous Huxley, *The Doors of Perception.* Ever heard of it?"

"I've read *Brave New World.*"

"Yeah, that's a good one, too. What Huxley was on to, long before the actual laboratory work had been done, was the connection between brain chemistry and what's called altered states. You feeling anything, other than sleepy?"

"You mean, is my state altered? I don't think so. Except for being nervous that someone is going to come in here, and we'll get reported."

"Then let me get rid of the evidence." Jason went over to one of the derelict science exhibits, which consisted of a large glass sphere filled with thin streamers of shredded paper in various colors. He dropped the remains of the joint through a small aperture in the top of the sphere. "Pure science," he observed, "often yields unexpected applications in our daily lives."

"What was the second reason, Jason? Come on, don't keep me in suspense."

"Look out the window."

William went to the window and looked out. The bright daylight saving sky was sliced in two by the jet trail of a plane slanting west toward the airport. Tall, elderly hedges of white lilac defined the horizon and the extent of the school's grounds. A squirrel darted for a tree trunk and spiraled up to peek out from behind the lowest branch. William felt he'd established a kind of understanding with the squirrel, a fellowship based on a shared, groundless fear. "What am I supposed to be looking *for?*"

"Don't you recognize any of the cars in the parking lot?"

There weren't that many cars left in the lot, and his eye lighted at once on a gray Honda Civic identifiable even this far away as his ex-stepmother's by its extreme grottiness. Madge never took the car to a carwash. What the rain didn't wash off gradually bonded itself to the paint.

"What's *she* doing here?"

"It's your birthday, isn't it? What do you think?"

"But why should *you* . . . I mean, you don't know her. Do you?"

"Can I help it if older women find me irresistible?"

"Seriously."

"It's a traditional birthday maneuver. She got my number from Judith, and asked me if I would keep you after school long enough so she could take you off and do birthday-type things with you. I can't tell you more without spoiling her surprise. Now, stick these inside your knapsack where they won't get crushed"—he tapped the cigarette pack that was not a cigarette pack—"and go cash in your birthday chips."

32

As soon as he was near enough to the mud-crusted Honda so that she didn't have to shout, Madge waved and said, "Happy Birthday, Billy."

"I'm William now," he announced, as he'd been doing all day.

"Really? As of when?"

"As of this morning."

She held out her hands welcomingly, and he caught hold of them and stood on his tiptoes to kiss her cheek as she pecked at his. She smiled. "I think you're a little taller every time I see you . . . William. But you shouldn't be in such a hurry to be a grown-up. It's overrated."

She seemed genuinely happy to see him, which wasn't always the case. As often as not when he came to visit, Madge would be off in another world, and nothing he said would register. She would ask him about school and then nod and go Mm-hm, Uh-huh, Isn't that interesting.

Today it was William who was in another world. During the entire drive to St. Paul, all the while he was telling her about how his friends and teachers at St. Tom's had reacted to the declaration of his new identity, and then while she was telling him the story of how she'd vacillated all through nursing school and for years afterward between being prim Margaret and brazen Madge, he kept glancing at her and wondering, uneasily, why she seemed . . . different. It wasn't a difference he could put into words. It wasn't, for instance, that she was so much fatter now than when they'd been living together. That change had taken place gradually, and William could no longer clearly picture Madge the way she used to be (which even back then hadn't been what you could call thin). It wasn't that she no longer wore the same basic black outfit every day as soon as she changed out of her hospital uniform. Now that she was working at a nursing home, she dressed like an ordinary person. Her hair was done up in the same loose bun as ever, and her face was made up with the usual bare minimum of makeup. The general impression was that she didn't *care* how she looked so long as she basically passed muster—but had she ever been otherwise?

Probably it wasn't Madge who'd changed, but himself. He'd got used to his mother's more stylish, more expensive clothes. Without knowing it he'd become the kind of snob that Judith accused Ben and Sondra of being. The kind who feels superior to anyone who's wearing the wrong clothes, wrong meaning cheap.

Or just as probably the "difference" was nothing but a side effect of the marijuana he'd been smoking. Because, in fact, everything seemed skewed from the way it usually registered: the traffic was too speedy, the trucks too loud, the sun too bright through the rifts of cloud. He examined his ragged fingernails and began to feel choked up with pity because his pink hands looked like two animals that had been skinned alive.

The Obstschmecker house, when they finally got there, was the strangest sight of all. It only needed a sign over the door saying "Beware of Ghost" to look like an official haunted house. The paint all flaky, the lawn already rank with weeds this early in the spring, a fallen branch from the elm in the backyard clinging to the ridge of the east dormer window, and the lower half of that window sealed up with a weathered sheet of plywood. To the right and left and across the street as well were new pink-brick condos with fake mansard roofs. The big FOR SALE billboard at the corner said that Calumet Manors had been built by the Golden Gopher Development Corp., a subsidiary of N.N.E. Each unit of the development had its own sunken garage and plot of not yet sodded lawn, and each lawn its own seedling maple. Even if it had been fixed up, the Obstschmecker house would have looked out of place amid these latter-day structures, having been built on so much larger a scale.

"They're awful, aren't they?" Madge said, parking the Honda outside the garage. "And would you believe each one of them costs more than they were offering Mother for the house five years ago? The ceilings are only eight feet high. And the plumbing's already shot in half the houses. Those developers are crooks, all of them."

This instant diatribe seemed to cheer her up appreciably, or else she was simply glad to be home. William followed her around to the back of the house (Madge explained that the front door was kept locked all the time, "just to be on the safe side") and then in through the back door. The wooden railing had broken off the back stairs and lay rotting in the leaf pile that had been a flower bed.

"Mother!" Madge called out from the kitchen. "We're home."

The kitchen reeked of air freshener. No forest, no lumber yard, had ever smelled so piny. Yet both windows were open and a breeze was turning the pages of a cookbook that lay on the table amid a clutter of newly dirtied bowls and pans.

Madge checked the stove to see that the burners and the oven hadn't been left on, and then called out again: "Mother! William is here."

In reply a door slammed shut.

Madge sighed. "I hope she's not going to be in one of her moods. Well, she can suit herself. Come in to the dining room, that's where your stuff is. I was going to have your friend set it up in your old room so you could test it out right off the bat, but he explained what that would entail in terms of wiring the whole thing together, and it sounded like more trouble than it was worth."

By the time this preamble was over William stood in view of his birthday present. It was, as he'd been hoping (but hoping to get from his step-father, not from Madge), an Apple. Not just an Apple, however, but an Apple garnished with all good things—a double disk-drive, a Soft-Card co-processor, a DOS 3.3 disk controller, and for the icing on this electronic birthday cake, a Silentype thermal printer, the first such (according to the note Jason had provided for the unveiling) that the dealer, the User-Friendly Computer Store in the Robbinsdale mall, had sold to anyone in the Twin Cities.

"It's *wonderful*, Madge," William said, after he'd checked off all the items on Jason's inventory, "truly. But I can't possibly accept this. I don't know exactly what it all cost you, but something on the order of three thousand dollars. At least. You could get a new car for what you spent on this. And I *know* if I bring it home, my mother wouldn't let me keep it."

"That's sweet of you, Billy—William, excuse me—but in fact I didn't spend a penny of my own money for it. It all came out of your own trust fund. Naturally, if you don't want it, I can take it back to the store. But both your sister and the nice Jewish boy she put me in touch with, both of them thought this would be exactly what you wanted. And that you'd probably learn to use it well enough to get your money's worth out of it."

"This is the first I've heard about my having a trust fund."

"Because you weren't told. Right after the accident I had a hard enough time just dealing with things like the funeral, and in any case there didn't seem to be any immediate need for you to know about it, not till you had to start thinking about college. Maybe I was wrong, maybe I should have told you before this. Or maybe I should have waited a year or two longer. But your mother tells me you might be heading to college ahead of the usual schedule. So you should know what's possible, financially. Basically, you've got enough money to draw on that you can go to just about anywhere you want to, including medical school, if that's what you're still aiming for."

"But Dad didn't have any money saved. How . . . ?"

"How!" replied Madge, lifting her right hand, Indian-style.

It was like a belly dive into the pool of memory. Madge and his father had played the same simple trick on him a hundred times, and the humor of the sudden derailment it created whenever it appeared had always cracked him up. And so it did again.

Madge smiled and, when he'd stopped laughing, said, "We did have some fun times together, didn't we?"

He nodded.

The telephone rang and Madge went into the kitchen to answer it. As soon as she was out of the room, the reality of the once familiar but so much changed scene bore down on William—the mustiness, the mess, the neglect. The floorboards in the alcove where the hanging plants were hung had warped from the water leaking, drop by drop, from the over-watered pots. Beside the rocker an ashtray of cigarette butts had been spilled on the carpet and never picked up. The place looked as though bums had been squatting there.

Madge came back into the dining room and said, "That was St. Malachy's, and I'm so pissed off. I've had this arranged for weeks in advance. You'd think that when I ask for *one* afternoon, but no, no, it's impossible to get anyone else. Lucy isn't answering her phone, and there's only the two aides on duty, and this is something that requires an R.N. Which means me. Sorry."

William gave an obliging shrug. "That's okay. I'm planning on getting into the same business, remember. So I better get used to this sort of thing. But I would like to know about this mysterious trust fund before you head off. Dad was not exactly a millionaire when he died."

"There's no mystery. He had insurance. It was our wedding present from my father, a fully paid-up life policy for $100,000. Henry was furious at the time. I remember him saying he'd rather have had a set of Tupperware than the damned insurance, and you could see his point. *He* was never going to enjoy any of it. The policy was drawn up in such a way that he couldn't even use it as collateral for a loan—if you know how that sort of thing works?"

William nodded. He didn't, but he wasn't interested either. "Does my mother know about the trust fund?" he asked.

Madge smiled. "She knows it exists, but not the amount. Right after the accident, your mother was a little . . . I guess the word is hostile. She seemed to think I was going to put up a custody battle for you. I mean, I do love you, and it broke my heart to have you move away so soon after Henry was gone. But she's your mother, I'm not. Anyhow, when we discussed your situation, I told her that there was a trust fund and that I was the executor but that I didn't want to tell you about it till you were nearer to college, and she agreed to that. But I never told her how much it was, and she never asked. She probably thought, knowing our situation, that the insurance was for a couple thousand at most, and didn't want to embarrass me by asking. While I was thinking that *your* long-term interests might be better served if Dr. Winckelmeyer wasn't aware that you stood to come into a lump of money like that. Sometimes, you know, a stepfather will want to take money from a trust fund to pay for things like high school tuition, even clothes. And Ben Winckelmeyer never struck me as an especially generous man. Maybe I'm wrong, but I'd advise you to keep this under your hat. Let him think the computer came from me."

William smiled agreement. He was always happy to join a conspiracy. And such a present coming from Madge *would* make his stepfather feel like a cheapskate.

"I gotta go now," Madge said. "And since I won't be able to drive you and this big gray Apple home to Willowville, let me give you money for a cab."

"No, no, I'll call Mom. She's always saying how I never visit you often enough, so she won't mind coming to pick me up. She's happy for any excuse that'll get her out of the house. But there's still one thing . . ." He hesitated, with an instinctively lawyerly prudence, not wanting to come right out and ask how much the trust fund amounted to.

Madge misunderstood his reticence. "Oh, I got my share, if that's what you're getting at. The pot was divided fifty-fifty. I put my half in a similar trust fund for Ned, so that if I go before he does, he won't have to be in the kind of ward I used to work in at the state hospital. That's always been my worst anxiety, and the insurance money has more or less put an end to it. Whatever happens, I know Ned will be taken care of decently."

A bell began to ring. It wasn't the doorbell, or the telephone, but a real hand-rung bell that produced a thin, silvery, irregular tinkling like the bell that an altar boy rings at Mass when the Host is lifted. It seemed to come from upstairs, which gave William an uneasy feeling, since he'd been assuming that Grandma O. had gone to her own room, and so the only person who could have been responsible for ringing the bell upstairs was Ned, and that, of course, was impossible.

"Damn," said Madge, reaching the only logical explanation, "Mother must have gone upstairs. That's the bell she rings when she wants me to bring Ned up his dinner, or for whatever other reason. And if those bowls out in the kitchen are any clue, she's put together some kind of birthday party. If I go up there now, I won't be able to get away for another fifteen minutes. Mother doesn't do that much cooking anymore, but when she does . . ."

"Hey, that's okay," William said. "I'll go up and say you've already left. If you want me to."

"Would you? I'd appreciate it."

"She doesn't let up with that bell, does she?"

"It's funny, I've got so used to it I don't even notice anymore. Mother has the idea that Ned likes the sound. She'll sit there sometimes five, ten minutes just holding the bell up in front of him and ringing it. Like now. At first it got on my nerves. Now, it's like . . . I don't know, hearing the water run for a bath. It seems natural. You're sure you don't want cab fare?"

"Don't waste your money. Mom'll come for me. After all, it's my birthday, I'm entitled to limousine service. Which reminds me, I can't thank you enough for the Apple and the printer. It's the best birthday present I ever had."

"Thank your father. The trust fund came from him." She took up her purse, and they smiled at each other but didn't try to kiss again. They were neither of them much for hugging or kissing. But when she'd gone and the back door had banged shut behind her, William felt a pang of sorrow go through his chest, a sorrow not simply over the fact that his feelings for Madge went deeper than his feelings for his own mother, but a further sorrow that came from knowing that deep as those feelings might be, they weren't finally deep enough. It was as though, inside, he was just like his brother Ned, but while in Ned's case it was his body that was immobilized and impotent, with William it was his feelings, or his soul.

And still that damned bell kept up its endless jingling, as though it was the sound of the sadness he was feeling, the silvery, incessant shrilling of his own emptiness. Little as he wanted to go upstairs and have a "birthday party" with Grandma O. and Ned, even that seemed preferable to staying down here and listening to that bell. How could she stand to hear it herself? Maybe her own hearing wasn't that good.

"I'm coming!" he called up the stairs. "Stop ringing the bell, I'm *coming!*"

The moment he'd mounted the first step, the ringing stopped. He felt embarrassed, since he hadn't thought Grandma O. would have been able to hear what he'd said.

—*Well*, said a voice that was not Grandma O.'s, but a man's voice, deep but seeming also somehow far away, like the bell. *I'm waiting, Billy. Come.*

"Billy?"

It was the voice, the real voice of Grandma Obstschmecker. The other voice, the man's, could not have been real. He must have imagined it, the way earlier he'd imagined the words on the blackboard in room 202.

"Billy!" Her voice was louder, with an exasperated ring to it. "Billy, I know you're up there, I'm not deaf. And your knapsack's right here on the table as plain as day. Billy!"

Reprieved for the time being from having to go up to Ned's room, he hurried back to the dining room. Grandma O. regarded him doubtfully, as though making up her mind whether or not to be angry.

"Hi, Grandma," he said, with a perfunctory smile. "I thought you were upstairs."

"Why did Madge leave?" the old woman demanded brusquely. "I heard the bell ringing, so naturally I supposed it was Madge. She has the idea that Ned likes the sound it makes. But then I heard the car drive off, and the bell went on ringing, so I knew she must have left you here." She grimaced at him, and touched her wig to be sure it was positioned properly. "Happy Birthday," she added. Somehow she made even that seem like a complaint. "How old are you this time?"

"Thirteen."

"I'll be seventy-three on my next birthday."

He didn't know what to do with this information except collate it: "That's sixty years' difference between us."

She nodded gravely, as having reached the same rueful conclusion independently. "I baked your favorite dessert."

"Lardy-slice?"

She nodded.

"Hey, I haven't had any lardy-slice for a long time."

"It's in the pantry, under a bowl to keep the flies off. I'm afraid it's a little burnt."

"Well, we won't have to eat the burnt parts."

The lardy-slice, however, had been half incinerated. Its blackened, pie-crustlike dough could not be pried from the tin baking pan even with the most heavy-duty metal spatula. They ate it by digging shreds and chunks from the soft middle with their forks. William was surprised at how much he enjoyed it. Even the dark brown parts tasted good. They ate without talking. Grandma O. was old enough not to have to pretend an interest in matters that didn't concern her, such as how William was doing in school, or the nature of the equipment in the boxes in the dining room.

"Now," she said, when the last edible morsels of the lardy-slice had been carved from cinders stuck to the pie tin, "if you like, *I'll* phone for your mother to come get you, and you can go back upstairs and see Ned a while longer. Maybe Madge is right, maybe he does enjoy company when they come calling. Maybe for him hearing that bell is like listening to a song on the radio. That's what Madge thinks. We'll probably never know, will we? You wouldn't mind ringing it for him a little while longer, would you?"

"But *I* wasn't ringing the bell. I was just starting to go upstairs when you called me."

"In some ways, Billy Michaels, you haven't changed a bit since you were six years old. Stubborn? I've never known a child to be so stubborn. Well, there's no point in arguing with stubborn people. It only raises your blood pressure. Though mine's not as bad now as it used to be. I guess I must be eating more healthily. Though I don't make any effort to. I eat whatever I like. The lardy-slice was good, wasn't it?"

William concurred in this with a sincere nod of his head. "Thanks for making it, Grandma."

"It was Mr. Obstschmecker's favorite dessert, too," she confided. "He could put away an entire pan at one sitting. So I always made two, one for him, one for the family. It has a different name in German, but I can't remember what. I don't remember any German now, except *Gesundheit!*"

"I'm taking German in school, did Madge tell you? St. Tom's is the only high school in the Twin Cities where it's possible to study German."

"I would go upstairs with you," she said, ignoring his attempt to capture the spotlight, "but right now I have to clean up in the kitchen. Madge gets conniptions when she comes home to a sink full of pots and pans."

Reluctantly he got up from the table. "I'll go up and see Ned now." Grandma O. nodded her approval. Passing through the dining room he saw his knapsack lying on the box containing the Silentype printer. Remembering the Camel pack inside and what a snoop Grandma O. could be, he took the knapsack with him as he went up the stairs. At each step he half expected the bell to begin ringing again, but the only sounds to be heard were his own footsteps and the creaking of the stairs.

33

There was a girl in New Jersey or somewhere like that called Karen Ann Quinlan, who had been in a state of coma and considered brain-dead for years. She had only been kept alive by the machinery she was hooked up to in a hospital, and her parents had had to fight with the hospital over whether to take her off the life-support machinery or leave her on. Theoretically that kind of equipment could keep a vegetable body like Karen Ann Quinlan alive for decades. As "alive" as the body of Ned Hill. But what kind of life could that be? Ned wasn't brain-dead. His eyes opened and closed; he could breath and swallow water and soft foods; he urinated and defecated, though he was not in control of either process. And his hair grew. In fact, Madge had such an aversion to shaving Ned and to cutting his hair that he was beginning to look like some kind of biker. He was also getting fat, since Madge would let him go on eating the things she whipped up in the blender as long as he'd keep swallowing—and he'd keep swallowing as long as something was being shoveled into his mouth. At this point he was no fatter than Madge herself or than Grandma O. In fact, the three of them looked like they could all have shared the same clothes, and maybe they did. The white nylon shirt Ned was buttoned into today had undoubtedly come from the nursing home where Madge worked, St. Malachy's Hospice. They let her have all the old uniforms she wanted for free, the ones with stains that wouldn't wash off. This one had a huge tan amoeba all down the front, representing, probably, the better part of a cup of coffee.

In another twenty years, maybe there'd be a case about this kind of situation. If the decision had been William's, he would not have hesitated: he would have Ned put out of his suffering and any healthy organs donated to people needing transplants. Surely Ned, if he were still conscious in some dim way (as Madge tried to believe), would have wanted the same thing for himself. Imagine lying here, day after day, with the flies settling on your face and crawling around your eyes (the way they were right now) unless someone was around to shoo them off (which wasn't worth the bother, they just flew right back). It used to be they'd at least haul Ned out onto the sun porch in the summertime, but he'd got too big for Madge to lug him out there by herself, so now the limits of his existence were this room, this bed, and *that* body. And it stunk—room, bed, *and* body. There was no way anyone was ever going to keep up with Ned's sanitary requirements. His waste products weren't produced at intervals, in neat bundles; they just sort of leaked out of him, the way the water leaked out of the radiators at school. At least with the radiators you could keep bowls under the leaks.

And it wasn't just Ned who suffered (assuming he felt anything at all). The situation was worse for the people who had to take care of a human vegetable than for the vegetable itself. Both Madge and her mother were obsessed with Ned. Their lives revolved around his requirements. The idea they had about the bell was only the latest bee in their bonnets. Madge also continued to waste a couple of hours every night doing "patterning" exercises, which meant her using Ned's inert limbs as a kind of human rowing machine. William couldn't see the point of it. Who needed a vegetable version of Arnold Schwarzenegger? But of course you couldn't say any of that to Madge. Ned had become the god she worshiped and the crucifix she was nailed to, and to call the worship into question was like suggesting that all the pain of her martyrdom was wasted effort. Her only hope, as far as William could see, was that somehow the vegetable would wither on the vine and die, but after more than six years of living death Ned seemed as vital—and as sickly—as the damned houseplants spilling out of their pots and planters all over the house.

—*Such cruel thoughts, Billy*, said the voice he'd heard before, at the foot of the stairs. The voice of the man who wasn't there.

Knowing the voice wasn't real did not make it less interesting. Just the opposite. The strange thing was not that he was hearing voices but that his reaction was primarily curiosity, not fear. Partly because the voice seemed friendly. Partly, maybe, because of the marijuana he'd been smoking. "Pot" you were supposed to call it, if you wanted to be hip.

—*Fear can be experienced in different ways. But it's true, you have no reason to be afraid of me. I am your friend.*

"Do you have a name?" William asked aloud.

—*Of course. Don't you remember it?*

William shook his head.

—*Then let me assist your memory.*

A hand, as much larger than his own as a grown man's would be larger than an infant's, gripped his shoulder, the thumb pressed to the nape of his neck, the fingers digging into the flesh of his pectoral muscle. He became rigid in that grip, unable even to lower his head to see the hand that had laid hold of him—to see *if* he could see it. Where the thumb and each fingertip pressed against his flesh he could feel a distinct but indefinable sensation, a tingling like the tingling of Ben-Gay. The sensation spread through his body in a twining filigree, like the interference patterns set up in a still pool as an insect, as many insects, skate across the surface. He feared he would pass out and concentrated on looking at what was before him clearly and steadily, ignoring the pulses of brightness that seemed to want to override his field of vision—and what was there before him to look at was Ned. His head had fallen back against the pillow, and his mouth hung open slackly, but somehow his eyes seemed focused and aware of what was happening. Even his slack-jawed expression could be interpreted as awe instead of mere idiocy. What was it that Ned could see that he could not? He twisted against the grip of the hand, and the ripplings of energy that spread from the fingers suddenly drew cable-taut, and along that cable—or rather, *through* it, like a wind channeled through a wind tunnel and amplified by that constriction—flowed the ruthless, discovering energy of the god. As a tornado sweeps up the prairie topsoil to reveal the rocks that have persisted beneath the detritus of the centuries, so the god, with a single pressure of his inhuman hand, dispersed the shallow sediments beneath which William's memories had lain buried. He felt overwhelmed and lifted up all in the same instant. The figure visible before him, Ned sealed in the sepulcher of his own diseased flesh, testified with equal eloquence as to the guilt of what, so long ago, William had done as well as to the power that had allowed him to do it.

Instinctively, as a hooked trout might writhe against the barbed steel in its mouth, William twisted to be free from the hand's grip—not, now, to escape the god but in simple eagerness to turn from the sight of Ned, and his own guilt, and to regard the god, and his power. The hand let him loose (though, it may be, only as the fisherman might pay out some line), and William turned round and saw, again, the god Mercury.

—*Even now you doubt me*, the god remarked, lifting the caduceus in his right hand with a little flourish, like the conductor of an orchestra, signaling for silence. *You would rather think me some delusion induced by your first whiff of a psycholeptic drug than acknowledge my power and accord the worship that is my due.*

"I do worship you," William declared earnestly. "Anyone seeing you like this would have to. But it's true that I don't believe you're here, in this room, physically, the same way I am. And I think the pot may have something to do with it, though I don't know how. Am I wrong?"

—*No, that's not too far off. You've lost that quicker apprehension you had in childhood that let me speak to you directly, as we are speaking now, but shall not again. In the future we will have to conduct these rendezvous when you are dreaming. Or when, as now, your consciousness has been suitably altered and you're not in, as they say, your right mind. But I must warn you: the Police Department is quite right, drugs are dangerous. And the more fine-tuned the spirit—the more poetical, if you prefer—the greater the potential for danger.*

"The caduceus," William said eagerly. "Can I have it back?"

—*It is where you left it.* The god took a step backward to allow William to precede him out of the room and up the stairway to the attic.

No sound of footsteps but his own followed William up the stairs, and he thought of what the god had said: "Even now you doubt me." So he must not turn around, as though doubting that Mercury were behind him. He remembered climbing these same steps on Halloween, lighting his way with the jack-o'-lantern. Mercury had called himself Lord Saman then, and the snake on his caduceus had been alive. He remembered the cold, wet coils of the snake wriggling in his hands, like a piece of liver when it comes out of its cellophane wrapping.

He remembered his father bleeding in the wrecked car.

—*But that was not your fault*, said Mercury, though his voice seemed to come from a distance now. *Indeed, you had secured his good health to the full extent of the caduceus's power, just as you did for the women who still live in this house and enjoy such good health here. But good health is no surety against accidents. Feel guilty for the bald bitch downstairs, if you must feel guilt. Feel guilty for those who lost their teeth eating the candy you cursed, but think who they were and whether you do not, in fact, take pleasure in what became of them. Feel guilty for the vegetable your brother. But for your father? In his death you are guiltless. Surely you know that.*

William crossed the attic from the top of the stairs directly to where, so long ago, he had buried the caduceus beneath a thin covering of loose insulation. And there it was still, as the god had promised and memory prompted, the brittle stick with the dessicated sparrow corpse affixed to it. He held it again, and again could feel, though diminished almost to extinction, the power of the thing.

My power, he thought, and felt for a moment as though his body were as the god's, a compact radiance that the words of his curse or his blessing could release.

The god did not correct this thought. Indeed, his purpose was accomplished, and he had departed.

34

The moment Sondra hung up the phone on old Mrs. Obstschmecker, who had rambled on nonstop for nearly fifteen minutes, it rang again. She could hear the Cuisinart whirring away in the kitchen, so it was no use hoping Judith would answer it. At this point she'd be up to her elbows in cake batter.

Sondra picked up the cordless phone from where it nestled out of sight behind the drapes. It emitted a shrill tweet and before she could say hello, Ben's voice boomed out through the whole room: "Damn, I thought we had that thing fixed!"

She sighed. "The man came in, he said it was working fine. How do I adjust it so it doesn't broadcast all through the living room?"

"You've got me, sugar. *And* you've got a guest for dinner. I hope that's okay."

"Ben! It's Billy's birthday!"

"I thought we were going to start calling him William."

"Who is it?" she asked, quickly running through the worst possibilities in her head.

"Dan Turnage. You remember him? From ATA."

Sondra, though she often did defend herself against her husband's business associates by forgetting or creatively misremembering their names, needed no further reminding as to Dan Turnage. Turnage was the champion asshole of the lot. She had loathed him at first sight, and closer acquaintance had only confirmed her first intuitions. Years ago Turnage had been a sports figure (twelve years as second baseman for the Twins,

and another two years as coach); now he was a vice-president for the organization that funded most of Ben's research, the American Tobacco Alliance. Turnage was ATA's chief figurehead, the person who had to make
all the poker-faced disclaimers and denials on TV whenever there was
some awful new piece of evidence about the dangers of smoking. Turnage
could look any camera in the eye and say that smoking did not present
any danger to health, as far as *he* was concerned, because he'd been smoking two packs a day from the age of sixteen and still did twenty push-ups
every morning. Then he would smile his thin-lipped smile and light a
cigarette and blow smoke at the newscaster. His most infamous moment
in the spotlight had been on "Sixty Minutes" a year ago, when Morley
Safer had done an utterly damning exposé about ATA and the new push
in the southern states to market chewing tobacco to children. On that
occasion Turnage had punctuated his remarks with streamers of brown
spittle into a big brass spittoon and, missing once, on Morley Safer's shoe.
"Sorry about that," he'd drawled, "I must be getting out of practice."
Nothing anyone said ever made a dent in his cool. Ben, behind his back,
called him "our cigar store Indian." Turnage was considered ATA's major
PR asset, and he was the single person in the world Sondra most hated
having to be polite to.

"No, Ben," she said. "Not him, not tonight. Explain that it's William's
birthday."

"I did. And he's got him a present. A baseball mitt."

"He's already given William *one* baseball mitt, if you'll recall. He
probably travels with a trunk full of the damned things. It's just public
relations. And William doesn't give a hoot about baseball."

"Well, he can pretend, can't he? It's about time the boy started learning to be a hypocrite."

"Ben, have you been drinking?"

"Nothing beyond what duty requires. Turnage is in a mellow mood,
and I want to continue that process, sugar. It's business, it's what pays the
bills. You never object to spending the money, so don't make it any harder
than it is already to earn it. I don't like the bastard any more than you do,
but I've just pitched a proposal for a new project, and he seems to like it,
but he's not exactly a quick thinker. He has to be coached, and buttered
up. A nice dinner, some wine and candles, a bit of flattering attention,
surely we can manage that."

"You mean, I should smile when he tries to feel me up."

"He's not as bad as all that."

"He also has *terrible* breath."

"True," Ben agreed. "But we'll put him at the far end of the table. Okay?"

"Do I have any choice?"

"I can see him heading back to the bar. We'll be home sometime between six and seven. See you then."

There was another electronic screech signaling that he'd hung up. Sondra dropped the phone on the floor, hoping it would break. It bounced once and lay on its side, buzzing angrily.

"To answer your question," said Judith, who was standing in the archway that opened onto the dining area, "no, you don't have a choice."

"Judith, you know it's not nice to eavesdrop."

"I wasn't eavesdropping, I was listening to your *broadcast* in the kitchen. There's no way that *I've* been able to discover to know when the phone is going to work like a public address system and when it isn't. If there were an instruction manual . . ."

"I think it got thrown out with the Christmas wrappings. Anyhow I'm sorry to snap at you. It's not your fault, it's mine, I should have put my foot down."

"He'd only have stomped on it."

"Aren't you in a mood. I hope the cake is all right."

"The cake is fine. It's just gone into the oven. And the dinner will be all right too." Judith stared defiance at her stepmother, waiting to see if she would be challenged in her declaration that she was still to act as the cook for William's entire birthday dinner.

Only then did it dawn on Sondra that she had no idea what Judith was intending to make for that dinner. She'd been delighted with her stepdaughter's offer to take on the chore. Cooking for Ben was hard work. He liked dishes in proportion as they were trouble to make, and he could always tell when Sondra tried to cut culinary corners by serving take-out and deli-type food, even when it came from Byerly's. Sondra did not exactly rebel against his demands, but she'd never learned to *enjoy* cooking. Julia Child and the rest of that lot were a mystery to her. And Judith was a greater mystery, for why would someone who hates to eat food have such a passion for preparing it? Judith said she did the cooking by way of trying to overcome her anorexia, and she did seem to make more of an effort to eat the dishes she cooked herself. But Sondra had seen her in the kitchen in the throes of rolling out the crusts of pies that she would never eat a bite of, since they were destined for church bake sales, and it was obvious from her absorption in such tasks that the girl genuinely enjoyed fondling dough, and paring vegetables, and chopping onions, and beating eggs, and performing all the other boring rigmaroles that were the bane of

Sondra's existence. No, she had no intention of reasserting her authority in the kitchen, certainly not on Dan Turnage's account.

"Ah, the dinner," she said. "That reminds me. I hope there'll be *enough* now that we have a guest. As I recall, Mr. Turnage is a man with a large appetite."

"There'll be more than enough," said Judith.

"And, um, what have you planned?"

"I showed you the recipe for the cake. It's a hazelnut upside-down apple cake, from the Cuisinart cookbook. And the rest is a combination of all William's favorite foods from childhood."

"And what are those?"

"*You're* his mother," said Judith smugly. "I wouldn't think you'd have to ask me a question like that. Anyhow, the whole idea is to make something that will be a surprise for everyone. So, can I go back to the kitchen now? It's going to take you at least an hour to go get William and bring him back, and that won't give you much leeway for being here to greet our guest."

"What a gift for personnel management you have, Judith. Yes, I suppose I should be off. Any last minute items you'd like me to pick up?"

"No, I have everything I need. But there is one thing I meant to ask. I couldn't help overhearing Winky remind you that the two of you mean to begin to call William by his proper name, instead of calling him Billy as you did before. Was that your idea originally, or his?"

Sondra hesitated. "It was Ben's idea. And speaking of proper names, Judith, you know Ben hates to be called Winky."

"And did *Ben* say what inspired *his* idea?"

Sondra avoided her stepdaughter's gaze. She knew very well what Judith was driving at. Ben had read the letter that Judith had slipped under William's door in the middle of the night. It would make little difference to Judith that her father approved the contents of the letter, that he'd become almost lyrical at lunchtime on the subject of his daughter's character. To Judith it would be a simple open-and-shut case of violation of privacy, a felony charge in the court of her own opinion. "No," Sondra said, improvising slowly, "or if he did tell me, I've forgotten."

"Had William talked to him, did he say?"

Sondra took the bait gratefully. "Yes, that was it. It was William's idea."

"That's strange, because I was in the room from the moment that William came down for breakfast, to the moment we set off on the school bus. And I don't remember William saying anything on the subject. We all just watched the news reports about Mount St. Helens."

"Then it must be that William had said something to him earlier, and that Ben remembered it today. Probably because of its being his thirteenth birthday."

"Oh. And what is the connection with his birthday?"

"You really will have to ask Ben these questions, dear. And now, as you've pointed out, I've got to get into motion, if I'm going to be back in time to welcome old Dragonbreath to our happy home."

Judith nodded, pursing her lips in a skeptical smile, the very image of a prosecutor dismissing an uncooperative (but innocent) witness and getting ready to examine the accused.

35

Judith, with a spotless chef's apron cinched tightly about her twenty-three-inch waist, appeared in the archway that opened onto the dining area and announced that dinner was served.

"Great!" said Dan Turnage, grinding out his fifth cigarette (Sondra had been keeping count) in the big free-form blue-and-white glass ashtray on the marbleized Chinese-type coffee table around which the sectional formed a kind of oxbow. Turnage had already consumed most of a package of Crispy Cheese Doodles, and despite much finger-licking his fingers glowed yellow-orange with Cheese Doodle coloring. He had also, since arriving forty-five minutes ago, consumed three generous glasses of bourbon. And who knew how much at the Hyatt's happy hour? He was the very definition, Sondra had decided, of a drunken sailor, and what *do* you do with a drunken sailor? Feed him, if you can.

They rose from the various sections of the sectional and followed Judith into the dining area, where, in the middle of the rosewood table, a fourteen-inch anchovy and pepperoni pizza had been cut with scientific accuracy into ten equal slices.

"You're there, Mr. Turnage," Judith directed, pointing to the foot of the table. "And William, you're here beside me." Her seating arrangement placed Turnage and her father at opposite ends of the table, which had been expanded by its middle leaf. Judith and William sat side by side across from Sondra, William next to Turnage, Judith by her father. "In theory there are two slices for everyone," Judith said, "but in practice there's more, since I can't stand anchovies and will have to pass on the pizza. But this is *only* the first course, so save room." She signaled the beginning of the meal by helping herself to a sliver of carrot from the lazy Susan beside the pizza.

As soon as he'd helped himself to a slice of pizza and picked up the trailing strings of cheese he'd let ooze down onto the tablecloth, Turnage continued his analysis of the prospects of the Twins in the season ahead. It was a subject on which no one else had any contribution to make, though Ben was able from time to time to think of leading questions that would rekindle Turnage's powers of speculation. "So how do you think our boys will stack up against the Royals?" Ben asked.

"Good question!" Turnage answered, having taken advantage of the pause in his own flow to bolt down half the slice of pizza. Then off he went through the permutations and combinations, comparing the pitching styles of the Royals' Rich Gale and Renie Martin and estimating how the Twins' best batters would fare against each of them. Sondra actually began to enjoy the situation, since both the children, instead of displaying overt hostility, had adopted her own tactic of giving the man endless rope. Once Ben had satisfied himself that Turnage wasn't aware of how he was monopolizing the conversation, or at least that he was content to do so, even he seemed to take a secret pleasure in leading Turnage on. The man's powers of insensitivity were truly amazing. But at last he reached a kind of conclusion, predicting that the Royals would take the American League pennant, but would then lose the World Series, probably to Philadelphia.

"Do you want to bet on that?" said William, in a tone suitable to a serious wager, neither friendly nor hostile.

"Why, sure." Turnage gave a condescending smile. "The Series is still a long ways off. But I'm game. Who do you favor then?"

"No one. I'll just bet that Philadelphia *doesn't* beat Kansas City in the World Series. I'll bet everything in this envelope—" From his back pocket he took the folded birthday card with Ben's gift and set it down on the stained tablecloth.

"William," Sondra pretended to object, "that's your birthday present."

"It's his money," Ben said, "and he's entitled to spend it as he likes. But it's scarcely a fair bet for Dan here."

"Why not?" Judith asked. "Mr. Turnage seemed very confident of his predictions, and he was able to give so many good reasons for making them. He convinced me. But perhaps he doesn't believe in gambling. We Catholics gamble so much we never stop to think that many other religions consider gambling a vice."

Turnage chuckled in just the pained, mirthless way he'd chuckled when he'd appeared on "Sixty Minutes." "I don't belong to one of those religions, Judy." He turned to William. "You got a bet, son. How much is in the envelope?"

William smiled. "I don't know. I haven't counted it."

That was a lie, of course, but such a nicely double-edged lie that Sondra could in no way find fault with him for it. It made his wager seem all the more flamboyant, and at the same time it was a reproach to Ben for not having bothered to get a proper birthday present. Such style, and only thirteen years old; she felt a genuine glow of pride.

With fingers greasy with oil from the pizza, Turnage counted the money enclosed in the birthday card. "Two hundred fifty dollars. You want to bet that much?"

"Sure."

After the bet was sealed with a handshake, Judith rose from her chair and said, "You'll have to excuse me, while I get the next course ready. It'll only take two or three minutes."

William pushed back his chair. "I'll help," he said decisively. Both Judith and Sondra gave him odd looks, but neither raised any objection.

When the three adults had been left to themselves, Turnage asked if he could have an ashtray. Sondra obligingly went into the living room and returned with the big blue-and-white glass ashtray from the coffee table. Ben, meanwhile, had opened a bottle of Almaden. Sondra had never known Ben to serve Almaden to company. Turnage lit a cigarette. Ben filled three glasses and, raising his glass to Turnage, proposed a toast: "Your health!"

Turnage knocked back half the glass of wine, and commented, "That's some sharp kid."

"You shouldn't have let him egg you on into that bet," Ben said.

"It was Judith who did the egging on," Sondra observed. "She's not such a featherbrain that she doesn't understand how the odds favor William. I'm sure she was leading you on quite deliberately."

"I'll admit I kind of admired their teamwork," Turnage said. "But what the hell, if I win, it'll be worth it. And if I lose, I'll deduct it as a business expense. I'll just put it down as 'dinner,' and speaking of dinner, I like the way you got 'em trained to do the cooking. The way they both hopped up to go out to the kitchen, you don't see that every day."

"It's something *we* don't see every day either," Sondra said defensively. "But Judith insisted that she make the entire dinner for William's birthday, and we try to go along with anything that encourages her to show an interest in food."

"She has anorexia," Ben said, by way of explanation. He refilled his own and Sondra's glasses, then placed the bottle where Turnage would be able to reach it by a long stretch.

"What's anorexia? A disease?"

"Not in the usual sense," Sondra said. "It's a psychological stage she's going through. It means she has no appetite."

"Oh, anorexics have an appetite all right," said Ben. "But they become obsessed with their own willpower. It starts out with dieting, and in the most extreme cases it can end with someone starving herself to death. It's almost always women who come down with it, usually teenage girls. We've become experts on the subject, haven't we, sugar?"

"Yes, unfortunately."

Turnage reached for the wine bottle. "What my folks used to do with me when I wouldn't eat my dinner was they'd make me sit with a plate of food in front of me until I'd eaten it. Ever try that?"

Sondra shook her head. "When she's forced to eat, she throws up afterward. Violently. It's not induced, she doesn't push a finger down her throat. I've seen it happen, it's completely spontaneous. But it's not something we should be talking about now. She'll hear us, and there's nothing likelier to make her finicky than being reminded of her problem."

Turnage stubbed out his cigarette and grinned. "Bobby Snyder, catcher with the White Sox, used to be just the same. He was usually a fair batter, but around '73, '74, he had a slump. I mean, he was batting zee-roe. And if anyone *talked* to him about it, that just made him play worse, he'd start messing up behind the plate. It was a no-win situation."

"It is," Ben agreed, "a no-win situation."

Sondra smiled and changed the subject: "And how is—" She tried to remember: Clara? Charlotte? She couldn't be sure. "Mrs. Turnage? Wasn't she able to accompany you on this trip?"

Turnage scowled. "If you mean my mother, she's doing fine. If you mean Cindy, we got divorced." He reached into his shirt pocket for a cigarette, then snapped open his lighter and tried to light it. The lighter wouldn't catch.

"I'm sorry to hear that," Sondra said.

"It's been two years," said Ben, with a glance to let Sondra know that he was on to her tricks. They'd already discussed Turnage's divorce and agreed that it had been one of those events, like the impeachment vote against Nixon, that makes a person believe that in the long run there is justice in the world. "Dan is probably over the worst of the shock by now."

"Oh no, every time I have to write an alimony check, the pain is as bad as ever." Turnage laughed at his own joke with a judicious amount of false gusto. Then he glared intently at the end of his cigarette and tried once again to scratch a flame from his lighter.

Sondra, though she smoked herself, hated people who smoked at the dinner table. She thought it gave a bad name to smokers in general. Even so, she was about to do the hostesslike thing and fetch the big silver lighter from the whatnot in the foyer, when Judith, stripped of her apron and looking to Sondra's stepmotherly eye more than usually like a concentration camp victim, returned to her place at the table.

"William," Judith said, sitting down and placing her fingertips on the edge of the table, as for a séance, "insists that because it's *his* birthday, he is going to serve the dinner. I tried to argue, but it truly *is* his birthday, so finally I was overruled."

"So, what's for dinner?" Turnage asked hopefully.

"It's a hot dish of Spam with scalloped potatoes, but it's also sort of Mexican."

"Spam?" Sondra asked, vaguely alarmed, as though at the mention of a distant relative serving time in prison. "Why Spam?"

"Well, I'd been planning to make tacos, because I know William likes them, but then on the bus coming home from school I heard from my friend Betty about the essay William had written for his German class. Betty's in the same class."

"German?" Turnage gave up on his unlighted cigarette and placed it in the ashtray. "What's he want to study German for? We won that war forty years ago." He showed, with a little bark of laughter, that this was meant as a joke.

"Thirty-five years ago actually," said William, who approached the table gauntleted by the quilted oven glove and bearing the four-quart Pyrex bowl, which gave off a powerful odor of scorched mustard. "And I really don't have any good reason for studying German except that I like the sound of it, and you have to have taken one language to get into most good medical schools. Mom, I can't serve you anything when your napkin's on your plate."

"Guests are served first, William," Sondra pointed out.

"Right." William went to stand by Turnage and sliced into the steaming hot dish in the bowl with a slotted metal spoon. He scooped out a large portion of potatoes in an ocher sauce complicated with diced bits of Spam, kernel corn, and flecks of green and red vegetable matter. Overall the impression was not promising.

After William had gone round the table serving the hot dish, Judith finished answering Sondra's question, *Why Spam?* "Anyhow Betty told me what William wrote in his essay about the earliest things he remembered, and one of them was Spam. In his essay William only mentioned Spam sandwiches, on Wonder Bread, but that didn't seem fancy enough for a birthday dinner. We don't usually have Spam in any form. I think Father thinks it's beneath us. Like eating Twinkies for dessert."

"Now, Judith," Ben said blandly, "you mustn't dig for compliments. Spam can be quite tasty, properly prepared. One could even wish you'd been more generous with it. The potatoes could use some stronger contrast."

"I used the entire can," Judith protested. "Plus a can of Mexicali corn niblets."

"The sauce is delicious," William said.

"Very tangy," Sondra agreed.

"Thank you," said Judith without looking away from the single pink die of Spam speared on the end of her fork. She seemed visibly to be bracing herself to eat it. She lifted the fork to her mouth, which opened just wide enough to admit the morsel of meat. The empty fork was returned to rest on the plate. She chewed, and went on chewing as though she were dealing with a hunk of gristly steak. At last she swallowed. Sondra could have applauded. Only then did she realize that both her husband and Turnage had been watching the performance with the same fascination.

"It's tasty," Judith said brightly, "if I say so myself. But maybe there's more mustard in the sauce than there should be. Next time I think I'll put in less mustard."

Ben laughed and then, his mouth being full of potatoes, began discreetly to choke. Once he'd stopped choking, he offered no explanation of what had provoked his laughter.

They began, all five of them, to eat, slowly and stolidly, as though under duress, as though wishing for doggy bags into which they might surreptitiously scrape the food from their plates. Sondra tried to think of a neutral subject of conversation. But not baseball, they'd done baseball to death.

It was Turnage who rescued them from the widening silence by turning to William and saying, "So tell us about this Apple computer. What are you going to be able to do with that that I can't do on my little old pocket calculator? Think it'll do your German for you?"

William gave Turnage a commiserating look of the sort that Sondra usually got for well-meaning but dumb questions. Then he proceeded to explain. Soon he'd become as big a bore on the subject as Turnage had been about the Kansas City baseball team. Ben was looking chagrined, but it would not have looked good if he'd tried to cut off the flow of William's enthusiasm for his birthday present from Madge Michaels, a gift that made his own envelope with $250 seem pretty paltry. So while William celebrated the new era dawning for the "computer literate," they went on eating their dinner.

There was something definitely peculiar about Judith's hot dish. Not just the sauce, which tasted as though half the spice shelf had been emptied into it. There were also little scraps of paper in among the soggy slices of potato. Sondra had found two so far. One might have been accidental; two indicated something else, but exactly what Sondra did not wish to know. The scraps of paper were barely recognizable as such, and she'd eaten them without comment, but she feared that Ben, if he were to notice the same thing, might not react as mildly. An explanation, if one were required of Judith, would surely lead to a family quarrel.

At last it was Judith who brought William's monologue to a stop by asking her father if he wanted a second helping. He didn't, but Turnage said he would (the poor man must have been starving), and while the oven glove and the bowl were passed to him, Judith introduced the subject they'd all politely been avoiding. Tobacco.

"Can we look forward to seeing you on TV again any time soon, Mr. Turnage?"

"I hope not, unless it's for my induction into the Hall of Fame."

"You didn't like being on 'Sixty Minutes'?"

"No one enjoys being publicly attacked, Judith," her father observed. "Or privately attacked, for that matter. So please let's preserve our usual truce tonight?"

Judith smiled at Turnage, and explained: "We're not allowed to discuss anything to do with tobacco at the dinner table. Or at any other time, really. Father finds it too upsetting."

"Upsetting? I *like* talking about tobacco. It's how I earn my living, after all." Turnage gave her just the sideways, mean-looking smile he'd given Morley Safer on the program. It had been such an expressive smile that they'd used it for the cameo shot at the start of the show when they previewed what each segment was going to be about. "Tell me, Mr. Turnage," Morley Safer had asked, "if you had a teenage son or daughter, would you want them to take up smoking, knowing the proven consequences?" Turnage had answered, "The only proven consequences that I know about is that smokers get treated like second-class citizens when they're on an airplane." "I was referring to the warning that is put by law on every cigarette package," Safer had said, "the warning that cigarettes are a danger to your health." "Well," Turnage had said, with that sneaky smile, "I don't believe everything I read."

"You see, Father, I knew Mr. Turnage wouldn't object to having a *discussion*. And really, there's only one question I wanted to ask him, and that's the one he avoided answering on the program. *Would* you encourage your own children to smoke?"

Turnage gave her an exasperated look. "I don't have any children, so I can't say."

"Well then, how about me? I'm sixteen. You said on the program that you began smoking at that age. Do you think *I* should take up smoking?"

"That's a choice you'll have to make for yourself."

"But would you, for instance, feel right about offering me a cigarette from the pack in your shirt pocket? What are they? Marlboros, I think."

"Judith, really!" Sondra said. "Mr. Turnage is in the middle of eating his dinner."

"Listen, kid, you can have the whole pack if you want. I always take a carton with me when I travel, so I got plenty. Here." He reached into his shirt pocket and produced the flip-top pack of Marlboros. He tossed them to her. "Catch."

Judith's reflexes were fast but not accurate. She dropped the fork in her right hand and grabbed for the pack of cigarettes. The cigarettes ricocheted from her clutching fingers and landed in what remained of William's dinner. Her water glass had been knocked over, dousing the tablecloth, and her fork had chipped the gilt edge of the dinner plate.

"Judith," Ben commanded, "go to your room."

She stared at her father. "Why? What did I do wrong?"

"Never mind, just go to your room."

Sondra looked at Turnage, hoping he would have the good grace to take the blame for the accident, which had, after all, been his doing. But he seemed quite impenitent. He had retrieved his pack of cigarettes from William's plate and was wiping the sauce off it.

"This is grotesque," Judith said, pushing back her chair. "This is truly grotesque."

Turnage took a cigarette from the pack, flipped the top closed, then thought better of it, flipped it open, and offered Sondra a cigarette.

"You've got to be kidding," she said.

"I'll have one," said William.

"You will not!" Sondra snapped.

"He's a teenager now," Ben said. "He should be able to smoke if he wants to. *You* were smoking at thirteen."

"No one knew any better when I was a kid," Sondra protested.

Meanwhile, ignoring Sondra's proscription, Turnage had offered the pack of Marlboros to William.

William took a cigarette and held it up to be lighted.

As earlier, Turnage's lighter would not produce a flame. Turnage kept snapping it futilely, until William said, "I think it's out of gas. Let me go get some."

When William had gone off to get butane for the lighter, Sondra stood up from the table. "If you two gentlemen will excuse me, I think I'll go speak to Judith."

"There's still the birthday cake," Ben reminded her.

"Enjoy it," she said curtly. Just before rounding the corner out of sight, she thought of a parting shot—to ask Turnage for the name of his wife's lawyer. But she bit her tongue. She'd only once before risked an argument on the subject of divorce, and this would certainly be the wrong moment, with Turnage looking on as an umpire, to open old wounds. Best let sleeping dogs lie.

Going through the gallery on the way to Judith's room at the eastern end of the house, she heard footsteps on the staircase. Thinking it must be Judith, she veered right.

But it was William, heading to his room.

"You have lighter fluid in your room, William? When did you start smoking?"

"No, Mom, nothing like that. I just wanted to get away from that creep Turnage. The same as you did, right?"

"If you agree that he's a creep, *why* did you ask him for a cigarette?"

"I just wanted to see how far he'd go. I was thinking I'd have a choking fit after he lighted it, or something like that, and then I'd throw the lit cigarette in *his* food. It really ticked me off, the way he did that to Judith."

"I feel just the same, but please, William, don't do anything to provoke a quarrel when you go back down there. Arguing with that kind of person doesn't accomplish anything."

"Yes, Mother, you're right. They should be shot."

She laughed. "Come here. Let me kiss you good night."

He came down the stairs, and they hugged, and she kissed him on the forehead and wished him a happy birthday, and even that became a joke to be shared, though this time without words. They just smiled at each other and nodded, and it was understood that a truly happy birthday was out of the question, but that people with good manners and a sense of humor would always pretend otherwise. She tried to think of something to say in parting that wouldn't sound entirely cynical, a nugget of worth-while grown-up wisdom, but all she could think to say was that as you got older, birthdays came to matter less and less. But she wasn't sure if that was true, and decided that the kiss would have to do.

36

From the moment Turnage's pack of Marlboros had landed on William's dinner plate and he'd looked at the man and seen the satisfaction he'd taken in Judith's misery, from that moment William knew the man would be his victim. He didn't know how he would do it, since the man was already, by virtue of having shared the hot dish that Judith had prepared, blessed with perfect health, and though it was a theory he'd never put to the test, William was certain that anyone whom the caduceus affected for the good could not later be blighted by its power. Certainly the reverse was true: Ned was the living, drooling proof.

Served with this spoon/ Health is your boon. The words of the blessing had been as simple as that. It had seemed important that before he used the caduceus in any other way he should first inscribe some such all-purpose protective charm about his family circle. It was like vaccinating kids against polio and measles at the earliest possible age. So even before Son-dra had come for him at the Obstschmecker house, he had found the serv-ing spoon in a kitchen drawer and framed the little rhyme of the blessing. That Turnage should have been on hand to receive a portion of that bless-ing was sheer fool luck.

He still couldn't quite believe that he possessed such a power. Yet the evidence was hard to refute: Ned's paralysis, Grandma O. going bald, the elms he'd preserved, the kids who'd lost their teeth eating the Halloween candy; even the continuing good health of Madge and Grandma O. Every test to which the evidence could be submitted confirmed the caduceus's power. But what *kind* of power was it? Where did it come from? As a kid he had taken his dreams or visions of "Mercury" at face value, believing the way that only a kid can believe. And it was probably because of the strength of that faith that the caduceus had worked. But was the power in the caduceus, or in him? Maybe the caduceus was like Dumbo's magic feather. Maybe he could fly without it. It would be easy enough to put that theory to the test. But even supposing the caduceus was somehow a necessary adjunct to his power, what a power it was! For the first time in history it would be possible to study the power of psychic healing *scientifically*. (And, necessarily, the opposite power, too.) It was an awesome responsibility.

It might also be a lot of fun. It would be dishonest to deny that, though it was the danger in the present situation. It was fortunate, in a way, that the power had been in abeyance these last five years, for no child so young, however intelligent, could be trusted to use such power wisely.

And now? At age thirteen?

He looked at Turnage's empty lighter, and smiled, knowing what he would do, and certain of its poetic justice.

37

When they'd been left to themselves, Ben Winckelmeyer allowed himself one small deliberate sneer at Turnage's expense. There was a limit to how much grief anyone had to put up with in the name of good manners, and that limit had surely been exceeded.

"If you're truly desperate for a cigarette," he said to Turnage, "there's a lighter on the shelf on the wall just to the left of the front door. It's basically there as decoration, but it probably works."

"I'm sorry if I offended the little lady, but I don't like to be put down on account of smoking. It's a sore spot with me, for obvious reasons."

"Oh, I think 'the little lady' was happy to have an excuse to get away from us."

Turnage hesitated, then got up from the table to find the lighter in the foyer. He returned, puffing intently, one eye half-squinted against the smoke. Bogart himself could not have smoked a cigarette more solemnly.

Though he knew he ought to leave well enough alone, Ben couldn't resist baiting the man some more, and aimed for the sore spot. "Tell me, Dan, how *do* you feel about this business we're in of selling addictive drugs? From an ethical point of view. Obviously, it's something we can't discuss with outsiders. But just between you and me, don't you ever have qualms?"

Turnage snorted a derisive double plume of smoke from his nostrils.

"Qualms?" The inflection he gave the word summed up his ethical position: qualms, like quiche, were something real men don't mess around with.

"For instance," Ben persisted, "do you ever worry about your own smoking?"

"Do you worry about driving? Or your weight?"

Ben nodded. "Certainly. But cars are a necessary evil if you want to live out here in the suburbs. I do what I can to minimize the risk—avoid the freeways, always use the seat belt, that sort of thing. Billy's father got killed in a crash because he hadn't buckled up. It can happen to anyone. As to my weight"—he paused to refill his glass from the bottle of Almaden—"my obesity may well be my downfall. My GP is always telling me I need to take off fifty pounds. Probably more like sixty now. Every so often I do go on a diet, and then fall off it."

"So how is smoking any different?"

"Did I say it was? Though, in fact, it *is* different. Eating's a necessity. Smoking is a gratuitous abuse of the cardiovascular system for the sake of a very doubtful pleasure."

Turnage took a defiant drag on his cigarette and, holding the smoke in his lungs, declared, "Seems a pretty real pleasure to me."

"Only because you're addicted. Nonsmokers like Judith or William would have a toxic reaction from a single cigarette."

"Jesus, Winckelmeyer, I can't believe I'm hearing this shit—from you, of all people. Addiction! Toxic reaction! You sound like some damned TV commentator. What is it with you? You smoke, your wife smokes, and you earn your living doing research for ATA. You've done more to disprove the Surgeon fucking General's Report than anyone alive."

"My research has never *dis*-proved that there's a link between smoking and the various illnesses to which it undoubtedly contributes. All my research has accomplished is to create a kind of smoke screen—no pun intended—for the industry. I've never imagined that anyone at ATA ever thought otherwise. Not at the executive level."

Turnage took this, as it was intended, as a personal insult, but he had no ready comeback. To argue the point would only confirm Ben's suggestion that he lacked an executive degree of cynicism; to concede it would have been tantamount to admitting that all the denials he had issued as an ATA spokesman were part of a nationwide conspiracy of deception. It would have been like saying straight out to Morley Safer that, sure, smoking causes heart disease, lung cancer, emphysema, and birth defects, but what the hell, it's a billion-dollar industry and nobody lives forever. That probably was his private opinion, but it was not for public consumption.

Ben said it for him. "It's an industry, Dan. *Caveat emptor*, right? And the devil take the hindmost."

Turnage tried to move to the moral high ground. "And that's all you can say for the research you've done, that it's a smoke screen?"

"No, the research has sometimes been quite interesting. The work on tattoos, for instance. Fascinating results, and very suggestive for further research. Though not, in all likelihood, with funds from ATA. Their motive in funding any project has never been altruistic. I'm not complaining, mind you. ATA has been, in many ways, an ideal sponsor. They're generous. They don't meddle in the design of experiments, and don't get fussed when they fizzle out, or even when they produce bad news."

Turnage scowled. "Yeah. Well, don't think everyone in the Baltimore office can't think of what to do with their money except write you out another fat check."

Ben realized he'd gone too far. Turnage was not on the ATA Board of Directors and probably never would be, but he was on confidential terms with all of them. He should not be provoking him for no better purpose than his own amusement.

"Oh, I realize that," he said placatingly. "It's a shame that there are so many curtailments on the direct PR side of the budget. I know MIMA's research gets better funding because of the situation."

"Well, it can't be helped," Turnage conceded. He ground out his cigarette in the ashtray. "Anyhow. I should be heading back to the hotel. Sorry if I put a damper on the birthday party."

William took this as his cue to appear with the birthday cake, its fourteen candles already burned down to within a half inch of the frosting. Ben tried to estimate from this how much of his conversation with Turnage the boy must have overheard.

"You're not going without a slice of birthday cake, are you, Mr. Turnage?" William asked.

"Sorry, but I've got . . . uh, an early flight." He looked to Ben for help. And truly, the man was helpless. Without his own car, in one of the outermost suburbs of the city, he was at his host's mercy. A taxi might take half an hour to get to the house. But to expect Ben to act, at just this moment, as his chauffeur . . . Even Turnage must appreciate that that would be asking a bit much.

Ben was kind. He took the keys to the BMW from his pocket and placed them on the table. "Here's the keys to the car. I hope you don't mind if I don't drive you back. Just leave the keys at the Hyatt reception desk, and I'll have Mrs. O'Meara pick them up in the morning."

Turnage took the keys with a look of astonished gratitude. He was the sort of man, Ben supposed, who enjoyed a jealously monogamous relationship with his own car. "Thanks. I really appreciate it."

William blew out the candles on the cake without any ceremony and set it down on the table. "Don't forget this." He reached into his pocket and took out the lighter. "The butane wasn't where I thought it was. It was in the kitchen. That's why I took so long. Sorry. But it's working now. See." He snapped a light from it and handed it, flaming, to Turnage, who responded to the stimulus of the flame with wonderful automatism, flipping open his pack of Marlboros, tipping a cigarette from it, and lighting up. As he did so, a glance passed between Ben and his stepson that was as good as a writ of execution. Turnage was an asshole, their glance declared, and should be got rid of with all deliberate speed.

Even so, it was another five minutes before Turnage, with directions as to how to get back onto I-94 and when to exit from it, had driven off and it was possible to offer William an apology for a spoiled birthday.

"Actually," William said, "it got so I was enjoying it. When Turnage threw his pack of cigarettes at Judith and it ended up in my potatoes, that was straight out of the Three Stooges." He poised the cake slicer over the birthday cake. "Small, medium, or large?"

"Medium. But shouldn't we sound an all-clear so Judith and Sondra can join us?"

"Mom's gone to bed, I think. And I was going to bring a slice up to Judith myself, a little later."

William plopped down slices of cake on two rose-festooned dessert plates that generally ornamented the sideboard in the far corner of the nameless and useless space between the kitchen and the dining area. The house was full of such wide-open, anomalous spaces that served no better purpose than to display pricey trash of the sort that served as prizes on "Wheel of Fortune." The Chinese-style umbrella stand in the foyer, the (electric-powered) grandfather clock in the gallery, the étagère in Sondra's bedroom with its tiers of Steuben "collectibles." Sondra bought all these white elephants under the impressions they were objets d'art, but it was Ben who cherished them as the glitzy, gloating assertions of affluence they were. Art had nothing to do with it. Sondra had a natural instinct for defining the Winckelmeyer level of income and the Winckelmeyer position in society by whatever she bought, and he loved her for it. He loved her for other reasons, as well, and he loved his home, and his children too (though with some reservations), and he had reached that precise stage of mellow drunkenness when his love extended beyond his immediate sphere of prosperity and embraced all Nature. "This is really delicious cake, isn't it?" he said, slicing into its spongy brown flesh with the side of his fork.

"Mmm," William agreed with his mouth full. Then, "You must be telepathic."

"How so?"

"You haven't tasted it yet."

Ben regarded the slice of cake on his plate, the morsel on his fork. "You're right. I haven't." He ate the morsel with conspicuous deliberation. "And I'm right, too. It's really delicious."

"Can I ask you a question?"

"If it's about my work, no. I'm feeling mellow."

"I wasn't intending to *attack* you. I was just curious. Are you supposed to never discuss it outside the office? Is it like working for the government, where everything's a secret?"

"There's that side of it, of course. Mostly it's habit. Judith declared herself an enemy of the tobacco industry something over five years ago. That's a year before she got to abortion, and two years before she became a vegetarian."

"Since when is she a vegetarian?"

"She isn't, anymore. The anorexia probably made it unnecessary."

"You think it's just obstinacy then? You think she just *refuses* to eat?"

"No, not at all. Anorexia is a medical disorder; I don't doubt that at all. It's also almost certainly psychogenic. But that is not to deny that it's a real disease. I tend to believe all diseases are psychogenic. You know what I mean by 'psychogenic'?"

"It's the same as 'psychosomatic'?"

"Not exactly. Psychosomatic refers simply to the interdependence of the mind and the body. Psychogenic is more specific: a psychogenic illness has its *origin* in some kind of emotional or mental conflict. The mind is the trigger of a psychogenic illness, but the final result can be as physiological as a bleeding ulcer."

William considered this for two more forkfuls of the cake. Then he asked: "So you think it's all in the mind? And cigarettes don't have anything to do with lung cancer?"

"That's not what I said. Cigarettes certainly have an effect, but just as certainly it's not a one-to-one cause-and-effect relationship. If that were the case, nicotine would be a poison pure and simple, like strychnine. But it's not. Some people, like Turnage, can go on smoking for years with relatively little ill effect. Others . . ." He shrugged. "It's a lottery. Or that's what smokers like to tell themselves, anyhow."

"What is it if it's not a lottery? A very slow kind of Russian roulette? That's what our gym teacher called it."

"It's a good analogy, but it begs the question of why people play Russian roulette, why they climb mountains or race cars, why they risk their lives in a hundred foolish and unnecessary ways and call it entertainment."

"Flirting with death," William said, savoring the words as though they were a morsel of the cake. "Why do they?"

"Every school of psychology, every religion has its own theory, and each theory probably has its own grain of truth. Freud calls it a death instinct and claims that it's a basic component of the subconscious. The trouble with that as a theory is that, almost by definition, it can't be proven. The subconscious is the part of the mind we *can't* be conscious of. We have glimpses in our dreams, that's probably the nearest approach. But dreams may be just the froth on the surface of the subconscious. And its depths? Who can say."

"But it sounds like you have a theory."

"Mm." Ben picked up his wineglass and lifted it to eye level so that the amber hemisphere of Almaden within condensed the light into a single bright node. The boy had never sought to draw him on this way before, and while it made him feel uncustomarily paternal and full of elder wisdom, he also felt uneasy. Circumspection had become a deeply ingrained habit. Sondra had no patience with any talk that smacked of philosophizing, and Judith had her own fully formed worldview in which he figured, monolithically, as the oppressor of her virtue. She was certain she knew his every patriarchal thought without his having to say a word. He had supposed that the boy, in his own quieter and less dogmatic way, had shared Judith's estimation of him. But maybe he had been wrong. The boy was bright, and Ben appreciated that, but he was a boy nevertheless, who still watched the Saturday morning cartoons on TV. A birthday did not possess such fairy-tale magic that a child of twelve can be transformed overnight into a young man of thirteen. And yet . . . William did seem different tonight. Perhaps it was not the magic of his birthday, but of his new name. Or perhaps (the likeliest hypothesis) the difference resided in the Almaden, and all the bourbon that had preceded it. "I'm sorry," he said, putting down the wineglass. "I've been woolgathering. And I've lost the thread."

"That's okay. We can talk about it another time, if you'd rather."

He would rather, and he appreciated being let off the hook. But he felt a sting in the kindness. A drunk does not like to be thought to be too drunk to carry on a conversation.

"In a nutshell, William, what I think is that there are more things under heaven and earth, and in the subconscious too, for that matter, than are dreamt of in anyone's philosophy. Once we've mapped every neural path of the brain, and charted every twist and coil of DNA, even then . . ."

"Even then?" William prompted.

"Even then we won't know everything."

It seemed—indeed, it was—a cop-out. Ben felt, absurdly, like a small rodent that has been chased into its hidey-hole by a larger predator.

"You're probably right," William said, and then, with the indifference of a cat that does not really need to eat the mouse it has pursued, he got up from the table and said, "I'll take a slice of cake to Judith now, before she turns in. See you in the morning."

Ben nodded. He knew he'd funked out. But why did he feel such inexplicable relief? What had he been afraid to say? To even think about? He glanced at the bottle of wine. There was nearly one glassful left. He waited till he'd heard William's knock on Judith's bedroom door and then poured the last of the wine, with gratifying precision, into his glass, filling it till only the surface tension kept the liquid from overflowing the crystal brim.

38

As soon as she was in her own half-bathroom, Judith stood in front of the toilet and waited for her stomach to revolt against the meal she'd eaten. Invariably after a dinner-table quarrel, her stomach would empty at the sight of the pink porcelain toilet bowl. It was as automatic as a windup toy, as reflexive as the bouncing of a rubber ball. But tonight it wasn't happening. Her stomach, like some dog jealously protecting its dish of Alpo, refused to surrender its contents to the toilet; it was actually processing the stuff. Judith would not, as a matter of principle (she'd made a promise to her therapist), induce vomiting artificially, and so, after dousing her face and neck with cold water at the sink, she returned to her bedroom, feeling a strange, diffused queasiness all through her body. Not the familiar queasiness that might precede the release and relief of a good puke. It felt like a bad sunburn that had soaked through her skin deep into her muscles. And stranger than this queasiness, she still felt hungry. Though she'd eaten twice what she usually did at dinner, she could have returned to the table and eaten twice as much again.

Hunger, however, was something she knew how to deal with. Indeed, it is the glory of an anorexic to combat hunger, as it is the glory of a saint to resist temptation. One simply turned one's mind to other matters. And there, on her worktable, was the perfect refuge—her poor wounded diary, and lying on top of it, like a suicide weapon still clutched in the corpse's hand, were the scissors she'd used to cut out its eight meager pages of entries.

She sat down and wrote:

Dear Diary,

What a foolish, self-defeating thing to do—& anger is no excuse. What I did was cut out all the Diary pages from January 1 to now—& served them at dinner! It wasn't easy to get the paper into a cookable state, but after I'd soaked it a long time in milk and then put it through the Cuisinart for a few spins it served quite well as the basis for a white sauce. It didn't taste exactly like milk anymore but I put a lot of spice in the sauce & I don't think anyone noticed. Maybe I should enter the recipe in the Pillsbury Bakeoff! Spam Casserole in Diary Sauce!

Why did I do such a dumb thing? Because I found out this morning that my father had read the letter I wrote & left under William's door. I was so furious at first I *almost* went into Sondra's room to smash one of her silly Steuben figurines. But I controlled myself & came here & saw you on the table, dear Diary—& I thought: I'll see to it that they don't read any of this at least. And right away I knew what I would do. I would make them *eat* my words. So I made my Diary Stew, but at the last moment I couldn't bring myself to spring my big surprise & tell them what they were eating. Partly because my father had brought home that awful Mr. Turnip from the Tobacco Alliance, who is so thick he would never have understood why I'd done what I'd done—imagine having *him* for a father!—and partly because it was William's birthday—& he was being so nice I couldn't spoil things more than they were spoiled already by having the Turnip for dinner. William actually insisted on being the one to serve the Diary

Stew—& at that moment I realized that what I'd done was mean
and spiteful and nothing else. But did that make me behave with
any more consideration? No, I deliberately provoked the Turnip
till he did something impossible—for which of course *I* was sent
to my room. Sondra came to see me right afterward & was as nice
as could be & apologized for Winky, saying he surely realized that
the fault was the Turnip's much more than it was mine but that he
had to avoid giving offense to the Turnip for "business reasons."
As tho that were any excuse! On the other hand, it's not a surprise
either. Everything he does is for "business reasons." I really do
hate him. I know it's wrong of me, but there it is, I can't help it—
& if he ever does read this Diary—which I won't lock up or hide
away but leave right here where he can violate my privacy any
time he likes—then he'll just have to swallow that fact. I've hated
him absolutely as long as I can remember having any feelings
about him at all.

She stopped there, with a feeling somewhere between shock and satisfaction at the awfulness of what she'd written. It was always like that
with the diary. She'd be writing a blue streak until such a thought would
come wriggling out of her pen, like an inky little snake, something perfectly impossible, and probably untrue. Just like her mother when she got
angry: "I hate you!" or "You're ugly!" or just some low obscenity. It had
to be hereditary, since she'd actually lived with Rhoda so little time and
most of that time while she was an infant.

There was a knock on her door. Not a knock, really, but a subdued
kick. "Come in," she said, and William answered, "I can't. My hands are
full." She opened the door, and there he was with two slices of the hazelnut upside-down apple cake on the hand-painted china plates from the
sideboard.

"I don't know if you still have any appetite left after the row at the
table, but I'd have had a guilty conscience if I didn't share some of this
with the person responsible. I can tell you already that it's delicious. The
apples make a kind of crust."

She laughed aloud, as though at a joke, and then felt obliged to explain: "It's weird, but you know . . . I really am hungry! I could eat both
slices. Come in, sit down. Did you get your wish?"

"I think it's only very old people who don't get their wishes on their
birthdays. It's really not hard to blow out fourteen candles. Anyhow, *he*'s
gone." William set the plates down on her worktable.

"The Turnip? I know, I heard them drive off." Self-consciously she cleared away the diary and the scissors. Then she fetched the second bentwood chair from its place by the window.

"Ben didn't go with him, actually. Turnage had to drive himself. That's why I couldn't bring you your slice of cake earlier. Ben and I were talking, just the two of us."

"Amazing. He actually gave you five minutes of his time. It must be because of your birthday." She could hear the spitefulness as soon as the words were out of her mouth. "I'm sorry, I shouldn't be so sarcastic. I know Father is not a total ogre. What did you talk about? No, that's not a proper question. It was *your* conversation. Asking you about it is almost as bad as eavesdropping, or reading a person's private correspondence. Let's have that cake. I really am famished."

To her surprise the cake was delicious, and her joke that she could have eaten two slices was not an exaggeration. As they ate, William kept looking up at her, as though expecting her to say something. But her mind was a blank. Sometimes he smiled as though she *had* said something and he were offering his silent concurrence. His lips seemed redder than lips would be unless they'd been painted with lipstick. She could not keep from thinking of the two false teeth in his mouth and the wires that held them in place—his flipper, he called it—and wondering how he kept food from tangling in the wires. She thought: *What if he asks me what I'm thinking about at just this moment?* If she were honest she would have to say, I'm thinking about the inside of your mouth.

"Actually," he said, as though continuing from where they'd left off a moment and not a minute ago, "Ben and I talked about the same thing you tried to get Turnage to talk about. But on a more abstract level. He thinks when people get sick it's all psychological. Not *all*, he didn't say that. But it begins that way. Psychogenic, that was his word. But we didn't really get into the subject. Just sort of skirted around it. I think he felt a little shy."

"What a convenient theory for him to have," Judith scoffed.

"But he was ready to admit that smoking has a connection to the whole thing. In fact, *he* got kind of nasty with Turnage on the subject. I could hear them from out in the kitchen while I was lighting the candles on the cake."

"You shouldn't eavesdrop," she said primly.

"Listen, if the person who designed this 'ranch' had put doors between one room and the other, it would be possible to avoid eavesdropping. Anyhow, my point is your father is not the complete hypocrite you seem to think."

"What kind is he then?" she demanded sharply. "A half a hypocrite?

A third? The fact remains that he is employed by an industry that earns money by getting people to poison themselves. I don't see that his working for the Mafia would be any better."

"I don't know, maybe he'd dress better if he were in the Mafia."

"Be serious, William."

"I'm being serious. Do you actually know what the research is that he does? Have you ever *read* any of the studies that MIMA publishes? The one on tattoos, for instance, have you read that?"

"I've heard him talk about it often enough, and call it his favorite statistical freak. But I can't say that I remember much about it, except that it had nothing to do with smoking one way or the other."

This was a lie, for she did in fact remember all too clearly the actual physical nausea she'd felt four years ago when the report had come out and she (then age twelve) had looked at the leather-bound copy of it that had been given a place of honor in the middle of the coffee table. It had been full of pictures of dreadful tattoos, all of them tattooed on prisoners awaiting execution or serving life sentences. What the study had shown was that prisoners who'd been tattooed with the nastier kinds of designs—skulls and devils and such—were likely to develop malignant cancers or have fatal heart attacks at a younger age than prisoners who'd been tattooed with pictures of animals or women. But both groups proved to be significantly healthier than those who had not been tattooed at all. Judith simply could not see the point of such "research." It seemed as immoral, in its way, as laboratory experiments on dogs and monkeys, except that in this case it had been human beings who were in the cages, not animals.

"The point," William lectured at her, "is that the differences from one group to the other had to be psychological differences. Unless you believe in magic. I don't suppose the research has any practical use. I mean, it probably wouldn't keep other people from getting cancer if they were tattooed with lions and eagles."

"What a thought!" Judith said, wrinkling her face into a mask of revulsion.

"But that's because the decision wouldn't have come from deep down inside them. From the subconscious. From inside the cells."

"They were inside their cells, all right," Judith said.

"You know what I mean."

"And I know how easy it is to make statistics lie. There could be a hundred other factors that could have accounted for the same results. And in any case, what does it prove? And why is ATA so eager to have Winky digging up these statistical freaks?"

"Okay, forget it. I didn't want to start an argument."

She realized that if there had been an argument it had all been of her making and looked down abashed at the crumbs left on her dessert plate. Somehow, as they'd been talking, she'd eaten the entire slice of cake without being aware of it. "I'm sorry. It's my fault. I do see your point. I'd have to be very dense not to. It just all seems so . . . ugly. It's the same with the research they do on animals. Forcing hamsters and rabbits to smoke until their little bodies are riddled with cancer."

"A lot of medical research has to be ugly. Because disease is ugly."

"Then why not do research on health instead of disease?"

"Sure, why not?"

Was he making fun of her? She could imagine her father making the same snap response, but there was no sarcasm in William's voice as there would have been in Winky's.

"I'm serious," he insisted, as though he'd heard her speak the question in her mind. "There *should* be research into lots of things that medical science usually ignores. Acupuncture, for instance. Or faith healing. Or wounds that heal overnight. The medical establishment ignores that whole area, because it doesn't fit in with their scheme of things."

Judith was amazed to be hearing her stepbrother say such things. She knew that he meant to be a doctor someday, but she hadn't really credited it as a serious intention. She'd thought he wanted to be a doctor the way a younger child might say he wanted to be a deep-sea diver or a fireman or a cowboy.

"But you don't—" she began, and then broke off.

He smiled, and again she became aware, to the point of distraction, of his lips and his teeth. "What don't I do?"

She had to look away from him in order to continue.

"You don't . . . believe in God. Do you?"

"Where'd you get that idea? Because I stopped going to church?"

"I suppose that's why."

"Just because I don't believe in everything the nuns taught us back at Our Lady of Mercy doesn't mean I don't believe in God. You never had to go to a Catholic school, so it's a lot easier for you to be a Catholic."

He paused, as though waiting for her to disagree. Another time she might have, because she did resent his assumption that her faith was somehow a flimsier thing than his skepticism. But she didn't want to get sidetracked into all that. They could discuss religion some other time. In fact, she realized with a sudden leap of joy, they would be able to discuss absolutely everything now! They were no longer limited to acting out the roles of older sister and kid brother. They could be equals!

"Let me ask *you* a question," he said. "But you have to promise not to get angry. It's something we've never talked about, and if you don't want to talk about it now, that's okay."

She smiled, for she was sure she knew what he would ask about. "I promise not to be angry. Or to count to ten at least."

"I was wondering what you think is behind your anorexia."

"I knew that's what you'd ask about. And I don't mind discussing it— with you; I do with Father or Sondra. Because really they're not interested in what I think. They just want to make me eat my vegetables. Do you *remember* having to eat vegetables when you were little? My mother— my real mother, Rhoda, who sends us the grapefruits every Christmas from Texas—was a sadist with vegetables. I would have to sit at the table facing a dish of cold peas until long after my bedtime. I hated peas. Which isn't at all unusual. Dr. Helbron says he's never known a single child who hasn't gone through some trauma over vegetables, and kids hate peas more than anything else. According to him."

"So do you think that's what behind the anorexia?"

"If it were, then we'd all grow up to be anorexic. No, Dr. Helbron's theory, and what you read in most of the books, is that anorexia is like a diet that's got out of control. You start off like everyone else just wanting to take off a few pounds or a few inches, but where for most people dieting is always a big difficulty, for *us* it becomes . . . Enjoyable isn't the right word. But it feels good the way that volleyball does when you're playing really well. That feeling that you're in control of the ball. Except that what I'm in control of is my body. I'm making it do what I want, not some authority figure out there telling me to eat my cold peas."

"You sound like you like it," William commented. It was what Dr. Helbron was always telling her, too, but somehow with William it didn't seem like scolding.

"At some level I suppose all anorexics do, or they wouldn't be anorexic. I realize it's unhealthy. But it's not a conscious choice anymore. Eating, the physical act of eating, disgusts me. I can make myself sick thinking about an English muffin with butter and jam, and I used to love English muffins. Yet rationally I know I'd be better off if I'd eat the English muffin."

"You didn't seem to have any trouble with the birthday cake. Or with dinner."

"You're right about the birthday cake. Dinner I had to force myself, and usually when I do that, I'll throw up afterwards."

"You didn't throw up tonight, did you?" he asked, in a tone of such concern that it almost was annoying—as though it would be all right for her to throw up any other time, but not on his birthday.

"No. I thought I would. But I didn't."

"It seems to me, from what you've been saying, that your anorexia is a perfect example of what Ben was talking about, a psychogenic disease."

"Thank you, Dr. Michaels, for your brilliant diagnosis." She waited for him to come back with a sarcasm of his own, and when he just sat there, like Dr. Helbron at his most infuriatingly nonjudgmental, she went on: "What you're saying is obviously true. But that doesn't mean it's just something in my head and that if I'd adopt a 'healthy attitude' I'd be cured. It doesn't work that way."

"I never supposed it did. But if you agree that anorexia is caused psychogenically, why can't it be cured the same way?"

"I would think that almost by definition that's what its cure would amount to. The only problem is, there are no psychogenic spas for the cure of anorexia, not that I know of."

"Didn't you ask *me* just a moment ago if I believed in God? Well, do you?"

"Of course I do."

"So, have you ever *prayed* to be cured?"

"Prayer isn't like that, William," she protested. "It's not like going to the Santa Claus in Dayton's toy department and giving him a list of what you want for Christmas. It's a conversation, like we're having, only it's God we're talking with."

"If you needed something from me that I could give you, you'd ask me for it, wouldn't you? Don't you think God can handle your anorexia? *Have* you ever prayed to be cured?"

"No. And I haven't prayed to be made a millionaire either."

"When I was talking, before, in general terms about how the one area that medical science has been afraid to investigate was the area of psychic healing, you seemed to agree. But when it comes to your own case, look how you react."

She felt trapped in his logic. It was only a variant form of what Dr. Helbron was always telling her, in his smug, pipe-puffing way, that to get well she had to *want* to get well. But Dr. Helbron had never had the bad manners to drag God into it. Even her confessor, when the subject came up, was only concerned with her anorexia insofar as it led her into sins of disobedience. Father Balch had never suggested that she should pray to be cured. Because (it dawned on her) he'd never thought God had any-thing to do with it; he'd never believed that the anorexia was an affliction, like being crippled or blind, that God *might* exert his influence over. He'd thought, as everyone else did, that she was simply being self-willed and self-destructive.

"You make it sound like voodoo," she said.

"If voodoo works, why not use it?"

"All right, I'll *pray*. Hail Mary, full of grace, cure me of my anorexia. There, do you think I'll be better now?"

"Maybe. It didn't sound very fervent, though. You weren't even kneeling."

She had to laugh.

William took no offense at her laughter. He even seemed, by his smile, to share the joke at his own expense. But he didn't let up either. "I think," he said, "if you were to put it in more positive terms, it would probably work better. Instead of asking to be cured, why not ask right out for a healthy appetite?"

"A *healthy* appetite?"

"You make it sound like a contradiction in terms."

Again, and more deftly than Dr. Helbron had ever been able to, he had cornered her. Appetite: the word, and the idea it represented, did make her feel queasy, even repelled. She could accept the need for food as a kind of fuel that kept the machinery of the body running. But appetite was another matter. People *surrender* to their appetites. And she did not want to surrender to anyone or anything.

"I see your point," she conceded, but she conceded no more than that. She did not kneel. She did not change the wording of her prayer, which had not been (she saw now) a real prayer at all, but a verbal formula without the force either of faith or of feeling.

"You want to be alone, don't you?"

"You're a mind reader, William."

"Okay, but before I go, I just want to do one thing. Okay?"

"What's that?" she asked guardedly.

"Just close your eyes."

"Why?"

"Just close them."

She closed her eyes, and when she did she felt his hands on her shoulders. She could feel his thumbs pressing into the muscles on either side of the bony knob at the base of her neck, while his fingers dug into the fleshy cavity just above her clavicle. At first she thought he meant to massage her, but the pressure he exerted, though firm, was unvarying. Then he removed his hands and said she could open her eyes.

"What was *that* all about?" she asked.

"I healed you."

She felt the blood rushing to her face, and with it a shock wave of feeling, of all possible feelings, so powerful as to literally take away her breath. She felt the shame of ridicule and the pain of betrayal; she felt the anger of violation and, worse than that, a horrible craven gratitude at having been, for even so little time, touched.

"Get out of my room," she whispered.

"It will work," he said, with no trace of a smile, with not a hint that he was making fun of her. "Give it time, you'll see, you'll be better. Soon."

When he'd left and she could hear his footsteps mounting the stairs to his own room, she prayed. Not on her knees, but from her heart. She prayed that it would not be so. She prayed that she would still be as she had been. Free. Autonomous. Untouched.

39

That night he had a dream. He dreamt he was in a large dark room with a high ceiling that sloped down right and left almost to floor level. The thick beams supporting the roof were exposed like the beams of Our Lady of Mercy Church, and like those beams these had words written on them in gold letters, but these letters were in the old German style and he could not decipher them. They glittered erratically, high overhead, as though reflecting the light of some far-off flickering candle. He was walking toward a small low window at the other end of this room across a thick gray carpet. At each step he took, the pile of the carpet would billow up like the very lightest snow, or like clippings of gray hair on the floor of a barbershop. It was weird but in the dream it didn't seem so, it seemed perfectly ordinary.

He didn't know where he was going, only that he didn't want to go there. Yet he had to, it was as inevitable as the bus ride to school. He felt angst. Angst is a feeling for which the English language has no equivalent. It is not the same as fear, nor is it quite the same as the English word that derives from it, anxiety. It is specifically the way you feel inside a dream when you have to do something that is nevertheless impossible. *Trotzdem:* nevertheless. *Unmöglich:* impossible.

The window at the end of the room was the screen of a computer. The prompt character was winking on the screen, insisting that he issue a command:

I

He didn't know what to type and pressed the RETURN key. A series of pastel squares tumbled about on the screen, as in a patternless kaleidoscope. Slowly they coalesced into a kind of face, though a face reduced to such simple masses of dark and light that it might more accurately be called a skull. The face's mouth hole gaped open to speak his name: "Billy."

It was not the resonant, movie-star voice of the god, but a voice at once more familiar and more terrible. He wanted to turn the computer off and erase the skullish face from the screen, but he could not, and, pixel by pixel, the face achieved a higher resolution to become unmistakably the face of his father, as he had seen him last, blood streaming from eye-sockets and mouth, flesh lacerated by the shattered windshield, bubbles of blood fizzing at the wound in his throat as he had struggled for his last living breath.

"Billy," the ghostly image pleaded, "is that you? If you can hear me, speak to me. Are you dead now, too? Is that why I feel you here beside me? It *is* you. But where are you? Are you alive? Speak!"

He could not speak, but his fingers touched the keyboard of the computer, and entered the name of the standard greeting program: HELLO.

"Billy, can you understand my questions? Do you know *where* you are? Can you tell me what *year* it is?"

He typed: 1980.

The ghost gave a rasping sigh and raised its hands to press its eyelids down over the bleeding sockets. "Then it is not too late. You can still destroy that wretched stick before it does more harm. Will you promise to do that?"

He realized at just this moment in the dream that he was having a nightmare, but the realization was not an exit door by which he might escape the dream world. Rather it was like one of those moments when you are walking in the middle of a city busy with people and cars and suddenly become aware of the immense size of the world about you, and know that your own little mote of consciousness is just a tiny flicker in a power grid of incalculable extent.

THIS IS A DREAM, he typed, frantic for release.

"Ah," Henry Michaels said, "of course. Tell me, how is Madge, is she well?"

YES, he wrote, yielding to the dream's authority, and by that yielding winning for his father a kind of release from his seeming torment. For now Henry, no longer an image on a screen, seemed to stand before his son, unbloodied, whole, and dressed in his everyday clothes. He put forward his hand, as though to touch William's face, then checked the gesture and, with a grimace, took a step backward.

"I have no physical existence now," he said in a tone of patient instruction. "No flesh. My senses are not as yours, though I can see you now. Now—and as you'll be, as you could become. You must destroy that thing. What is the word you call it by?"

CADUCEUS

"The harm it has done your brother is only an atom of the evil that it can bring. I can *see* that evil ahead of you like a cloud of smoke. You must not let its power grow. Burn it. Tonight. Take it out to the barbecue and burn it."

William shook his head.

His father caught hold of his wrist, his stony fingers forming a bracelet of physical, panicking horror in which William's thinking, dreaming mind had no participation. It was as though his flesh had been invaded in a single onslaught by all its biologic enemies, by every virus and bacteria that can enter and deform the vital tissues of muscle and nerve, every horrible parasite that may be hatched from the flesh of a human host. He screamed, but the scream did not win him relief from the dream or from his father's ghostly grip.

"I am sorry," Henry said, "that I must do this. But you must be made to understand what you are doing. I would spare you the pain, if I could. But to see what I must show you, there must be such pain. That is something I cannot alter, for I am as little in control of this process as you."

"But I *am* in control!" William insisted aloud, struggling to break loose. "And the caduceus can be a force for good as much as for ill. I can *heal* with it. I can cure diseases that medicine has never been able to cure before. And I can *learn* what I am doing and pass on that knowledge. Believe me, I will be careful."

The ring of pain about his wrist passed, in spasms, up through his arm and metastasized into a thousand vector quantities of death, needles of malignity that pierced lungs and heart and lodged there, pulsing. It felt as though a lifetime's possibilities of pain had been summarized and then, like a long-held high note, extended into an endless howl of damnation.

Yet, looking down, he found that that howl had lifted him high above Willowville, which had become a circuit diagram of roofs and treetops and asphalt streets. One of the neighbors' houses was burning, and the smoke fanned out from the blaze in a plume that spread southwestward toward the city. The horizon tilted, and he was flying, guided and powered by the pressure of the hand about his wrist, in the same direction. The traffic below them zipped by along the long double curves of the expressways at impossible velocities, a clockwork speeded up by trick photography. The pains were now suffused with a sense of exultation, as though they had been the seeds of this new power, seeds sending roots into his chest and soul, and bursting from his slender back as wings, invisible but exquisitely sensitive.

Henry pointed to the winding streets and low tents and buildings of the State Fairgrounds ahead of them. A block wide perimeter of leveled houses formed a ring around the Fairgrounds, and this ring of demolition was demarcated by high barbed-wire fences and patrolled by guards in gas masks and protective uniforms. At intervals along the outer fence were observation towers manned by more armed guards.

Within the inner fence a mob of men, women, and children wandered about listlessly or sat on benches and curbstones, reading, talking, playing cards. They all (except for a few workmen in civilian clothes) wore the drab cotton pajamas and gowns that are the uniform of hospital patients.

Inside the oval of the grandstand's raceway, its three tall chimneys screened from the view of the Fairground's denizens by the tiered seats of the bleachers, a large crematorium had been erected. Parked at its entrance were flatbed trucks piled with the bodies of the plague dead that had been gathered from the quarantine precincts. The stacked corpses had been sprayed with white powder so that they seemed to form immense composite plaster sculptures.

"Poison," Henry explained. "Otherwise the quarantine would be completely ineffective. Vermin would carry it throughout the city."

"Did you know that in German the word for poison is *Gift?*"

"These horrors mean nothing to you? You care only for yourself, for your 'career'?"

"This is only a dream."

"Yes—but a dream that will come true, unless you stop now. Destroy the caduceus."

"I'm sorry, Father. I can't."

"You won't."

"You never understood what it is to be ambitious. That was the real difference between us. You don't know what it's like to know that you're built on the same scale as the world. That you can be part of history."

Henry shook his head sorrowfully, but it was only, once again, a head on a television screen. "Remember me," he whispered, almost as an afterthought.

William nodded. He felt guilty for what he'd just said, but it was true. His father had never wanted to amount to anything. "Sure, Dad."

"If you want to get in touch again, you know my file name."

The screen went blank, but William continued to sleep restlessly for another three hours, and when he did wake he'd forgotten everything about the dream except that his father had been in it and that they'd flown together above the city and that at the end of the dream he had told him the name of the file to access on the computer if he needed to see him again. But what that name was he could not remember.

BOOK FOUR

40

With luck Jimmy Deeters might still be let off. Even though he was nine-teen now and had graduated from the Family Court to this dump, he looked a lot younger. There were places downtown where he got asked for his ID when he wanted to buy a pack of fucking cigarettes, and as for getting a drink in a bar outside his own neighborhood, forget it. But to-day, according to Wiener, the dipshit Legal Defense lawyer assigned to his case, it might turn out to be a plus that he didn't look his age. The dipshit thought the D.A. had messed up on Friday when he let the old lady with the bandaged foot be on the jury. She was a grandmother of five, and maybe she would take it in her head to hold out against a convic-tion, seeing as Jimmy was still basically a kid and shouldn't have to be sent up for two to five years, which was what he was facing, less for the snatch than for assaulting an officer and resisting arrest. So when he'd come in to the court today he didn't wear the camo he wore on Friday, when they were picking the jury, but a Twins T-shirt that belonged to his kid brother and a pair of chino pants. But the old lady had also come in wearing a different outfit. The bandage was off her foot and she was dressed in a baggy black dress like she was coming to a funeral. Which was not, Jimmy thought, a good sign, 'cause whose funeral would that be but his?

The old lady's sympathy was about all he had to bank on, because there was no way to deny that he'd done what he was charged with. The bitch he'd grabbed the purse from had been a police decoy, and she had two partners who witnessed the whole thing. He'd been set up, but it was all supposed to be legal, as the county prosecutor had explained to each person who was examined to be on the jury, and each one of them, includ-ing Granny, had to agree that they didn't see anything wrong with using decoys. So really all he could hope for was sympathy on account of his looking like a slightly older Gary Coleman. He would have plea-bargained if they'd let him, but because of his record they wouldn't. They were out to nail him and send him to Stillwater for two to five.

His record was what would wreck him, even with the grandmother of five, but Wiener said they wouldn't be able to bring up all that shit if he didn't take the stand in his own defense. Anyhow, according to all the guys he'd talked to, that was almost never a good idea. But as it turned out they got to read his whole Family Court arrest record to the jury anyhow, and Wiener only made it worse shouting out "Objection!" each time, and each time the two lawyers would go up and whisper to the judge, and the judge would say "Objection overruled" in this real bored voice, and the other lawyer would smile this smile of his at the jury and read the shit on this sheet of paper the size of a fucking newspaper: February 2, 1976, second degree arson; August 14, 1976, third degree attempted burglary; November 20, 1976, attempted rape. Et fucking cetera. What Jimmy hated more than the look on the asshole's face when he was reading through the list was how almost everything was "attempted." Like he'd never actually been able to carry through on anything. Which wasn't true, those were just the times he was caught. But what could he say? Objection, Your Honor, I'm better than that!

At a certain point Jimmy got depressed and forgot what he'd been told by Wiener, always to try and look innocent. Which meant not to react to what was being said about him but just to keep his eyes on the table in front of him like he was in school. Not an easy trick when everyone in the room was staring at him like he was a fucking werewolf. None of *them* were hiding the way they felt about him. They all wanted to nail him, even the grandmother of five. You could tell from the way her lips had got all squeezed together, the way she wouldn't look at him anymore. Fuck looking innocent! Fuck the jury! Fuck them all!

When the decoy started in on her testimony, Jimmy turned round in his plastic chair and looked at the people in the back of the courtroom. Wiener nudged him, and he told Wiener to fuck off. This might be his last act of freedom for two to five years. There were not many familiar faces. His own mother had taken off, and the only person he knew was Ms. Tough Titty, his old probation officer, who must have come for the sheer enjoyment of seeing him shafted. That's what was going to happen, no doubt about it. This was not Family Court, this was the real thing. This was Stillwater, and for what? For a fucking purse with nothing but fucking confetti in it.

A courtroom they called it! He'd seen courtrooms on TV and he knew this was no fucking courtroom. This was just a waiting room where everyone had to sit on plastic chairs, everyone but the fucking judge. And the judge was no judge, just some kid out of college, still so young they wouldn't have let him on a golf course except as a caddy. Two to five years, because he'd been carrying a piece! He hadn't tried to use it, he hadn't even reached for it, even when he'd got loose from the decoy's first partner. So he was carrying a piece, what did they think? That some bitch was going to say, "Oh sure, honey, here's my purse, just help yourself to what's in it." He'd never *used* the fucking piece, and never meant to, but they were going to nail his ass anyhow. Unless someone on the jury agreed with Wiener that there was a reasonable doubt.

Which there wasn't.

Now it was the decoy's partner's turn to tell his story. He was some old Uncle Tom who didn't look like a cop at all. He might have been the twin brother of the grandmother of five. Jimmy wished he *had* used his piece, even if it had meant thirty to life, just so as not to have to listen to the bastard recite his answers to the D.A. Yes, he could point out the perpetrator. Yes, the perpetrator was here in courtroom. Yes, that was the weapon he had removed from the defendant.

But the absolutely worst part and what made the whole thing seem like a nightmare was that all the while they were setting him up for his two to five years there was this goddamned little *student* sitting in the back row of plastic chairs taking *notes* like he was in a fucking classroom. In a fucking Izod polo shirt. A schoolkid. Every time Jimmy turned round to look at him he looked away, but when he looked again the kid would be staring at him, with his lips squeezed tight like the old lady on the jury. Jesus Christ, wasn't there a *law* to keep kids out of courtrooms?

The judge announced there was going to be a recess, which meant the jurors got a free lunch. For Jimmy it meant he could go to the toilet, which was down at the end of the hall on the right. On the left were the elevators, and the stairs, and the guard. Wiener, who had been full of talk up till now, suddenly didn't have anything to say. He sat at the table and avoided Jimmy's questions by working a crossword puzzle in the newspaper.

Jimmy went out into the hall. The guard was there in front of the elevators where he always was, looking like he wished Jimmy would make a dash for it and give him a chance to lay into him. At the other end of the hall the kid who'd been sitting in the back row of the courtroom with the notebook was standing in front of the men's room holding the door open, as though he couldn't make up his mind whether to go in or go out. When he saw Jimmy, he let go of the door and started walking toward the elevators, looking down at the rubber tiles, as though if he'd looked straight at Jimmy, he'd have caught some kind of disease. Jimmy moved out into the middle of the hallway, so the kid would have to walk around him, and the kid, with his eyes glued to the floor, didn't even notice till he was just a few feet away. He stopped and said "Excuse me," and when Jimmy didn't move, he walked around him and went back in the courtroom.

Jimmy thought of going after the kid, but if he did, what then? Wiener was in there. Fuck them all. Jimmy just wanted to be by himself. And the only way to do that, with the guard watching him like a hawk, was to go down the hall to the men's room. He figured he would take one last small revenge on Hennepin County by pissing on the floor. But as soon as he'd gone inside, he forgot all about what he'd meant to do, because lying on the tiled floor just in front of the door to the first of the toilet stalls was a small red change purse. He almost laughed out loud, because he *knew* that it must have fallen out of the kid's pocket when he'd come out of the crapper. Who else but a wimp like that would keep his money in a change purse? At least, he hoped there was money in it.

There was. A five-dollar bill and some change. He hadn't really expected more than that, not in a fucking change purse.

He pocketed the money and threw the change purse into the waste bin. Then, feeling a little peculiar, he went into the toilet stall, locked the door behind him, and sat down on the toilet seat without even bothering to take down his pants.

When the guard was dispatched, a few minutes later, to bring the defendant back to the courtroom for the conclusion of his trial, he was discovered in the locked toilet stall, dead. The County Medical Officer was summoned at once from his office two blocks away and declared that the cause of death was apparently asphyxiation. As a drug overdose seemed to be the probable underlying cause, an autopsy was performed within hours, but there were no traces of any drug in his system. His asphyxiation seemed to have been entirely spontaneous. Mrs. Deeters was interviewed on the Evening News and denounced her son's death as a clear case of police brutality. The Urban League backed her demand for an investigation, but really there could be no suspicion of foul play. There were no signs of a struggle, and the toilet stall had been locked from inside. Even Mrs. Deeters came to accept the fact that her son's death had been an act of God and, very likely, a punishment for his sins.

41

The ambulance pulled up to the main entrance of the courthouse at two forty-five, according to the clock on the tower of the building. William had been pacing back and forth alongside the wall of endlessly cascading water in the plaza of the Government Center across the street. The attendants wheeled a stretcher in through the courthouse's low, barrel-vaulted entrance. William was sure that Deeters was dead, but he wanted to see them bring the body out of the building. If they didn't turn the siren on when they drove away, that would mean Deeters had died right there in the bathroom, as soon as he'd opened the purse.

He hadn't expected it to happen so fast, and he was shaken up, not so much on account of what he'd done, but because it hadn't gone according to plan. From what he'd read in the medical book, he'd supposed that Deeters would continue breathing regularly until he fell asleep that night—probably in a jail cell. William had counted on being present to hear the jury deliver its verdict and the judge hand down his sentence and to see Deeters produce one final scowl. After Deeters's guilt had been officially recognized in that way, William's unofficial death sentence would have seemed less of an act of vigilante justice. But now that Deeters was dead, those scruples didn't disturb William's conscience. Deeters had been a dreadful person, and he would surely have gone on being a dreadful person for the rest of his life. A couple of years in prison wouldn't have changed that. Arson, burglary, rape—all before he'd turned eighteen. And a look in his eyes all through the trial like he'd have liked to add murder to the list of his accomplishments. The world would definitely be a better place, and Minneapolis a safer city, without James Deeters.

But he shouldn't have died there in the courthouse, with William still in the vicinity. That had been a major error in judgment of William's, and that's what had set his heart to pounding so that even now, an hour and a half after the courtroom had been cleared, he still couldn't trust himself to think clearly. What if the guard had noticed him coming out of the bathroom just before Deeters had gone in? What if someone remembered him being in the courtroom and simply tried to locate him as a witness? But a witness of what? He was being panicky about nothing. Still, it had been a mistake to be present in the courtroom, even with the excuse ready to hand (an excuse that was halfway true) that he was watching the trial as part of a report he had to make for a summer school Civics class. As it turned out, no one had seemed even to notice his presence in the courtroom except the defendant, who had scowled at him a couple times when he wasn't scowling at the D.A. or the witnesses. The reason he'd felt he should be at the trial was that he didn't want to zap anyone—even someone who was guilty as hell—who seemed to be basically a good person. Which had turned out to be the situation at the first trial he'd started watching, on Thursday, a man who'd got drunk and stabbed his wife in the shoulder and then threatened two policemen with a gun. Not a nice thing to do, but the man seemed sorry for it, and he was not someone who made his living preying on innocent people. Like Deeters. Deeters had deserved what he got.

But why had it happened so soon? According to what he'd read in the textbook, apnea (which was the general condition that Ondine's curse was just the most extreme example of) was always connected with sleep. The commonest kind of apnea and what the textbook mostly discussed was snoring. And from the definition of Ondine's curse it seemed logical to suppose that it was also connected with sleeping. Without even trying to, just by having studied it so carefully, William had memorized that definition: "*Ondine's curse*, a primary insensitivity of the medulla's respiratory center, of unknown origin, which impairs the reflex drive so that breathing becomes voluntary and no longer automatic." Or, in the simpler words of the "Stranger Than Fiction!" column of the *Green Magician* comic book where he'd first learned of the existence of Ondine's curse: "The doomed victims of Ondine's curse never realize the danger they are in until it's too late! This rare disorder short-circuits the part of the brain that makes you go on breathing without having to think. With Ondine's curse you can only keep breathing *as long as you think about it!* And when you finally can't keep from falling asleep, then it's *Lights Out*—forever! You stop breathing—and Die of Asphyxiation!!"

When William had first read that in "Stranger Than Fiction!" almost a year ago, he'd dismissed it as a fabrication. But he kept remembering the accompanying half-page drawing of a blue-faced corpse with one hand clutching at the collar of his pajamas. And then, on Tuesday, when the phone call had come from Rhoda Winckelmeyer in Florida and he realized that he would have to act quickly to help Judith, he'd recalled that picture again and, on the hunch that Ondine's curse might be a real disease after all, he'd gone into his stepfather's study, where he kept his medical books. Ben liked to claim that he had a better medical library than most doctors, and he subscribed to a dozen medical journals and had them bound in buckram bindings. It seemed a fair bet that if Ondine's curse was more than a comic book artist's fantasy, there would be something about it in one of these books. But a library without a librarian can be as useless as a computer without software. Tracking down a single rare disease among all those tomes had been like looking for a needle in a haystack, and William had almost given up the search when, in the index of a two-inch-thick *Introduction to Neurophysiology*, he had spied the needle's glint: "Ondine's curse: see *apnea*." Looking up "apnea" he was directed to page 465, where in a long paragraph about breathing disorders, for which "apnea" is the technical term, he'd found the short definition of Ondine's curse that proved that the disease existed.

But the medical book had not said in so many words that someone with Ondine's curse only stopped breathing when he went to sleep. Even the comic book said you only went on breathing as long as you *think* of it. Deeters must not have realized what was happening to him. It was hard to believe that someone could be dying of asphyxiation and not start gasping for breath. It would be like drowning, a reflex. But a person with Ondine's curse didn't have that reflex anymore. Deeters must have died in the courthouse bathroom almost as soon as he'd opened the change purse William had cursed with the caduceus:

> *Take the money from this purse*
> *And you will suffer Ondine's curse.*

He'd drowned in the open air without even knowing he was drowning.

At three o'clock, just as the bells of the tower began to ring the hour, the two medics wheeled the stretcher out of the courthouse. The body on the stretcher was covered with a sheet, and when the ambulance drove away it did not sound its siren. Deeters was dead.

He thought that being a murderer would have made more of a difference in the way he felt. He'd expected he'd have to contend with guilt or remorse or an urge to confess what he'd done. But all he felt was relief that it was over, as though he'd been traveling for days and days on an endless bus ride. He took a long, lung-filling yawn and then another deeper yawn, and even as he did so it came over him what a strange and wonderful mechanism the human body was. The heart pumping the blood round and round, and the lungs working like a microscopic filling station fueling the red corpuscles with oxygen, and the brain's mainframe firing off its strings of commands to all parts of the system. Was there anything else in the world so profoundly beautiful, so endlessly, intricately interesting? He stretched his arms up high over his head and clenched his fists and drew another, deeper breath, bending back his head to feel the muscles in his neck, drawing his elbows down slowly, conscious of the flexions of his shoulders and his back.

Out of nowhere came an intense urge to run. Not away from anything, but from the sheer joy of inhabiting his flesh. Or better still, to swim! To feel his muscles meshing together in a single smooth continuous effort. To feel cold water slide across his skin, defining its geometries. Suddenly the statue he had passed in the courthouse lobby, the statue of a naked, bearded man sitting on top of an alligator (a sign had identified him as "Mississippi—Father of Waters"), instead of seeming ridiculous, seemed to make sense, completely and logically, though it was not a logic he could have explained. There was something in the whiteness and smoothness of the marble and in the calmness and the strength and the size of the figure on the pedestal that declared that the body, in itself, was like a god. The Greeks had understood that and had filled all their temples with statues of naked bodies for that reason.

He had to go back there. It was not really a matter of volition. He had to look at the statue again, to be in its presence and feel its power. Even as he passed between the low, squat granite columns of the entrance, he realized that he was doing just what every murderer is supposed not to do, but inevitably does: he was returning to the scene of the crime.

There it was: "Mississippi—Father of Waters." And it was just another marble statue of a naked man, and even sillier than he'd first supposed. When he touched it, no power emanated from the stone, but from the other side of the lobby a guard called out, in a tone of routine prohibition: "Hey kid, get away from the statue!"

42

When she heard the car pull up to the house, Sondra lighted one of the butts in the ashtray and blew puffs of smoke about the living room, as though it were air freshener. She was probably the only person in the world who had to pretend to be a smoker instead of the other way round, pretending to have quit. It still amazed her how easy it had been, once she'd had the motivation. All those years she'd agonized over being unable to kick the habit, and now all at once, because she was pregnant, stopping smoking had been as easy as falling off a log. She had no more craving than if she'd never smoked at all. The taste of cigarettes actually repelled her. The reason she lit cigarettes and left them burning in ash-trays was that she didn't want Ben to know she'd quit, not yet, not till she was ready to tell him she was pregnant. She'd always said that was the only thing that would convince her to give up smoking, and if he noticed she'd quit, he might guess why.

It was a false alarm. The car pulling into the driveway hadn't been Ben, but a pair of Judith's fellow crusaders against abortion stopping by to see if she would come along to the Willowville mall to hand out leaflets. Sondra explained that Judith had extended her visit to Florida an extra week, but she didn't volunteer the information that Judith was in the hospital. When the car drove off, it was as though its bumper sticker—ABORTION IS MURDER—had been dispatched to the house specially for Sondra's benefit, a sign from on high.

Personally Sondra did not share her stepdaughter's unconditional hor-ror of abortion. She had had an abortion the first time Ben had got her pregnant, and though at the time she'd let Ben assume that she was doing it for his sake and despite her own finer feelings, the fact was that the prospect of pregnancy and diaper pails had not been any more appealing to her than to him. But that was in 1970, when she'd been eager to make up for the time she'd lost by marrying Henry as soon as she was out of high school. This was 1980, and time had smoothed over the rougher edges of memory. Now it wasn't the morning sickness or the nights of infant colic that she remembered, but the mystery and the amusement of having made another human being out of her own body, a little burbling milk-mad mammal that slowly evolved into a genuine human being. It seemed, once again, worth the effort. More than that, she had a *craving* to be a mother again, a physical lust to feel her belly filling with another child, to nurse it at her breasts, to see it crawl about this barn of a house, smearing food on the furniture and crayoning the walls and making it a home in those drastic ways that are the privilege and the genius of the very young. She didn't care about its sex, it could be a boy or a girl, she just wanted a baby, and if she was to have one, it should be now. She wasn't too old yet, only thirty-four, but with every year she let slip by the odds grew worse of some kind of irregularity.

These were not feelings that Ben shared. Ben had no fond memories of fatherhood, and Sondra was sure he would want her to get an abortion. There would probably be fights, and almost certainly it would mean the end of the recent renaissance in their sex life. Ben had never been a great lover, certainly nothing like the Beauty-Rest gymnast Henry had been, but in the last few months since he'd been feeling his Cheerios again, Ben had actually advanced from Beginner to Intermediate. He'd even developed a taste for eating pussy, and if he was still a little tentative in the way he went about it, by comparison to the old days it was a genuine sexual revolution. At first she had suspected he was taking drugs (you heard all this talk nowadays about cocaine in suburbia), and then she thought the old dog might have learned his new tricks as a result of having had a mistress, but the simplest explanation was that he was having his mid-life crisis. He was forty-five, and the articles she'd read said that that was the age when men were most likely to have a mid-life crisis and to take a fresh interest in sex. Whatever the cause, she enjoyed its effect and didn't want to put a damper on it prematurely.

It was a beautiful day, unusually cool for midsummer, and Sondra decided she would take a walk. From the first days of her pregnancy, even before she'd realized what was happening, she had been brimming with physical energy. Before Judith had gone to Florida to visit her mother and William had started his summer school classes, she'd taken them almost every day to the pool at the country club, and when she no longer had that excuse for exercise, she'd begun jogging! But when the tests showed she was pregnant, her doctor had advised her to discontinue that. Instead, for an hour every morning when there was no one else in the house, she did the stretching and breathing exercises recommended in the book on natural childbirth that she kept hidden among the paperback romances stacked sideways on the bookshelf in her bedroom. (Ben couldn't make fun of the titles if he didn't see them.) With William she had meant to have a natural delivery, but she'd got lazy about doing the exercises and when the time had come she had funked out and let them give her an anesthetic. She'd always reproached herself for that. It was like flying over the Grand Canyon in broad daylight and being asleep. This time she was determined to do it right.

Willowville was not a stroller's paradise. Few of the houses had smooth concrete sidewalks, the preference being for paths of gravel or crushed rock, and there was rarely anything to take special notice of. People did their flower gardening, if they did any at all, around their patios in their backyards, and the front lawns featured evergreen shrubberies and trees just out of the nursery. She walked the length of Pillsbury Road until it veered west into Willowville Drive, then up Willowville as far as the Sheehy house, a center hall colonial with a full acre of lawn and the tallest trees in the neighborhood, seven huge willows that surrounded the white clapboard house like a shimmering dusky-green veil. Sondra envied the Sheehys their willows, but not their house, which was spacious only from the outside; inside it was old-fashioned and boxy. Though, of course, it helped with that many children (the Sheehys had three) to have a good supply of bedrooms. When the new baby came, Judith would have to move upstairs and take the room next to William so the baby could have hers, and then there wouldn't be a guest room. Ben would object to that, but when did they ever have guests?

She was tempted to cut across the Sheehys' lot to her own backyard but, resisting the temptation, returned the way she'd come and was rewarded by discovering, under one of the low junipers that bordered the gravel path in front of 1232, a lost Frisbee. It was printed with the name of the company Mr. Sheehy worked for, TECHNO-CONTROLS, and with a motto in smaller letters, "Designing Machines with Souls." Obviously, it was a promotional giveaway and just as obviously belonged to the Sheehy boy, who was a few years younger than William. Properly she ought to take the Frisbee back to the Sheehys' house and leave it somewhere in plain sight on their lawn, but the heft of it in her hand, its lightness and its promise of effortless flight, made her reluctant to return it without sailing it a few times across her own backyard. She returned home, Frisbee in hand, just as William was putting away his bicycle in the garage. "William!" she called out, and when he looked up, startled, she threw the Frisbee toward him on a slow lofting arc that hooked in its last instant of flight right into the hand he lifted to receive it.

"Hey, nice," he said. "Techno-Controls? Where'd you get this?"

"I found it in some shrubberies. I think it belongs to the Sheehy boy. Do you want to play with it a while in the backyard?"

William seemed to take as much pleasure as she did in tossing it back and forth. As they gained confidence, they sailed the Frisbee across wider and wider spans of lawn but without either of them having to trespass beyond the invisible boundaries of their own backyard. It was wonderful all the different flight paths you could make it trace. She had no idea what twist of wrist or flick of the fingers made it follow one trajectory instead of another. It was all done unconsciously but with such a strange precision. You'd almost think the plastic disc had a volition and intelligence of its own, as though it were some species of bird that had been fined down to this bare aeronautical minimum, a living discus skimming the lowest branches of the maple, whirling toward the patio and then veering away, settling down on the mown grass with a whoosh of deceleration like a waterfowl coming to rest on a lake. Before today she had only ever played Frisbee with Henry, and that was years ago, on days when they'd taken William, still in a stroller, to Brosner Park. Now William was almost as tall as his father had been then, and beginning to share his good looks. He'd be dating soon. Possibly even off to college in another year: it was the hope of entering the U in the fall of '81, after only another year at St. Tom's, that had lead him to take the summer school courses.

Where did he get such ambition—at age thirteen? In that way he was much more like Ben than like Henry, but even Ben was in awe of the way the boy kept his nose to the grindstone. He was deliberately taking the very dullest course the school offered, Civics, because he wanted to get it over with. And the teacher, Lilah Gerhart, was apparently a real pill. Judith had had her this last year, and she would come home at least once a week infuriated with some new work of tyranny perpetrated by Miss Gerhart. But William, so far, had not breathed a word against her. He just memorized all the dull facts and figures about city government and state government (and really, was there anything as dull as Civics?), and wrote his term papers and book reports, and generally behaved like a prisoner bent on earning time off for good behavior. She wished there was a way to explain to him that he didn't have to be so *grim*. High school—even one like St. Tom's—could be fun, if you didn't confuse it with getting an education. That could come later, but in the meantime the boy should really learn to throw a Frisbee better. A thirteen-year-old whose mother has better aim with a Frisbee than he does should be taking an exercise class, not a course in Civics.

As though to confirm this judgment, William's next throw went wildly askew and the Frisbee came to rest, gracefully, high on the roof of the garage. Even standing on a lawn chair and reaching for it with a rake was no use.

"I'm sorry," William said. (Though it occurred to her that perhaps his aim hadn't been wild at all, but perfectly accurate. Maybe he'd got bored with playing catch but didn't want to say so.) "Do you want me to get the ladder?"

"No, leave it. It was fun, but I'm tired. The doctor says I shouldn't overexert myself now that—" She caught herself, but not in time. William was no dunce.

"The doctor?" His eyes had narrowed.

The embryo of the idea was already there. She might as well be candid. She couldn't keep it secret much longer in any case.

She nodded. "I'm pregnant."

William grinned and sprinted across the lawn to hug her and spin her around in a little impromptu polka. "Mom, that's wonderful! When is it going to be?"

"Sometime between Thanksgiving and Christmas most likely."

"That's terrific. Can you feel it inside you yet? Is there a lump or something?"

She smiled. "No, not yet. I'll let you know as soon as there is."

"Have you told Judith yet? She's going to be so tickled. She used to tell me how she kept hoping you'd have a baby. So she would know what it was like to have a sister. She said she knew all she needed to know about brothers from me."

"So far, William, I haven't told anyone but you. And I hadn't intended to do that, it just slipped out. I suppose I'll have to tell Ben tonight."

William crinkled his brow, and it was as clear to Sondra what he was thinking as if the thoughts had been printed out between the furrows on his brow. He understood what she feared and the reason she hadn't spoken with Ben.

She kissed the crinkle. "Don't worry. It'll work out. Ben may be a bit peeved at first. This wasn't an event we were planning on. But it is— what's the old expression?—a *blessed* event. Every baby is a miracle. But a woman probably has an easier time accepting the idea of the miracle. For a man it's probably like when the angel came to Joseph to tell him what was in the works. It's still a miracle, but it takes a while for the idea to sink in." It sounded nice. She hoped it was true.

43

When Ben finally came to bed at ten thirty after watching the local news on Channel 11, Sondra was there, sprawled on the bed listening to a tape on her Walkman. Her eyes were closed, and her pedicured toes flexed in time to the music. Ben stood in the doorway smiling, trying to imagine from the rhythm of her toes what she was listening to. It was never classical music, she had a reverse snobbery about that, but it wasn't rock either: her toes were moving too slowly. Her Zampir tape, probably. She loved the sound of panpipes when she was feeling sexy. And so did he, for that matter. The problem was, he wasn't feeling all that sexy, not after the day he'd had today. Though with a little encouragement he might get into the mood. For the last so long he'd been in a state of perpetual rut. Something had happened to his testosterone level. And the feeling was mutual: Sondra was a bitch in heat. Pheromones? Was it as simple as that?

She opened her eyes, and turned off the Walkman, and smiled. "I was just thinking about you."

"I was just thinking about you."

"You looked upset when you got home. Did something happen at the office?"

"Several things. When it rains, it pours. I finally got through to the attending physician at the hospital in St. Augustine, and it was like talking to a wall. According to him, Judith can't leave the hospital for another two weeks, minimum. When I asked what treatment she was receiving, he tried to flimflam me, and then, when I started to ask about his financial relation to the hospital, an emergency developed very suddenly. Then I got a call from Rhoda, who wanted to know if I remembered what day it was."

"What day was it?"

"Our anniversary."

"Yours and hers?"

"Apparently she still celebrates it. It's the source of all her alimony, after all. She was gloating."

"About your anniversary?"

"About having Judith under her thumb. I'm probably going to have to fly down there myself and hire an attorney to spring her from that Blue Cross snakepit."

"I hope it's not as bad as that. I mean, all doctors are a little greedy or they wouldn't be doctors, but that doesn't mean the hospital is a snakepit."

"There's more. After the call from Rhoda, I finally got through to ATA. They've 'declined' to fund the research on skin staining I wrote up last spring. Kearns wasn't there for the meeting when they made the decision, and when I asked why not, I couldn't get a straight answer from anyone. So I called him at home, and you know what I found out? He's gone to Mayo Clinic for a checkup. A checkup! No one flies halfway across the country for a 'checkup.' Anyone who goes to Mayo has got a damned good reason."

"Well, I'm sorry your project didn't go through, but you said yourself it probably didn't stand much of a chance. You'll think of other ideas, you always do. But I'm more sorry to hear about Mr. Kearns. From the few times I met him he always seemed the nicest person at ATA. The only actual human being. What do you suppose is the matter?"

"Cancer is what I suppose."

"Oh no, I hope not. Why immediately suppose the worst?"

"Because everyone I talked to at ATA was so damned pussyfooting when I asked about him. They sounded worried, and what do you suppose the main worry is at ATA? The board members are all pushing sixty, they're all heavy smokers, and they know the odds."

"For getting lung cancer, you mean?"

"Not Asian flu, honey."

"Well, it would certainly be ironic, but I hope you're wrong about Mr. Kearns. There's all sorts of things that can start going wrong at his age. Now, is that *all* the bad news?"

"Isn't it enough?"

"Because if it is, I've got some good news." She pushed herself up into a sitting position with her back against the headboard of the bed. "I've given up smoking."

"You have! Since when?"

"Over a month now. I didn't tell you before, because I wanted to be sure I'd really quit."

"Over a month? Honey, that's terrific! Congratulations. Tell me your secret."

She smiled in an odd way, lowering her eyes down to her hands where they rested on her stomach, clasped together as though to cradle some small invisible animal. And when, after a long pause, she spoke, she seemed to address that animal and not Ben. "I'm pregnant."

Jesus, closing his eyes and slumping back against the doorframe, admitting defeat before the fight was even under way. From the tone of her voice he knew she would not be amenable to arguments or bribes. She meant to have the baby. The pregnancy had sprung some biochemical spring in her endocrine system, in some gland probably no bigger than a garden pea, and the result was a will enslaved to the needs of the fetus inside her, a faith as fervent and fanatic as any Shiite Muslim's.

"Congratulations," he said drily.

"I knew your first reaction would be dismay. So was mine. The idea takes a while to sink in."

He agreed to this with a weak smile, thinking how the same might be said of the hook of a lure that a fish takes in its mouth. Perhaps, as in the fish's case, he would come round to her frame of mind more quickly if there was a fight, if he did reproach her for carelessness or deceit (for she was supposed to have been on the pill), if there were curses and tears and the balm of a final reconciling embrace.

"It wasn't deliberate. I hadn't *told* you I'd stopped taking the pill, because it would have seemed like I was complaining about our sex life. And then when all of a sudden we were going at it again, I did start back on the pill, but then it was too late. It must have been that very first morning that did the trick, remember, the morning after William's birthday?"

He nodded. "I remember."

"I don't want an abortion. Not this time. I want this child, and there's no reason we can't have another child. Money certainly isn't a problem. Compared to most people we're rich."

"Sondra, I did not utter the word 'abortion.' You're arguing with yourself."

"It's the word you were thinking."

"No, I was remembering Judith as an infant. She was a crier. For about six months she seemed to cry nonstop. Then she moderated to a whine, and whined till the age of four."

Sondra laughed, for it was exactly what she would have imagined Judith to have been like as a baby.

"Well, maybe this one will take after William," she said softly. "William was a darling baby, the kind other women coo over. At eight months he already had two teeth and was climbing the stairs. And the intelligence in his eyes, even at that age, it was like a lamp that never went out. He was only two when I left Henry. Two years, five months, and just starting to form sentences."

"You don't have to remind me of that, Sondra."

"I was a stranger to him during the years when children are at their most beautiful. When a mother can make the biggest difference in the kind of person the child will become. Madge Obstschmecker was William's mother more than me. And he loves her in some deeper way as a result. Maybe not deeper, but different. I don't blame him for that, he can't possibly help it. But I want a child who will be mine *totally*. It's like that word they use in church, a vessel. There's a kind of emptiness in me that has to be filled. Men don't feel that. Do they?"

Ben shrugged. He did not want to be drawn into a discussion of the joys and wonders of procreation. "I feel empty often enough, that's not gender-specific. But I can't entertain the same literal hope of filling that emptiness with an embryo. That is certainly a woman's prerogative."

It made no difference that Ben refused to have an argument. Sondra had foreseen whatever objections he might raise, and she was determined to counter those objections, whether he spoke them aloud or not. "It's not as though we led the kind of life where another child would represent a real inconvenience for either of us. I'm at home all the time, and I've no wish to have a 'career.' We don't go out much. Judith graduates from high school next year and will be going to college, and so may William if he gets approved for that accelerated studies program."

"More emptinesses to fill?"

"No, in fact William will probably be around the house more once he's in college. But they *will* both be grown-ups before we know what's happened. We'll be less important to them. It's like . . . early retirement."

"Sondra, you're arguing with yourself."

"Oh, you're being very tolerant and good-natured, and I appreciate that. But I want you to *want* the baby, I want you to feel good about it."

"When the time comes, when I can see it and feel it and talk to it, I probably will become a doting father. I'm only human."

Sondra smiled. The mantle of complacent maternity already had enveloped her securely as a cocoon. All of creation seemed cozy and warm, and at the center of that coziness and warmth was herself, and centered in herself, the sun that generated all this radiance, was the seed of life in her womb.

"And what's wrong," she demanded, sliding forward in the bed, inviting him to her, "with your being human? I never noticed it before, but I think it makes you kind of cute."

He surrendered to the sheer biologic power of the event. He had always admired the salmon leaping up waterfall after waterfall, mad to spawn. Why should he be any different?

"I hope it's a girl," he told her, knowing it was what she was waiting to be told, "and that she's just like you."

44

Icksy the witch was sitting in the middle of the misty clearing William had come to in his dream, a large black woman in a red cotton dress. He didn't recognize her at once, thinking her to be the mother of Jimmy Deeters, whom he'd seen only a little while earlier on the Evening News, when she had accused the police of killing her son. ("And the woman's probably right, you know," Ben had commented, in his John Chancellor tone of voice. "Not that anyone else but his mother is likely to miss the little bastard, by the sound of it. That boy was bad news." To which William had murmured a cautious *Mm-hm*, not wanting to become involved in a discussion. He'd felt relieved when the brief account of Jimmy Deeters's mysterious death was followed by the latest news concerning the hostages in Iran.) Icksy sat there, rocking back and forth woefully and calling out her son's name in a tone sometimes of lamentation and sometimes shrill with accusation. The name she called out was not "Jimmy" but "Reinhardt," and that was how he knew that she was Icksy and not Mrs. Deeters. That, and by the color of her dress, which was the same bold red as the bowling pin who long ago had triumphed over Dundor and seen her son Reinhardt assume the crown of the decapitated king and reign over the kingdom of Wyomia. Why then was she grieving?

As though he had spoken the question aloud, Icksy looked up and fixed her eyes on him, eyes glistening with tears and black with malevolence. "Why do I grieve! You dare ask me that—you, his murderer?"

"I never!" William protested.

Her laugh was like the cawing of her raven Karn. "Oh no, you never!" she mocked. "And the train? The train that was wrecked just days after Christmas—you never did that either, I suppose. No, not an innocent child like Billy Michaels. And Dundor impeached and beheaded, you had no hand in that, I'm sure. And his people enslaved and forced to worship false gods, that had nothing to do with *you!*"

"They were *your* enemies," he protested. "I did it for you, so that your son would be king."

"Some day, William Michaels," she prophesied darkly, "some day your people will honor that king, and make the day of his birth their holiday. And the name of his assassin will be reviled, and a nation shall mourn and not be comforted. Some day your own mother will bear a child, and that child shall have no name. And some day, William Michaels, mark my words, some day *you* shall be put in the balance, and your crimes shall be *judged* and your guilt made known. And your judge's name is—"

—*Enough!* It was the voice of Mercury.

William turned round to find the god standing just behind him. His right hand was raised against Icksy, and it bore the caduceus with its twining serpents, which hissed their own wordless confirmation of the god's command.

"I will *speak!* I will publish the name of the wicked and rejoice in his accuser's glory."

—*I say you will be silent. For you are nothing but a piece of painted wood, a bowling pin, a child's toy.*

The god had only to step forward and it was true. On the boulder where she had sat there was nothing but the red bowling pin that William had used in his childhood games of make-believe. Mercury picked it up and tossed it underhand to William, who caught it and put it in his pocket.

"I'm glad to see you," William said eagerly. "There are some things I wanted to ask you."

Mercury looked amused.—*Do you suppose curiosity is one of the charms of youth? On the contrary, William, it's what the young don't know, and can't imagine, that beguiles their elders. But ask your questions—three is the usual allotment—and then we'll go down to my surgery for some practical hands-on instruction.*

"I was going to ask why you visit me at certain times but not at others, but if I only get three questions . . ."

—*What a bargain hunter you are. Very well: That answer won't count toward the three. I visit you as a gardener might visit the garden he has planted, to observe your growth and foster it. Sometimes I come and find you're not available. Last week, for instance, I dropped by and found your spirit closed to my approach. "What's this?" I asked myself. "Has he come to disbelieve in me so soon? Has he been able to dismiss all the memories that I've restored? Can he hold the caduceus in his hand, and feel its power, and deny its source?"*

William was abashed. He'd hoped his crisis of faith might have passed unnoticed by the god. He felt obliged to offer an explanation, though the god seemed to understand him, in many ways, better than he understood himself. "I didn't really ever disbelieve in you. I *doubted* you."

—*A subtle distinction.*

"What physical proof did I have? A stick with a dead bird tied to it. I would take the thing out of the box of comics where I'd hidden it, and it seemed as silly and childish to believe it could do all the things I seemed to remember it did as to believe the stories in those comic books. I could remember it vibrating with some kind of invisible energy, but it wasn't doing that any more. Of course, there was Ned, and Grandma O. going bald, and the rest, but all those things could have happened naturally."

Mercury accorded William a disdainful look.—*The gods of Olympus have never dealt in overt miracles. When we visit mortals we assume familiar forms. The arrows with which Apollo slaughtered the children of Niobe took the form, to human apprehension, of a plague. This is tedious. Ask your questions.*

"Okay: *Why* wasn't there any power in the caduceus? Why didn't the curse I'd put on Turnage's lighter have any effect?"

—*Those are two separate questions. The answer to the first is that you had simply drained the caduceus by putting too large a demand on it. Unqualified good health for five people—do you have any idea what that costs in terms of an equal and opposite reaction? Evidently you don't. It will take more than the death of a Jimmy Deeters to pay that medical bill. Your account is heavily overdrawn. Mean-*

while, just as with the debts you owe elsewhere, interest accrues. There is even the possibility, if the debt isn't paid within a reasonable amount of time, that you may forfeit your credit privileges altogether. So to speak.

"You mean—" William began, and then, realizing this would constitute a third question, stopped short, for it was quite clear what Mercury meant. If William did not work some further harm with the caduceus, it would stop functioning for good *or* ill.

—*Yes? You were about to ask?*

"I understand what you mean."

—*As to your second question, many things might account for the curse on the lighter not yet having taken effect. Cancer can be like the bulbs that gardeners plant in the fall. They may lie dormant many months before the first leaves spring from the thawed ground. Or it may be that Turnage hasn't used the lighter since the curse was put on it. It may still be in the pocket of the suit he wore that night and the suit may have been hanging ever since in the back of his closet. Or the flint may have fallen from the lighter and not been replaced.*

William felt cheated. He'd thought of those possibilities himself.

—*Your third question?*

"My mother is pregnant."

—*I am aware of that.*

"I want the baby to be healthy."

—*Naturally.*

"Can I do that while it's still . . . inside her?"

—*Yes, once the caduceus's power is fully restored. And within the wee thing's constitutional limits.*

"What do you mean by that?"

—*Properly, that is another question. But my meaning's plain enough. I mean the primal event that determines the structure of a human embryo is beyond the power of the caduceus to alter or correct. In that, even the gods must be fatalists. What will be, will be.*

"Are you saying there's something already gone wrong?"

—*I am only declaring the limits of the caduceus's power. The chromosomes twine together as fate determines. Were it otherwise, men would have become gods long ago, for anyone possessing such power would see to it that his offspring, and his offspring's offspring, were all genetic paragons. Even great Jupiter had a gimpy son. Now, come along, the bell is tolling, and there is something you must see in order to believe.* Mercury smiled a knowing smile, as though he'd said something clever, but clever in an obscure way only he could appreciate. Then he pushed aside the boulder on which Icksy had been seated to reveal a rough-hewn stairway that descended into the earth.—*Down this way,* he bade William, *and take care, these steps can be slippery.*

As they went down the stairs, the god's luminescing body cast a pale light on the curving stone walls. William strained to hear the bell that Mercury had spoken of, but the only sound he could make out was a muffled drumbeat that seemed to come from far below. It was the beating, he realized, of his own heart.

—*Ecco!* said Mercury, as the staircase opened out into a vaulted chamber. Echoes of the Latin word skittered about the darkness like bats. And there directly before him, on a raised slab of polished white stone, was the object William had been commanded to behold: the corpse of a well-proportioned young man, his toothless mouth gaping wide and bleeding at the gums, the hollow eyesockets stuffed with fleecy balls of cotton batting. A tray of surgical instruments had been placed on a stainless steel trolley beside the stone slab. After a single glance at the naked body on the slab William had to look away.

—*Come, come*, Mercury chided. *Doctors must be made of sterner stuff. Afraid of your first cadaver? You won't get far in medical school at that rate.* He lifted the corpse's hand and let it fall back limply to the stone.—*You see, quite harmless. Though you should, as a precaution, be wearing gloves. There's a pair there on the cart.*

Reluctantly, William put on the surgical gloves. They were made of a thick translucent plastic and it took a good deal of wiggling and coaxing to get each finger snugged into place.

—*Why don't we begin by exploring the abdominal cavity? A right paramedian incision should do the job. Start here.* He placed his finger just below the cadaver's lowest rib.

William placed the scalpel on the spot indicated but could not bring himself to exert the least pressure against the dead flesh. Mercury rapped the back of his hand, and the flesh parted. There was no blood. The tissue beneath the skin was a pale pinkish-gray.

—*Continue*, Mercury said, *to about here*. He touched the cadaver's crotch just above its penis, where the pubic hair had been shaved away, all but a faint stubble that had sprouted up in the time since the cadaver had been prepared for dissection.

William continued the incision, trying to take an intelligent, dispassionate interest in the procedure. Mercury helped by calling attention to various features revealed by the opening of the abdominal cavity.

—*Note the filmy adhesions over the ascending colon, and the dilation of the bowel. There would also seem to be gas within the transverse colon and into the sigmoid colon area.*

As the incision lengthened, the dermal tissues seemed to spread apart of their own volition, like a too tightly packed suitcase that has come unlatched. The viscera began to slip loose from the abdominal cavity and spill out onto the stone slab.

William replaced the scalpel on the trolley. "I'm sorry, I can't go on."

—*Nonsense, you're doing fine. Only a few more inches, and the incision will be done.*

William made himself look again at the cadaver and saw that its penis had become erect and that a thick, clotted white fluid was being discharged from the urethra in irregular spurts. The initial shock of horror quickly yielded to an intense, morbid fascination. As the discharge continued, it came to have the color and consistency of small-curd cottage cheese.

"Jesus," William whispered, "what *is* it?"

Mercury laughed.—*That, my boy, is a question you will have to answer yourself.*

45

"William? William, are you in there?"

William woke with a start. The room was dark, and the phone was ringing, and his mother was rapping at the door.

"William, would you *please* answer your phone. It's been ringing the longest time."

"I got it," he called out, and picked up the phone.

"Thank you," Sondra said. "And will you point out to your friend, whoever he is, that it's almost one a.m.?"

"I have a collect call," an operator announced in a strange accent, "for William Michaels, from Winky Meyer." She pronounced the name with a precision denoting disapproval. "Will you accept the charges?"

"Uh." The receiver of the phone was covered with some kind of glop. William switched the phone to his left hand and wiped his right hand on the bedspread. As he did so, he realized that the glop had not been on the phone, but had been on his hand before he'd picked up the receiver. "Just a second, operator." He used the corner of his bedsheet to wipe both hands clean and then wiped off the receiver, but it was still sticky when he picked it up again.

"Are you there, Mr. Michaels?" the operator inquired.

"Yes, operator. I'll accept the charges."

"Go ahead, Miss Meyer."

"William?" It was Judith. Why had he thought it was Ben? Because the operator had said Winky Meyer. He was still half asleep, and he could feel the dream fading and there were things he'd been told in the dream that he had to remember. And it wasn't just on his hand: his pajamas were a mess, too. It dawned on him that he'd been having a wet dream, the first he'd ever had, and the stuff on the phone and in his pajamas was *sperm*, the first genuine sperm he'd ever produced though he'd been jerking off pretty systematically for more than a year. But the dream hadn't been anything like wet dreams were supposed to be, it wasn't about sex at all.

And now Judith was on the phone.

"Judith?"

"I'm sorry, did I wake you up? It's an hour earlier there, I thought you might still be up."

"Is something wrong? Where are you?"

"I'm in the Greyhound station in Miami. But don't tell Father, not for another half an hour anyhow. By then I'll be on a bus. I'm coming home."

"But Ben just talked to your doctor today. He said you'd be in the hospital another two weeks."

"I left the hospital right after lunch. My mother always comes in the afternoon, and I couldn't face another one of her visits. She does nothing but complain about her health. *I'm* the one in the hospital, though it's really more of a mental institution, but *she* spends the whole time whining about her health, and not having money for her own hot tub. She was always like that, but she's worse now. It was such a dumb thing to do, coming down here."

"But Judith!"

"Don't be angry, and don't worry about me. I'm really quite well. In fact, I've never been better. That's one of the reasons I had to call you. I couldn't call from the hospital, there was never any privacy. And the food! It was just like everyone says about hospital food. It was so unwholesome. And I was starving, but even so, when the meals came, I would just look at the little shreds of meat in cold gluey gravy and cry. From hunger! And the food at my mother's was almost as bad in its own way. Microwave junk food, with the same awful gravy only piping hot. And endless pints of ice cream! Rhoda can eat a whole pint of ice cream while she's watching a game show. And breakfast? Breakfast is sugar-coated cereal *and* croissants. It would have made *anyone* bulimic to be with her for a week. I mean, Burger King would look like a health spa in comparison. Unconsciously I think that's why I came down here. Because I knew I'd get sick. But I'm *not* sick anymore, not really. I was *making* myself throw up. That night when you said you cured me? You really did! But I refused to accept the fact." She paused for breath, and added: "I must sound hysterical."

"You sound wrought up," William agreed.

"Do you know what it was?"

"What what was?"

"The problem, the anorexia. It's just what all the books about anorexia said it was. Sex. I refused to accept the idea that I was becoming a woman, that I was going to have breasts, and boyfriends, and all the rest of it. I didn't want to have a woman's body. And I *starved* myself so I wouldn't."

"Judith, you haven't been drinking, have you?"

Judith laughed. "Is that what I sound like? I sound drunk? Maybe I am, but not on alcohol. I'm drunk on movies. That's all I've been doing today. When I walked out of the hospital, I took the bus downtown, but I still didn't have any idea what I was going to do. So I went to see *Romeo and Juliet*. Oh, William, it was so beautiful. Not just beautiful, but— I don't know, I can't describe it. About fifteen minutes into the movie I started crying, and I didn't really stop crying till it was over, and then I stayed to see it a second time, and it was just the same, I couldn't stop crying. It made me realize that I'm not in touch with my own deepest feelings. Anyhow, at that point it was seven o'clock, and I was famished, so I went to the restaurant nearest to the theater, which was a Cuban restaurant, but not at all lower class, though my mother goes into a panic if she sees a word of Spanish anywhere, I don't know why she lives here, but the people in the restaurant were all very well dressed, and I ordered the first thing I saw on the menu on the wall, which was arroz con pollo, which turned out to be half a boiled chicken with a great heap of *beans* and *rice*, and all the while I was wolfing the stuff down I kept remembering scenes in the movie, and I would start crying all over again, right into my beans and rice, and at the same time I was enjoying the meal like no other meal I've ever eaten. I'm sure the waiter thought I must be crazy. *You* probably think I'm crazy."

"No. But it sounds like it must have been a great movie."

"Oh, William, it is! As soon as I'm back I want to take you to see it, if it's still playing somewhere. I never understood what all the fuss was about Shakespeare. When we had to read *Julius Caesar* and even when they showed us the movie, it was like being taken to a museum to look at all those battered old statues. I don't know, maybe I'm growing up. Maybe I should go back and look at the statues again."

For just a moment William thought he might try and stem the flood of Judith's monologue by telling her about the statue of "Mississippi—

Father of the Waters" he'd seen at the courthouse and the similar but less lasting impression it had made on him, but really he was more interested in hearing Judith rattle on than in trying to calm her down. "So then what happened?" he prompted.

"*Then* I went to another movie, though first I thought to call the hospital and explain that my mother had taken me out to dinner and I would be spending the night at her house—the hospital is really very lax, since you pay for the room you're in whether you're in it or not—and then I called my mother, who wasn't home, as usual, she's always out at a bar drinking, so I left a message on her machine saying I had a headache and please not to call till late in the morning. And then I went to see *Grease*. Have you seen *Grease*?"

"It's another movie?" He knew it was, but it was easier to ask leading questions than to spoil her story by explaining that he'd seen the last fifteen minutes of *Grease* on a double feature, but hadn't stayed to see the beginning.

"William, what century are you living in? I thought everyone at St. Tom's but me had seen *Grease*. It's a musical comedy with John Travolta and Olivia Newton-John. Who are both so wonderful! But then I started crying again! It was as though it was the same movie, but everyone was dressed in different costumes. They were singing these beautiful songs, rock and roll songs, which ordinarily don't have much effect on me, but tonight for the first time in my life I understood them!"

William was completely outside his own dream at this point, but it was as though he'd entered Judith's. What she was saying was so classic it was hard to take her seriously. "I didn't think rock and roll was supposed to be difficult to understand."

"No, of course not. Not for anyone in the world but me and Olivia Newton-John. God, did I *identify!*"

"Judith, I'm sure *Grease* is an unappreciated masterpiece, and when it's showing on a double feature with *Romeo and Juliet* we can see them together and compare notes. But I still don't understand why you're at a Greyhound bus station."

"I didn't have enough actual cash for an airplane ticket, unless I went standby, and I thought if my mother had found out I wasn't at the hospital, she might have them check the airports but not the bus station. Who would ever take a bus from Florida to Minneapolis?"

"No one. And maybe you shouldn't either."

"Oh, I guess I should have explained all that part right at the beginning. The thing is, my mother and this doctor, who I think she must have had an affair with at some point, are keeping me here as some kind of hostage. Isn't that awful? Like those poor captives in Iran. The thing is, when I got here I was determined not to let go of my anorexia. When you touched me that night and said I was cured, I got very upset. And angry. But I gradually did start to feel different about eating. I *wanted* to eat. All *sorts* of things I wouldn't have touched before that. Hamburgers! One day I went to Burger King and ate a Whopper! And I liked it! And didn't throw up afterward. But I did not want to give in. So when my mother phoned and said why didn't I come down for a visit, it seemed like a perfect excuse. I mean, I really do *hate* the way my mother eats, which is a classic anorexic syndrome. But I would get so hungry that I would eat all the same things she did, which did make me feel genuinely sick, but even at that I wouldn't have been vomiting after every meal if I hadn't made myself do it. Which is the next stage for most anorexics, bulimia. So, she took me to this *sinister* doctor who's a friend of hers, and he *incarcerated* me in his dreadful clinic. And I was stuck. Either I admitted there was nothing wrong with me, which I was still too stubborn to do, or I stayed on at the clinic and had to eat their terrible food. And all the while my mother was just gloating, because she figured she could keep me a hostage in Florida and get who knows how much money in child support."

"So you just up and left the hospital?"

"Finally. Today. Yes."

"Good for you."

"I don't know how you did what you did, William. But I am so grateful."

"Hey, listen, *you* did it."

"It would be silly for us to argue about it. How is summer school going?"

"Terrible. You were right about old Lilah Gear-heart. She's a lunatic. But I think Civics would be a pain even if Joan Rivers taught it. The Minnesota state constitution is inherently dull. The German class is dull, too, but only because I have to keep memorizing new vocabulary."

"You're going to grow up to be the world's most hardworking workaholic."

"Oh, it's not all nose to the grindstone. Today Mom and I had a grueling workout with a Frisbee that she'd found under somebody's shrubbery. And after I'd declared myself too tired to go on by sailing the Frisbee onto the roof of the garage, she let it be known that she's going to have a baby. Sometime before Christmas."

"How wonderful! Tell her how thrilled I am for her—but don't tell her till tomorrow morning. William, they're announcing the Nashville bus, I've got to go."

"Nashville?"

"That's where I transfer. I just thought: there's no reason you have to tell them I'm on a bus at all. Just say I called to tell you about the movies. Okay?"

"Yeah, but when Rhoda calls up to say you're a missing person, they'll start to worry."

"I'll phone them myself from Nashville. William, I've got to go: I love you."

"I love you too."

Judith hung up.

It was true then, all of it. Not that there had been any doubt after what had happened today to Jimmy Deeters. The only thing, really, that had given him to doubt at all had been the way that Judith's anorexia had seemed to get worse ever since his birthday, and then her being put into a hospital. That, and the fact that the caduceus had seemed inert. But in his dream Mercury had explained about that. What had he said? Listening to Judith on the phone, the dream had got all hazy. He could remember the last part, having to dissect the corpse that was laid out on some kind of tomb, or altar, and the corpse's penis shooting off the sperm, and then his embarrassment waking up and finding out that that much of the dream had not been a dream at all.

He got out of bed and went into the bathroom to wash his crotch, but he did it in the dark so as not to dispel any fragment of the dream he could still get hold of. A bowling pin: Mercury had thrown it to him and he'd put it into his pocket.

Then it all came back, the three questions he'd asked and the answers Mercury had given. His account was overdrawn, and interest charges were accruing. He would have to find another Jimmy Deeters or the caduceus would lose its power. And he had to do it soon if he wanted to give his unborn baby brother (for some reason he was certain it was going to be a boy) the birthday present of a clean slate of health. The prospect of finding new victims made him uneasy. When he'd seen Jimmy Deeters's mother on the Evening News, he'd begun to feel guilty about what he'd done. And maybe the death penalty was too drastic a punishment for Jimmy's crimes: blindness would have kept him from becoming a career criminal as effectively as death. In the future he would do well to temper his justice with a little more mercy. Also, he shouldn't use his power on strangers. Perhaps there'd been a worthwhile side to Jimmy Deeters that his court record would not have revealed. Maybe he had musical talent. Maybe he'd have joined the army in a year or so and turned all his aggressions to some constructive purpose. From now on, he vowed, he'd be more responsible in the ways he exercised his power.

By the time he'd arrived at this laudable conclusion he'd toweled himself dry and had changed into a fresh pair of pajamas. Then he got back between the bedsheets and dove effortlessly into the pool of a deep and dreamless sleep.

46

Lilah Gerhart was not vain about her appearance, but she was aware that her good looks were a professional asset and tried to dress accordingly. Adolescent children could be merciless toward the teachers they considered dowdy. Today, though she had no teaching duties per se, she'd worn her best summer dress, a striking cotton print with gigantic red flowers exploding on a field of white. Her lipstick precisely echoed the red of the flowers, as did the barrette that secured her jet-black hair in place above her left ear. Miss Gerhart's features were inherently dramatic—strong cheekbones, a firm chin, and a Roman nose—and she emphasized that drama quite consciously with makeup and a hairstyle that commanded attention. Teaching was a form of theater, and in the theater there is no place for reticence or false modesty.

Summer school had been over for a week, but she had agreed to come in to the office and help Mr. Paley, the new principal, prepare the schedule for the next school year. She had also agreed, reluctantly, to speak with the insufferable Michaels boy about the grade he'd received in Civics. The boy's stepfather had had the nerve to go directly to Mr. Paley with his complaint, but Mr. Paley had been quite firm and insisted that the matter properly was the concern of the teacher and the student, not of the principal and the parent. And so the appointment had been set up. Of course, it was not the grade in itself that was at issue but the boy's preposterous ambition of skipping from freshman to senior year and graduating from St. Tom's at the unheard-of age of fourteen. A C+ in Civics did not automatically doom the possibility of his entering the Early Admissions Program, but in combination with Miss Gerhart's strongly worded advisory note (she was the senior member of St. Tom's Early Admissions Program Committee) the boy could count on at least two more years before graduation. At least two.

At five minutes to ten, Miss Gerhart (who was always punctual herself, since she expected the same consideration from others) locked up the principal's office (Mr. Paley had not arrived yet; he, evidently, did not practice the courtesy of kings) and went down the hall to the Counseling Office. The Michaels boy was already there, waiting outside the door.

"Good morning, William," she said cheerfully. "Have you begun to enjoy what's left of the vacation, now that summer school is over?"

"Not a whole lot, Miss Gerhart. Not after I got my grade from you."

"Yes, I understand that you're not used to receiving anything less than an A. But I can assure you some of your fellow classmates would envy you your C plus. Dick Larsen, for one. The hockey team is going to have to find another goaltender this year, I'm afraid. But I don't consider myself to blame for that, or for your C plus, for that matter. A student's grades are based on his or her performance."

"I performed well enough on the final."

"And that's why your grade is as high as it is. But I would trust a bright young fellow like you to do well on any multiple-choice test. Personally, I think such tests have little place in a humanistic discipline like Civics. Fortunately for you, that is not how the State Board of Education views the matter."

"You mean you'd have flunked me if you could?"

"What you speak of as 'flunking' can also be regarded as an opportunity for growth, and yes, I would have liked to give you that opportunity. One of the essential tasks of secondary education, and in particular of the study of Civics, is to prepare the nation's young people to become concerned, responsible citizens. On the evidence of your term paper I feel I've failed at that task, while *you* have passed the course. I won't have another opportunity to correct my failure, and I regret that, for I think that if I could have had you again in my class for an entire school year, I might have begun to get through. Civics really ought not to be squeezed into two months of hard cramming, but again the State Board has other views. However, I'm not the only teacher here at St. Tom's. Perhaps Mr. Raab or Miss Milman will be able to succeed where I've failed. I hope so."

"And that's the reason you gave why I shouldn't be admitted to the Early Admissions Program—so Raab and Milman could have a chance at me?"

"Have a chance at you? That's a rather self-centered way to put it, isn't it? In any case, my note to the committee is a confidential matter. Yet the gist of it is easily summed up: I don't think you are either socially *or* intellectually mature enough to meet the challenges of an unstructured environment like the University."

"What about my SAT math scores? They look pretty intellectually mature, I'd say. They're better than the average grade that's required to get into Harvard."

"My, what a lot of research you seem to have done on the subject!" She pushed back the half of her hair that was not held in place by the barrette, a gesture that commonly precluded her more definitive statements. "Obviously, you're gifted in the area of math. But there are enrichment programs available right here at St. Tom's for our math prodigies. You're not the only one, you know. In any case, William, I did not agree to meet you to discuss my *confidential* recommendation to the Program Committee. I understood that you wished a fuller explanation of your grade in Civics."

William glared at her. His hostility was barely under control, and Miss Gerhart had to make a conscious effort not to tease him or to seem amused by his futile effort to adopt her own tone of implacable objectivity. She, after all, had had years to practice that tone. For someone so young and so aggrieved, he really was handling himself rather well.

"I would like to know why I got an F on my term paper." He took the term paper in question from his knapsack and placed it on the desk before Miss Gerhart.

Miss Gerhart placed her fingertips symmetrically at the back of her jawbone and craned forward in her chair to look at the term paper with an expression of polite curiosity tinged with repulsion, as though she'd been asked to examine a collection of insect specimens.

"I can see that I've written comments just beside the grade. In what way do you find them unclear?"

"For one thing, the comment on the front seems to contradict the shorter ones at the end of the paper. On the front you say I refuse to take a moral position, but on page seven where I talk about triage, you say, 'Repugnant,' and on the last page you wrote, 'This is cynicism pure and simple.' It sounds to *me* like I took a moral position, but you don't happen to agree with it."

She could see that she would have to be careful. The real reason for his F was that all but the last two pages of his paper had been copied verbatim from a reference book. She had seen too many such plagiarisms over the years to be mistaken about that, and the topic William had chosen to write on, "The Population Explosion," was one well calculated to expose such deceits, since the writers of children's reference books became more than usually bland and euphemistic on subjects with a potential for controversy. She'd spent an hour in the library trying to track down his source, but he'd had the foresight to copy from a book the school didn't possess, which meant that she had only her suspicions to go by. Had she been able to prove him a cheat, the boy would have had a lot more to regret than his C+. Lacking such proof, she'd had to content herself by giving the paper a failing grade. Her grounds for that grade were not indefensible, but she had been distinctly relieved when Mr. Paley had rejected the boy's stepfather's suggestion that he read the paper and judge its merits for himself.

"If there seems to be a contradiction, William, it is in your paper. The first several pages, in which you define the problem, struck me as simplistic and not at all up to the level an 'exceptional' student like yourself ought to be aiming for. You go to great lengths to explain the difference between an arithmetic and a geometric progression, but when it comes to the actual social issues involved you get very fuzzy and vague. What were your principal sources for your paper, by the way? There are no footnotes, and no bibliography."

"I used the *Encyclopaedia Britannica* mostly. Though I didn't just copy it out. I put it into my own words."

"Did you, indeed?" She smiled knowingly, as though inviting him to share her amusement at his lie, but he was not that easy a nut to crack. "Well, you'll remember, when I spoke in class of what I expected in your term papers, I emphasized the need to deal with the *ethical* dimensions of the topics you chose. And through most of your paper you seem to be exerting all your intelligence to do just the opposite. But then, when you begin to talk about 'triage' and you suggest that medical assistance be *withdrawn* from Third World countries that don't achieve Zero Population Growth at once, it's as though another writer had taken over. And that is where my first response was simply to say 'Repugnant.' That doesn't mean, however, that your paper constitutes a moral position. If anything, it's amoral, and it doesn't represent a 'position' at all, since your conclusions don't follow logically from your first statement of the case."

"But they do," William asserted loftily. "I'm not saying anything Malthus didn't say almost two hundred years ago. If famine doesn't get them, then epidemics will, or they'll kill each other fighting for dwindling resources. All that is already happening. Would Malthus have got an F, too?"

"If Malthus had written *this* paper"—she dipped her head toward the offending document—"he would have. You simply didn't work hard enough, William, and you know it. When your first project for a report on the operation of the Hennepin County Courthouse proved to be too much for you to handle, and there were only two weeks left till your term paper was due, you changed horses in the middle of the stream, thinking that you could recycle someone else's prose through your word processor and add a few paragraphs of cheap cynicism and that I wouldn't know the difference. But I'm not that dumb, William. I've been teaching a long time, and I know when a preadolescent Machiavelli is trying to pull the wool over *my* eyes." She concluded this peroration with a triumphant smile, leaned back in the swivel chair as far as its spring permitted, and waited for one of two possibilities: his surrender or his retreat.

"I don't think there's another teacher in this school who would have read this paper and given it an F."

"Thank you, William, I consider that a compliment. But in fact I think there may be a few others who can detect a rotten egg when it's put right under their noses. I expect you'll have ample opportunity in the next two or three years to discover for yourself whether or not that's so."

"You really have it in for me, don't you, Miss Gear-heart?"

"I think our discussion is over, William. I'm not obliged to sit here and listen to childish epithets. You can go now."

When he was halfway to the door, she said, "Aren't you forgetting something?"

He turned around. "Am I? What?"

"This." She picked up the term paper between thumb and forefinger and held it out at arm's length, as though it were a source of contagion. "You seem to value this much more than I do. I think you should keep it for future reference."

William took the paper and hesitated a moment, as though expecting her to say more. When she did not, he left the room.

There was a strange, tingling sensation in her hand, the kind of pins-and-needles feeling one gets when a limb goes to sleep from being held too long in an awkward position. She flexed her fingers until the sensation went away. "Pig piss!" she exclaimed with a vehemence that coated the desktop with a fine spray of spittle. She pursed her lips with distaste and looked about for her purse, in which there was always a packet of Kleen-exes, but of course her purse was back in the principal's office.

She got up from the desk, pulled at the seams of her dress to smooth away any wrinkles, and stuck out her tongue at the framed photograph of John Dewey, the great philosopher of education. Then she went back to the principal's office, where Mr. Paley had just begun to perform the ritual pencil sharpening with which he began his day's work.

"Good morning, Miss Gerhart. I see that, as usual, you've got a head start on me."

"Good morning, Mr. Paley. Eat shit and die."

Mr. Paley put down the pencils beside the pencil sharpener and regarded Miss Gerhart with alarm. She could not have said what he thought she had said, it was simply not in her nature. He tried to imagine what she could possibly have said that could be confused with such an obscenity.

She had sat down at the worktable on which she had already spread out an array of three-by-five cards, each representing a particular schoolroom and period of the day. She had explained her system, but Mr. Paley had not given the explanation much attention at the time. As she sat there, studying the cards, her thin red lips suddenly retracted from her teeth and the muscles about her nose and eyes convulsed. The effect was uncannily like the snarling of a dog, except that it was soundless.

She became aware of his attention, and looked up with a sunny smile. "Yes, Mr. Paley? Do you have a question?"

"I was wondering if you were feeling . . . entirely all right."

She sighed. "In fact, I have just had a rather trying encounter with the Michaels boy, who I was telling you about yesterday. Poopy-pot! Or I should say 'whom,' shouldn't I? About whom I was telling you. I'm afraid he became rather rude."

Mr. Paley did not know what to make of Miss Gerhart's behavior. He'd been warned by the assistant principal, and by his predecessor as well, to expect a certain amount of eccentricity from Miss Gerhart, but surely this went beyond the bounds of eccentricity.

"My colleague Miss Milman has a saying: 'Hell hath no fury like a straight-A student the first time he gets a C.' That's so true, isn't it?"

Mr. Paley nodded.

Then Lilah Gerhart leaned forward, clutching the sides of the desk, and began to bark. It was a high-pitched yapping bark, like a terrier's. She continued barking for a little after Mr. Paley had turned his back on her and hastened from the room, at which point it finally struck her what she had been doing. She had been *barking* at the principal. He must have thought she'd lost her mind!

But she knew that was not the case. Her mind was as lucid as ever. She had had a nervous breakdown, four years ago, but that had been nothing but a case of frayed nerves, and after a few weeks in less stressful circumstances, she'd been fine. This was not the same thing.

She had always had an extraordinary memory for any phone number she'd called more than a few times, and she was able to dial the number of her old psychotherapist without having to consult the address book in her purse.

After three rings a receptionist answered and said, "Dr. Helbron's office. Can I help you?"

Miss Gerhart took a deep breath and said, "This is Miss Motherfucker Piss Cunt. I seem to be having some kind of . . . speech problem. And I'd like to—"

But the receptionist, who had never before had to deal with a patient suffering from Tourette syndrome, had already hung up in indignation.

47

When school began again, the Wednesday after Labor Day, Miss Gerhart was no longer on the teaching staff. Her last action as a faculty member had been to revise the memorandum she'd written for William's file, urging much more earnestly that he not be allowed into the Early Admissions Program. The language of the memo was so intemperate that the remaining two members of the Early Admissions Program Committee had to wonder if it were not a further symptom of her disorder. One of the members, Mr. Thorsen, who had tutored William in math and seen him accomplish four years' work in one without any apparent strain, was so incensed by the tone of Miss Gerhart's memo that he became William's champion. He obtained a fresh printout of the term paper (the original with Miss Gerhart's comments on it had been used as kindling, William confessed, to start a fire in the backyard barbecue) and insisted that Mr. Paley read it.

Mr. Paley was cautious in such matters, slow to move, and being moved, not likely to move far. He had a strong conviction that a principal should never override a teacher's decision, especially in regard to grades. Inevitably, some teachers would abuse their power, but so long as their actions did not inspire insurrection, it was better not to challenge them. The alternative, in his view, was anarchy and a return to the sixties. However, there were reasons why this case could be considered an exception. Miss Gerhart no longer taught at St. Tom's and so would not feel the slight to her authority, while Mr. Thorsen's advocacy ought to be accommodated before it got any fiercer. He'd known other men of Thorsen's apparently mild disposition to get some such bee in their bonnets and become perfect fanatics. The boy was obviously bright enough, and while the loss of even a single student's tuition was not to be regarded lightly (St. Tom's had a very tight budget), there was the possibility for some discreet publicity that would suggest St. Tom's was a breeding ground for young overachievers. Mr. Paley allowed himself to be persuaded: the disputed Civics grade was quietly emended to a B, and William was allowed to enter the Early Admissions Program.

William could not have been happier, not on a regular day-to-day basis. His classes were much more interesting as a senior than when he was a freshman. He wasn't in over his head, but it wasn't so much like wading at the kiddie end of the pool. American History, with Miss Gerhart's old crony Mr. Raab, was the only class he felt any real aversion for, and even that wasn't as bad as Civics had been, since he was able to keep a low profile and not become one of Raab's preferred sparring partners and the butt of his sarcasms against "Mondale Me-Too liberals." That had become Judith's destiny, but she actually seemed to enjoy the little "Socratic" dialogues that Raab engineered, and to do Raab credit, her grades didn't suffer for her services as strawman and scapegoat. At the end of the first six weeks she had an A, while William's careful neutrality got him only a B.

At home everything seemed as bright and cheery as if they all were auditioning to appear as the average happy family of four featured in an ad for absolutely anything. Sondra had spent a small fortune on maternity clothes and glided around the house looking like a medieval fashion show, while Judith had filled out with the same almost-overnight blossoms-on-the-bough suddenness to become a hypothetical candidate for St. Tom's Homecoming Queen, hypothetical because St. Tom's didn't have a football team whose coming home could be celebrated with a dance. She looked terrific, but beyond looking terrific she radiated good feelings, high spirits, and (in her own account of it) joie de vivre. "I feel just like Cinderella," she confided to William one night after a game of fast but noncompetitive Ping-Pong. "The only difference is the clock never strikes twelve."

Even Ben was swept away by these spring tides, to the degree at least that he, too, stopped smoking. Lacking Sondra's powers of self-command and her sense of decorum, Ben's battle against the weed was conducted at center stage of the family theater, with much moaning and groaning, and momentous falls from grace when a late night brandy would tip the scales of willpower and send him out of the house in a panic to find a cigarette vending machine, forays from which he would return repentant and crestfallen. Gradually, however, the crises became rarer, and the lamentations diminished to ordinary kvetching and self-deprecation. Ben even began to use the exercise bicycle in Sondra's bedroom and to partner her in the exercises recommended in the book on natural childbirth. However, Judith proved to be a better partner, as Ben had no knack for relaxing.

Through it all William experienced the delight, all the keener for having to be kept secret, of knowing himself to be their benefactor. When he saw his mother sitting cross-legged on the living room's white carpet rocking back and forth in time to "Puff the Magic Dragon," it was as though *he* were singing the tune that had enchanted her. And when he came upon Judith whirling about the house in a black leotard augmented with a red tablecloth while *The Rite of Spring* blared at top volume from all three sets of downstairs speakers, it was as though he'd been conducting the music and summoning with flicks and jabs of his baton all her contortions and dashings about.

When Judith saw William in the doorway, she didn't interrupt her gyrations (the music had come to the "Evocation of the Ancestors" and had momentarily calmed down) but gestured for him to join her on the floor where she was spinning around alternately on her knees and on her behind. He declined, on the grounds that he had homework to do but really because he would have been embarrassed to make such a fool of himself, even though it did look like fun. He'd never been able to cut loose that way, even with rock music. "I'm too *inhibited!*" he shouted out over the music, and Judith just nodded and paid him no more attention, flicking her sweat-drenched hair about like the mane of a horse, then bending backwards slowly and flailing her arms convulsively when there was a bleat of brasses or a cymbal crash. William himself could never predict just when these explosions would come, but Judith connected with almost every one and seldom got faked out. William was impressed, since even though *The Rite of Spring* was one of his favorite pieces of music, he was always going *blip* when Stravinsky was going *blat!* and vice versa. This was all the more remarkable since Judith had never been known to dance so much as a two-step until this fall, when she'd started taking a course in Interpretive Movement in order to meet St. Tom's Phys Ed requirement.

The overall change in Judith since she'd returned from Florida was almost spooky. She seemed another person. It wasn't just that her face and figure had filled out, but the animating spirit within this new and ampler flesh had changed, too. She moved differently. There was still something abrupt and birdlike about her, but the bird you might be put in mind of was more likely now to be a swan than a stork. She had started wearing makeup and doing inventive things with her hair. Gone were the Peter Pan blouses, the droopy pastel cardigans, the pleated tartan skirts. In their place was an array of clothing that seemed to present a different hypothesis of the essential Judith Winckelmeyer every day. Sondra's drawers and closets were filled with years of impulse buying, clothes that had been worn once or twice (or never at all) and then retired to mothball status: shirts and sweaters in all the colors fashion had ever thought to decree; pounds of bracelets, bangles, pins, and beads; the jeans of all major designers; miniskirts and maxiskirts and skirts that formed spiraling, caressing draperies as you walked. Sondra tended to buy off the rack, and many of these old purchases, when they were exhumed from their mothballs, proved to fit the new Judith better than they'd ever fit the old Sondra. Without having to spend a cent of her father's money, Judith had a wardrobe to rival any at St. Tom's, and she'd taken to it like a duck (or a swan) to water.

Meanwhile, since some time in mid-September, the caduceus had begun to regain its former power. Each time William took it from its hiding place in a box of Saran-Wrapped comic books, the tingle he felt on touching it seemed perceptibly greater. Though he could not measure this increase, he knew that the power involved was more than the power of suggestion and that somewhere out beyond William's ken the caduceus was doing its work. Turnage, with each flick of his 24k Cartier lighter, had been planting seeds of carcinoma in some smoker's lungs, and those seeds were growing. The effect of this impending harvest on the caduceus had not become apparent until (as Mercury had explained) the outstanding debt for Turnage's and William's family's "health insurance" had been paid in full. Now at last the shifting balance of plus and minus had been restored and soon, as further seedlings ripened to mature cancers, it would be possible to bring William's unborn sibling within the charmed circle inscribed by the caduceus about the Winckelmeyer household.

On the whole William was glad that the office of the American Tobacco Alliance was so far away, and that his victims, however deserving they might be of their fate, were not known to him personally. Whatever their sufferings, they had only themselves to blame. The warning was there on every pack of cigarettes they'd bought: SMOKING CAUSES LUNG CANCER, HEART DISEASE, EMPHYSEMA, AND MAY COMPLICATE PREGNANCY. They had not only defied that warning, but (those who worked at ATA) had denied it, as well. William had only accelerated the process of justice. He felt no guilt, but neither did he feel any curiosity, except for the effect all this might be having on Turnage himself. Had he become aware yet of the shadows gathering round him? How long could he maintain his bluff facade before the TV cameras, staring down the truth and spitting tobacco juice at his accusers?

The question was answered on the same evening that William had come upon Judith performing *The Rite of Spring*. Ben called from his office, saying that he would be home late and urging them all to watch, and to make a tape of, a TV program called "The *Good* News Hour," which was broadcast on a cable channel at seven thirty. He wouldn't say why, only that they were certain to be astonished.

"The *Good* News Hour" was sponsored by the Son of Man Foundation of Wilmington, Delaware, and was devoted, in the words of its hostess (and the copresident of the foundation), Bess McKinley, to "all the news you'll never see on NBC." For the first fifteen minutes of the program this news consisted of strange portents prefiguring the soon-approaching end of the world (a tornado—or very nearly a tornado—in Delaware's Kent County, where no tornado had ever been reported before; and strange red stains that had appeared overnight on the screen of a drive-in movie theater outside of Macon, Georgia, that showed X-rated movies) and of the wonderful cures effected by faith in Jesus through the healing ministry of his servant, and Bess's husband, Hal McKinley. There was also an inspirational story about a Girl Scout troop in Wilmington that had tied over a thousand yellow ribbons to their neighborhood trees by way of demonstrating the nation's concern for the hostages in Iran, and this was followed by a personal, off-the-cuff declaration by Bess concerning her own lack of confidence in the leadership of President Carter. "Are you sure," Judith asked Sondra, "that this is the program that Father wanted us to tape?"

"This is it, I wrote it down." Sondra seemed just as puzzled. "There must be a reason. Be patient."

After a brief but earnest appeal for contributions to the Son of Man Foundation, Bess McKinley patted the blond beehive of her hair and smiled intently at the camera. "Tonight's special guest on 'The *Good* News Hour' is a man who needs no introduction to any sports fans who are watching. He is none other than Dan Turnage, longtime second baseman for the Minnesota Twins. Welcome to 'The *Good* News Hour,' Dan."

The camera shifted to the right to show Dan Turnage, who said something that his lapel mike did not pick up. Bess leaned forward carefully to help him adjust the mike. Turnage seemed much less self-assured and brassy with Bess McKinley than he'd been during his infamous appearance on "60 Minutes," a clip from which was shown by way of illustrating the work he'd undertaken since leaving the baseball diamond acting as a spokesman for ATA. When the clip was over, Bess smiled at Turnage and asked: "Well, Dan, do you still feel the same about smoking now?"

The camera moved in until Turnage's face filled the whole screen. "May God forgive me, Bess. May God forgive me for all my lies."

"Do you mean to say, Dan, that there really is a link between smoking and cancer? And that you knew it at the time of your appearance on '60 Minutes'?"

"Is there anyone who doesn't know it in his heart of hearts, Bess? I only denied it because I was paid a large salary to do so by the tobacco industry. I figured *every* smoker knows what he's doing and so the fact that I was saying, 'Hey, kids, smoking is okay,' didn't really fool anyone. Well, maybe it didn't fool them exactly, but it did something just as bad. It showed them how to harden their hearts, how to defy the judgment of the Lord. I can see that now, because I've been born again, but I couldn't see that then. Sin made me blind."

"Praise the Lord. That's quite a turnaround for you, Dan."

"It certainly is, Bess, and I'll tell you how I came to it. It wasn't the Surgeon General's Report, and it wasn't any so-called scientific experiments on mice and rats. It was the living hand of God. He plucked my friends from me, one by one, the men I worked with, and played golf with, and dined with at expensive restaurants. All of a sudden, Bess, they started to come down with lung cancer, one after another, like ducks in a shooting gallery."

"Could you tell us who some of those men were, Dan?"

"I can tell you three that've died in just the past two months. The first was Sid Kearns, who was one of three top men at ATA. Sid used to smoke like a chimney. Then there was my secretary, Rita Baker, who was also a heavy smoker and the mother of three kids. Finally, just the Monday before last, the president of ATA himself, Maurice Myers, died. His obituaries just said 'due to natural causes.' ATA doesn't want any of this getting into the newspapers, and the names I've mentioned are only the tip of the iceberg. They're doing all they can to hush it up, and so far they've succeeded. I happen to know the whole story because I personally know the persons involved."

Bess nodded and turned to the camera. "I guess I should have explained right at the start of our talk that Dan is no longer working for the tobacco industry. He left the American Tobacco Alliance three weeks ago, and from now on I'm happy to say he'll be putting his talent to work for the Son of Man Foundation. And that's one reason why 'The *Good* News

Hour' has been able to bring you this important news story before any of the national networks."

"And the other reason," Dan put in, with some of his former feistiness, "is that none of the networks dares to touch it. And why do you think that is? It's because *they* are smokers, and they refuse to see the sign the Lord is showing us. They are the same as I was before the scales were lifted from my eyes. 'Oh, it's a coincidence,' they'll say. Or they'll say, 'Well, they were all old men, they had to die of something.' Or they'll say, 'So you know three people who've died from lung cancer, so what? There's thousands more dying from the effects of smoking every day. Only at ATA would that be considered news.' And they laughed at me, Bess! Behind my back, they were laughing at me. As though I were still just a PR man, trying to drum up publicity for a client. I'll tell you, Bess, I know now what it must have been like for Jonah when the Lord came to him and said, 'Jonah, you've got to go right now to those sinners in Sodom and Gomorrah, and tell them to stop their wickedness and fornications.' Jonah knew if he did what the Lord told him, they'd just laugh at him, but he had to do it anyway. That's my situation exactly."

"Actually, Dan," Bess said in a tone of gentle reproof, "it was to Nineveh that the Lord sent Jonah: 'Arise, go to Nineveh, that great city, and cry against it; for their wickedness is come up before me.' Jonah, chapter 1, verse 2."

"Sorry, Bess, it's been a while since I've read the Good Book. But you get my idea."

"I understand that you were a smoker yourself, Dan."

"I was, but not anymore, Bess. And never again. It wasn't easy to stop, even with the Lord's help. I still wake up in the morning and reach for that pack of cigarettes, but then I remember Sid and Rita and Maurice, and other good friends who are sick right now, some already in the hospital, and I know I'd be there, too, if it weren't for the grace of the Lord."

"Yes," Bess agreed, "the Lord is our refuge and our strength, and he *will* spare the sinner who comes to him with a contrite and repentant heart. There is more joy in heaven over one sinner that repents than for the ninety-nine just persons who need no repentance. That is the good news we're here to tell you today on 'The *Good* News Hour.' Thank you, Dan, for being with us, and I hope you will be back soon to tell us more about these remarkable developments. And thank you, good people, for your prayers and contributions."

A hymn tune swelled up from the background, and Bess's face faded from the screen to show a slowly spinning globe banded at the equator with the name of the show, and below that the address to which contributions could be sent to support the continuing work of the Son of Man Foundation.

The next program—"Ever Since Noah," an educational series on Creation Science—was well under way before Sondra thought to lean forward and turn off the recorder. The movement made her grimace with effort. Her pregnancy was well advanced, and even in her billowing maternity gowns she seemed immense and ungainly.

There was a long silence. They all went on looking at the blank screen of the TV so as not to be looking at each other. Finally Judith said aloud what they had all been thinking: "He may be born again, but *I* can't tell any difference."

Sondra lifted her eyebrows in ironic agreement, but felt obliged to say, "We mustn't judge."

"It is a weird coincidence though, wouldn't you say?" Judith ventured.

William and Sondra had to agree.

48

On October 21 the Philadelphia Phillies won the World Series as Steve Carlton and Tug McGraw pitched them to a 4–1 victory over the Kansas City Royals. Within minutes of that victory, as William, in his own room, was computing energy changes in various reactions for the next day's chemistry class, he got a long distance phone call from Dan Turnage in Philadelphia, reminding him that he now owed Turnage two hundred fifty dollars. William had long ago spent the money Ben had given him on his birthday and he didn't have ten dollars to his name, let alone two hundred and fifty. It seemed mean of Turnage, and even slightly threatening, to be so quick to demand a settling of the score. In fact, ever since the Series had started and there seemed to be an even chance that Turnage's long-shot prediction might come true, William had been hoping their bet would quietly be forgotten, out of deference to the fact that any official, business connection between Turnage and Ben had been severed by his departure to the greener pastures of the Son of Man Foundation. Instead, Turnage, who was calling from Veterans Stadium, positively gloated over his having won what had seemed, back in April, a sucker bet.

William got more and more resentful as Turnage did his own précis of the major plays of the day's game, but he did promise to mail Turnage a check as soon as he could, for which purpose Turnage dictated his new address at the office of the Son of Man Foundation in Wilmington, Delaware.

"We saw you on TV last week," William remarked before Turnage could hang up.

"Uh-huh."

"You certainly have changed your mind about cigarette smoking."

"Yes I have."

Turnage didn't seem disposed to discuss his new views, but William persisted. "How many other people at ATA have actually come down with lung cancer, besides the three you named?"

"A few."

"Is it classified information? Is there some reason you can't tell me?"

There was a long pause, and when Turnage answered it was in a different tone of voice, "Okay, I don't know why I'm telling you this—I don't owe you any favors, or your dad either, but the situation in Baltimore is pretty desperate. ATA is going belly-up. They're rushing through the paperwork so they can officially cease to exist a day or two after the election, when they figure there'll be the least attention from the media. I don't suppose there's much your dad can do about it with that little advance notice, but for what it's worth, now he knows. Any more smart questions?"

"You didn't really answer the question I asked."

"I answered it, you just weren't listening. Get that check off to me pronto, you understand? And next time think twice before you bet against a pro." Turnage hung up.

Ben was not home yet, and William didn't look forward to being the messenger of Turnage's news. ATA funded most of MIMA's research; if ATA sank, it didn't seem too likely that MIMA could escape being dragged down with it. In hindsight the logic of this seemed so inevitable that William wondered how he had failed to foresee the results of the curse he'd placed on Turnage's lighter. There were not that many dominoes involved.

He decided he would tell his mother the bad news and let her pass it on to Ben. He also decided that at the same time he would take the caduceus from its hiding place and use it for one final benevolent action—and then, never again. He would extend to his unborn brother the birthday present of a lifetime of unfailing health, and trust that the havoc being wreaked in the corporate ranks of ATA would suffice to cover the cost of such a generous gift. He'd long ago worked out a rhyme that seemed in its thoroughness and categorical simplicity to be secure from being construed to mean something it wasn't intended to mean, and now, as he grasped the caduceus tightly he pronounced the words of that rhyme:

> *To the child within my mother,*
> *Whether my sister or my brother,*
> *This hand imparts a long and healthy life*
> *Unthreatened by disease or surgeon's knife.*

The idea of using simply his own hand to channel the power of the caduceus had come to him as he had watched "The *Good* News Hour" and seen a montage of healings performed by Hal McKinley. In each shot the camera had been focused tightly on McKinley's right hand as it rested on the forehead or arthritic hands or crippled legs of the person to be cured. It seemed an efficient technique.

William found his mother in her own room, sitting up in bed and eating dry-roasted peanuts directly from the jar. A paperback romance, open to where she'd stopped reading, rested precariously on the basketball of her belly. William told her about Turnage calling to collect on his bet and what he'd revealed about ATA.

Sondra sighed. "That is bad news, but I doubt Ben will be surprised. Surely, it was only a matter of time. ATA couldn't have kept going on with business as usual much longer. They were lucky that Turnage's story didn't receive any more notice than—oh!" She drew a sharp breath, and the paperback on her belly fell to the bedspread.

"Aah!" She let out the breath in a long sigh.

William looked alarmed. "It's not starting now, is it?"

"No, this is just practice. Braxton Hicks contractions is what the book calls it. Oh! Oh, feel how *hard* it is now." She took his hand and placed it on her abdomen, then closed her eyes and bent her head back. William closed his eyes too, and under his breath he recited again the words of his fraternal blessing. Slowly the flesh beneath his fingers grew less rigid, as though it were a leaking balloon. Sondra sighed a deeper sigh.

It was done.

"Isn't that strange?" Sondra said. "And now I can feel its little feet kicking at my rib cage. It doesn't like it when I'm on my back, because then it's resting on my spine."

William felt overcome by a strange shyness, almost a sense of shame. "I'd better go finish my homework," he said.

"Here, take these peanuts." She handed him the jar. "I've eaten too many already."

When William was back in his own room, he dialed the old St. Paul phone number. He let the phone ring more than twenty times, hoping if Madge was at work that Grandma O. would eventually stir herself to answer it, but she never did. He was hoping to be able to get the money to pay Turnage from the trust fund that Madge set up for him from the insurance proceeds. Then, when he visited the house, he meant to return the caduceus to the place where he'd found it, buried in the loose insulation in the attic. He couldn't bring himself to deal with it in any more irrevocable way, but at least in the Obstschmecker attic it would not be tempting him to take some spur-of-the-moment revenge. He wanted the caduceus out of sight and out of mind, as it had been until his thirteenth birthday.

Why did he want that? That was a question he managed pretty well to evade. If he had had to give a reason, he would have claimed it was the working of his conscience. In fact, he was beginning to be afraid.

49

There is another darkness than the darkness of the night, an inner darkness that corresponds to what is called the inner light, and this darkness (the light, as well) is visible only to spirits who have passed beyond this life and, sometimes, briefly, to those with whom such spirits are able to communicate. Henry could see such visible darkness now, curling like the surf of some immense black ocean over the rooftops of Willowville, engulfing and blotting out the incandescent lights of the houses, the street lamps, and the moving cars. Mountain climbers can witness a similar sight, looking down into a valley as it fills with turbulent vapors. It was beautiful, but only as the coilings of a very large and deadly snake might be beautiful viewed in a documentary movie or through the thick glass of a vivarium.

Henry enjoyed no such safe vantage with regard to the darkness that flowed across the lawns and seeped into the houses arrayed below him. Within those mists, invisible to living eyes, he would be blinded; their fumes, undetectable by mortal senses, could suffocate and infect a spirit's incorruptible flesh. Even from this distance he was filled with abhorrence, and yet he must, for Billy's sake, enter that miasma and try to prevent what the roiling darkness declared, by its very presence, to be a predestined and unavoidable fate.

From within that darkness flesh tugged at him. The long chain of chromosomal causality that links the living, the dead, and the yet unborn invited his descent, spiderlike, along its trembling filaments. That attenuated thread was all that still linked him to the brutalities, hungers, and horrors of physical life, and he did not wish to trust himself to it. There was a defect in the thread that only his own early death had prevented him from experiencing within his lifetime. But the thread still might snap, unable to support his passage down into the black surf of mortal life, and he would fall into the darkness and be dissolved into a flux of immaterial energy. Or, worse, the thread would come untethered at its farther end, and the tainted chromosomal heritage would unspool through another life still more ill-fated than Billy's or his own or any of the other spinners of the thread. Should that come to pass, should the bloodline be perpetuated, the consequences would be felt, as an infection and convulsing pains, all along the length of the thread: for in eternity the ancestor suffers for the evils of his progeny—unto, in the prophetic words of Exodus, the third and fourth generation. And so it was not only solicitude for his son that moved Henry to attempt to avert what now could clearly be foreseen; it was, much more, a fear for what he would suffer himself if the thread were spun out to a longer length.

50

"Do you know," Judith said, assuming a kneeling position on the cowhide laid down as a hearth rug over the white carpet, "my first real memory of you is from Halloween. It was years ago, when Sondra and I came visiting the place on Calumet. Remember?"

"Vaguely. I remember you brought over a jack-o'-lantern bigger than the one my dad had already made."

"You were dressed as a doctor."

"That's right, Young Frankenstein."

"But I can't remember how I was dressed."

"A witch, I think."

She shook her head, and the fake diamond pin in her hair twinkled in the darkness. "That doesn't sound right."

William poked at the embers and produced a brief flaring up of the flames that gave Judith's bare arms and shoulders a wonderful tawny glow. She was still dressed in the flowing saffron-colored tunic she'd worn to the school's masquerade dance, but she'd taken off her long-thonged sandals the moment she'd got back to the house. The sandals and the crescent-shaped pin in her hair had come from Sondra's endless supply of junk clothes; the tunic Judith had made herself. She was the Greek goddess Artemis.

She had wanted William to go to the dance as her brother Apollo, even offered to make his costume for him, but he'd balked at the suggestion. Instead he'd dug up an old green track suit, smeared his face and hands with green hunting makeup, added an 89-cent green shower cap, and said he was a Martian. It was easily the least fussy and cheapest costume at the dance, and it had the further unplanned advantage that since the makeup rubbed off at the lightest touch no one had wanted to dance with him. Judith had not danced much either, but that was because the thongs of her sandals kept slipping down from her thin calves unless they were tied so tightly they were painful. They'd left at the first offer of a ride.

"I remember now: I was St. Clare. St. Francis's sister." She laughed in the nervous way of someone looking at an old and unbecoming family snapshot.

"That's right. You had on some kind of gunnysack. Quite a change from tonight."

"From a saint to a goddess? It's a logical progression. And besides, Clare and Artemis were both virgins."

William poked at the fire some more, by way of steering the conversation in some other direction than sex. Sex was fun to talk about only with boys his own age, where the rules were clear as to what lies you could get away with and how far you could carry certain lines of speculation. But with your own three-years-older sister, what could be spoken of? You could tease her about boyfriends or about her vanity, and that was it. But Judith didn't have any boyfriends, and though she was beginning to be beautiful, she wasn't vain about it. Happy, in a Cinderella-ish way, but that wasn't the same as vain.

"Speaking of virgins," Judith said, "have you heard what they're saying about Elizabeth Naughton?"

When he shook his head, she leaned closer and lowered her voice. "She was pregnant."

"And she isn't now?"

"They say she had an abortion. In August!"

"Is that a bad month for abortions or something?"

She smiled, but at once corrected it to a frown. "Abortion isn't something to joke about."

"So what is the proper way for us to deal with it? Should we go up to her after English class and tell her she's guilty of murder and insist that she wear a big M on all her clothes?"

"William, abortion is a serious crime."

"Liz isn't a Catholic, is she?"

"That doesn't make any difference."

"Not to you. It probably does to her. Seriously, Judith, lots of women have had abortions, and if you're going to live in the world with them, you can't go around staging a protest anywhere you've sniffed out a sin."

"Well, how would you feel if I told you she'd murdered Mr. Paley?"

"I'd be curious to know why. Was he the father, is that what you're implying?"

"Will-yum! I just chose Mr. Paley as a random example. Be serious."

"You always say 'be serious' when I start to win an argument. And it's always the same argument. If *you'd* had an abortion and felt guilty about it, I could understand your being so obsessed with the idea."

"I don't deny it's an obsession and that my own feelings get tangled up in it. This summer when I went down to visit her, I found out that my mother had had an abortion before she had me. She told me that the last time she visited me in the hospital, and she added that if Father had had his way I'd have been an abortion, too."

"I guess, if you look at things from an either/or point of view, we all of us can be considered failed abortions."

Judith clamped down on the impulse to laugh so that it emerged as a kind of muffled sneeze. "You're just trying to provoke me. Why do you always have to act out the part of a bratty kid brother?"

"Did *I* bring up the subject of abortion? Anyhow, I wouldn't necessarily credit everything your mother says on the subject of Ben. She obviously holds a grudge against him, and I wouldn't put it past her to have made up the whole thing, knowing how you'd react. Besides, that's all ancient history. Ben's certainly not guilty of promoting abortion these days, is he? Speaking of which, isn't it getting late for them to still be at their party? Mom's in no shape to party all night long."

"Actually, sometimes at the end of a pregnancy there's a period when you get this great charge of energy and you feel up to anything. That's what the book says anyhow. It's such a miracle, isn't it? The more I think about it, the more amazing it is. Two little cells connect and the result is everything we think, everything we do."

Somehow, no matter what she said, his impulse was to contradict her. He knew he should stop it, but it was like chewing fingernails or scratching poison ivy. "If you're speaking of *us*, there'd have been four cells. But a miracle? Why is what ova and sperm cells do any more miraculous than what cancer cells do? Or hair follicles? Any cell just does what it's programmed to. It's like a robot with a minicomputer telling it, 'Now do this, now do that.'"

"Oh, William, you're such a romantic. It gives me goose bumps when you talk that way."

"I'm not saying that miracles don't happen down at the level of the individual cell, only that it's hard to tell the difference between a miracle and business-as-usual. We just don't know how things happen down there."

"We could find out," Judith said in a tone of mock suggestiveness, which she couldn't quite bring off. When William looked up in surprise, she blushed and turned her head.

The easiest thing to do was pretend she hadn't said it, or at least that it didn't mean what it seemed to. William erected an impromptu barricade of philosophy, trotting out a neat idea he'd discovered in a book in the school library called *Six Before Breakfast*, a collection pointing out the paradoxes that were involved from a scientific viewpoint in the various miracles reported in the Old and New Testaments, such as the quantity of water it would have taken to produce a global flood or how the sun could not have stood still in the sky without the earth stopping its rotation and what the results of that would be, according to the laws of inertia. This particular paradox had to do with the Virgin Birth and the nature of Christ's genetic makeup. Was he a haploid, with chromosomes only from his mother? Or did he also have a set of chromosomes from God the Father, and if so, wouldn't it be possible, at least in theory, to create a genetic map of God's chromosomes? Admittedly, there are a lot of genes in the makeup of any individual, millions, maybe billions, but still a finite number. And once gene splicing became an exact science, would it then be possible, in theory, to duplicate what God had done and create another Jesus in the laboratory?

Judith listened patiently to his whole account, and when he was done her only comment was: "It's Young Frankenstein all over again."

Before he could insist that it was a serious theological problem the phone rang. The cordless phone was not in its cradle, so William went into the kitchen to use the wall phone. It was Ben calling from the Reagan fund-raiser to say that he and Sondra would be spending the night downtown at the Radisson, since Sondra insisted that he was too drunk to be allowed to drive home, and she was too tired. "And anyhow we're still having fun. What have you kids been up to? Any ghosts come to the door begging for candy?"

"Not so far. We've just been sitting in front of the fireplace, talking. Did you want to talk to Judith?"

"No, just have a happy Halloween." Ben hung up.

When William returned to the fireplace, Judith's saffron tunic lay on the carpet, but Judith had left the room. "Judith?" he called out.

"You don't have to shout, I can hear you quite clearly. And I heard everything Father said over the phone." Her voice was coming out of the speakers set into the bases of several of the phones in the house. She had the cordless receiver and was using it as an intercom. In the darkness it was easy to think of her voice as ghostly. It made him remember the times, back in the Obstschmecker house, when Ned would turn off all the lights and hide and start talking in the voice he used when he wanted to be scary.

"Did I ever tell you what I did when I was in Nashville?"

She hadn't, and you couldn't help wondering. Her bus ride from Florida to Minnesota had taken almost a day longer than it was supposed to. Judith had described her journey at such epic length that no one had pressed for further details, but William had noted the discrepancy. "No," he said, returning to the fireside, "you never did."

"The bus arrived in Nashville late at night, and I just couldn't face sleeping another night sitting up. So I went to a hotel. And then I went to a bar and ordered a grasshopper. I was sure they wouldn't serve me but they did. Have you ever had a grasshopper?"

"It's a kind of mixed drink?"

"It's just delicious. Would you like me to make you one? I know how, and there's crème de menthe in the liquor cabinet."

"Sure, why not."

Carefully, he lowered a split log onto the andirons and heaped the embers beneath into a mound high enough to crisp the white flesh of the log. While he tended the fire, the phone broadcast muffled bumpings and thumpings and then a subdued gurgling, which must have been the blender. A green flame fanned out from the back of the log and seemed to waver in sync with the blender.

Judith appeared, wearing a kimono in Halloween colors and carrying a tray with two parfait glasses. They clicked their glasses, and William agreed that a grasshopper was better than an ice cream soda.

"So that's how you spent the night in Nashville, drinking grasshoppers?"

"Not the whole night. But I did feel rebellious, sitting there in my Miami T-shirt and waiting for John Travolta to come over and ask me to dance. The only problem with that was that it wasn't a bar where people ever danced, and John Travolta wasn't there, or any other male under the age of fifty. Anyhow, I didn't want to dance. I wanted to be kissed. Ever since I saw those two movies I couldn't think of anything but the fact that I was almost old enough to vote and that I'd never been kissed. Have you?"

"Been kissed? Not like in the movies."

"It always seemed like such a repulsive idea to me, putting your tongue into someone else's mouth. I couldn't see what purpose it could serve except to stop the other person from talking. But then, seeing those movies the day I phoned you from the bus station, I realized there had to be more to it. Do you know, sometimes people spend *hours* kissing each other, and not doing anything else, just kissing."

It dawned on William that Judith was not speculating in any idle way, that she was leading up to something. "Judith," he protested, "if you're thinking that you and me . . ."

"Why not?" she insisted. "It wouldn't be incest, for heaven's sake."

"Why wouldn't it?"

Judith chuckled in a superior way. "Because our biological parents are completely different. Suppose Father hadn't ever met Sondra, and *we* met each other instead and got married, and then *they* met for the first time and fell in love. Would it be incest for *them* to get married? Of course not."

"Sounds like you had that all thought out ahead of time."

"Anyhow, I wasn't suggesting that we have sex. But I don't see why we couldn't kiss each other. Aren't you curious to know what it's like?"

"To be perfectly honest, I find the whole idea embarrassing."

"More embarrassing than covering yourself with green paint and wearing a shower cap to a dance and saying you're a Martian?"

"Maybe not more, but equally. Oh, okay, why not? I'm willing to try it. But if it's not really pleasant, we don't have to keep trying, agreed?"

"Agreed."

"Should we be sitting up, or lying down, or what?"

"Right the way we are is fine, but you better give me your glass first. There's more grasshoppers in the blender if you want some more later."

She placed the two parfait glasses on the floor off to the side of the fireplace. The new log was burning nicely, and the bark was crackling. Judith positioned her hands on William's rib cage and on the side of his neck, but she couldn't bring herself to bring her lips nearer his. They remained in that position some time, motionless as two mannequins in a store window, smiling stiffly, as for a photographer, and avoiding looking into each other's eyes. It was like being poised to dance and waiting for a record to play.

"I think it would be easier," he suggested, "if we closed our eyes."

She nodded in agreement, and closed her eyes, and waited for him to take the last few centimeters of initiative. He brought his lips closer to hers but not quite touching. His nose and upper lip were tickled with warm feathery blasts of breath from her nostrils. Something in his chest resonated sympathetically, as though her exhalations were the softest and lightest of mallets a musician uses to touch the bars of a xylophone, and their kiss, when the music came to it, was the sound that issues from that touch: involuntary, clear, and low.

51

In death Henry could not keep from yielding completely to the embrace of all his morbid fascinations. Combustion, dissolution, the sudden rending or wrenching of any complex tissue—these were spectacles that lured him like a moth to a flame. Indeed, before the flaming log in the fireplace, the likeness amounted to identity. He was himself that log, those glowing gases, the reckless, ecstatic release of years of slow stockpiling of cell on cell. Simultaneously—indeed, with no sense that the burning log and the awakening of the two children to sexual maturity were distinct processes—he shared in and even, in a sense, directed that first kiss and the motions flowing from it. When William's hands pressed Judith's breasts it was with a certainty of experience and a reverence for the flesh that were his father's inadvertent gift and that gave his touch a grace, a tenderness, and an authority they would not otherwise have possessed. William did not know this, and Henry, having come this near the flame of mortality, could not have kept from the final joy of immolation, and so his visitation on that Halloween night, far from serving to warn William away from what he was about to do, had helped precipitate the action. The log was reduced to soot and ashes in only a few hours; it took four days for the parallel process to be completed. Yet to Henry, outside of the arithmetical chronologies that govern mortal life, the two events seemed to begin and to end in the same moment. He was more fortunate than the moth in that he was allowed a little time to appreciate his final brightness. He could witness the first quick uncoilings of the filaments from which the fibers of his grandson would be knit. He saw them double and redouble, and then with a sense of both sorrow and horrible hilarity—as though only now after so many years' experience of death had he finally understood the joke that all skulls are grinning at—he turned away and let himself be pulled down into the darkness from which even the dead cannot arise. Henry's spirit was no more.

52

Sondra knew within moments of the delivery that something was wrong. She had remained conscious throughout, cooperating with the doctor, breathing just as she'd practiced through the months, and riding the pain when it came like a rodeo rider on a bull, or a surfer on a curling wave. When it was over she felt that moment of supreme relief, more precious than any pleasure, by which our nerves seek to excuse the fact of pain, and then she waited for her maternal rights to be accorded her. But instead of *showing* her the child, the two doctors and the nurse seemed to have formed a kind of barricade of their white-gowned bodies to prevent her seeing it. It was alive, she could hear its squalling, why wasn't she allowed to see it? She tried to frame that question aloud, but already the second doctor—the anesthesiologist—was administering the gas she'd had no need for during labor. She wanted to protest, it seemed so unfair, and then with that strange lack of transition between fading away and coming to that can happen in a hospital or a dentist's office she was in a small bright room and Ben was lying asleep in a chair by the foot of the bed. Something awful had happened, but she no longer wished to know what it might be. She let Ben go on sleeping, and when he began to stir, she pretended to be asleep herself. The child was not dead, she had heard its first cries; there must, in that case, be something wrong with it, something visible. It must be deformed.

Three days she remained in the small bright room, grateful for the unofficial quarantine she'd been placed in and for the medications that allowed her to avert whatever horrible truth was waiting to be announced the moment she seemed sufficiently alert. Perhaps in the meantime it would die and she'd be spared ever having to know what the doctors and Ben knew, to see what they'd seen that had made them unable to answer her unasked questions. Then on the morning of the fourth day, when she awoke without even a wisp of tranquilizer on her mental horizon and when the nurse brought her no medication before breakfast, she knew they had decided to put it off no longer.

It was the doctor, not Ben, who performed the grim duty, beginning with a little scientific lecture on the subject of genetics, the drift of which seemed to be to reassure her that it was *not her fault*, nor Ben's fault either, but simply a very unfortunate "roll of the dice." A recessive gene could be passed on for a hundred years or more without anyone the wiser, and the rarer the gene, the more unlikely that a man who bore it would have a child by a woman who also bore it. The odds in their case had been on the order of one in twenty-five million. Impossible, therefore, either to have predicted or prevented such a contingency.

Even then the lecture continued, as though there might be something worse to know. Then she realized that in fact the doctor was offering her the only hope left to offer, though it was couched in pieties about the need to accept the likelihood that the child would not live long, that even with the best care the hospital could provide, it would probably be dead before the New Year. In that case, she asked, did she have to see it? Yes, he said, he had discussed it with her husband, and they thought it would be best. The hospital bills in these cases could quickly mount up to an extraordinary sum. Even with their hospitalization the intensive care that such a child required could be ruinously expensive, and since, in the long run, there was little to be hoped for from such treatment . . .

Sondra understood: the child would be likelier to die at home than if they left it in the hospital. She agreed to see it, and a nurse brought it to the room, wheeling it in a little crib, as though she could not bring herself to make any closer physical contact. The corner of the sheet that formed a kind of hood over its face was folded back to reveal features so grossly misshapen, so literally horrible, that even braced by the doctor's warnings she could not repress a cry of revulsion, as though it had to be put on the record at once and incontestibly that she recognized no claim of mother-hood or of humanity.

Every facial feature had in some way or other been skewed or twisted awry: the squinting eyes wide-spaced and slanting, the nose a bony beak, the ears misshapen and misplaced, but worst of all the hare-lipped and cleft-palated mouth with the white funguslike growths where lips should be—the mouth that at the very moment of her own cry of revulsion and denial opened to scream in seeming sympathy, or else to demand that which she would rather have died than to allow, to be given suckle at her breast.

"Take it away," she told the nurse in a whisper, and then, to the doctor, "Leave me alone." The squalling of the thing in the crib seemed to continue long after it had been wheeled out of the room, and indeed it never really was stilled from that moment on, but, like some horrible advertising jingle that replays itself even in our dreams, it went on hour after hour, day after day. In the middle of being fed its formula it would pull away from the nipple that had momentarily gagged its misshapen mouth to scream with renewed energy, flailing its warped, polydactylous hands at the bottle, as though protesting being forced to drink the artificial milk, forced to be alive and in pain.

For that must have been the reason it cried—it must be in constant pain. It was not only its face and limbs that were abnormal. Beneath the rough, red, flaky skin its body was a nest of anomalies—the heart congenitally diseased, the kidneys and other organs pitted with lesions. The doctors professed to be amazed that it was still alive a week after it had been taken home. And Sondra, who had been able to endure the horror of its presence only because of the doctor's unspoken promise that it would not live much longer, began to doubt that promise. She found that no matter how long it went on screaming, no matter how many hours since it had last been fed, she could not make herself go into her own bedroom, where it was kept (and into which neither Judith nor William was ever admitted). A nurse had to be hired, Mrs. Ruddle, an elderly, dwarfish, terribly cheerful practical nurse who seemed to develop an actual affection for the child. Soon Sondra felt a horror of Mrs. Ruddle almost equal to that which she felt for the thing in the crib, but Mrs. Ruddle could not so easily be avoided. Meals had to be made for her. Her questions had to be answered, and it was necessary from time to time to pretend to take an interest in the condition and behavior of Mrs. Ruddle's charge.

The nights were the hardest to bear. Then Mrs. Ruddle wasn't there, and Sondra had to lie alone in her room, listening to the rasping irregular breath of the thing in the crib. She did not have the concentration to read, and she could not sleep, so she would watch movies on TV, using earphones to keep the thing from waking up and howling. It did anyhow, of course, at least twice a night, and then she would have to go over to the crib and roll it back and forth till the howling abated. She would not, could not bring herself to take it from its cocoon of blankets and hold it in her arms, and if its diaper was wet, it stayed wet until Mrs. Ruddle appeared at 7:00 a.m.

She slept in the daytime, when the kids were away at school and Ben was at the office. When they were home, she made a conscientious effort to maintain a business-as-usual attitude, cooking favorite recipes and during dinner asking one preemptive question after another about *their* lives, *their* problems, and whether because Ben had coached them in how to deal with her, or from their own sense of tact, both William and Judith respected the unstated ground rule of all these dinnertime conversations, that they were never to refer to the thing in the crib or anything associated with its presence in the house, including the unfortunate Mrs. Ruddle.

Christmas approached and was allowed to go by with the most minimal festive observance: an artificial tree assembled, by William and Judith, on Christmas Eve and disassembled on New Year's Day; a modest exchange of presents that developed inadvertently into a comedy, as it turned out that almost everyone had got almost everyone else a sweater (there were no presents, of course, for the thing in the crib); and for dinner, in defiance of all tradition, a roast beef. The one major breach of decorum had come on Christmas morning itself when only Judith got dressed to go to Mass, and then had begun to urge her family to go with her. Finally, more angry than distraught, Sondra had had to explain to her stepdaughter what ought to have been too obvious to need underlining, that she did not intend to sit in a packed church and listen to a priest go on about the wonder and glory of the "Nativity." The idea seemed an obscene joke. Judith went to Mass alone.

Through it all Ben paid her the compliment of not interfering or offering "advice." What advice could be given? Obviously, she was cracking under the strain; they both were. But what could be done but to wait for the thing to die, as the doctors had assured them it would? In a way it helped that it looked so utterly inhuman: it was impossible to feel love for it, and so she would be spared the pain of mourning. Though perhaps when it did finally die and had been cremated, she might feel differently. But guilt seemed more likely than grief. Already she could feel that guilt, like another fetus inside of her, not low in her stomach but higher, near her lungs, clawing at her rib cage as though trying to escape, to be expressed by some *visible* action. She began to be able to understand stories of penitents who had torn out their hair or whipped themselves with thorns.

In lieu of such certifiable excesses she took to going for long walks along the ice-slicked Willowville streets. The sidewalks were rarely shov-

eled out here, except the walks connecting front doors to the driveways.
You had to walk in the street itself alongside the mounds built up in the
gutters by the snowplows. The traffic was light in the daytime, and it was
seldom necessary to step aside for a car to go by. The wind was wonderful, cold and brutal, a thief determined to snatch her fur coat away from
her. It forced tears from her eyes she would not otherwise allow herself to
shed. It numbed her feet and penetrated the thin leather of her gloves so
that, by the time she returned home, an hour, two hours later, her hands
would be stiff and red. She would go into the kitchen then and plunge her
hands beneath a stream of hot water and gasp with the splendor of the
pain. But she never came down with a cold or the flu, nor did the little
monster, though at night she placed its crib directly in the path of the
steady draft from the partly open bedroom window.

They really were called monsters in the medical books, though of
course they used Greek—*terata* was the word—to smooth over the fact.
There was an entire branch of medicine devoted to the study of monsters,
teratology, and Ben had brought home a thick textbook on the subject. In
it there was a picture of another infant monster like theirs, though the one
in the photograph hadn't lived an hour beyond its birth. The book said
that no infant afflicted by Bradley-Chambers syndrome had ever survived
more than ten weeks. It was reassuring information, though she wished
Ben had copied only that one page and not shown her the book. The
pictures were upsetting, but she couldn't keep from looking at them. And
thinking. As soon as she was well enough, she would demand to have a
hysterectomy. She did not want to risk becoming pregnant ever again. If
she did, there would be a one in four chance that any child she and Ben
had together would also be afflicted by Bradley-Chambers syndrome.
That was how it worked with recessive genes. She had learned a lot about
heredity since she'd come home from the hospital.

As the ninth week passed into the tenth and the thing in the crib was
showing every sign of setting a new record for survival with Bradley-
Chambers syndrome, a visitor called at the house in early afternoon, rous-
ing Sondra from the comforting void of a deep, dreamless sleep. At first,
confused, she thought the ringing of the doorbell was the smoke detector
in the kitchen. Then Mrs. Ruddle appeared in the archway leading to the
gallery, clutching a piece of knitting the same sickly pink as the sweater
she was bundled in, as though she were in the process of knitting herself
into existence. "Mrs. Winckelmeyer?" the little woman inquired in her
piping Munchkinish voice. "Are you awake? Do you want me to get the
door?"

"No, no, Mrs. Ruddle!" Sondra said, alarmed at the thought of a visitor encountering the dwarfish nurse. Mrs. Ruddle, like the thing she tended, was a source of shame to Sondra, a skeleton in the closet, and must be kept a secret as much as possible. "Please, just . . . go back to the bedroom."

Mrs. Ruddle crinkled her thickly lipsticked lips into a smile of compliance and disappeared back along the gallery.

Sondra adjusted her sleep-mussed hair in front of the foyer mirror and then opened the door to confront, through the hoarfrosted panel of the outer door, the silhouette of a man in black. "Mrs. Winckelmeyer?" he inquired in the soothing tones of a professional sympathizer. A funeral director? she wondered, with a brief unreasoning sense of elation. Then, through the obscuring hoarfrost, she saw the Roman collar.

"Yes?" she replied, through the still closed door. "What do you want?"

He tipped his hat. "I'm Father Youngermann," he said, "from Our Lady of Mercy parish in St. Paul. I'd like to talk with you, if I may."

Youngermann, she thought, as she watched him shrug off his topcoat in the foyer. How odd that he should be called that. The first thing she'd thought, after noticing the Roman collar, was that he seemed too young to be a priest. He might well have been younger than she was. She couldn't remember ever having encountered a priest younger than herself. It was disconcerting.

Without being invited, the young priest went into the living room. He looked about, like a guest arriving at a party and hoping not to find himself the earliest. "I don't suppose that Mr. Winckelmeyer would be home at this hour?"

"No. He's not."

"I realize that Our Lady of Mercy is no longer your parish, and properly I shouldn't be trespassing on Father Durling's territory here in Willowville."

Sondra shrugged. "It's no concern of mine. I wouldn't really say that I have a parish—since I was divorced."

Father Youngermann nodded gravely. "But I understand you *have* been bringing up your son William in the church. And that your stepdaughter, likewise, is a practicing Catholic. Even, I'm told, an ardent Catholic."

"What is your point, Father?" Father: The word grated. He was not her father, and she resented having to address him as such.

"Only that I understand, from my work at the hospital, that you've had another child."

She regarded him levelly, neither agreeing with nor contradicting his statement, simply waiting for him to continue.

"And there seems to be no record of that child's baptism. Indeed, the birth certificate says only 'Male child.' *Has* he been baptized?"

"Who sent you here?"

"No one at all, Mrs. Winckelmeyer. I came on my own initiative. As I've said, this is not a parish matter. I'm here because of my own personal concern."

"I'm touched."

"I realize, of course, that you must have felt—and must still be feeling—shock and emotional distress. Even when there are no complications, childbirth can be—"

"Spare me the sympathy card and get to the point."

He grimaced. "Very well. The point is simply this. I would like to baptize your child, if he's not already been baptized."

"I'm sorry, that's out of the question."

"And *I'm* sorry, Mrs. Winckelmeyer, but as a representative of Holy Mother Church, I really must insist that some arrangement be made for the child's baptism, and it really can't be postponed. Father Durling has tried to reach you on the phone, and I've tried. But we get only an answering machine. I respect your wish for privacy at this time, but my understanding is that the child is in daily peril of dying without having received the sacrament of baptism. Your duty as a mother, and as a Catholic—"

Sondra had been waiting for the priest to have his say before she got rid of him, and the last thing she wanted was a quarrel, but his offering to instruct her in her duty as a mother was one too many. She held her hand up like a traffic cop, signaling him to stop. "I have a proposition for you," she said. "You want to baptize that thing in there, then you *adopt* it."

The priest gave a little snort of incredulity. "I'm sorry, Mrs. Winckelmeyer, but obviously, as a priest, that's not a possibility I could even consider. In any case, it's beside the point. The point is the salvation of your child's immortal soul."

"I'm sure I've read in a magazine just recently about a priest adopting a kid. Anyhow, that's my proposition, take it or leave it."

"I'm sorry, Mrs. Winckelmeyer, but I don't understand your unwillingness to have the child baptized. The very sufferings it has gone through here below can add to its glory in Heaven—but if it's denied any hope of salvation through the lack of the sacrament of baptism—"

"Do you know, until today I never realized what an insane idea that is. A little water on the forehead and a few words and it'll go to Heaven. And without the water and the words, what? Hellfire? Millions of babies must die without getting baptized. All the ones that get aborted. They all go to Hell? That's God's idea of being fair?"

"It's not for us to question the will of God, Mrs. Winckelmeyer. We must accept the Church's teaching on faith. Without faith we have nothing."

"Really? Without faith—without *my* faith—you're out of a job, I can see that. Anyhow, I don't want to get into dumb arguments. God didn't have anything to do with . . . I refuse to even say it's a child. It's not, it's a monster. It should never have been born, and it *can't* live very much longer, and I don't want it baptized, I don't want it even to have a *name*. It's like a tumor that I've had removed, as far as I'm concerned. A tumor that screams and shits in diapers. I'm just waiting, that's all."

"Waiting?"

"For it to die. And for you to leave."

The priest took a deep breath. "Can I at least see the child?"

"I've asked you to leave."

"Father Youngermann?" It was the piping voice of Mrs. Ruddle, who stood once again in the archway leading to the gallery. "I have the baby here." She held out the bundle cradled in her arms.

The priest crossed the living room toward Mrs. Ruddle. Sondra did not object at once. She was curious to watch his reaction when he saw the thing's face. It was not exaggerated, just a clenching of the jaw and a narrowing of the eyes. Then he reached into his right-hand jacket pocket and took out a strip of colored cloth, which he kissed and draped scarflike about his neck. From the other pocket he produced a small silver flask. It was clear that he meant to go ahead with the baptism despite her having said that he could not.

Sondra considered trying to wrest Mrs. Ruddle's bundle from her by main force, but her aversion to physical contact with the thing in the nurse's arms was greater even than her anger. Instead, without having to take thought, she ran into the kitchen and opened the cupboard below the sink. There beneath the leaking drain that Ben kept saying he would fix and never did was the plastic bucket that caught the leaks. It was three-quarters full of stagnant water. She eased the bucket out from under the U-shaped curve of the pipe, spilling only a little, and hurried back to the living room, where she found Mrs. Ruddle supporting the thing's mis-shapen head above the big blue-and-white glass ashtray on the coffee table so that the ashtray would serve as a kind of basin for the baptism. The priest was already beginning to pour the water from the silver flask, and to pronounce the words of the sacrament: "I baptize thee in the name of the Father—"

Sondra heaved the dirty water from the bucket, and it arced out across the living room to drench the priest, Mrs. Ruddle, and the still unbaptized, still nameless child, which now began its usual caterwauling. The priest stood his ground a while, glaring in speechless rage at Sondra, so aghast at the sacrilege against his own person that he quite forgot to continue with the rigmarole of the baptism. Mrs. Ruddle, with less resources of self-confidence, retreated, the child in her arms, to the safety of the bedroom.

"I baptize *thee*," she said with satisfaction, placing the empty bucket on the floor and kicking it, football-style, in the direction of the priest. Then, feeling inspired, she added, "In the name of the Mother!"

"I could have you charged. For assault and battery!"

Beads of water were rolling down the black fabric of his jacket, and a bit of wet scuzz had glued itself, neat as a postage stamp, to the square of white collar beneath his chin.

"I asked you to leave, you wouldn't leave, I was defending my property—and my child. And if you don't leave right now, *I* will call the police."

He considered this a moment, then his face shifted gears. "God forgive you, Mrs. Winckelmeyer. God forgive you." Having secured the moral high ground, he retreated to the foyer and began to put on his coat, but a regard for its silk lining decided him, instead, to carry it off draped over his arm. He hesitated in the doorway, as though he were forgetting something, and Sondra had the final satisfaction of slamming the door in his face.

Only when his car, a black Audi 5000, was out of sight, did Sondra notice what it was that he'd forgotten. While he was dealing with his topcoat, he'd placed the silver flask of holy water beside the decorative lighter on the whatnot, and there it remained. She picked it up and sniffed at the contents, but the holy water did not have a distinctive smell. The screw-on cap, connected to the spout by a chain of delicate links, clinked dully against the silvered sides of the flask. She looked at her face in its distorting mirror. Her forehead bulged. Her eyes warped out of symmetry. She bared her teeth in a beauty contest smile and tilted the flask to exaggerate the effect of fangy ferociousness. Now she looked the true mother of her monster child. Now . . .

But she didn't have to think what she would do now. She could simply do it, the way she'd flung the water at the priest. She could still feel, in her arms and deep within the muscles of her back, the satisfaction of that act, a tingling and aliveness as though she'd just had a good swim.

She capped the flask and snugged it into the back pocket of her jeans. She returned the plastic bucket to its place beneath the kitchen drain. There was nothing that could be done for the stains the water had made on the white carpet, but it was overdue for a shampooing in any case. She went to the bedroom and knocked at the door.

Inside, the baby started to cry, and Mrs. Ruddle emitted a quavering "Yes?"

"Mrs. Ruddle, I have to know if it was you who arranged for that priest to come here."

Mrs. Ruddle didn't at once reply. The baby left off its howling as though sensing that its own fate was at stake. Sondra had begun to feel a strange compassion for it. Not love in the usual sense, and certainly not "motherly" love. More what one might feel for a character in a movie—a foreign movie, in another language, filmed in black and white.

"Mrs. Ruddle?"

Mrs. Ruddle opened the door. She had put on her quilted anorak and a winter cap with furry earlaps, and was carrying her purse and a plastic shopping bag brimming with paperbacks, knitting, crossword puzzle magazines, and the other paraphernalia of someone who is paid to sit alone and be bored for days on end.

"I'm not sorry," she said, looking up at Sondra defiantly. "I did what my conscience told me to do. I wouldn't treat an animal the way you treat that poor child. You won't even let it have the dignity of a name of its own. Even a dog has a name!"

"I don't intend to argue with you, Mrs. Ruddle."

Mrs. Ruddle pushed past Sondra and stalked down the gallery and across the living room to the foyer. Sondra felt a real regret that she couldn't thank the woman for having anticipated her dismissal and for offering no protest or resistance. She had been expecting to have to make a scene. Instead, Mrs. Ruddle was practically ice-skating out of the house. It was too bad she could not offer her a kind word in parting, some token of her appreciation, but to adopt a tone of understanding or appeasement now might delay or even prevent her setting off.

The front door slammed.

Sondra went over to the crib. The child—she had begun to think of it as a child, and that seemed ominous, a sign of relenting, she could not delay any longer doing what had to be done—the child was staring at her with its bug eyes, its deformed fist pressed against its lipless mouth. It was silent, as though it knew it was in danger.

She tried to think what to use. A pillow from the bed would be too unwieldy. The comforter! The comforter Mrs. Ruddle had knitted from her endless skein of pink yarn and that hung now on the back of the slat-backed chair at the head of the crib. She took the comforter's satin-bound hem in her hand and pulled it free from the chair. It could not have weighed more than a pound. Had there ever been an unlikelier murder weapon?

There really was nothing else to be done. The thing showed no sign of sickening. It might live on for years, in constant pain itself and making a nightmare of everyone else's life. You could see what it had done to Madge Michaels to be burdened with her bed-bound vegetable of a son, and Ned was no monster. But this one, if it lived . . . Always, before that "if," Sondra averted her imagination, as she averted her eyes whenever she saw its face.

She draped the comforter over the headboard of the crib and from her back pocket took the flask of holy water. Now that she'd finally resolved to kill the child, she was willing to concede that it was, legally, theologically, human. She would baptize it herself, and if there was a heaven that only the baptized had access to, then it would arrive ticket in hand. She trickled the holy water over its head and recited the simple formula she'd not allowed the priest to complete: "I baptize thee in the name of the Father and the Son and the Holy Ghost." Then she took the pink comforter, folded it to a fourfold thickness, pressed it to the child's face, and held it in place firmly till the feeble flailings of its arms and legs had ceased and it had stopped breathing.

After all the weeks of agonizing, how easy it had been. As though death were a sunlit room that one entered by a door that said KEEP OUT. You only had to ignore the sign and enter. She felt a hesitant confidence, like the first time she'd driven a car after two months of drivers' training classes—more a hope than a confidence, a hope that suicide would be no more difficult than murder. She located the bottle of sleeping pills, still nearly full, at the back of the drawer of the bedside table. She took five of them at once, using the holy water remaining in the flask to wash them down. Then she remembered her doctor's warning never to take alcohol and the Tuinal at the same time, since the combination was a recipe for instant oblivion. She didn't want to leave the bedroom: the corpse in the crib lent the room a steadying sense of peace and finality that she would not find elsewhere in the house. But it wouldn't do to put off getting the liquor, she might fall asleep—merely asleep—if she didn't act at once.

The sideboard that served as a liquor cabinet had been substantially depleted in the past few weeks. She and Ben had both been drinking heavily, and neither had bothered to restock it. She had a choice of sherry, crème de menthe, vermouth, a Christian Brothers brandy, and tequila. The brandy seemed least vomit-making, and the fact that it had been a present from one of her own poor relations, an uncle visiting the Twin Cities for a family funeral, gave it a spice of poetic justice. She poured some into a snifter, added the last of the holy water to take away the worst of the sting, and washed down another ten tablets. Then she refilled the snifter and considered whether to return to the bedroom or to remain in the living room, which seemed, now that she was here, the most suitable part of the house to die, with its oversize, waiting-room-style furniture, its chilly colors, its stripped-bare anonymity. What a comment it was on their life. She slumped down on the sectional and stared up at the nubbly stucco of the ceiling. She could feel the first wave of wooziness dimming her thoughts. It was a surprisingly pleasant sensation.

She'd always wondered what it would be like to die. Everyone must. You hoped it wouldn't be too painful or go on too long. She'd thought a sudden violent accident might be best. The way Henry had died. She'd almost envied him the ease of it. Cancer must be the worst. Crabs eating you up from inside. Horrible.

She took another sip of the brandy and felt some delicate digestive balance tipping from well-being to queasiness. She must avoid throwing up. If she botched her suicide, she would almost certainly end up in prison for murdering the baby. She couldn't expect a jury to be sympathetic. People said suicide was a way of cheating death, but she'd always been a cheater, she didn't mind that. She'd cheated on Henry, and it hadn't bothered her at all. If she hadn't cheated on Ben, it was only because she hadn't been tempted to. Her life had been comfortable, she was lazy. One day just followed the next. Problem-free, no complaints. But characterless, like this room.

She decided that, after all, she'd rather die in the bedroom and placed the snifter, carefully, on the coffee table, beside the blue-and-white glass ashtray. Getting to her feet took all the concentration she could muster, walking was next to impossible. Her body seemed to want to tip forward from her hips. The white carpet stretched out in front of her like the sands of some vast desert. The light had become much too bright. She had a nagging sense of having left something important undone, and as she reached the bedroom door, she remembered that she'd not said "Amen" at the end of the baptism. Would it work without the "Amen"? Was it too late to add it now? Her hand was on the doorknob, but she wasn't able to twist it round so that the door would open. She began to tip forward at her hips and this time she couldn't keep from falling forward. As she lay on the carpet, she tried to whisper the "Amen" of the baptism, but not even her lips and tongue would do what she asked now. It didn't matter, really. God couldn't be as stupid as all that. She closed her eyes and yielded, gratefully, to the ease and comfort of her death.

53

Ben asked Mrs. Ruddle to wait in the car until he'd had a chance to talk to Sondra and be certain she'd calmed down. Mrs. Ruddle was herself in such a state of fretfulness that, though normally taciturn and unforthcoming, she had already twice recounted the tale of Father Youngermann's visit and his abortive attempt to baptize "the poor child." One moment she would be effusively apologetic for having contacted the priest, the next she would be fuming at Sondra for having emptied the bucket of water on the priest. "I was soaked through myself, but that's no matter. I don't blame her: she was so upset she didn't know what she was doing. But a priest, to do that to a priest!"

Mrs. Ruddle's two declared objects in returning home with Ben were to offer an apology to Sondra (and try to get her job back) and (if the apology failed of its desired effect) to retrieve various of her possessions that she'd forgotten in the excitement of her first leave-taking: an umbrella, overshoes, a box of decaffeinated tea bags, and a hand-knitted comforter she'd left by the baby's crib. "And what's going to happen to that poor child without me there I'm sure I don't know!"

Ben had managed to keep the lid on his own temper through Mrs. Ruddle's nonstop monologue, though the cumulative effect of it was almost as maddening as being kept awake by the baby's screams. She had arrived at his office in midafternoon and refused to take Mrs. O'Meara's hint that he was in a meeting. She'd simply outwaited him until, at four o'clock, he'd agreed to see her, and the long whine began. Listening to Mrs. Ruddle carry on was like hearing the baby's strident, nonnegotiable demands rescored for an adult voice. No wonder Sondra had finally cracked under the strain of having to contend every day with the pair of them, the baby and its nurse. By the time they had got back to Willow-ville, Ben was inclined to think that of the two, Mrs. Ruddle was the worse.

Though it was after sunset, there wasn't a light on in the house, not even the flicker of a TV screen. But that only meant (Ben supposed) that Sondra was taking a nap, and that the kids had stayed late after school. "Sondra?" he called out, as he went round the living room from lamp to wall switch, turning on the lights. There was an almost empty snifter on the coffee table, standing in a puddle of spilled brandy. "Sondra?" he repeated, raising his voice. He looked into his office, where she would sometimes nap on the leather sofa in order to be away from the baby, but there was no sign of her there, or in his bedroom.

Even when he found her sprawled in the hallway outside the door to her own bedroom, his first assumption (remembering the snifter) was that she was drunk, and when he stooped to lift her up and carry her to bed, it was with a smile of commiseration and indulgence. Only as he entered the room with the weight of her in his arms did he realize, from the utter limpness of her neck and arms, that this was not drunkenness but death. He placed her on the floor so as to administer mouth-to-mouth resuscitation, though he knew from the coldness of her hands and face that it was too late. Then, as he drew the first breath that he meant to force into her stilled lungs, the thing in the crib began to cry. Just a feeble whimper at first. Then a second cry, louder, but with a catch in it, as though it were having some mechanical difficulty.

Even before he'd looked into the crib and seen the folded comforter still covering the child's nasty little face, Ben understood what had happened. Sondra had thought she'd put the thing out of its misery and then, unable to bear the guilt of her action, had committed suicide. But the guilt was his. He'd known for weeks what he ought to have done. He should have murdered the brat himself, not left it to his wife. Infanticide is a man's job, and he could have done it with as little qualms of conscience as Herod himself. It was only the fear of being suspected and brought to trial that had stopped him. And now Sondra was dead and the little fucker was still alive and ready to continue the long scream of its existence.

No. He would not allow Sondra's death to have been nothing but a bad joke. He lifted the screaming infant by its throat—and squeezed. The grotesque face turned cherry red, and its tongue protruded from the doubly deformed mouth. He shook its carcass until he felt something snap and then, resisting the urge to hurl it for good measure against the wall, he dropped it into the crib, wishing that crib were a bottomless pit, an incinerator, a grave. He hadn't realized, until his hand had been about its neck, the depth of his hatred for the thing. Sondra's suicide seemed more comprehensible now. She must have felt the same satisfaction in the thought of its death. Instead of remorse or guilt or some more morally appropriate response. Instead, this obscene elation. This pride, as though he'd defeated some enemy in single combat! What a cesspool the human heart is. Or, as someone famous had said, probably Shakespeare in one of his plays, "What a piece of shit is man."

He replaced the comforter on the baby's face. Again he took up Sondra's body (it had seemed light before, now it was almost beyond his strength) and carried her from the room.

Despite his having told her to stay in the car, Mrs. Ruddle had come into the house. William and Judith were with her. At the first sight of Sondra's body in her husband's arms, Mrs. Ruddle became officiously professional, ordering Ben to place the body on the sectional for her to look at, ordering William to phone the hospital.

"I am taking her to the hospital myself," Ben insisted. "That will be faster than waiting for an ambulance. William, would you open the door for me?"

"The baby," Judith said. "How is the baby?"

"The baby's dead."

"No," Mrs. Ruddle insisted, with calm nursey authority, "that can't be."

"Don't you understand?" He glared at the nurse, trying to assert his own authority. "Sondra killed the baby, and then she killed herself."

"No, the baby's still alive. I heard him just moments after we came in the door. He was crying, and then he stopped, suddenly. We all heard it." She turned to William. "Didn't we?"

William shook his head. "I didn't hear anything."

"You must have mistaken what you heard, Mrs. Ruddle. The child is dead. See for yourself. But there might still be hope for Sondra. I must get her to a hospital." In fact he was desperate to get out of the house and away from Mrs. Ruddle.

William went to the front door and held it open.

Mrs. Ruddle grasped Judith by the arm. "*You* heard the baby crying. Didn't you? *Didn't* you?"

Judith looked at her father, and looked away. She needed no further explanation. She understood everything that had happened.

She nodded her head. "Yes, I heard the baby crying."

Mrs. Ruddle tightened her crimsoned lips in a grimace of triumph and went to the telephone. She dialed 911, and when the operator came on the line she asked for the police.

Ben lowered Sondra's corpse to the sectional. He looked at Judith. Judith looked down at the stain on the carpet. William, in the foyer, closed the door.

From this point it all seemed inevitable: the arraignment, the indictment, the trial. And the verdict. Ben Winckelmeyer had killed his nameless infant son. That had been established. The only question that remained was whether he'd be allowed to plea-bargain down from a charge of murder in the first degree.

With chagrin for his own stupidity, and admiration for her own larger courage, Ben kissed his wife and waited for the police.

54

So far, two weeks into the month, April had not represented much of an improvement on March. The streets had stopped being slushy, and most lawns had progressed from tawny to green, but the weather was weather that only a garden could love, with one gray day after another, and the temperature seldom rising into the fifties. The last two weekends had been cold and drizzly, and now on the first day of Easter vacation there was a steady, coat-sopping rain that had been coming down since early morning. He ached to be away from the house, where he felt as much a prisoner of his bedroom as if he were Ned. The Obstschmecker house no longer registered as a great mansion the way it had when he was a kid. He missed the wide-open, unpartitioned arrangement of the Winckelmeyer ranch house. This place was like the house for small mammals at the Como Zoo, a honeycomb of separate little burrows, each generating its own peculiar smell, which mingled into a single overwhelming mammalian stench. Theoretically after you've lived with any smell long enough, you're supposed to get acclimatized to it so that it becomes as undetectable as your own bad breath, but William had been back here for two months already and every time he came in the house he recoiled at the amalgamated smells of Ned's bedside diaper pail, woodrot, burnt milk, ashtrays, in pungent and varied association with the twice-daily mistings of Grandma O.'s favorite pine-scented air freshener.

Usually he was able to focus on schoolwork. Even with his knack for assimilating science textbooks directly into his bloodstream as systems of self-evident truths, even with the Apple assisting at his homework, there was a certain amount of drudgery that had to be accomplished to meet the demands of his physics and chemistry teachers; for English there was an unending slog of books to be read: *Pride and Prejudice*, *Portrait of the Artist as a Young Man*, *1984*, preachy, long-winded novels that you had to "appreciate" according to the lights of the English teacher, Mrs. Simms. It was a lot like catechism classes back at Our Lady of Mercy, only you had to be able to produce the correct answers "in your own words" instead of just reciting them. American History was much the same, except that Mr. Raab prudently had retarded the march of time so that his class would not encounter any living controversies that might get someone's parents fussed. It was halfway through April, and they had just arrived at the causes of World War I. He had to produce five hundred words on that subject for Monday's class. It wouldn't do to say stupidity or greed and leave it at that. Mr. Raab required heroes and villains and ethical problems with three reasons in favor and three against, and that meant an elaborate paraphrase of the official version set forth in their textbook, *Sea to Shining Sea*. Which he would do, just as he'd done it for the Greatness of Theodore Roosevelt and the Importance of the Railroad in the Winning of the West, with the intended result that he was now pulling down an A- in Raab's class, though probably more as a mark of sympathy than because of his perfunctory, paint-by-the-number essays. (Lilah Gerhart, to do her credit, had had his number on that score.) His mother's suicide and Ben's being sentenced to five years in prison had made both William and Judith pariahs at St. Tom's—not out of meanness on anyone's part but because no one knew what to say to them. And then, when it began to be clear, on top of all the rest of it, that Judith was pregnant, and when the rumor sprang up, natural as a weed, that the father of her child was her own father (who'd already pleaded guilty, after all, to killing his infant son), it had become impossible for Judith to remain at St. Tom's. If her pregnancy became known to the press, the publicity would be fatal. Mr. Paley was too much the diplomat, however, to *expel* an honor student with a chance at becoming valedictorian. Instead, she'd been given her diploma early in March, whereupon she'd flown off to her mother in Florida, beyond the reach of scandal. And so, after all those years, Rhoda Winckelmeyer had at last won the long-fought battle for the custody of her daughter.

William had not asked for, nor would he have accepted, an early discharge from St. Tom's, since it would have entailed his leaving the Early Admissions Program, diplomaless, and having to go to another school for a retread of his senior year, a grim prospect. In any case, the easiest way to avoid being buried by an avalanche of bad feelings was to concentrate on nailing down good grades. He studied the way that kids in Japan are supposed to study, to the exclusion of everything else, as though his life depended on it. It wasn't that he didn't feel real grief. He felt terrible about what had happened and dreaded that worse might still be in store. But what could he accomplish by dropping out of school? It helped to have something to do, a routine to follow, meals to eat, tasks to complete, a life he could pretend to live. If you pretended long enough, it would start to be real. Six more weeks and he'd have his diploma, and then he would start his first courses at the U, and never mind summer vacation. Six weeks was nothing. There were people in the *Guinness Book of Records* who'd lived in cages filled with poisonous snakes for longer than six weeks.

Such were his good intentions, and usually his willpower could be counted on to carry them out. Sometimes, though, he did get antsy, or angry, or depressed to the point where he had to do something, not just sit around and study or fool with the Apple or watch TV, but to feel himself exert an influence on the world. He had to use the caduceus and feel its power.

But not (he'd promised himself) on people, not anymore. Reminded by the continued well-being of the elm in the backyard, and of the other elms in Brosner Park whose lives and limbs he'd saved, he confined the use of his power to strictly arborial ends, tying bits of yellow yarn to the trees he meant to doom (often beside frayed yellow ribbons left over from the hostage crisis) and bits of red yarn to any surviving elms. Only in the past two weeks, as the first buds had opened on the trees, or not opened, had the results of his ministrations become apparent. All along the row of newly built condos that Madge had taken such a dislike to, the seedling maples had expired, their brittle young skeletons lifeless as the tiny plots of sod about them. But against those plants that William would most liked to have seen perish—that is, the dense curtains of hanging plants darkening so many rooms of the Obstschmecker house—the caduceus's power was unavailing, for it had been through that power originally that these plants had acquired their extraordinary vigor. Pot-bound, malnourished, cut back, and cursed, nothing could inhibit their kudzulike vitality. Whether for good or ill, what the caduceus once had done it could not later undo.

He had not, therefore, used the caduceus to confer the gift of unfailing good health on the fetus in Judith's womb, as he had blessed his brother. Any infant suffering Bradley-Chambers syndrome was supposed to be unviable, but who knows how long it might have gone on living—or what it might have become—if Ben had not murdered it? And because William was his mother's son and Judith her father's daughter, there was a chance (a lesser chance than with their parents but not negligible) that a child born from their union might also have Bradley-Chambers syndrome. The odds when both parents had that recessive gene was one in four, and the odds that you would pass on the recessive gene to otherwise normal children was one in two. So, a one-in-sixteen risk—and there was no test to determine whether either he or Judith carried the gene. The proof was in the pudding.

It was, however, possible to determine, by amniocentesis, whether the fetus was afflicted with Bradley-Chambers syndrome. But this Judith refused to do. "It would be pointless, for me," she'd said when they'd last discussed it, the night before she was to fly to Florida. "It would only make the remaining months of the pregnancy more difficult, if the test results were positive. You certainly can't suppose that I'd have an *abortion*. Not after all you've heard me say on the subject."

"You never saw what that thing looked like," William had said darkly.

"Whatever it *looked* like, it was a human being. Anyhow, that's not true. I did see it. I paid Mrs. Ruddle five dollars to let me come in when Sondra wasn't there and to hold the baby. I felt guilty going behind Sondra's back, but I felt I had to know."

"You've heard the thing screaming. It was always in pain, every minute of its life. If you had a pet that was in constant pain, you'd have the kindness to put it out of its misery. But to another human being you wouldn't show the kindness you'd show a pet."

"As I recall, that was one of the arguments that Father's attorney used at the sentencing. It didn't convince the judge, and it doesn't convince me. I'm really disappointed in you, William, that you should stand there and argue in favor of your own child's *murder*. I thought you had more decency than that."

"I'm only arguing in favor of amniocentesis, of our *knowing* where we stand."

"Wherever it is, it's me who's standing there, not you. And there is no valid *medical* reason for undertaking such a risk. There is a risk with amniocentesis, you know: one chance in a hundred and fifty of inducing a miscarriage. And no benefit to be derived."

"Except knowledge."

"We'll know soon enough in any case. In July, my doctor says."

When they'd had that conversation, abortion had still been a theoretical possibility. Now, with the pregnancy just two weeks short of the third trimester, that hope was gone.

And William had entertained the hope. Not that Judith would ever have agreed to it, he knew quite well she never would, but there was a good chance with Bradley-Chambers cases that the fetus would abort spontaneously. Beyond that worst-case possibility, even if the baby were as normal as one of the Waltons on the TV show, William did not want to be a father at the age of fourteen. And if he ever did become a father, he didn't want Judith to be the mother of his child. Technically it might not be incest, but it felt like incest, and it would look like incest to other people. Marrying Judith would be a lifelong embarrassment, even supposing it was what they both wanted, which it wasn't.

He couldn't understand now how they could have been so dumb or so careless. It wasn't as though they'd been driven by some overwhelming passion: it was more like a project they'd undertaken for a science class, at least in the preliminary stages. Judith hadn't taken any precautions because that was against her principles, but she had let William do what he could on his own by way of avoiding a baby. And except for one time—the night of Reagan's election, when Ben and Sondra had been out of the house to another fund-raiser at a downtown hotel—William had always been wearing a condom. But that once, obviously, had been enough.

So far Ben didn't know anything. He'd been too wrapped up in his own legal problems to pay much attention to anything that was happening around him, and now he was in prison and Judith was in Florida, and all their visits were over the phone. Rhoda knew Judith was pregnant—that was unavoidable—but Judith had promised William not to tell her mother who had played Romeo to her Juliet. However: *If* the baby should prove to have Bradley-Chambers syndrome, then Judith's silence would be beside the point. The chances that anyone but Ben or William could have been the father were on the order of twenty-five million to one. Talk about leaving fingerprints at the scene of the crime!

Sometimes, thinking how *unnecessary* all this anxiety was, how easy it would have been to have taken a simple test and known for sure, William wanted to climb the walls. Several times he'd phoned Judith in Florida, but whenever he'd worked the conversation around to the subject, Judith would say they couldn't talk because her mother might be listening on the extension line. And now she'd stopped answering the phone at all. When he called he got either an answering machine or Rhoda.

He was helpless. There was nothing he could do. Nothing but wait. Wait for the rain to stop raining. Wait for graduation. Wait for the baby to be born. One in sixteen wasn't bad odds. In Russian roulette your odds were only one in six, and lots of people played Russian roulette and won.

At noon he shared a can of chicken noodle with Grandma O., and then he put on rubber rainboots and a plastic poncho and went out to brave the elements. Under the poncho a nylon backpack produced a hunchback-shaped bulge. Inside the knapsack, wrapped in Saran-Wrap to keep any more of the original bark from shredding off it, was the caduceus. Without even having to touch it, he could feel the power stored inside, a constant tingling in the small of his back, as though his nerves were wired into it. He could almost see himself as one of those battery-operated robots that had replaced model trains as every kid's favorite Christmas present. For a while he lurched along the puddled pavement robot-style, not bending his legs at the knee, swiveling his head from side to side in quick, ratchety twitches. But that got dull, since there was no one else out of doors in such weather to pay attention, and anyhow he was too old now (only a few months from starting at the U) for that kind of goofing off.

The rain got worse, and he decided to get himself a quarter bag of potato chips, then admit defeat and head back home. He went into the little grocery at the corner of Coughlin and Austin and took a bag of Old Dutch potato chips from the bottom shelf of the crunchies rack. Only when he got to the counter and was digging into his pants pocket for the quarter, did he realize that he'd forgotten to transfer his billfold, change, and the house key from yesterday's pants to today's. Madge was at work, and Grandma O. had gone up to Ned's room after lunch to watch "As the World Turns." Once she'd settled in her rocker, she would probably stay with Ned until "General Hospital" was over at three o'clock, and William knew from past experience that she was deaf to the doorbell, knocking, and even the telephone when she was upstairs with the TV on. No doubt that was why she was willing to make the effort of going upstairs.

He looked up at the old man behind the counter, who was waiting for the quarter, and explained: "I'm sorry, I left my money at home."

"That's okay," the old man said, with a prissy smile, like Mr. Whipple in the toilet paper ads. "You can leave your money home and that bag of chips *here*." He bent forward over the counter and appropriated the bag of potato chips.

William was peeved. "I've bought all kinds of stuff here, I'm in here almost every other day, and I can't have credit for a quarter bag of potato chips?"

"Store policy," the grocer said, nodding his head knowingly. "The sign's right up there over the cigarettes. I'll read it for you if the print's too small: IN GOD WE TRUST. ALL OTHERS PAY CASH." He repeated his mean little smile: "Sorry."

"Yeah, sure, I can see you're real sorry."

William stalked out of the store and stood fuming in the shallow recess of the doorway. The rain had got heavier in just the little while he'd been in the store, so heavy that even wearing the poncho he'd be soaked by the time he'd walked a block. For that matter he'd soon be soaked standing here in the doorway. There was a big canvas awning that spanned the front window of the store that would have served quite well as an umbrella, but it was rolled up tight. Whipple probably only opened the awning if you paid him admission.

Sorry! William could have made the old asshole know what sorry was—if he hadn't made it a principle not to use the caduceus on people anymore, whether for good or for ill. In the past few weeks, since moving back to the Obstschmecker house, he'd come to have second thoughts about almost everything he'd done with it. Not regrets, exactly: Jimmy Deeters, Miss Gerhart, the bigwigs at ATA, they'd all got what was coming to them. But maybe his punishments had been too drastic. Maybe he'd been what's called a hanging judge. It might have been better to have gone easier on some of the people at ATA and given them just a smoker's cough—what is it called, emphysema—instead of terminal cancer. A temporary problem that would go away after a while, or that could be reversed. How often, hearing his little brother screaming in endless irremediable pain, he'd wished he could have taken away the perfect health that for him had been only a curse. Health is no blessing when you live in a torture chamber. If he could take away what he gave, or give back what he took away, if each curse or blessing could be like a door that could be gone in or out of, locked or unlocked by the caduceus's power . . .

There was a sharp rapping on the glass of the door. He turned around to see the grocer gesturing at him to move away from the doorway. "You're blocking traffic!" the old man shouted through the glass.

At the same instant as the rapping he felt in the small of his back a zap of something that was neither electricity nor warmth. As though the caduceus itself were reacting to the possibility of its being used as a key. He smiled at the old man behind the glass, and walked off into the rain with a genuine sense of delight, happy to pay the price of a soaking for the idea (which he might not have had in any other set of circumstances) of a curse (or a blessing) that worked like a lock.

He began to work out the details as he walked through the pelting rain, which was no enemy now but the outward and seemingly inevitable expression of his own state of mind. By the time he'd got to the next corner everything was in place but the rhymes. And then, noticing a pay phone that shared the same pole as the traffic light, he had an inspired hunch and reached in to the coin return slot to see if there was a quarter someone had left inside. When he found that there was, he wasn't even surprised at the world's being so ready to fall in with his plans. The glow that still radiated from the mid-small of his back, making every muscle a conscious entity, that glow seemed also to guarantee the success of any action he might undertake. He felt infallible as a pope. If he'd had a basketball in his hands and aimed it at a hoop all the way at the other end of the court, he'd have made a basket at that moment. If he'd been playing cards, he'd have drawn the card he needed to complete a royal flush. There was a great flash of lightning and then a splendid, long, lingering roll of thunder. Heaven itself seemed to agree.

Across the street, catercorner from the phone booth, was a shelter for a bus stop. There were two people in it, and then, by another act of Providence, the Coughlin-Como bus came along and scooped up the two people and carried them off. He crossed the otherwise untrafficked street and took refuge in the bus shelter, where, in no time at all, he had four lines that would do the job. Deftly he slid the knapsack off his shoulders, and, crouching, took out the caduceus and stripped off its protective cellophane. He touched the caduceus to the quarter he'd found in the pay phone and spoke aloud the verses of his improved, reversible incantation:

How much will my quarter buy?
A sty, a sty, beneath your eye.
There shall it swell until the day
My second quarter takes it away.

Then he returned to the store and bought himself a bag of potato chips.

BOOK FIVE

55

Launce Hill was sitting on top of his black sample case on the shoulder of State Highway 32, some twenty-five miles southeast from Crookston and almost exactly a hundred miles south of the border. He was waiting for a ride, without any immediate hope of getting one, but that didn't matter. There'd be more traffic later in the afternoon. Meanwhile, counting his blessings, he figured he was beyond the range of the border patrols, plus he'd managed to keep down the breakfast he'd eaten at the truck stop outside Crookston: dry toast, oatmeal, and skim milk. Each swallow of milk had felt as luxurious as slipping on a cool silk pajama top after a hot bath. All the time now he felt he was burning up. Not his skin, he'd been careful to keep from getting a sunburn, but inside, as though his flesh were slowly being roasted in a microwave.

A car appeared at the far horizon, and Launce hauled himself to his feet and held out his thumb. The car didn't even slow down. The fat woman behind the wheel knit her brow and squinted dead ahead, so intent on the highway that she didn't know he was there. If her husband had been driving, he'd probably have given a hitchhiker the finger. Men have an easier time expressing feelings of hatred and naked aggression. It's their early training with toy guns. As the car sped by, Launce shot the fat woman with his trusty fingertip .45, then sat back down on his sample case. Even as small an effort as that made him wheezy, and the dust raised by the car attacked his eyes like a swarm of gnats and released a slow trickle of poison tears.

The Minnesota weeds were beautiful, higher and bushier than Canadian weeds, and the tears in his eyes acted like lenses to bring far-off flowers into focus. The splinters of death in his soul gave them a gleam of ineffable beauty. Everything turned to poetry when you knew you were dying, even the road kills.

But—he had to keep reminding himself—he wasn't dying. He had survived AIDS, despite testing HIV-positive for six long years, and he would survive ARVIDS, for which AIDS had been merely an appetizer. He'd hung in till they'd come up with a cure, at which point along came mystery plague number two. But Medical Defense Systems had cured cases more advanced than Launce's. All he had to do was get there. Another 250 miles.

A mud-spattered yellow pickup with an unmatched gray left fender approached from the south, slowed as it passed by Launce, and executed a U-turn fifty yards up the road. This time as the pickup drew near, it came to a stop.

Launce picked up his sample case and approached the window of the pickup with misgivings.

"I'm only going down as far as the turnoff to Ada," the driver announced in a tone of challenge. He was a squat, red-faced old fart with a visor cap that advertised Chippewa Bait & Tackle.

"Uh, that's okay." Launce set his case down on the shoulder of the road. The guy had a mean face, and it didn't make sense, his changing direction to accommodate a hitchhiker. Only a highway patrolman would do that. "I'm going a lot farther."

"Into the Cities?"

"Uh-huh."

"Well, you'll have a better chance getting a ride going south after Route 200. So get in. Just be careful with the coffee can on the seat there. It's full of worms."

Reluctantly Launce got in the cab of the pickup, setting the rusted Folger's can on the floor, positioning his sample case on his lap, folding his hands atop the sample case. Without prompting, he began to reinvent the story that had already served to allay the suspicions of three earlier drivers: the family reunion at the Agassiz Wildlife Refuge, the fishing accident, the dead battery, a plausible, slightly farcical mix of family crises and automotive treasons leading to his present carless dilemma.

His audience didn't seem amused. From time to time the driver would swivel sideways to glower at Launce, but never cracked a smile or said a word in response, not so much as "Is that so?" As a salesman, Launce was familiar with the type. Someone like this who combines raw ugliness with other social disadvantages must actively resent smiles and small talk. The man was probably only happy at a lynching. Add to that the incalculable element of pheromonal response: some straights had a nose for gays that was like a bird dog flushing out pheasants from the corn stubble.

When they reached Route 200, the driver took a right turn and kept on driving.

"Hey," Launce pointed out. "That's where I get off."

The driver didn't say a thing, just gave Launce another sideways glance and stepped on the gas. The speedometer needle edged up to its high-noon position of 50 mph.

Launce knew, without the driver's announcing his intentions, that he was being escorted to the local health authority, who would only have to test his saliva and Launce would be on a greased slide to the nearest plague camp. He sighed.

Then, since there was no real alternative, he dipped his hand inside his jacket pocket, thumbed off the safety of the Lady Winchester, a pretty little handgun manufactured at the end of the eighties for the defensive needs of the fair sex, and held it up to the plastic webbing of the visored hat. "I think you're driving *too fast!*" he shouted into the old fart's ear. "I wish you would drive *more slowly.*"

When, instead, the old fart floored the gas pedal, Launce pulled the trigger, and the bullet went right through the man's skull and out the open window of the pickup. The hands did not at once lose their grip on the steering wheel, and the foot continued to bear down on the gas pedal. This went on long enough for Launce to wonder if he'd fired a blank, and then the head drooped to one side and blood seeped out of the bullet hole and dripped on the bib of his overalls.

Launce got hold of the wheel just in time to keep them from going into a tailspin. He was as much concerned to keep his jacket from getting bloodied as with keeping the truck on the road. He didn't have a second suit with him.

As the pickup coasted round a bend, the watertower, trees, and rooftops of the town of Ada came into view. Launce managed to nudge the corpse's foot off the gas pedal and toed the brake. The pickup rolled to a stop beside a sign welcoming Launce to Ada, population 784.

Make that seven hundred and eighty-three, the eternal proofreader in his soul corrected.

He got out of the cab and, after he'd unloosed the corpse from the safety belt, he tugged it to the passenger side of the car, grasping only the unbloodied bib of the overalls. In the process he overturned the can of worms he'd been warned not to spill. He'd always had a horror of worms, and these were nightcrawlers, fat as garden snakes, and all in a frenzy of hope now that they were out of the coffee can. Launce could sympathize with them—who better?—but he could *not* bring himself actually to pick them up in his fingers and drop them into the ditch beside the road. He positioned the corpse's booted feet carefully on the floormat so that none of the worms were injured, then slammed the door shut, and went round to the driver's side of the car.

The engine was still running, and the road was clear in both directions. For the first time in his life since taking his driver's license exam at the age of seventeen, he executed a perfect K-turn. The corpse tipped first to the right and then to the left. Launce pulled to the side of the road, fastened the corpse's seat belt and his own, and headed back to State Highway 32 at a moderate 45 mph.

This was the first time in his life he'd ever killed anyone, and he felt a rush of pit-a-pat hyperkinetic coming-of-age glory, which was also, like an inappropriate hard-on, a little embarrassing, since theoretically he didn't approve of the machismo of homicide. He'd been sincere, in his draft-dodging days, in wanting to make love, not war. It occurred to him that the corpse beside him might well be (or rather, the proofreader amended, have been) a Viet Nam vet. He was the right age and social class and the kind of good citizen who follows the rules, such as the rule to report suspicious strangers to the health authority.

It further occurred to him that he ought to find out who his victim was (had been) and what (such as money) he might have on him. In any case, not to show some curiosity at such a time would add insult to injury. He had not yet sunk to the subhuman level of some mass murderer who just sprays bullets willy-nilly, killing anyone in his path. If he killed someone, he should at least know his name.

His name was Ray Bonner, and he was, like Launce, a Leo. Which figured: it's never wise for one Leo to thwart another. Now he knew.

Forty-six dollars in cash. Two useless credit cards. And a Gas-O-Mat credit card with the confirmation number written right across the back, just the way you're warned not to do.

There were sunglasses in the blood-sodden pocket of the overalls bib, and these Launce fitted over the corpse's nose and ears. From the same pocket he took a pack of cigarettes and lit (his fingers were beginning to tremble) two, one for himself and inserted the other, dangling, into the corner of the corpse's mouth. It seemed a proper sort of funeral pomp for someone like Ray Bonner.

After the foolish indulgence of the cigarette (but when you think you're dying it's hard to just say no) Launce unwound, focusing on the muscles of his neck and shoulders, humming his own private mantra he'd paid one hundred and fifty dollars for at the start of his TM course back in the lost paradise of Toronto 1975: *Shamoo Urmee Zama!* The fellow who'd run the course had been a perfect charlatan but a perfect hunk as well, and Launce hadn't in the least regretted spending one hundred and fifty dollars for three nonsense words. Indeed, they'd always worked quite well for him: *Shamoo Urmee Zama!* His spiritual leader had chanted it along with him, his fingers digging into Launce's trapezius muscles. *Shamoo Urmee Zama:* it always did the job.

56

On the Sunday before Memorial Day, it had rained all day long, and the rain had continued through the next day, and the *next* Sunday it had looked like rain again, and Madge had said she had a headache and disappeared as soon as the sun came out, so here it was, two weeks after Memorial Day, and Mrs. Obstschmecker had yet to visit Mr. Obstschmecker's grave at Veterans' Cemetery or even make it to Mass at OLM. For the first time in how many years? She took down the notepad from its holder beside the phone on the kitchen wall and did the arithmetic: 1999 − 1970 = 29. Twenty-nine years she had faithfully visited Mr. Obstschmecker's grave bringing him irises from the backyard, and now there wasn't one iris left. She felt peeved. It would mean buying flowers at a florist, and the price of even a small bouquet these days was outrageous. Not that Mrs. Obstschmecker had been to a florist recently, but Madge was always bringing home these gigantic arrangements and claiming to have paid fifty or sixty dollars for them. For flowers! Mrs. Obstschmecker suspected that she was making off with them from the clinic and that these were the bouquets of patients, who were all vegetables like Ned and so couldn't really have appreciated them, and they did make the house look lovelier, so why make a fuss? That was Mrs. Obstschmecker's philosophy.

The boy was supposed to arrive at nine o'clock, and it was only seven thirty now. Madge was still asleep, but Mrs. Obstschmecker always awoke once it got to be light, which meant six thirty these days. She blamed the early sunrise on daylight savings time, though Madge said it was the other way round. Maybe she was right. In any case, six thirty was just too early to be waking up if you didn't have a job to go to or somebody's breakfast to make. Already the dawn had brightened to full morning, and the X's of the security gates were sharply defined against the lowered window blinds.

Now a new silhouette appeared on the blinds. A squirrel! It scampered up the iron lattice and paused at the point from which it could best launch itself toward the bird feeder hanging from the lowest limb of the elm. "Shoo!" Mrs. Obstschmecker called out. "Shoo! Go away!" She shuffled in her slippered feet toward the window, but before she could get there to raise the blind and rap a protest against the glass, the squirrel made its leap.

And there the nasty little thief was, when the blind was up, clinging to the swinging plastic cylinder, stuffing himself with birdseed and staring back at her with his beady little black eyes blazing defiance. She rapped and shouted for the squirrel to go away, but of course he stayed right where he was, shoveling the seeds out of the feeder. She wished she could have opened the window and thrown something at him, but at her own insistence the windows were sealed up tight with caulking at every crack, though Madge insisted it didn't do a bit of good. Still, Mrs. Obstschmecker felt safer knowing the outside air was outside, just as she felt safer with the security bars in place, even though they provided the squirrels the ladder they needed to get to the feeder. And there was nowhere else the feeder could be hung, she and Madge had gone through all the possibilities and there was nothing to be done. You couldn't poison the seed, because that would kill the dear little birds as well as the squirrels.

Lisa Michaels had remarked some time ago that Mrs. Obstschmecker could solve her problem by thinking of the bird feeder as a squirrel feeder. Weren't squirrels just as cute as birds? she'd asked in that superior tone of voice. Lisa was Jewish. Whenever she came visiting with her twins (which wasn't that often, thank goodness), Mrs. Obstschmecker had to remind herself that the woman was no relation. Not an Obstschmecker, not even a Hill, only Madge's stepson's wife. Madge said it was un-Christian to point out that Lisa was not family, but a fact is a fact. Just because William had become Mr. Big Shot with a Cadillac car and had his picture in magazines didn't mean Mrs. Big Shot hadn't grown up with the last name of Schechner.

But there was no need to dwell on unpleasantness. It was the fault of that squirrel. Mrs. Obstschmecker turned away from the window and turned on the TV. "Fill in the Blanks" was on, and for a while Mrs. Obstschmecker tried competing against the contestants, but they played too fast, and the solution of the first puzzle, SNUG AS A RUBBER, was supposed to be a popular saying. Mrs. Obstschmecker had never heard such a saying, but she could guess what it meant. There was dirty talk *everywhere* these days—on the TV, in newspapers, and the boy who was coming to take her to church, though he was otherwise the politest young man and claimed to be a born-again, even he used four-letter words like he'd never been taught any otherwise. And with a nun for a mother! Not that that made a speck of difference these days, not with a Lesbian nun

running for the state assembly right here in the Twin Cities and conducting kneel-ins at the Cathedral so they could be Lesbian priests instead of
Lesbian nuns! And all of it discussed on the TV like it was today's
weather!

She blipped off the TV. And sat and stewed.

Upstairs the toilet flushed. Madge was up. But that didn't mean she'd
come downstairs any time soon. She had a microwave in her bedroom and
her own separate phone line, which connected to the computer, and the
computer connected to everything else, so Madge could lock the doors at
night without leaving her bedroom. She could even talk to Mrs. Obstschmecker on the television set, since there were gizmos now that let you
do that, though Mrs. Obstschmecker wouldn't let one be connected to her
TV. How would you know when someone was looking at you and when
they weren't? Sometimes Madge left the camera on in her room and Mrs.
Obstschmecker could see her on the TV screen walking around without a
stitch of clothes. The computer revolution! Progress!

Mrs. Obstschmecker pressed the Intercom button. "Madge," she
shouted into the little microphone, "do you want me to make breakfast
for you?"

"No, Mother, thanks just the same."

"That cantaloupe you brought home last week should be ripe by now.
I've had it on the windowsill."

No reply.

"That squirrel was back at the feeder again."

Nothing.

"There's still time for you to change your mind and come along to
Mass and the Veterans' Cemetery. You haven't visited your father's grave
for I don't know how long."

"I took you there last year, Mother, if you'll recall."

"What's that? You know you have to talk into the microphone if you
want me to hear you."

"I said, 'No thank you!' "

"You took me there, but you stayed in the car the whole time."

Silence.

"I don't think it's right I should visit your father's grave on Memorial
Day with a stranger."

"Judge is not a stranger, Mother. He's a member of our family."

"He's the illegitimate child of someone who is no relation to any Obstschmecker, so how is he our family I'd like to know!"

"Mother, you know very well William and Lisa have adopted Judge as
their son."

"And *they're* no relation either."

"Mother, really. After all that William's done for us."

"And what about all we did for him? Who looked after him after his mother killed herself and that Winckelmeyer man went to prison for murdering his own little baby? Family! And the daughter's just as bad. A nun with a son in reform school for setting buildings on fire. And that's who you're getting to take me to see my husband's grave because you're too busy to take five minutes to honor your father's memory. Well, I guess that tells me what *I* can expect!"

Another silence, but this one Mrs. Obstschmecker interpreted as abashed. At last Madge said, "As to who's going to bury who, that remains to be seen. You'll probably outlast me, the way you're going."

"That's because I take care of myself," said Mrs. Obstschmecker, who prided herself on doing without extra salt on her food and for limiting her intake of cholesterol.

"I've got to go wash up Ned now and feed him his breakfast. Make sure you're ready to go before Judge gets here. I got down your best wig, it's on your dresser."

Mrs. Obstschmecker hated being told what to do by her daughter but went about doing it nonetheless. By the time she had showered and dried and powdered and got into her best summer dress and then decided the white dress was more suitable for a visit to the cemetery, it was time to begin to worry whether the boy would be late.

But then the doorbell sounded, and Mrs. Obstschmecker felt the same little tingle she'd felt sixty-five years ago in Anoka the first time Mr. O. had called at the house with a bouquet of flowers. This boy had come with a bouquet, too—roses, no less, which Lisa Michaels had picked from her own rosebushes—so they would not have to waste good money at the florist's, after all.

It was hard to catch everything the boy said, since he kept forgetting to speak up, and even when he did, his Florida accent made him hard to understand. But he was a proper southern gentleman in terms of opening the car door (he was driving William's sky-blue Cadillac) and helping her into the safety belt. Looking at him sideways as he sat behind the wheel, with his back scarcely touching the seat behind him, Mrs. Obstschmecker could almost suppose it was her husband as he'd been in the 1930s, the hair short but still neatly parted, the Clark Gable–type mustache, the *size* of him. Even the stiff white collar and the bow tie, since that was the fashion again.

"You would have liked my husband," Mrs. Obstschmecker said in a burst of generosity. "He was a lot like you."

"I'm sure that's so," the boy answered, never turning sideways, keeping his eyes on the street, a responsible driver.

"August 20, 1970. I'll never forget the day. A stroke. No warning. One minute he was watering the lawn, the next minute, gone! Madge—that's Madge Michaels, my daughter, you've met her at the house—"

"Yes, ma'am, many times."

"Madge was at the hospital, and I called her, and they sent an ambulance right off the bat. But there was nothing they could do."

"We'll all be called to Judgment sometime," said the boy, "and usually sooner than we think. That's God's way."

Mrs. Obstschmecker tried to take some comfort from this reflection. The boy's tone of voice made it sound as though it *should* be comforting, but the idea seemed almost the opposite, a threat. Protestants had their own slant on things, which didn't mean that they were right, but they thought they were, so you had to be polite discussing religion.

"I hope you don't mind my asking," she began with an exaggerated delicacy, "but how is it that you came to be a Protestant. I mean, your mother, after all, Mrs., um, Winckelmeyer—"

The boy made a loud snorting sound, which had been just the way Mr. Obstschmecker had laughed at something when he didn't want to laugh out loud.

"She's a Catholic, isn't she?"

"That's hard to say, ma'am. She says she is, but I guess the pope off in Rome says she isn't. She's one of these skiz-matics."

The boy made it sound like a kind of appliance, or a car, and Mrs. Obstschmecker had to smile. There could be no question about the pope questioning *her* faith. Whatever the Holy Father wanted her to think she thought. She was against birth control and abortion and pornography and priests getting married and women becoming priests. She didn't go to Mass every Sunday, but at her age that wasn't to be expected.

"And were you sent to a Catholic school?" Mrs. Obstschmecker pressed on.

Again, the boy made his snorting sound. "Just about everything I did had some Catholic connection. I grew up in this big com-mune outside of Miami. We grew our own pesticide-free Catholic vegetables and brewed Catholic beer by the barrelful. They are all drinkers, those Catholics down there."

"So how is it that you left the Church? You must have been very young."

"I'll be eighteen on the Fourth of July, and I been a follower of Brother Orson since I was fifteen." He turned sideways to give Mrs. Obstschmecker a significant look. "We don't call ourselves Pro-*test*-ants. The time for pro-testing is over. Now's the time for Judgment."

Mrs. Obstschmecker waited for an answer to her question, but none was forthcoming. The boy turned his attention back to the road, and two blocks further on they pulled into the OLM parking lot, once the school playground. The school had closed down years ago for lack of funds and students.

The boy locked the car and offered his arm for the walk round the corner to the church. Everything seemed as nice as could be, but then, the moment they came to the church steps, the spell was broken. A crowd of colored people had gathered about the main door, as though they were waiting to throw rice on a bridal couple. Mrs. Obstschmecker couldn't see over their heads and wondered why they were all just standing about.

The boy tapped an older black man on the shoulder and asked, "Is there some problem about going in the church?"

"There's protesters blocking the doorway. Some of them got themselves chained to the railing."

"Why's that?"

"They don't like Father Sinclair bringing in the Imani Temple people."

"And having the women say 'Our Mother who art in heaven' instead of 'Our Father,' " added a black woman.

"Uh-huh." Judge turned to ask Mrs. Obstschmecker, "You still want to go to Mass?"

"Are they having Mass?"

The boy passed the question on to the black woman. "They having Mass?"

"If you can get into the church, it's already started."

"Shit, that's no problem."

The boy stooped down and scooped up the short, portly body of Mrs. Obstschmecker like a groom on his honeymoon sweeping up his bride to carry her over the threshold of their new home. She was utterly flabbergasted but not to the degree that she forgot to secure her wig with both hands. The boy mounted the steps, saying "Scuze us, please," and "Stand aside, please." The crowd on the steps parted to either side, revealing the row of demonstrators sitting, arms locked together, on the top step of the church. They had a bedsheet banner spread out before them that said, NO MORE VOODOO MASSES. GOD IS OUR <u>FATHER</u>!!!

It dawned on Mrs. Obstschmecker as she saw the demonstrators, and they saw her, cradled in Judge Michaels's arms, that they were all whites while all the people they were keeping out of the church were black.

Judge began walking up the last two steps across which the bedsheet banner was spread. "Please don't go in Our Lady of Mercy," the oldest of the demonstrators shouted, a man whom Mrs. Obstschmecker recognized by his beard and his Roman collar as Father Youngermann, the church's pastor. "The archdiocese does *not* approve of the new liturgy. Father Sinclair has no right to be saying Mass here. Please do not cross—"

"I'll tell you what," said Judge. "I'm going to kick you in the face if you don't move your ass. I got this lady here wants to go in, and I mean to take her in."

"Just stay where you are, everyone," Father Youngermann said to the other demonstrators. "We will not be moved."

A woman at the far end of the line began to sing "We Shall Overcome," and the others took it up.

Judge aimed a kick at the priest's solar plexus. He doubled over, and the men on either side of him didn't try to keep their arms locked in his. They even slid sideways to make room for Judge to pass between them.

"No violence!" shouted the woman who had started the singing going. "There must be *no* violence."

Once inside the big doorway, Judge set Mrs. Obstschmecker back down on her feet. The blacks who'd been kept out by the demonstrators were coming into the vestibule single file, through the breach Judge had made.

"Well now," said Judge matter-of-factly, as though nothing out of the ordinary had happened, "where do you generally like to sit—up close by the driver or back here by the door?"

57

Father Lyman Sinclair looked down from the pulpit of Our Lady of Mercy Church and waited for the spirit of prophecy to give him a jump start. The congregation was used to Father Lyman's ways and knew his long pre-sermon pauses were not signals to them to be quieter, as they would have been from Father Youngermann. Almost the opposite: Father Lyman actually encouraged people to whisper and confabulate and get comfortable around each other. "Half of communion," he liked to say, "is communication. And who says the Mass has to be a military exercise?" So, while they waited for Father Lyman to come to a simmer, many of the parishioners turned to their neighbors to tell what they'd seen of the demonstration outside and how the tall white boy with the old lady in the third pew from the front had kicked Father Youngermann in the stomach.

Father Lyman himself knew nothing of the fracas, but he was aware of the two strangers. Not that many white parishioners attended the ten o'clock service at OLM, not since the Imani Temple people had been invited to move their worship service here from All Souls' Parish, from which they'd been removed by force after they'd lost their long legal battle with the archdiocese. For almost five years the leaders of the African-American Catholic Church (the official name for Imani Temple) had been ordaining their own independent clergy and developing their own liturgy, modeled partly on that of their fellow heretics and apostates, the American Catholic Church. The main practical difference between the two movements was that Imani Temple claimed the right, even though its members were excommunicated, to share all Roman Catholic places of worship, a privilege not generally accorded them. In all the Twin Cities only Our Lady of Mercy had opened its doors to the Imani Temple, and here only because of Father Sinclair's political savvy. With the parish council's help he'd been able to make an end run around Father Younger-mann on one of the latter's periodic retreats to his favorite Josephan detox center in Phoenix, Arizona. Father Youngermann had returned to the so-bering discovery that OLM had opened its doors, and its ten o'clock Sun-day service, to the Imani Temple. Still more sobering had been his discovery that the doors couldn't be closed. Now it was Youngermann and a small band of ultramontane rednecks who had taken up civil dis-obedience as the court of last resort.

But these matters, just because they were uppermost in the minds of the congregation, were not what Father Lyman wanted to speak about. A good sermon should be a lesson in prayer. That had been the constant theme of Monsignor McKibben, the Jesuit who had taught homiletics at the North American College in Rome.

So there it was, like a door opening before him, the way to begin. He began: "When I was in Rome, studying to be a priest, I had a teacher, an Irish Jesuit who'd been a missionary in Zimbabwe and Taiwan and I can't remember where else, and this man had a favorite saying about sermons. 'A good sermon,' he said, 'is like a lesson in prayer.' Now most of you have probably heard me preach a few sermons that didn't exactly follow that prescription. Some of my sermons have been more like political speeches than like prayers. What's prayer, after all? It's talking with God. Which isn't easy. It's a lot easier talking with other people, 'cause they'll talk back and you can tell if you've made a connection. With God it's more like you're on the phone with someone who's listening so hard he forgets to say even 'Mm-hm,' or 'How's that?' "

"Mm-hm," said someone in one of the front pews, and right on top of it, from the back of the church, Kristi Aldritch called out, "How's that, Lyman?"

Father Lyman joined in the laughter.

Then, after a beat, "The Bible says there's one prayer that's all anyone ever needs, and you know how it begins: *Our Father—*"

"Or Our Mother—don't forget her!" It was Kristi again, always to be depended on to look out for equal opportunity for her sex, always alert to patriarchal ploys.

"Well now, Kristi, you've got a point. I guess we won't any of us know what sex God is till we get to Heaven and see for ourselves. But let's suppose that Jesus wasn't just an old-fashioned sexist who didn't know better than to suppose the Almighty Alpha and Omega might transcend questions of gender. Let's suppose he meant something by starting off his prayer to our *father*. Fathers and mothers are different kinds of people."

There were several low *Mm-hm*s and *Amen*s.

"Mothers are just plain closer, for one thing. When you're a baby you suck milk from her breasts. She hugs you. She loves you. She's *there*. Fathers . . . they can't be counted on the same way. They're not always around when you need them. They're off at their jobs—"

"Or in jail!"

"True enough, Kristi. Anyhow, he's away. Maybe far away. Like the prayer says, *Who art in heaven*. Though, just as a side note, the Protestants say *Which art in heaven*, and in terms of the gender problem, that's interesting, 'cause 'who' is for people but 'which'? 'Which' is like saying God is something else besides a person. Anyhow, who or which, he's in heaven, far away from human shit and misery. It's all blue sky and sunshine, and your prayer is like a kite you're sending up there—"

"Kites again, Lyman?" This from Jerry Stiller, who was sitting with the other members of the parish council around the communion table. It was true, and no accident, that kites were a regular feature of Father Lyman's sermons. His first consciousness both of sin and of redemption had come in the form of a kite.

"Mm-hm, kites again. And what's written on the kite is just the basic message man has to send to God. *Hallowed be thy name!*"

"Amen, amen!"

"Oh no, not so fast. We got a lot of the Our Father left before we hit Amen. We got *Thy kingdom come*. Not *came*, it's not here yet. But it will come. It's the first thing we've got to believe. It's faith and hope rolled together in one big promise. It will come, it is coming. And I believe it's got to be very close. Just think what year it is. One nine nine nine. A few months now the odometer of history will be turning over its last row of zeroes, and then—*The trumpet shall sound, and the dead shall be raised incorruptible, and we shall be changed.*"

"Hallelujah!"

"Hallelujah, indeed. But that trumpet is sounding not just glory hallelujah, it's sounding judgment, and there's not going to be anywhere to hide from the sound of that trumpet, no safety perimeter sealed against the plague he'll send down, the plague we already can see mowing people down around us. No fallout shelter, not against the radiation God has got. No sterile labs, no millionaire mansion with its air pumped in from tanks of oxygen.

"So we better all shape up. We better mean it when we say *Thy will be done, on earth as it is in heaven.* 'Cause that's what the judgment will be about: Have we done his will? Have we loved one another? Not just said nice things about love on Sundays in church, but got out and done some actual hands-on love. 'Cause he knows, God knows, he knows for sure."

He paused and smiled and caught the eye of Jason Beale. Jason was the main security officer at the A & P. "What comes next, Jason?"

"Daily bread," Jason muttered, pretending shyness but pleased to have proved he was actually following the sermon.

"Right. And that's the part of the prayer everyone understands: Gimme. That's what people mostly think prayer is about. Gimme this, gimme that. Once you got the bread you need some butter. Anyhow, in the daily bread category we seem to be doing pretty well and I'll bet most of the people Jesus was dealing with weren't exactly starving. Not with the wedding feasts and loaves and fishes. So maybe the daily bread he's talking about means something else. Maybe it's like the bread of God, in John, chapter six, verse thirty-three: *The bread of God is he which cometh down from heaven, and giveth life unto the world.* Or, in a nutshell, *Jesus said unto them, I am the bread of life.* That's clear enough. What the prayer is asking is for God to be *here*"—Lyman gave the side of his gut a solid slap—"every day, inside of us, where we can feel him like a full belly of food."

Another pause, and then the verse, "*And forgive us our trespasses, as we forgive those who trespass against us.* Another version has 'debts' and 'debtors,' *Forgive us our debts.* I wish I knew which bank would do that, and that reminds me at some point we've got to discuss the building fund. That ceiling up there looks so pretty, with those big rafters, and the stained glass either side. I read in the *Star-Tribune* that considered purely as a work of architecture this church has got it over the Basilica downtown. A landmark of the twenties Byzantine Revival no less. But structurally the roof is a borderline case, and the inside of the dome needs more than a can of paint. So that's one debt that'll have to be paid and not forgiven.

"Trespassing, on the other hand, I've always thought is an essentially harmless activity. You see all those woods when you drive north a ways out of the city with the signs tacked on the trees, NO TRESPASSING. And I will confess that I have sometimes trespassed—*as* I've been trespassed against, which I try to deal with forgivingly, such as when a basketball game starts up at eleven p.m. just outside my bedroom. Loud noise late at night is definitely trespassing. But evil? No, evil is something else, which the prayer comes to next. Trespassing can get you into trouble, even into jail, but it means well. Trespassing is just looking for fun. A joint, if I may say so, is a trespass. But evil . . ." Lyman shook his head.

"Evil *hurts* people, and it may not even know it's doing so, like a tank that just runs over innocent bystanders in a crowd, or a banker investing millions of dollars in cigarette companies. Oh, you start looking for evil and it shows up all over the map, and all you can hope for, really, is that fate doesn't put you in a situation where evil starts to look tempting, where it looks like an easy score but it ends up homicide. *Lead us not into temptation.*" He paused again.

"*But deliver us* . . . from *doing* the evil we might be tempted to? Or from the evil that's out there like Jaws or this damned plague that's keeping everyone but us sitting home locked up in their houses, this plague that doesn't sniff around for sinners like old AIDS did, but just strikes down anyone it takes a fancy to, like some psycho sniper? The prayer doesn't specify which kind of evil it has in mind, and what I think is that there's no real difference. The evil that gets hold of you when you decide that nothing but your own ass is worth saving, that is the same evil as the one that chews you up directly. Now, I could be quite wrong about that. In fact, that's probably a heresy. It's like saying evil is too big and too bad to break loose from once you get to be a sinner. And I know, or I hope, that has not been true for my own particular sins, some of which definitely passed beyond the category of No Trespassing. That part of the prayer I still haven't scoped out, but maybe that's why Jesus said this prayer would last a lifetime. 'Cause all the problems we've got to discuss with God, all the ones nobody's got an easy answer for, they're all there, built in—fathers and children, power and glory, heaven and earth, bread and the national debt, and the knowledge of good and evil. God bless you."

Father Lyman smiled and stepped down from the pulpit and nodded to Sister Fidelis in the organ loft, who was ready to hand with her own rendition of the Lord's Prayer.

58

"Judge," Mrs. Obstschmecker urged in a commanding whine, "are you sure this is a good idea?"

Judge heeded her no more than Madge would have. He just stood there at the edge of the crowd funneling through the church doors and wouldn't budge. "Won't take but a minute, ma'am. Then we'll zip right off to that cemetery and get those roses to your old man. Anywhere I ever been to church you stop by after the service even if it's only to shake hands."

This was precisely what Mrs. Obstschmecker was dreading. There had been a period, years back, when they'd tried to make people *kiss* the person sitting next to them in the pew, no matter who they were or what disease they might have. The Kiss of Peace it was called. Mrs. Obstschmecker would only go to church then when she had someone she knew sitting on each side of her. Finally in the eighties things returned to normal and you only had to nod and smile at people at that point in the Mass.

The crowd diminished to where only Judge and Mrs. Obstschmecker and the people who'd been sitting up at the communion table were left inside the church.

Judge shook hands with the black priest.

"You must be the young man who dealt so roughly with Father Youngermann. From everything people have told me it seemed unprovoked and unnecessary."

"I was out of line an' I admit it," said Judge, "and I beg to apologize for my hasty action. I would've never used my feet against a man if my arms were free. I have a bad temper, but I know that is no excuse."

"I will convey your apology to Father Youngermann. I'm told that he wasn't seriously hurt. Are you . . . visiting the Twin Cities? I don't think I've seen you at OLM before."

"I'm from Florida. But this lady here has been going to your church for a while, I believe."

"Oh yes, hers is a familiar face." The black priest held out his hand. "Mrs. . . . ?"

Mrs. Obstschmecker offered her fingertips (but not her name) for a gingerly handshake.

"I am not a Catholic myself," Judge volunteered.

"No?" (The black priest was not letting go of Mrs. Obstschmecker's fingers, despite the hint of a gentle tug.)

"I was brought up a Catholic by my mother, who is now a nun."

"Really?" (She tugged again, and the priest responded by clamping her hand inside both of his and flashing his dentures in a priestly smile.)

"I am a follower of Brother Orson. Praise God."

"I always praise God." (At last he let go of her hand.) "But I can't say I'd do the same for Brother Orson."

"Maybe not, but there was things you said from the pulpit about the Lord's Prayer and the Judgment soon to be that could of come right off one of Brother Orson's audio cass-ettes. I was wondering if you had seen his TV show."

"No, I can't say I have. I've read *about* him."

"Then you've read lies, prob-ly. That's all you ever hear in the media about him, seck-uler humanist lies."

"Judge!" Mrs. Obstschmecker tugged on his coat sleeve. "We should be getting to the cemetery."

"This is my great-grandmother, by adoption," Judge went on, un-budged. "I am taking her to the cemetery where her husband is buried. If you would like to come with us, I will tell you about the promises the Lord has made through his prophet. As you said, in the pulpit, we are living in the Last Days. A Judgment is approaching. All men will not be saved."

"Do you know, I think I'll take you up on that."

"Father, please!" Mrs. Obstschmecker acted as though the smoke alarm in the kitchen had gone off. "There's no necessity!"

"What's the old saying? Opportunity knocks but once. I've never had a chance to speak with a follower of the famous Brother Orson. None of my parishioners"—he turned to wink at the members of the parish council who'd been hovering at the edge of the conversation—"are likely to become heretics in that direction. As I understand it, Brother Orson holds out little hope of salvation for the sons of Ham."

"That's true. But we are not forbidden to testify unto the heathen."

"And you will be heading back this way after a while?"

"After this lady has had time to pray beside the grave."

"Judge, *really!* I'm sure the father has more important things to do."

"The name is Lyman," said the priest, holding out his hand again to Judge. "Lyman Sinclair. No need to call me Father."

"I didn't mean to. I got but one father, God Almahty." Then, with an odd smile, as an afterthought, "Which art in heaven."

Mrs. Obstschmecker was too flustered to reprimand Judge for showing so little appreciation to William for having adopted him as his own legal son. It was true, of course, that the boy had no real father (unless it was Ben Winckelmeyer who'd got his own daughter pregnant, which Mrs. Obstschmecker had heard Madge speculating over the phone when she thought her mother wasn't on the line), but for *him* to say he had no father was certainly an act of ingratitude.

Judge led them to the Cadillac, and the priest was suitably impressed, which led to Judge's explaining who his adoptive father was, and the priest was suitably impressed at that, too. It never ceased to astonish Mrs. Obstschmecker that the name of William Michaels—*Dr.* Michaels—should be known by so many people who'd never met him. But in fact this black priest had met him, for as they set off for the cemetery (Mrs. Obstschmecker had insisted she'd be more comfortable in the backseat), he explained that he'd gone to school with William at OLM.

"Well, isn't that something. You and Billy classmates, my goodness."

But the men in the front seat continued talking to each other as though she hadn't said a word. The priest was interested only in hearing Judge go on about one thing, Brother Orson. Judge, however, wanted to explain about the Rapture and the Last Judgment and some book that was sealed with seven seals, and some horses connected to that. All a lot of nonsense as far as Mrs. Obstschmecker was concerned, and after a few minutes the priest got tired of it, too.

"Actually, Judge—that's your name, 'Judge'?"

"Since I was baptized into Chrahst, Judge's been my name. Praise God."

"His real name is John," Mrs. Obstschmecker said, leaning forward to speak directly into the priest's ear. "John Winckelmeyer."

"Actually, Judge," the priest continued, "I've read the Book of Revelations myself, and I've got my own ideas about what it may mean. What I'm more interested in is Brother Orson himself and your, uh, relationship with him."

"I relate to him every day. Praise God."

"On the TV, you mean?"

"And in my heart."

"But the image you *see* on the TV, you realize, don't you, that it's like a cartoon. And when Brother Orson is talking with that angel who's got so many opinions—"

"The Angel Lazarus. Praise God."

"That's not a real angel, that's a computer-generated program. And when you ask them questions—if you've got that interactive capability—"

"When I ask the Angel Lazarus a question, the Angel Lazarus tells me all I need to know. When I was in prison, like Paul, for testifying to my faith, the angel came to me and said I would be redeemed from my bondage. Soon, the angel said. And so I was, not two weeks later. That's when the Lord sent me here."

Mrs. Obstschmecker sighed and gave up trying to keep the boy from making himself look worse than he had to. He talked about his time in prison without an ounce of shame.

"But you was asking about do I know what I see is a kind of cartoon. Well shit, any fool knows that. But is the pope off in Rome any different? Doesn't he have his Cistern Chapel with all its graven images of what God's supposed to look like?"

"For one thing," the priest said, starting to sound like the boy was getting to him (which he always did eventually; Mrs. Obstschmecker had seen him drive William right up the wall), "it is the Sis-*teen* Chapel, not the Cistern Chapel—"

"I know *that*. I was making a joke. Now let me ask you: you think when you see your pope on TV that those little dots sprinkled on the TV screen is a real person? Isn't that a *picture* the same as Brother Orson's picture? Only difference is, Brother Orson is more careful *how* he gets his picture taken."

"Are you aware of the stories that have been in the newspapers? Do you know about the trial going on right now in Florida? It's not the media who are saying the man is a fabrication. It's people in his own organization. People who were officers. The chief of the studio where the programs are put together has said, and I quote, 'Brother Orson is no more real than Mickey Mouse.'"

"Well then, I guess Mickey Mouse must be more real than we knew." He turned sideways to smile at the priest. "That's another joke. Praise God."

The boy did have a wicked smile. It always put Mrs. Obstschmecker in mind of the nice young senator who used to work for President Reagan. Oliver North. Except that Judge's hair was shorter and he had a stockier build.

"The obvious answer to your question," Judge said, in his most serious and reverent tone of voice, "is Paul to the Corinthians: *For now we see through a glass, darkly; but then face to face.* That is a clear prophecy of Brother Orson. And as for the lies in the media, it's no news that Brother Orson has got enemies. And enemies spread lies."

"You have an amazing faith," said the priest.

The boy smiled. "When I have spoken with Brother Orson, he has said to me, *Judge*—he called me by my name, Judge—*you have a per-fect faith.* And I guess if he said it, it must be so."

59

Valerie Bright was the perfect administrator: brusque, incurious, a benevolent martinet toward her staff, who either loved her or left, and discreetly obsequious to her superiors; to Ben Winckelmeyer on a daily basis, to Dr. Michaels whenever her duties took her within the perimeter of his personal regard. She understood his need for privacy. Creative natures require solitude, and it was one of Ms. Bright's primary duties (though not one listed in the official job description of the administrative director) to create that solitude for him.

Ben had discovered her at a Christian Fellowship Breakfast in Eden Prairie some time after his release from prison. Even then she had seemed to him the incarnate spirit of the eighties, one of those plump, gilded assistant directors of a government agency who would appear on the nightly news denying guilt, glaring at the cameras through enormous glasses, shameless and unconfoundable. This had been during a troubled period for the breakfast's sponsor, the Son of Man Foundation, and Ms. Bright had shown the stuff she was made of by proclaiming her undiminished faith in the copresidents of the foundation, Hal and Bess McKinley. If the Lord had bestowed unusual bounties on them, surely that was a mark of his grace and no reason for a media witch-hunt. When less confident voices expressed misgivings and even repeated the media's allegations, Ms. Bright had held her hands over her ears and declared, "I don't want to hear any more so-called facts." Then, lowering her hands and smiling warmly, "I thought this was supposed to be a *fellowship* breakfast."

She had been much cast down when the McKinleys, at their sentencing, had acknowledged some degree of guilt with regard to the funds that had disappeared, though they still insisted that they'd always tried to follow the promptings of the Holy Spirit. The judge had said he'd try to do the same in meting out their sentence, which was eight to twelve years, or half that term if either of the copresidents was able to help in locating the missing funds.

Ms. Bright had been furious. "I just know that man was being sarcastic," she'd confided to Ben on their first date, two months after the fellowship breakfast. "Mean and sarcastic."

"Try not to think about it," he had urged.

"You're right, I know. But when I think of those two beautiful people in some terrible prison . . ."

"Prison doesn't have to be terrible. If I hadn't been in prison, I probably wouldn't have found my way to Jesus. Prison can lead sinners back to God."

Ms. Bright had squeezed his hand. "You are such a brave man, Ben Winckelmeyer! And you're right, too. The Lord doesn't send us more grief than he knows we can handle. In the long run, it probably will be a blessing."

A month later, Ms. Bright had found herself unemployed, when it developed that the Eden Prairie Development Fund (EPDF) in which she had served as executive secretary, represented a significant part of the vanished assets of the Son of Man Foundation. Ms. Bright had accepted this stroke of fate without a murmur of protest. Ben believed her when she said she'd never had the faintest suspicion that EPDF had been anything but what it seemed, a real estate developer. The woman was a jewel, and Ben had offered her a position with Medical Defense Systems at a salary matching what she'd been earning at EPDF.

She expressed her gratitude at the job offer with a hug and a kiss. "But no more than that, mind you," she'd said, lowering the protective barrier of her glasses to peek out over the top of the frames flirtatiously. "That's all *any* man gets till I'm wearing a wedding ring!" This to a man who'd rounded the bend of sixty, a man almost twice her own age. And she was in earnest: if he'd proposed, she'd have accepted. To Ms. Bright marriage represented only a more intensive form of management.

At Medical Defense Systems headquarters Ben addressed her as Ms. Bright, an appellation she preferred to Miss. Ms. represented her commitment to feminism, albeit a fundamentalist feminism. She believed in women's right to equal pay, and was alert to any sign of on-the-job sexual harassment, including the use of loose or insinuating language, as more than one former employee of MDS had learned to his cost.

Except in her dress, which was unexceptionally drab, costly, and ladylike, Ms. Bright avoided stereotypically feminine behavior. If a man held a door open for her, she froze in her tracks and would not go through it. She prided herself on doing no cooking that could not be done in a microwave. The only magazines she read were *Fortune*, *U.S. News and World Report*, the *Journal of Hospital Administration* and, until it ceased publication, *The Good News Gazette*, the McKinleys' monthly newsletter. She loved baseball and attended the Twins' home games on Sundays.

At all other times, so far as Ben could determine, she worked. She worked not only as administrative director for Medical Defense Systems, but soon was acting in a similar (though unacknowledged capacity) for other businesses that nestled under MDS's capacious umbrella. For MDS was much more than a simple research facility in the war against ARVIDS; it was also, in some sense, a chain of hotels, a prison system, and a realty and construction company. Indeed, the profits of these related businesses—the Minnehaha Hostels, the MedSec Group, and the Northwestern Development Fund—rather dwarfed, as financial entities, their parent (or host) organization, MDS, and Ms. Bright soon was devoting considerably more attention to these affiliates and offshoots than to MDS itself, which in its nature could not be administered efficiently. For if one's business is research, and there is no guarantee that the research will achieve results, and if that business defines itself as not-for-profit, then what can an administrator do? There was only one supplier for the ten thousand mice that MDS purchased every year, at twenty-five dollars apiece, and that supplier did not give discounts for quantity. If Dr. Michaels approved a particular experiment, then MDS had to bear the expense. Funding sources seemed not to be a problem. In its not-for-profit infancy, with a staff of only the good doctor and some two dozen technicians, MDS had played a significant role in developing the vaccine that had brought the AIDS epidemic to an end. Now, with ARVIDS cutting its much wider swathe and wreaking proportionally greater havoc, MDS had virtual carte blanche both from the government and the big foundations. Whatever Dr. Michaels wanted, Dr. Michaels got—from twenty-five-dollar mice to twenty-five-thousand-dollar incinerators for the disposal of said mice's infected corpses.

For the profit-oriented concerns, especially for Northwestern Development, Dr. Michaels's word was not so inevitably taken as law. Indeed, his connection with this side of things was generally deemphasized. He was known to be a member of the board in all three companies, and a shareholder, but so were many prominent figures in the medical world and in state government. Minnesota hoped to set an example for the rest of the country in operating a system of treatment and security that would be fair to both the victims of the plague and the community at large. If the investors who helped create that system also realized a profit in doing so, that was one of the benefits of the free enterprise system—and none of anyone else's business.

But even in a medical emergency on this terrible scale, there were people who insisted on monkey-wrenching the system, and it was another of Ms. Bright's unwritten duties to deal with such troublemakers. In most cases, this meant reaching an understanding with former long-term residents of one of the Minnehaha Hostels who wished to take back a benefaction (freely given) to MDS, now that they supposed themselves recovered and out of reach of ARVIDS's scythe. Less numerous but more troublesome were the disgruntled heirs of those whom MDS had been unable to help (some 46 percent, alas), who threatened to litigate to recover a testamentary endowment. No such litigation had ever succeeded, but it always looked bad, and there were certain confidential documents that it would not do to have subpoenaed, so sometimes an out-of-court settlement was the wisest course. In all these matters, Ms. Bright and her legal staff could be counted on to realize the organization's overall goals with a minimum of fuss.

But there were some matters beyond Ms. Bright's scope, some forms of trouble for which her years of experience working for the McKinleys were of little use. State Senator Lester Burton was one such form of trouble. Politeness was no use against him; though he came from one of the poorest counties in the state and dressed deplorably, Senator Burton could be as polite as Ms. Bright at her politest and yet not yield an inch. He had also made it clear that he was not to be deflected from his purpose by being offered a position on the board that would administer the project whose development he was hindering, lucrative though such a position might be.

"He is just bound and determined to spoil the entire project," Ms. Bright had lamented to Ben, in their regular Wednesday morning meeting. "I've pointed out all the long-run benefits that Onamia itself stands to gain. The facilities that will be built, the employment opportunities, the health benefits for those who choose not to relocate."

"Not to mention the benefit to the thousands who will be treated there."

"I've been over every detail. I've shown him the lovely scale model that the architects built with the teeny little pine trees. I've shown him the actuarial projections over a five- and ten-year period, and he actually spent half an hour reading the text while I twiddled my thumbs. Then he wanted a photocopy! But he wasn't willing to make a single concession. He insists that he is going to bring the matter up at the next session of the legislature, and he means to call a press conference before then."

"To what purpose?"

"To keep Northwestern out of Onamia."

"He lives there?"

"He was born there, and he's been holding onto the building the drugstore is in."

"I trust we've made a reasonable offer? At this point we can afford to be generous."

"Our people have offered him twice the building *and* the business's market value, and firm guarantees that it will continue to operate as a pharmacy. That was his first concern. He said he didn't want Onamia becoming another ghost town. That was when he thought Northwestern was going to be building a mall outside of town. Then he started doing title searches. Basically that's what he's done for a living most of his life. A small-town lawyer."

"With a seat in the state legislature," Ben pointed out.

"That doesn't seem to make much difference. I've had Lucille Borg, who represents the greater Mille Lacs Lake area in the state house, approach him and explain what a really good thing for Onamia and the whole region the development could be. She probably told him more than she should have. Because after he talked with her, he got interested in MedSec, and now he has this whole *theory* about everything we're doing, and I really can't cope with the man. I'm sorry."

"So, what *is* to be done, do you think?"

Ms. Bright took a deep, bosom-lifting breath. "He says he wants to talk with Dr. Michaels. About what, I asked him. About his real estate investments, is what he answered. I told him Dr. Michaels is too busy but that he could talk to *you*, and he said 'That's too bad,' and started walking out the door. I'll tell you, if I were not a Christian woman, I would have liked to—" She made a claw of her false fingernails and made a cute growling sound.

Ben nodded agreement. "Sometimes it's hard to love our enemies."

"I realize that Dr. Michaels hates to be bothered with business details. But this goes beyond details. This could undermine the whole Onamia project."

"We can't let that happen. I'm sure William will agree to see the man and smooth his feathers."

"I hate to take him away from his real work."

"Tell Stan to set up an appointment ASAP."

Ms. Bright touched her gold chain and gave a little bow of fealty. She knew the problem posed by Senator Burton would be taken care of once Dr. Michaels turned his attention to it.

"He has," she often said of him, "a magic touch."

60

William at that moment was in his office but not at work, unless it is that the play of creative spirits is their true work. He was playing with a favorite piece of software, a flight simulator, and just stoned enough that the graphics on the monitor seemed realer than real. The white clouds in the blue sky shredded into fractal geometries at their edges, abraded by a western wind, their dissolution in sync somehow with the CD on the player, Scott Ross playing Scarlatti. He dipped the nose of the imaginary biplane (and dipped his own to a line of coke), and in a moment the clouds parted, and he spiraled downward to the dark airfield with a spacy feeling that the plane's extended wings were his own. A perfect three-point landing. "Exit plane," he commanded, and found himself at once in the airport lobby, which was neither more nor less generic than any other airport lobby. There was an IBM news kiosk with that morning's genuine headlines scrolling across the screens (the software had windows open to the MDS databank, Compu-Serve, and a pager). Armed security guards in green uniforms stood beside the main exit, above which a banner proclaimed WELCOME TO THE GREEN HILLS OF WYOMIA.

He felt the warm sag of happy relief that comes at the first instant of surrender to a favorite sitcom or the fizzing water of a hot tub. He was home in his own private Wonderland, his Tara, his alternate universe, where anyone he met was the projection and reflection of his own imagination.

He went to retrieve his suitcase from the slowly revolving luggage carousel. The suitcase was filled with a jumble of paraphernalia that had proved useful over the years in coping with the perils and puzzles of Wyomia: knives, scalpels, forceps, tweezers, rope, glue, blowtorches, antibiotics, and placebos. And at the bottom of the bag, wrapped in a silk handkerchief, his most potent resource, a caduceus, whose potency was not limited to the imaginary realm encoded in the program's software, but which could share, like a rechargeable battery, some small portion of the total zap available to its original, which William still kept in the Obst-schmecker attic and brought to his Medical Defense Systems office only when the icon in the software program needed to be reenergized.

It was somewhat worrying, therefore, to have his luggage delayed, but there were a variety of instructions in the program that might account for a delay. Stan might have summoned him on the hot line (but then his pager would be beeping). Or there might be a news headline of such urgency that UPS had flagged it for the immediate attention of subscribers. He went to the news kiosk to check that possibility and used his mouse to select PRINT. Then NATIONAL. Then TOP STORY. His subjective camera zoomed in on a screen of the news kiosk, and, via the window to Compu-Serve, the top story of the day appeared: COUNTRY RECKONS MEMORIAL DAY DEATH TOLL.

There followed a black-bordered list of the latest celebrities to have died from ARVIDS-related causes. Death had assembled a varied cross-section of the rich and famous over the past two weeks: a novelist, the mayor of Sacramento, the head of the nation's second largest bank, a mass murderer awaiting execution in Arizona, a pop singer, an opera singer, the four-year-old daughter of a TV sitcom star, the president of an Ivy League university, a Catholic archbishop, and the owner of a baseball team. The president had rebuffed critics who objected to flags over the Capitol and White House being flown at half mast, and she defended the surgeon general's proposal for more intensive random testing in primary schools.

All that related to the epidemic was in some sense flagged for William's special attention, but no item in the roster of the recently deceased would have activated an override delay. He switched tracks to state and local news, where the top story concerned the state legislature's rubber-stamping the governor's decision that there would be no State Fair again this year (the State Fairgrounds having been converted to a quarantine facility) or for the duration of the health crisis. Counties were being urged to follow the state's example.

—*It comes full circle*, said a familiar voice.

William turned around and there was the god, in a gray business suit, looking down at him and smiling.

William knelt to kiss the hand the god extended. The action of kneeling was not accomplished by any command of keyboard, wand, or mouse. By that act of fealty William had crossed the threshold between simulation and the god's own realm. He knew that what he saw now— the god's archaic smile—was not an image formed by the pixels of the computer screen but a phantasm visible only to some inner organ of vision. He knew that the touch of the god's hand, prompting him to rise to his feet, was an impalpable touch, and that when he seemed to stand, he yet remained seated at his desk in a kind of trance. But he knew this only as we sometimes know, when we are dreaming, that we dream.

—*It was at the State Fair, wasn't it, where the seed was sown from which all these interesting events have sprung?*

"Of course. I have no secrets to hide from you." He waited for the god to say more, but he only smiled. Rather than ask a question (invariably, the god would depart when three questions had been asked), William observed, "It has been quite some time since I last saw you."

—*But not for want of your keeping the channel open. You have been abusing controlled substances rather recklessly of late.*

"Stan has good connections. And I see to it that every gram is guaranteed nonaddictive with no deleterious side effects. Pure euphoria and no hangover, no dimming of the wits—and no sweat."

—*Twinkies are never good for you, William, but I did not come here to lecture you on personal hygiene.*

He would have to ask. "Why are you here, then?"

—*To warn you of a very imminent danger.*

William bit his lip, unwilling to waste a question on what he was sure would be forthcoming without his asking.

But the god did not define the danger he was to beware. Instead, he added:

—*And of broader dangers contingent upon the first, dangers from father, brother, and son.*

"My father's dead."

—*The same is often said of the gods, but we still exercise a certain influence on the course of events. You're looking well, I must say. The strain of your work hasn't etched noticeable furrows in your brow. Even your conscience, what can be seen of it, seems clear. A very trout stream of a conscience. It's as the Greeks have said:* Mens sana in corpore sano. *That's Latin, of course, but the sense is the same: good health breeds tranquillity. Even so, William, I'd advise you to be careful. Within the next few days you will be tempted to use the power of the caduceus in a manner that may have unforeseen and unfortunate results. Therefore, forbear.*

William knew he was being taunted. His conscience was no limpid stream.

—*Further questions? I don't want to keep you from your magic kingdom. Wyomia awaits you.*

"I have dreams," he said reluctantly.

—*And?*

"How do I get rid of them?"

Mercury laughed.—*As the physician said to Macbeth, "Therein the patient must minister to himself." Really, William, that was too easy. Don't make a face. Would you rather have me tell you to confess your crimes against humanity and take your punishment like a man? The cure for any nightmare is an altered point of view. Learn to enjoy what appalls you.*

"I do."

—*No, you've simply grown numb. It's an occupational hazard. Over the years most doctors become more cold-blooded than generals. It's the training: cutting up cadavers, learning to operate all the chemical switches for pleasure and pain, poking about in open wounds, being the first to know the worst. You succumb to the fascination; to do otherwise would be inhuman. But you don't enjoy your power. Not as I would. Not as a god.*

Before William could frame a reply, his pager began to beep.

—*Duty's calling, William.* The god held out his hand to receive William's fealty.

But instead of kneeling to kiss the proffered hand, William, partly from pique at having been taunted and partly from habit, typed SAVE.

The image on the screen shrank to a single glowing mote and disappeared.

William picked up the phone.

"It's the senator from Onamia," Stan announced. "Ms. Bright says you got to see him. And he says it has to be now. Sorry, Doc. I know you got better things to do."

"Send him in, Stan, and I'll do what I can."

61

Lester Burton, the senator from Onamia, was fat as the mature Marlon Brando, a marvel of obesity, jowled and dewlapped and huffing and puffing, his tan summer suit banded with the broad mottlings of his perspiration, his sagging face and pudgy fingers roseate with the blood his heart strained to supply, his edematous ankles, as he lumbered toward a chair, scarcely flexing. Before the man had said a word, William felt the satisfaction that comes with knowing the answer to a problem the very moment it is posed. Lester Burton was a stroke waiting to happen. Should it come here and now, in William's office, there would be nothing to wonder at.

William adopted a tone of formal courtesy. "Senator Burton, how do you do, sir. You've chosen some nasty weather to visit MDS. What can I do for you?"

"I didn't come here to discuss the weather. I didn't come here to *discuss* anything. I came here to tell you you can't turn Mille Lacs County into a goddamned quarantine ward. You can buy off the rest of the legislature, but you're not buying me off."

"I don't believe any offer has been made, Senator."

"Oh no?" The man's jawbone tucked in, his lips pursed, and his jowls trembled in an action that may have been experienced inwardly as a smile. "Twenty-five thousand for letting you put my name on the list of the politicians you've got in your pocket, that isn't an offer? That isn't a bribe?"

"Perhaps it isn't enough." William made the suggestion in a bantering tone, but it was there to be taken up if that was what Lester Burton had in mind.

It wasn't. "I hope that was meant to be a joke, Dr. Michaels."

"Of course, Senator. And *I* hope that you don't mean to imply that the other members of the Community Relations Board have been venal or corrupt in accepting their positions. Mayor Kuula? Representative Borg? Dr. Wempke?"

"Oh, they've been earning their salary, Doctor, no doubt about that. Lucille's been calling me up two, three times a day, trying to smooth my feathers, and according to Dr. Wimp, you're another damned Mother Teresa. As for Mayor Kuula, he's had his hand inside of one cookie jar or another since he got a seat on the school board back in '73, and I said so both times he ran against me for my seat in the senate."

"So that's what it is. You have a grudge against Emil Kuula."

"Don't you just wish that's all it was."

"Senator, I can understand your distress at the thought of your hometown becoming a quarantine area. No community can be expected to welcome such a prospect, no matter what the economic incentives may be. Doubtless, some of your constituents are unhappy with the choice of remaining in the development area or moving to equivalent homes elsewhere in the state. No undertaking on this scale can be accomplished without some distress and personal sacrifice. When highways are built, the same thing happens."

"But you're not exactly hurting, are you, Dr. Michaels?"

"It is the oldest irony of the medical profession that physicians seem to profit from other people's misfortunes."

"You can say that again. This place you got here couldn't've come cheap. I'll bet just those two marble snakes over the front entrance must've cost a million dollars. I'll bet they're thirty feet high."

"As it happens, Senator, MDS, as a nonprofit organization receiving public funds, was *required* to spend one percent of its construction budget on public art works. I'm not responsible for this state's laws: you are. And by the way, those 'snakes' are elements of a caduceus, an ancient symbol of the medical profession."

"Snakes are snakes, as far as I'm concerned, but that's no matter. It's your so-called nonprofit organization that's the problem. It seems to me you've got yourself a whole lot of profit already, Doctor, and if this development scheme for Mille Lacs County gets under way, you're going to be setting on top of a medical oil field. That's what it seems to me."

"Senator Burton, if you wish to audit the books of Medical Defense Systems, you're free to do so. As its director I receive a salary of $750,000—but no share of the money MDS brings in through contributions or service operations. Those moneys aren't profits—they go back into research. Research uses lots of money, Senator, but until there is a cure for ARVIDS, or a vaccine against it, that money has to be found. And MDS is finding it."

"If it was only MDS, Doctor, I wouldn't be wasting your time, seeing how valuable it is. But there is also an outfit called the MedSec Group that bought up St. Andrew's Seminary, six years ago when it was shut down, and now it looks like part of the plan you want the state to rubber-stamp calls for this MedSec Group turning the seminary into a medium security prison for prisoners with ARVIDS. And that isn't any nonprofit operation."

"If the state refuses to open its own facility, then the state will have to pay someone who's willing to do the job for it."

"Meaning you."

"I own shares in MedSec, that's true."

"And in Minnehaha Hostels, too—right?"

William nodded. Senator Burton definitely represented a threat to the Onamia project. He was grateful that Ms. Bright had insisted that he meet with him.

Burton continued. "And back in '88, when Minnehaha Hostels was still the Mille Lacs Lake Investment Group, you were buying up all kinds of properties around the lake. Real cheap."

"It didn't seem that cheap then."

"But they sure as hell are going to be worth a hell of a lot more once the MDS project goes through, and every cabin and motel room is rented to outpatients at a hundred dollars a day and upwards. And not just in the summer season, but year round, according to the prospectus I read."

"Minnehaha Hostels hasn't been the only investment group to foresee that possibility. The building boom has been going on for a couple years now."

"But Minnehaha was the first, by a few years, and it's still the biggest. That is, if you don't count Northwestern Development Fund, which has just about gobbled up every acre in Mille Lacs County that's gone onto the market since 1993. Now you can't tell me that's all just a big coincidence."

"In a way, it's been the biggest possible coincidence. The Northwestern Fund was started up in response to the prospect of the global climatic changes that are going on right now. The Great Plains are drying up. Saskatchewan and Manitoba and the northern counties of Minnesota are going to be the Iowa and Kansas and Nebraska of the next century, and Mille Lacs Lake stands at the south edge of that new corn belt. It's a big enough body of water that it may survive through the period of transition. That made it look like a good investment then, and that's why the Northwestern Fund was started up."

"I've read the brochure."

"The need to establish a research community has only made that investment mature earlier than expected."

"Conveniently for you."

"For everyone who's invested in the fund."

"And you wouldn't care to say just what percentage of the stock in Northwestern, and in MedSec, and in Minnehaha Hostels is owned by you and your relatives?"

"All my investments are in a blind trust."

"Blind trust, mm-hm. Well, maybe some people have blind trust, but not me, Michaels. I think I lost mine when I was around twenty-one, twenty-two years old and watching Watergate on the TV every night with my folks after dinner and hearing my old man say, 'If the president says something, I think we got to believe it. If you can't believe the president, who can you believe?' I got into politics back then because I decided the only answer to that question was myself. I don't trust politicians, or preachers, or big business, or even high school quarterbacks who swear they don't take drugs. It was me who got the law passed that started random blood testing at any high school or college sports event in the state. Everyone said what an invasion of privacy that was, and ACLU fought it all the way to the state supreme court. And when they finally started running the tests, do you know what percent tested out that they'd been using steroids? Thirty percent."

"It must have been a heady experience for you, Senator. And now, I imagine, you're hoping to get back in the headlines again with a new cause célèbre you can drag through the courts for a few years."

"We'll get into the headlines together, Doctor."

"Of what exactly do I stand accused? Of having invested too wisely?"

"Mille Lacs County belongs to the people who've been living there. Not to some investment group that comes in and sucks up all the real estate on the market and then just warehouses it for a few years so there's less tourist business than before, less business in the stores, and stores folding. And you think now that you've sucked it almost dry, you can turn us into a human waste disposal facility, and have the whole country ship all the ARVIDS patients here that they're afraid to keep in their own hospitals. Well, twenty years ago, there was a company tried to turn the north part of the county into a toxic waste dump, but the people didn't let that happen, and the people won't let this happen either."

In the course of the senator's diatribe, William had eased open the drawer of his desk to survey the possibilities. There was a small stack of business cards printed up with an extension of William's home phone number that was operative but never answered. These were his most reliable medium, as they had two built-in safeguards: they were effective only upon the individual who first was handed the card and took effect only after that person had dialed the number on it. William had only to specify the particular affliction he wished the card to transmit.

Finishing his peroration, Senator Burton smiled as though listening to silent applause.

From his shirt pocket William removed a gold Mark Cross fountain pen that bore a transferred charge from the caduceus. He touched it to the topmost card in the pile, and beneath his breath intoned a curse he'd used many times before:

> *When next you sleep, before you wake,*
> *A massive stroke your frame will shake;*
> *Paralyzed, no speech but tears,*
> *You'll linger half-alive for years.*

Senator Burton rumbled some phlegm in his throat and demanded, "Well, Doctor?"

"You must give me some time to think—and to speak with my associates."

"I intend to issue a statement to the press tomorrow."

"Then why did you come to see me? Simply so you could threaten me in person? There are many people besides myself with a stake in the Mille Lacs development. I don't have standing authority to speak for them or make decisions for them. Indeed, the project already has so much momentum, I doubt it could be stopped, even if Medical Defense Systems withdrew."

"That's all the more reason for me to act right away."

"Would a week make so much difference?"

"I don't know. Would it?"

"Let me find out." William rose and extended the business card that bore his curse. "Meanwhile, if you'll take my card—this has my home phone number on it—and let me know beforehand, at that number, if you mean to make any statement to the press."

The fat man levered himself into an upright position cumbersomely, like a balky construction crane. Then he held out his hand to take the card offered him, but the pudgy fingers were not quick enough, and the slip of pasteboard fluttered to the Persian carpet with a butterflylike motion that seemed willfully evasive.

William and Senator Burton looked down at the card on the carpet, each uncertain what to do. Even if he had been equal to the task, the senator was reluctant to bend down and pick up the card from the floor. And William, at the very instant the card had sprung to life and flown away, had remembered the god's advice of only minutes past, that he would be tempted to use the caduceus but that he must forbear.

"Here," said William, dipping back into the desk drawer and taking out a second card, "is another."

Burton accepted it and tucked it into the breast pocket of his suit.

When he had left the room, William retrieved the card that had fallen to the carpet. For a moment he considered destroying it (an ashtray and lighter were ready to hand), but then he reconsidered. It had been weeks since he'd visited the Obstschmecker house to renew the charge in his pen. There was untapped power still in the business card, and William's was a frugal nature. He put the card in his own suit pocket, wedged behind the handkerchief, in case he might need it.

62

Except for its high-gloss state of maintenance and the flag atop its flagpole, the Henry Michaels Memorial Clinic did not declare its institutional character from the sidewalk. It appeared to be no more than the amplest home along Luckner Boulevard. Inside, however, it was a model of health care management with facilities sufficient for the care of sixty patients, though only thirty-seven beds were filled at the present moment. Madge Michaels kept it going with a staff of twelve nurses and male aides and a maintenance crew of five, mostly black, who served her with a military esprit de corps.

In some ways the Henry Michaels Memorial Clinic was a lot easier to run than a nursing home that catered to geriatric or terminally ill patients, since all its residents shared the same perplexing incapacity as Madge's son Ned, a condition for which there was no certain etiology nor even a commonly accepted name. (The clinic's promotional literature referred to it as Colmar's syndrome, after its most famous victim, the astrologer Gloria Colmar.) The thirty-seven patients, of both sexes and a wide range of ages and backgrounds, were almost as easy to tend as a row of cabbages, and they afforded similar long-term satisfaction with regard to their response to the therapy they received. These improvements were slow to manifest themselves and rarely dramatic: Mrs. Johnston in bed 12 had begun to be able to refuse food spooned into her mouth by spitting it out; Mr. Reiner in bed 6, who had been in the clinic since it had opened in 1994, suddenly developed the ability to follow a moving object with his eyes, a sign not only of muscular regeneration but of some kind of mental life as well. (All the victims of Colmar's syndrome displayed a steady, if low, level of alpha rhythms, much as though they were yogis in a state of trance instead of semicomatose, catheterized vegetables.) None of the patients had yet achieved the big breakthrough that was the object of the staff's unceasing efforts (and Madge's unreasoning hope): none had regained muscular control sufficient to communicate—by the blinking of an eyelid or the stirring of a finger—that there was still intelligence behind the dull-eyed, slack-jawed mask of Colmar's syndrome. But Madge was certain that someday, when enough data had been amassed, the pieces would fall into place, and medical science would find the cure for the disease and Ned would be well. All that was needed was the data and the patience to gather the data and the money to fund the research effort.

So new patients were always welcome, even those who had to be received as charity cases, and the newest, Robert Corning, was the most welcome of all, since his medical history bore a striking resemblance to Ned's. They were approximately the same age (Ned was thirty-seven, Robert thirty-nine), and they had both, atypically, developed Colmar's syndrome as children. Robert might, in fact, be the first actual case of the disease, having manifested some symptoms as early as 1969. In his case, however, there had been a progressive degeneration of his capabilities, from an initial condition of spastic imbecility to the general incapacity characteristic of other victims. Because of this, and because he had been tended at home by his parents and received little professional attention, Robert Corning had not been diagnosed as suffering from Colmar's syndrome. Only after the death, a month ago, of his surviving parent, when he had become a ward of the state, was Robert's condition properly diagnosed. The clinic had been notified at once, and his transfer effected.

And here he lay, in bed 38, the most pathetic patient in the clinic, wasted to a skeleton, muscles the thinness of twine. How could his own parents have let him come to this? Almost all the patients had been in some way victims of neglect before being brought to the clinic—vitamin deficiencies and bedsores were common—but none had presented such a spectacle of wretchedness as Robert Corning. According to the social worker who had spoken to the Cornings' neighbors, the parents in their last years had lived at the extreme edge of destitution, rarely leaving their home on Kuhn Avenue. They'd avoided the attention of charities for fear their "Bubby" would be taken from them and had subsisted on a diet made up mostly (to judge from the mounds of detritus in their kitchen) of powdered milk, strawberry Jell-O, sardines, and canned peas. It seemed amazing that Robert had survived so long under such a regimen.

Now, as though she were atoning for his parents' years of neglect, Madge gave at least an hour of every workday to Robert's particular care. Sometimes she would feed him, sometimes bathe his matchstick limbs; most often she undertook the task of patterning, exercising the muscles he could not exercise himself. Years ago, when she had first begun to do the patterning for her own son, the endless repetitions had been a purgatory of boredom. Lift the foot, bend the knee, tilt to the right, tilt to the left, pull the leg straight, flex the instep, stretch the toes. Then the other leg. But now, after performing these rituals for almost half her lifetime, they'd become a source of inner peace. She'd read once, in a book about Gandhi, that he'd insisted that all his followers spend part of each day, as he did, operating a primitive spinning wheel. These bodies were Madge's spinning wheels, and the hours she spent in patterning exercises were her devotions.

She had finished with Robert's lower limbs and begun the more delicate work on his neck's wasted trapezius and sternocleidomastoid muscles—tilting the head back, then lowering the chin to the clavicle, tilting it, turning it to left and right, lowering it—when her stepson and employer appeared at the doorway of the room.

Being at work, she addressed him in her capacity as an employee. "Dr. Michaels! I wasn't expecting you."

"I'm not here as 'Dr. Michaels.' I was on my way home with Ben—Lisa's planned an Official Family Dinner—and I thought I'd drop by here and see if I could tempt you to join us. Lisa and the boys will be off to visit her brother soon, and I know she'd love to have you come. The boys, too."

"Oh, you know I'd love to. But there's Mother."

"She'd never have to know," William inveigled. "You could say an emergency came and you had to stay late."

Madge snorted amusement. "I can't imagine what emergency could happen *here*, unless there was a fire."

William looked down curiously at the withered carcass of Robert Corning. "Who's this? I don't think I recognize him."

Madge knew he was not just being polite. William had a wonderful memory for all the patients in the clinic. Madge had just begun to fill him in about Robert Corning's history when her secretary, Gail Robins, came to the door to say she had a *very* urgent phone call, and Madge had to excuse herself, adding, hopefully: "If you can wait just a minute, William, I really would love to take you up on your invitation."

"I'll still be here," he assured her.

In her own office, she picked up the phone and said, "Nurse Michaels here."

"Madge, is that you?" It was her mother: surely, by now, Gail should know that all Mrs. O.'s calls belonged in the "She's in a meeting" category.

"Yes, Mother, it's me. Is this *you*?"

But Mrs. O. was invincibly literal-minded. "Of course it's me. Can't you tell my voice on the telephone? The reason I called is there's someone at the door and he won't go away. He's been here half an hour. I called before, but that secretary said you were in a meeting. I swear, you must not do anything else at that place but go to meetings. Finally, I told her it was an emergency. He won't go away. He says he's your husband."

Madge did a silent doubletake: not Henry, Henry was dead. Could it be Lance? After all these years?

"Madge?"

"Do you mean my first husband, Mother? Lance Hill? Is that who's there?"

"He's out on the porch."

"Why don't you let him in?"

"For one thing, how can I tell he's who he says he is? He looks like any other old man on the street."

"We all age, Mother."

"I mean"—Mrs. O. lowered her voice to a scandalized whisper—"he doesn't look very clean. And he wants to park his car in the garage, and it isn't even a car, it's a pickup. And he wants to use the toilet."

"All the more reason."

"He could go to a filling station."

"Filling stations don't have public toilets anymore, Mother. Not even bars do."

"Well, that's not my fault. He can just hold his horses."

"Mother, if you're using the cordless phone, I would like to have a word with Lance. So would you slip the phone through the mail slot?"

"And what if he takes it and goes off?"

"Mother, we've been through this before. Please."

There was a longer silence, punctuated by the noises marking the phone's passage through the mail slot. Then, like turning a corner and finding herself back in the year 1965, she heard Lance's voice say, "Madge?" and there was no doubting it was Lance and that his voice had the same power over her that it had had when they'd started dating in high school.

"My God, it really is you."

"That's what I've been trying to tell your mother, but she's been a lot harder to convince. From what I can see through the window, *she* hasn't aged a day since I saw her last. Thirty-two years ago."

"Thirty-two years ago," Madge marveled. Tears were starting to form at the corners of her eyes, and in her chest the first clenchings of the fist of love's old misery. In a way, her feelings were in perfect accord with her mother's: she didn't want to let Lance into the house.

"I guess I should've phoned in advance. But I wanted to surprise you."

"You succeeded."

"Do you think you could convince your mother to let me go to the toilet? I'd hate to get this far, past the border patrol and everything, and then be arrested for creating a public nuisance. Which I will any minute if I don't get to a toilet."

"Aren't you here legally?"

"I'm not here as Lance Hill. I'm Launce, with a U. That's what's on all my ID now, and I guess it was enough of a difference to let me slip past the computer at Customs. You got to admit it sounds a whole lot classier: Launce."

Madge chuckled. He didn't seem to have changed one iota.

"Do you still have a mustache?" she asked.

"Yes, and chewing on it is the only thing keeping me from shitting in my pants at this point. *Please*, tell your mother to have mercy on me."

"Okay, but Lance?"

"Launce."

"It's going to take me a while to say 'Launce' without giggling. There's just one thing. Would you wait till I get home before you go up to see Ned? It's just that . . . it could be upsetting, and I'd rather be there."

"I guess if I've waited this long, I can wait a few hours longer. What-ever you say."

"Thanks. Now slip the phone back to Mother, and I'll have her let you in."

The connection did not survive the phone's return trip through the mail slot, and Madge had to wait for her mother to redial and Gail to reconnect. Time enough to collect her wits and settle her nerves. There was no reason in the world to suppose Lance had come back on her ac-count, no reason to suppose they'd even like each other again after ten minutes together. Love was like some damned sliver of frog tissue in a tenth-grade science class: the frog may have been dead who knows how long but the tissue still twitches when it gets zapped.

"Madge?" her mother whined, the moment she had got through the switchboard again. "Madge, he's still out there."

"Mother, you know Lance. Why make such a fuss? Just let him come in and use the toilet. For heaven's sakes."

"I don't trust him."

"Mother, you don't trust anyone."

"Oh, very well!" After a spell of silence, Mrs. O. announced, "It's not working, I can't get that thing to unlock the door."

"That's strange, you never have trouble with the security system when there's a delivery."

"It must be broken."

"What did you press?"

"Just what's written down on the pad. Oh-five-two-four-nine-nine."

"Mother, I've explained before: you've got to punch in today's date. The number on the pad is from three weeks ago."

"So tell me what numbers I'm supposed to use."

"Oh-six-one-four-nine-nine."

"Wait, wait, one at a time."

Within five minutes Madge had talked Mrs. O. through the process of releasing the security bolt on the door. She felt the same glow of high-tech accomplishment an air traffic controller must feel after coaching a passenger in landing a 747.

Lance took the phone from Mrs. O. just long enough to say, "Thanks. See you later." Just four words as he ran for the toilet, but it was as though she'd felt his hand touch her in the dark.

Back in room 38, she had to beg out of the dinner invitation, offering her mother's health as an excuse and saying nothing about Lance's sudden reappearance. She wanted to see him again before she broadcast the news.

William seemed skeptical about Mrs. O.'s purported indisposition. He probably assumed that Madge was being tyrannized by her mother, a reasonable assumption. Before he left, he wanted to know everything she could tell him about Robert Corning, and while she told the story, he kept playing with his Mark Cross pen, screwing the ballpoint tip in and out nervously.

"From all you say his life's been hell," William said with a thoughtful frown. Then, with a faint smile and a tap of the gold pen on the man's bare shoulder, "But now that he's here, he may get well."

Madge smiled, and repeated one of Henry's favorite stock phrases, "You're a poet, William, and you don't even know it."

When he'd left, Madge looked down at the inert body of Robert Corning and felt an overwhelming sadness and sense of futility. All these years of moving limbs and kneading flesh that could not move or knead her in return. All these years without love.

63

Dinnertime was sacred in the Michaels household, in theory. But like so much else nowadays that was supposed to be sacred, its day-to-day ritual observance was left to the women and children. Two nights out of three Lisa would preside over a rite attended only by Jason and Henry and their nanny. William's absences were dictated by the demands of MDS, even, in a sense, by history, both higher priorities than hearth and home. But when Judge did not appear at dinner it wasn't because he was away from the house (by the terms of his parole he couldn't be); it was simply to accommodate his and Lisa's mutual aversion. The only way Lisa could keep from seeming a wicked stepmother was to reduce direct contact to a minimum. Let the boy spend all his time at the screen of his monitor, interfacing with his cartoon prophet Brother Orson. It was too late, in any case, for Judge's rough edges to be smoothed by the civilizing influence of dinnertime conversation. As well try civilizing thistles.

But this evening William was to be home for dinner, and he was bringing Judge's grandfather with him (the only person in the world, Lisa suspected, who actually liked the boy). Lisa had gone to her stepson's room and laid down the law. He would be at the dinner table at seven thirty, and he would dress properly. Not that Judge ever dressed any other way. Indeed, more than one of his fights with Lisa had been over his objections to the immodesty of *her* wardrobe, which was such a droll reversal of the usual sartorial standoff between the generations in suburbia that sometimes Lisa, for her own amusement, dressed on purpose to provoke him. It wasn't hard: a bare shoulder would do the trick, or jeans that hugged her ass too closely.

So tonight they would have a family dinner by the book. William had phoned from the limo that he and Ben were already en route; Henry and Jason were being scrubbed and polished by their nanny; and Judge, from within the fastness of his bedroom, had acknowledged her summons. In the kitchen Dorey was in a whirl of varied purposes, as the venison roasted and the soup simmered and the celery root soaked in a remoulade, and here, in what Lisa liked to think of as the atrium (because of its showy, energy-saving skylight), Lisa was trying to achieve a balance between opulence and excess in the arrangement of the bushels of roses William had gathered from the garden this morning. A holocaust of roses.

Such profusions might represent an overflow from the morning's other pleasures (they'd been rutty as two goats all through the weekend), or they might simply reflect William's sometimes naive faith in conspicuous consumption. Lisa was not herself averse to immodest display, but only when there was an aesthetic program behind it. William spent money like a televangelist or a third-world dictator, and he just *stuffed* roses into anything that held water. It was Lisa's executive duty as an upper-middle-class wife to protect her spouse from such self-parody.

When the roses had been recomposed to best effect, Lisa sat down and did a quick skim of the news, avoiding obits and shortages and other material in the category of depressing, and scouting out interesting local crime stories. The Buster Johnson child abuse case from nearly a year ago was still in the news, and there was a wonderful clip of Johnson's ex-wife fuming at the judge in front of the courthouse. Then a story about an unidentified (because decapitated) corpse presumed to have been murdered, which had been deposited in the parking lot of the House of Pancakes on Lake Street. The dumping of mutilated (and untraceable) plague victims on roadsides and back alleys had become so common that the body had almost been carted off routinely to the big crematorium at the State Fairgrounds without having been tested for ARVIDS. Lisa felt she'd scored points against the Zeitgeist, since she'd already proposed to two of her friends, both mystery buffs, that the easiest way for a murderer to dispose of a corpse these days was to chop off the head, bury it or freeze it, and leave the carcass for the municipal health authorities to take care of. She had the printer make a print copy of the story so she could document her perspicacity.

While the printer purred, Lisa shot a spritz of soda into a snifter and let the cable choose the news by its own set of priorities. It switched to 39, the live news channel, and the first image on the screen was a mural map of the Mille Lacs Lake with an anchorwoman in front of it in a flame-bright yellow-orange blouse, and speaking in a tone of voice reserved for serious trouble. "Senator Burton's allegations, if they prove to be true, spell big trouble for Twin Cities medical miracle maker Dr. William Michaels and his prestigious research foundation, Medical Defense Systems. MDS spokesperson Valerie Bright denies that the foundation and its board have committed any improprieties. But questioned about the Northwestern Development Fund, Ms. Bright was less forthcoming." The newscast cut to a close-up of Valerie Bright wearing her invincible

Nutra-Sweet smile and painted thick as a de Kooning. "There is nothing in what Senator Burton says that in any way reflects on the conduct of MDS. Obviously, he is looking for any pretext he can to keep the state's project out of the area he represents in the state legislature."

"*Does* Dr. Michaels have a financial interest in the three companies Senator Burton cited?" an unseen reporter insisted, and even before Ms. Bright could begin to equivocate, Lisa could feel it coming. Don't ask for whom the bell tolls, no indeed.

She'd told her brother, when he'd involved his own company in the undertaking, that he was moving too fast. But the prospect had proved irresistible, and Jason had taken the plunge, and he'd brought in other major investors, banks and retirement funds, all desperate to invest in the one growth industry in a collapsing market: death.

She had better phone Jason right away. He was in Boston and a Minnesota state senator's news conference would probably not command the same immediate media attention. There might not be anything Jason could do at this point, maybe nothing he would want to do. It wasn't a crime to make money, after all. There had been fortunes made during the AIDS crisis by those (including William) who had recognized its investment potentials. The Mille Lacs project had already acquired so much momentum mere scandal might not be able to derail it. At least that seemed the best hope for the moment and the tack to take with William.

The phone rang. Could it be telepathy, was Jason calling her?

No such luck. It was Her Holiness Judith Winckelmeyer. To Lisa's mind Judge's mother was as much of a trial as Judge himself, and for much the same reason. They both acted as though anything they might have to say to you was just a parenthesis in their permanent long distance conversations with God. Judith's God had somewhat better manners than Judge's, enjoining her sometimes to seem to listen to other people. But finally there was no reasoning with either of them.

"Judith, how nice of you to call, where are you?"

"I'm at the bus station."

"In Minneapolis? Or . . . ?"

"Tampa. Is Judge there? I'd like to talk to him."

"Judge has his own phone line. Don't you have the number?"

"Of course. But it's always busy."

"He must be interfacing with Brother Orson."

"Still? After all the stories there've been?"

"He won't listen to anything anyone says on TV. Except for Brother Orson, of course. In him his faith is perfect."

Judith sighed. "That's so like William."

Which seemed (Lisa thought) an odd remark. "Like William?"

Judith had no answer ready to hand, and Lisa let it go by. She asked what she most wanted to know. "Are you coming here?"

"I wish I didn't have to."

Which meant Judith was under orders from her god and not to be argued with.

"When?" Lisa asked. "By bus?" Of course, by bus, since Judith was opposed on principle to air travel because of the carbon-emissions-per-passenger-mile ratio. She asked only because she enjoyed rubbing Judith's nose in the sillier consequences of her high-mindedness.

"Yes, by bus. It doesn't take that much longer, and it's safer. As long as I get there before the Fourth. I'm worried about Judge."

The Fourth of July was Judge's birthday. He would be eighteen.

"How's that? Do you think he'll self-destruct? Commit new acts of arson? I think he's grown out of that, Judith. Kids go through these stages. Murder, perhaps. But that will be less of a danger once he's moved out of here. For both of us."

"Has he said that's what he means to do?"

"He hasn't threatened me in so many words. But it's there in his body language."

"I mean leave home. Did he say he's moving away?"

"I think that that goes without saying. Judge isn't happy here. He considers all Willowville a prison, and it is, for him. For two years almost he's had to keep within a half mile of this house when he hasn't been in school, and I know from my own experience that there is nothing to be done within a half mile of this house but mow lawns. The boy's stir crazy. Anyone would be, but for him it's a little worse, because none of us share his fixation with his ridiculous prophet. None of us, to be perfectly truthful, *like* him. Except possibly for your father."

"You can say that and ask me why I'm worried?"

"Do you think your appearing here is going to be a bright candle on his birthday cake? The last I heard you and Judge were not on speaking terms."

"But he can't refuse to see me. Not while he's a minor and I'm his mother. After the Fourth I'm afraid it'll be too late. He'll be swallowed up by the Orsonians and I'll never see him again."

"Speaking of religious organizations, Judith, how is the convent?"

"It isn't a convent, Lisa. It's a community of sharing."

"I imagine Judge would regard the Orsonians much the same way, don't you? *If* that's what he opts for. He might just as easily go into the Marines. His sense of the approaching Apocalypse has a large guns-andammo component. You should see him practicing with his throwing knives."

"Oh dear."

"Oh dear, indeed. But come and see for yourself. As you say, for two more weeks he's still a captive audience. Do you know when your bus gets into town? Shall I send our car to pick you up?"

Judith gave the details of her arrival on Wednesday morning, and Lisa agreed not to give Judge advance warning of the visit. Little as she liked Judith, Lisa rather looked forward to seeing the two of them at loggerheads. The immovable object versus the irresistible force. A perfect match.

There was still time to call Jason. She dialed the number of Fein, Schechner & Joseph, and was routed to Jason's home line, where a machine answered.

"Jason, if you're there," Lisa said, shouting down her brother's recorded voice, "please pick up. It's important."

"Lisa," he said. "I know why you're calling. You heard about that Senator Burton. Am I right?"

"I didn't think you would have heard so quickly."

"My spies are everywhere."

"Is it serious?"

"Do you mean will it sink the project? It could. But I doubt it. There are too many people involved, too much money already in the pipeline. But there'll be some kind of scandal. And it looks like William will bear the brunt of it. That guy Burton has done his homework. In fact, he's dug up some stuff our own staff never knew about. Some of William's earliest real estate deals in that area go back to '86. How old would he have been in '86?"

"Is that a serious question? Am I supposed to get a calculator?"

"He was nineteen, in his first year at medical school. An orphan. Where'd he get almost half a million to buy up a bungalow colony?"

"You probably know better than me. He had some insurance money from his father, he was lucky on the market, and he got out before the crash. William occupied Ground Zero of the American Dream. How do you think I was *wooed* so quickly?"

"I always thought you married him for his pheromones."

"What I'm worried about, Jason, is if things do turn sour, what kind of trouble could William find himself in? What does he stand to lose, if his project *is* scuttled?"

"In that let-us-hope-unlikely event, just about everything. Except MDS. And if there's a real scandal, he might even lose control there."

"Jail?"

"It's a possibility."

"On what grounds?"

"A project on the scale of the Mille Lacs Lake thing requires cooperation at every level of government. Money buys cooperation. But I would bet that William has kept from becoming directly involved in that side of things. William is smart, he'd see to it that he'd have deniability."

"Jason, would you be an angel and call Mother and explain the situation and tell her I may be bringing the boys to the Berkshires for the Fourth. Possibly for the rest of the summer."

"Are you thinking of a preemptive divorce?"

"I don't know. I might leave him. And if I do, I shouldn't dally. As Lady Macbeth says, 'If it were done when 'tis done, then 'twere well it were done quickly.'"

"You mean you want the settlement made before he's gone bust?"

"That would seem a reasonable objective."

"He'll know why you're doing this, Lisa. It's transparent."

"I've never told him how to run *his* business. The marriage is my business."

"And what about 'For better or worse'?"

"Jason! Whose side are you on?"

"Just curious. Okay, I'll talk to Mother. I hope it doesn't have to come to that. I like William."

"And so do I. Enormously. He's as bright as anyone I've ever known, and he's good company, and he's actually quite good in bed, though rather more athletic than tender. We have what you might call aerobic sex. And as a parent he's been concerned and responsible, and the boys are undoubtedly fond of him. Though I wouldn't say they were that *close*. William and I have brought them up on the English model, and their nanny is probably the largest adult presence in their life. If *she* were to leave, Jason and Henry would be desolated. But William's absence would affect them not much more than the discontinuance of their favorite TV show. I'm exaggerating, of course. But not that much."

"It sounds like you've been considering this for a long time."

"I suppose in some ways I've had it in mind from the day we got married. Or engaged, rather. We neither of us ever claimed to be in a condition of romantic passion. We discussed the practical, assets-and-liabilities side of what we were doing."

"But it doesn't sound like you're intending to have a similar discussion this time."

"No, I confess it, I'm a coward. I'll discuss it with him once it's a fait accompli and I'm with Mother. And I'd better not discuss it any longer now with you. William will be home any moment. Give my love to Abigail, but don't say a word about this to her. It all may come to nothing."

But she knew, even as she expressed that pious hope, that the marriage was over.

It wasn't even that upsetting. She'd been more fraught, more agitated, during the president's impeachment. Though of course that had gone on for several months, and this was only beginning.

If it were done when 'tis done, then 'twere well it were done quickly.

Tomorrow. Otherwise she would have to contend with Judith Winckelmeyer while she was packing the bags.

Tomorrow! She felt as giddy as a teenager. The one thing nobody had ever told her about divorce was that it could be such fun.

64

If you looked at the screen in a certain way you really couldn't tell the difference between Brother Orson and a real person looking into a TV camera. Sometimes Brother Orson even came across as *more* real. But you had to be connecting with what he was saying, with the meaning behind the words. Then his eyes were like two tunnels opening at some infinite faraway distance into heaven's direct light. You looked into those eyes and you were already part of the way there. Or when he said *I will open my mouth in parables; I will utter things that have been kept secret from the foundation of the world.* Then you could see, in the very shape of his lips as he spoke, the edge of that secret. It was like a joke that he was sharing with everyone who was saved, like an amazing punch line that makes it clear that all the terrible things that were happening now during the Last Days were actually a blessing and a gift, and the plague a cleansing fire, and the scorn of unbelievers a precious raiment for the adornment of the righteous.

That's why the more people ridiculed Judge's faith, the stronger his faith became. They could subject him to their shrinks and deprogrammers, they could bombard him with phone calls from people who claimed they'd been involved in Brother Orson's operations, who claimed he didn't exist, they could fix an electronic trigger round his ankle to keep him caged like a dog inside his bit of suburbia. But they hadn't made a

dent in Judge's faith. Finally, when Judge had threatened to call the local
Ma Bell hotline and post a bulletin to the effect that the son of the big
celebrity doctor William Michaels was being denied his basic freedom of
religion, they'd backed down completely and let him interface directly
with Brother Orson on a 900 line. His stepmother had been ready to call
his bluff (though it wasn't a bluff, he would have done it), but the famous
Dr. William Michaels was too concerned for his media image.

It pissed Judge off a little that his stepfather was so indifferent to
Judge's involvement with Brother Orson. Judge knew William thought
Brother Orson was some kind of consumer fraud like savings and loans or
Scientology, but had he ever told Judge to be careful or just said to stop
watching Brother Orson? No, he was a permissive parent, he couldn't
care less. Brother Orson came down hard on permissiveness. He liked to
quote Colossians, third chapter, twentieth verse: *Children, obey your parents
in all things: for this is well pleasing unto the Lord.* But then he would say, in
almost the same breath, *Suppose ye that I am come to give peace on earth? I tell
you, Nay; but rather division: The father shall be divided against the son, and the
son against the father.*

Luke's lines reflected Judge's own experience much better than Paul's.
Once, interfacing with Brother Orson on the 900 line, Judge had had the
nerve to point out what seemed to him the contradiction between the two
verses. Brother Orson had bowed his head and wrinkled his eyebrows
into a frown of thoughtfulness, as though the question had never occurred
to him till just that moment. Then he'd looked up, right into Judge's eyes,
and smiled one of those tunnels-to-heaven smiles, and that's when he'd
said, *You must ask yourself, Judge, who are your true parents. Your true parents
are your parents in the baptism of the Gospel. You have a father in heaven and one
on earth, and another in the water of your baptism.* Judge would have liked to
know more about his true parents in the baptism of the Gospel, which
was the first he'd heard of that idea. But Brother Orson didn't always
spell out his deepest meanings. You had to take what he said and think
about it.

One thing that was immediately clear was that Paul's injunction to
obey one's parents in all things referred to one's parents in the baptism of
the Gospel, not to the two adults who happened to be Judge's legal parents. It was about them that Christ had been talking in the parable of the
unjust steward. *Make yourselves friends*, Christ said, *of the mammon of unrighteousness.* Meaning it was okay to accept the money and other advantages
that came from living with the Michaelses and to be polite to them. Judge
gave their mammon the worship they required, neat haircuts and shined
shoes, thank-yous and excuse-mes, passing grades in all his classes, even

if that meant repeating the lies and deceits of atheistic humanism when he took exams, whatever had to be done to get through the system.

But it didn't mean they owned him. It didn't mean that they hadn't drunk the wine of Babylon. They were partakers of her sins, and God knew their iniquities, and so did Judge. Partly he knew them just by instinct, but he also knew them by listening to the tap he'd put on the house's main optical fiber cable. Mostly what Judge heard wasn't that interesting. Over the phone William never talked about anything but business, sometimes medical business, usually wheelings and dealings connected with his real estate projects around Mille Lacs Lake. If Judge had realized those deals had had the potential of bringing his stepfather to financial ruin, perhaps even sending him to prison, he might have paid more attention. He'd just seen them as evidence of mammon doing business as usual.

It was Lisa's calls, much more, that he liked to listen in on, especially when she was going on about how much she couldn't stand him, which was one of her favorite topics. Like just now when she'd joked about his murdering her. That was something he had thought about, in fact. Not his killing her himself but what was likely to happen to her after the Judgment. Brother Orson had spelled out some of the details pretty graphically. In many ways Lisa understood him a lot better than his real mother, who seemed to think Judge was like a defective TV set and that if she could just find the right knob and fiddle with it, Judge would suddenly slip into focus and be just like her, another renegade Catholic do-gooder serving up shitty food to brain-damaged addicts in soup kitchens. Brother Orson had no use for people like that. In the last days Judith would be burnt up in the same fires that would consume Lisa and William, and all her so-called good works wouldn't abate his wrath one bit. The crusades against fur coats and abortion and killing nuns in El Salvador and quarantine camps—the Lord God Jehovah didn't give a shit about any of that. *Where were you when I laid the foundations of the Earth?* he would ask her. *Who shut up the sea with doors?* And then he would zap her straight down to the garbage pits of Gehenna where Moloch rules and the fires are not quenched.

Till that day came, however, Judge was under the thumb of their unrighteousness. This close to his eighteenth birthday and legal freedom Judge still couldn't try and make a break for it. Even if his credit card was valid for purposes of travel, the trigger banded around his ankle would go off any time he crossed the invisible perimeter set by the parole board. He would not hear it, but somewhere in some security office a blip would appear on a screen along with his name and social security number and automatically a federal parole officer would be on his case. Judge had tested out the system twice. The first time he'd got as far as Brother Orson's downtown Minneapolis office, where he sat in the waiting room twenty minutes before being cuffed and returned to the Michaelses'. The second time he'd headed north away from the city, and they'd picked him up even faster. So there was no way of escaping his mother's visit and all the lectures he was sure she meant to deliver, all the psychological gobbledygook and Catholic bullshit.

It upset him.

Judge did not like to admit that the forces of unrighteousness, including his mother, had the power to stir him up like this, so that his muscles felt like they were being roasted in a microwave (not his skin, his *muscles*), so that his head felt like there were calipers squeezing closed round his skull. He knew it was just his emotions, but it *felt* like his body. Back in the bad old days, at the Florida State Correctional Facility for Juvenile Offenders in Starke, he'd been made to take pills that had dulled down the feeling but dimmed his thinking processes at the same time. So since then, to avoid the medicine, he never complained about the burning-up feeling when it happened.

What he did instead—what he did now—was dial Brother Orson's 900 number.

And Brother Orson would appear—he appeared now—and he would lift up his eyes till they met Judge's own gaze levelly, and his lips would part in a little smile of recognition.

—*Why if it isn't my old friend Judge. Howdy, Judge. Welcome to the arms of Jesus.*

"Howdy, Brother Orson," Judge replied.

He didn't even think to enter his greeting on the keyboard, he was that off-kilter. But it didn't seem to make any difference to Brother Orson, for his brow furrowed, as though sensing Judge's unexpressed distress. He leaned forward in his high-backed chair, and a ray of light struck his silvery-gold hair, dazzled a moment, and dulled to a shimmer.

—*I think I know what's troubling you, Judge. It's the lies the media are spreading about us—lies, doubts, distortions, they're impossible to escape. The unbelievers saying that I don't exist, that I am nothing but a computer-generated image. That when I'm talking with you, it's just a script written by a whole stable of paid writers. That when I respond to your questions, my answers come from a computer programmed to provide one-size-fits-all wisdom. They're saying Brother Orson is just a new style of Santa Claus, a fiction, a myth, a lot of nonsense. And you know what else they'd say if they dared to, Judge? They'd say the same about Jesus Christ and God Almighty. They'd say there's no devil, he's just a superstition from the Middle Ages, so don't worry about him, go and have yourself a good time. There's no devil, no hell where sinners will pay for their sins, no Ten Commandments handed down to us, and the Bible is just another book like the books they make you read in school,* Huckleberry Finn *or* The Catcher in the Rye. *They made you read those two, didn't they?*

Judge nodded. He didn't remember ever having complained to Brother Orson about the secular humanist brainwashing he received at school, and he certainly hadn't mentioned those two books in particular. Brother Orson had known without being told; it was not unusual.

—*Well, woe unto them, that's all I can say. Woe unto them. Because hell exists, and there are devils in it, waiting to make the acquaintance of those unbelievers. One of those devils looks at a sinner and that sinner starts burning up inside like he was a cigarette the devil lit up.*

"Brother Orson," Judge said, unaware that he was interrupting, "*I* am burning up inside. That's why I phoned you now."

—*Judge,* said Brother Orson, *do you believe in me?*

The question didn't seem to connect to what Judge had just said, but the connection was there in Brother Orson's eyes.

"Yes, sir. Absolutely and completely."

—*Absolutely and completely,* Brother Orson repeated, though Judge had not typed the words out on the keyboard. *I knew that, Judge. And now I am going to unfold a mystery. I want you to reach behind your computer to the power switch.*

Judge leaned forward and put his finger on the computer's power switch.

—*Now if I were what the unbelievers say I am, I would disappear from the screen you're looking at, if you turned off the electricity, isn't that so? But I am not what they say. My voice is not sound waves, it is not broadcast signals, it is not wiring inside a microchip. It is the voice of faith, and when there is faith in your soul you will hear that voice, with or without electricity. Do you believe that, Judge?*

"Yes, Brother Orson, I do."

—*Then click the switch off. And I will be with you still.*

With no hesitation, like a diver bounding from a familiar springboard, Judge turned off the power switch. The image on the screen seemed to undergo a shift of hue, as though a shadow had passed over Brother Orson's face, but when the shadow had passed, Brother Orson's face was still there, bright as an angel's. Even his clothes were like an angel's, a kind of short white dress like marble statues wear in museums.

In an instant, in the twinkling of an eye, the burning-up feeling inside his body was gone. His mind was suddenly crystal clear. He hadn't realized how clouded and staticky it had been before, the way you get used to wearing smudged glasses until, just as in First Corinthians: *Now we see through a glass, darkly, but then face to face.*

Brother Orson smiled, and this time the secret that his lips had always seemed to hint at became known to Judge. Brother Orson had put on the flesh of incorruption. That was why he had to appear on television screens as though drawn by an animator. He was no longer a physical person. It was as Paul had written: *We are confident, and willing rather to be absent from the body, and to be present with the Lord.*

And Judge *was* present with the Lord, here in his suburban bedroom, with its shelves and closets loaded with junk, apparel for his mortal flesh. The very walls about him had been reared by the wages of sin, which is death. But when this corruptible flesh shall have put on incorruption, as Brother Orson had, then death is swallowed up in victory, and the old law was overthrown and a new law declared. That was the prophecy of Paul. And now the prophecy was fulfilled.

Judge, who had refused from an early age to kneel at the ringing of the bell when his mother had made him come with her to church, knelt now on the beige carpet.

Wordlessly, Brother Orson held out his hand. Reverently Judge kissed it.

He felt his own flesh change. Flames rose from the carpet and from the white Formica of his desk, but they were without heat or hurt. The room became unbearably bright, as though its air were gases fluorescing in a neon bulb.

Then the bulb blew.

65

During the two and a half years that Ben Winckelmeyer served of his five-year sentence, he had developed a fascination for the Book of Job. This was due in part to the fact that his reading matter had often been limited, by the whims of the warden, to the Bible, but mostly because he genuinely shared Job's sense of outrage and puzzlement. The more he read the story and thought about it, the more bizarre it seemed, particularly God's final set-piece of self-congratulation, after he'd ridiculed Job for being a ninety-eight-pound weakling, after he'd delivered his natural history lessons on vultures, ostriches, and whales, when he got to the crocodile: "Consider," God had said, "the chief of the beasts, the crocodile, who devours cattle as if they were grass: what strength is in his loins! what power in the muscles of his belly!" On and on God goes, for two pages of small print, about the sinews of the crocodile, its thick skin, its terrible teeth, how weapons are useless against it, how even its sneezes are to be admired. God doesn't come right out and make the comparison, but it seemed clear to Ben that God was proposing the crocodile as an emblem of his own awful power, to which the noncrocodile part of creation must make an unconditional obeisance. Which Job does, repenting in dust and ashes, whereupon there is an unlikely restoration of the status ante quo, as though to say nobody ever really has to suffer, it's only a phase you pass through. Just hang in there, show due respect for crocodiles, and all will be well.

What could God, or the author of the Book of Job, have been thinking of in singing the praises of the crocodile at such length? To Ben it was on a par with Stalin's having his portrait hung in every jail cell in Russia. What do crocodiles have to do with justice? Jesus! It wasn't that Ben had a different opinion than God. He agreed that justice was a mug's game, and that the likeliest way to recoup one's losses was to kiss the crocodile ass of constituted authority. And as much as Job, Ben had done so by following the canny advice of his old friend Dan Turnage and being born again under the auspices of the right-wing evangelical group that Turnage had pimped for since the American Tobacco Alliance had gone belly up. Ben became a role model of a whited sepulcher and, just as Turnage had promised, was released at his first parole hearing.

Even after his release Ben continued to be an active member of the Son of Man Foundation, for he'd discovered the secret wisdom of the Book of Job, that it is exciting and profitable to work for crocodiles. He found he had a talent for inventing the kind of nonsense people could pretend to believe in order to feel that *they* were on the side of the crocodiles. He became an expounder of Creation Science and an enthusiastic supporter of Pat Robertson, and as a private joke between himself and the Almighty he took to wearing Izod shirts.

Meanwhile, like Job, his fortunes were restored and his possessions doubled. Those were the eighties and the market had been kind to most investors, but to Ben's teenage stepson the market had been a very genie. During the time Ben was in prison, the boy had made a small fortune playing the market. His first big killing came from National Biodynamic Labs, a private, for-profit research hospital offering an experimental cancer treatment that involved the use of monoclonal antibodies. The technology for creating monoclonals had only come into being in 1975, and the therapy it made possible was time-consuming, incredibly expensive, and virtually untested. NBL represented a literally desperate hope. Prudent investors naturally had shied away from the stock until the first test results began to be published showing significant rates of remission. Then the gold rush had begun, and William Michaels's initial investment of $95,000 (insurance moneys he'd received at his father's death, which he'd been allowed to invest at his own discretion) had grown to almost a million.

Ben had looked on in wonder, as the boy had moved with an unerring instinct from stock to stock, always buying into companies like NBL at just the moment their fortunes were about to take off. After William's third great windfall, Ben, just out of prison and feeling the recklessness of conscious freedom, had put his own fortunes into William's hands. It was like riding a winner's coattails at the roulette table, except that William's successes seemed too consistent to be ascribed to luck. If William's profits had been the result of mergers and takeovers, one might assume that he was dipping into the databank of some inside trader, but that could not be the case. William's talent had nothing to do with the market, and everything to do with medicine. He seemed to have a dowser's instinct, even before becoming a researcher himself, for knowing from the bare outline of a medical experiment whether or not it would succeed or fail. After a while, Ben simply accepted William's gifts as God-given and no more to be questioned than the sufferings and deaths that were the rich loam, so to speak, from which these profits sprang. Having toiled in the service of the American Tobacco Alliance so many years, it wasn't hard for Ben to set a limit to his curiosity concerning the ultimate source of his income. In the last analysis, he supposed, all money came from crocodiles.

"Do you remember," he asked William, who was seated in back of the chauffeur and watching the traffic (quite as though he'd been doing the driving himself), "a cartoonist called Saul Steinberg?"

"There was a financier called Saul Steinberg. I read an article in *Fortune* ten, twelve years ago."

"There was a cartoonist by the same name. He was in *The New Yorker* a lot."

"I remember *The New Yorker*. Anyhow, what about him?"

"He used to draw scenes of highways filled with cars that looked like crocodiles. I never got the point till just now."

"And what's the point?"

"'His bones are tubes of bronze, and his limbs like bars of iron. He is the chief of God's works, made to be a tyrant over his peers. If ever you lift your hand against him, think of the struggle that awaits you, and let be.' That's Jehovah's view of crocodiles, and it fits the automobile perfectly, if you think of the highway as a kind of river. The way everyone *accepts* cars as a fatal necessity, and even admires them. It's just the way God told Job to think of crocodiles. Steinberg was brilliant, he really was."

"I thought you were against automobiles," William said, turning sideways and inviting Ben to resume the argument that had been going on between them now for almost two decades, the argument about technology and where it would all lead.

"But that's just it. One *can't* be against automobiles, any more than one can be against crocodiles. Here we are a decade after the hole in the ozone layer was documented, and the greenhouse effect is a daily reality, and the cars are still on the road pumping more carbon into the atmosphere. 'His nostrils pour forth smoke like a cauldron on a fire blown to full heat.'"

"That's the crocodile again, I take it."

Ben nodded. "Who was, if you think about it, the last surviving relative of the dinosaur. So in a way, the automobile is the dinosaur getting the last laugh. They've been refined to their irreducible molecular minimum, but they haven't given up against the mammals."

The Rolls was slowing down for no apparent reason, and William picked up the intercom to ask the chauffeur what the problem was. The chauffeur theorized it was a Public Health roadblock. William whispered, "Shit."

Ben poured himself a second glass of wine and held the bottle up with a questioning look to William, who nodded his assent.

Outside, in the ninety-four-degree heat, the traffic snarled to a complete stop. A blond teenager alone in the backseat of a Honda began combing her hair, using as her mirror the Rolls window through which Ben watched. She seemed an allegory of youth, its genuine, ingenuous assumption that all the world reflects its own bland values. It did not occur to her that there might be someone behind her mirror, studying her. Once, in Ben's own youth, the entire country had seemed like that. He still remembered the tune though not the exact words of the wonderful ad from the seventies about wanting to give the whole world a Coke. And why not? It was a realizable hope. Let them drink Coke!

"What's so funny?" William asked glumly.

"I was thinking about Marie Antoinette."

"Guillotines amuse you?"

"There won't be any guillotines for us. If Senator Burton had made his stink two years ago when the project was first proposed we might be in trouble. Now there are simply too many others involved. We have achieved full bureaucratic inertia, we are unstoppable. That's the beauty of being an institution instead of a person."

Ben was spared from having to produce any more positive thinking by the appearance at the chauffeur's window of a white and tan uniformed PHA officer, who explained that the Public Health Authority was conducting a random sampling, and that the riders in every seventh car had to submit to a blood test. The chauffeur tried to explain that such rules didn't apply to Dr. William Michaels. The officer was adamant.

William rapped on the window and told the chauffeur to yield to the inevitable.

The PHA officer directed their car over to the right, where the Rolls took its place in line just behind the Honda with the blond girl in the backseat. The PHA van where the blood tests were being administered was fifty yards ahead. One of the intervening vehicles was a school bus full of kids.

"We are going to be here an hour, minimum," Ben observed.

William sighed a philosophic sigh. "I can't complain: I was on the board that drew up the guidelines for operations like this. The more holes you allow in a net, the less effective the net will be, it stands to reason."

"At least we've got air-conditioning. If Judith were with us, she'd want us to turn it off out of respect for the ozone layer."

"It's too late to worry about the ozone layer."

Ben went him one better: "It's too late to worry about the atmosphere."

"Or the rain forests," William added.

"Or whales."

"Not to mention several hundred varieties of phytoplankton."

"You read about that one, too? That sounds like the scariest so far, if it's true. Half the known species of algae in the Antarctic are dying off—half!"

"Now that's the pessimistic way of looking at it. An optimist would say that half of them have survived."

Ben laughed and lofted the bottle. "Your glass is half empty. But now"—he poured—"it's full."

Ben leaned back and regarded the sere grass at the road's edge as though it were emblematic of what they had been discussing. Which, quite possibly, it was: the corn belt was well on its way to becoming an extension of the Badlands, the topsoil drying up in the dry summers and blowing away in dust storms that were slowly scouring the earth down to bedrock. The world was coming to an end just like his crazy grandson was always saying.

"You've got to look on the bright side," William said in a tone of considered equanimity.

"Right," Ben agreed. "Where is it?"

"In a way, we're in the middle of it right now, as we wait in this line. What is the basic problem, after all? The basic problem is too many people. It's people, billions of people, who burn the coal and gas and forests, too many people. The only long-term solution to the overall problem is to reduce the level of the population to what it was about a hundred years ago, a hundred million tops."

"Oh God, another deep ecologist. Spare me."

"No, not in a political sense. No society will ever be convinced to trim its own numbers to a half or a quarter of what they are now. But ARVIDS, potentially, is the ultimate Malthusian equalizer."

"Unless a cure is found—Dr. Michaels."

"That's what I meant by potentially."

"Does that mean you're in *favor* of the disease? If so, please don't ever discuss this topic in front of a TV camera. We can survive Senator Burton. We couldn't survive that."

William gave a wince of annoyance. "Every doctor has a kind of vested interest in disease, just as dentists thrive on tooth decay."

"Do you know, there are some people, including my grandson's guru, Brother Orson, who think that ARVIDS has been custom-designed by genetic engineers for just these reasons, that the government decided ten years ago to institute its own covert population-control program."

"There were people who thought the same thing about AIDS," William noted. "And that actually makes more sense, since the people who would have implemented such a policy would not have been putting themselves at risk. ARVIDS, on the other hand, doesn't confine itself to marginal social classes. It's as democratic as the Black Death. It would take a fanatically principled leadership to let loose an epidemic that was as liable to kill them as anyone else. No, if ARVIDS was engineered, the engineer had to be someone who had it in for the human race right across the board. Someone, I suppose, like God."

"Which takes us right back where we started, to the Book of Job. Or how I learned to stop worrying and love . . ." Ben paused to see if William would hit the ball back.

"The crocodile."

"Exactly," Ben said.

At just that moment there was a gunshot. Ben looked up in time to see the blond girl who had been sitting in the Honda running in front of the Rolls. There was a second shot that shattered the limo's windshield and the front seat window on the passenger side. The chauffeur began to moan. Ben crouched down behind the bar. There was a third shot and a fourth, and a crashing sound that made the car shake. Ben peeked up over the front seat to see what had happened. The PHA officer who had made them pull over had jumped onto the hood of the Rolls to take aim at the girl who was running away. His fifth shot connected. The girl collapsed into the yellow grass beside the road.

The chauffeur continued moaning.

66

Sgt. Janet Beale looked down at the limp body of the protester with a familiar rush of satisfaction and fear. Satisfaction for the obvious reason. Fear because any time you had to incapacitate someone in the line of duty you were inviting an inquiry, and an inquiry could always go the wrong way. This guy had said he was a doctor, and he'd been riding in a limo so he probably hadn't been bullshitting. Who but a doctor would go out of his way to become involved with someone shot down trying to escape a PHA checkpoint? It was a complex they had that made them look for trouble, and then when they found themselves *in* trouble, it was always the same story, "I'm an M.D., you can't arrest me, I was following my Hippocratic oath." Well, they could follow it all the way to Evaluation & Detention and on to the camps, as far as Sgt. Beale was concerned. Doctors weren't any better than anyone else. They could come down with ARVIDS as quick as the next person, and *this* doctor had got blood on his hands from the girl who'd been shot, so there was every chance he'd been infected. The stupid asshole.

To make matters worse, the asshole had panicked when he'd seen the chauffeur and the other passenger from his limo being driven off in a police car. He'd starting yelling at Sgt. Beale and then tried to push her aside from the door of the shed, and when he wouldn't obey a simple command to desist, she had been obliged to use a choke hold.

This was not the first time Sgt. Beale had faced a possible charge of using excessive force. Fortunately there were no witnesses. The incident had taken place inside the GHA detention shed while the guy had been waiting for the results of his blood test. Though he must have realized that whatever the results were, he was on a greased slide to E & D, since the girl's blood was all over him. And she'd been saturated with ARVIDS. The guy had only himself to blame for the fix he was in, and Sgt. Beale could see no good reason why she should take any heat for what had happened.

What she must do now was a simple matter of routing her problem to the farthest possible bureaucratic distance from herself. Beginning with ID.

She went through his pockets and was happy to discover that William Michaels (that was the name on all his plastic) did not live on credit alone. She took five of the six crisp hundred-dollar bills, leaving the sixth for Larry, who drove the meat wagon. Then she disposed of the billfold and assorted scraps of paper in the pyrolyzer. She didn't bother taking the watch, even though it was a good one. Likewise a ring and a fancy fountain pen. It had become more trouble than it was worth to unload that kind of junk. No matter what the experts said about how such things weren't contagious, fences were about as interested in secondhand jewelry as in old underwear.

Then the paperwork. What mistake could be more natural than writing him up as M. Williams instead of W. Michaels? She printed the reversed name on a yellow and black band and fastened it to his wrist. Larry's first drop was at Como Hospital Admissions. With a yellow and black band around the guy's wrist, and without instructions to the contrary on the envelope attached to the stretcher, it would be a natural enough mistake to leave him at Como instead of at E & D, where there were always do-gooders (the so-called ombudsmen) going around looking for trouble. At Como he'd be processed like anyone else.

In the register, however, Sgt. Beale noted that M. Williams was being sent to E & D and she used Pvt. Cullen's key and code number to log it in, Pvt. Cullen having conveniently left these at her disposal when he'd panicked after killing the girl, his first such experience in the line of duty. Now, even if there was fallout from leaving the guy off at Como, it would be the driver who got blamed, not Cullen and certainly not herself.

Larry arrived with the meat wagon at half past six. Sgt. Beale helped load the girl's black-bagged body into what had been the luggage compartment in the wagon's first incarnation as an interstate carrier. Then they hauled "M. Williams," strapped to a stretcher, into the wagon and slotted him into a middle berth.

Seven other berths were filled, a couple of them being obviously symptomatic cases.

"Busy day?" Sgt. Beale asked, when they were back outside the wagon and had peeled off the black plastic snouts you had to wear whenever you were handling meat.

"So-so. There was a pickup at a school this morning. Kids are always a pisser. You can't sedate the whole lot of them, so you just got to put up with the hollering."

"You know if you've got any darts left it wouldn't be a bad idea to give this jerk another dose. He was a real hell-raiser when we pulled him over."

"Will do."

"Have a good run."

After Larry had driven off with the bodies, Sgt. Beale poured herself a cup of decaf and rolled her neck around five times clockwise and then in reverse to take out the tension. Then, because the phone log was one of the first things they checked when there was an inquiry, she called the number on the card she'd taken from the breast pocket of the man's suit.

She was in luck: after the fourth ring, a machine answered and said she'd reached the number she'd dialed and to leave a message at the beep. At the beep she held the receiver up to the speaker the Muzak came out of and left the doctor's machine a minute of cheery polka music.

The rest of the work was routine, cleaning up, shutting down, peeling off and disposing of her protective under-uniform. Sgt. Beale generally followed the procedures as they were set down, since their purpose was to protect her from the possibility of contagion. She was not such a fanatic, though, that she was about to put the day's windfall of $500 into the pyrolyzers. None of the PHA guards she'd ever known were that scrupulous in following the rule book.

By seven o'clock she was done, and by eight she was home with a big bucket of fried chicken and all of the extras. She dished up the chicken and potatoes and slaw and then joined the kids in front of the TV. She let them watch their Star Trek cartoon through to the end, but then she insisted on tuning to the religion channel and watching that. Sgt. Beale wasn't particularly religious herself, but she believed religion was something kids should have, like milk.

At eleven o'clock she turned in, having smoothed the way to sleep with a pint of blackberry brandy.

When the children went into her bedroom the next morning, summoned by the nonstop ringing of the alarm clock, they found their mother on her back in the rumpled bed, staring at the ceiling through tears that welled up and pooled at the sides of her eyes and trickled down into her tightly braided hair. She wouldn't move, and nothing they said to her seemed to register. Later the social worker would explain to them that the reason she couldn't move was because she had had a stroke in the middle of the night. But he assured them it wasn't ARVIDS, and that was a great relief, since they had always expected that because of her job their mother would eventually come down with the plague and they would all be sent to the State Fairgrounds and put into quarantine and die.

67

There was a child seated on the steps of Medical Defense Systems, a boy no older than his own sons. He was playing with a radio-controlled turtle, making it emit nuts onto the sidewalk, then backing it off a little way, daring the squirrels to go after the nuts and, when they tried, sending the turtle to attack them at its top speed. On the sidewalk the turtle was almost as fast as the squirrels, but it could only inch along through the grass, so eventually the squirrels got all the nuts the turtle produced.

He was dressed in the unwary T-shirted style of only a decade ago, but the skin his clothing left exposed to the sunlight had the creamy, protected pallor of a child of the present fin de siècle, whom direct sunlight has no chance to tan.

The boy looked up at William with eyes as black, and a gaze as intent, as the squirrels' he was teasing. —*Hi there, Dr. Michaels. What are you doing up so early?*

William knew that he knew the boy from somewhere but couldn't think where.

The boy smiled in a mischievous way, biting the tip of his tongue. His lips and tongue were the bright, unnatural ripe cherry of red dye number two. —*Have you forgotten my name?*

William had to admit that he had.

—*That's all right. It'll come back.* He pointed the zapper at the turtle, which emitted, this time, not a nut but an inch-long brown turd. Then the turtle slowly lifted its head to take in William's reaction.

William smiled the kind of smile he allotted to the similar merry pranks of his sons, ostensibly indulgent but in fact as unamused as if he'd been watching cassettes of "Pee-wee's Playhouse" and the "Muppet Babies," cassettes that Jason and Henry had played over and over until William had memorized the timing of every pratfall, explosion, and canned laugh by heart. Children can be terrible bores, even the brightest, even his own. The only solution to the problem, as to most, was to ignore it. Let children lead their life apart in Nannyland. Lisa agreed.

Meanwhile this problem refused to be ignored. The turtle grinned up at William insistently, its lipless mouth looking like some small gardening tool, a hedge clipper or pruning shears. Its neck slid out from its carapace to almost swanlike length before William realized that this was no turtle at all but a large, black, wormlike snake.

—*Don't you remember Rottencore?*

"Yes, of course. Then, you're . . ." He felt confused.

—*When the Wise Men finally got to Bethlehem, what did they do?*

William ignored the question, as being rhetorical, and marveled: "The other times I've seen you, you were an adult."

—*Gods are any age they want to be. Jesus, for instance. At Christmas he's a baby. A few months later he's a dead grown-up. I think it must mean something, but the truth is, Dr. Michaels, I didn't come here to discuss hermeneutics.* He tilted his head to the side and smiled the same tongue-biting smile as earlier. —*That's a pun: Hermes, hermeneutics, get it?*

William said nothing.

—*Oh, you're not any fun. I was going to show you something, but now I don't think I will.*

"They worshiped the Christ Child. Is that what you were after?"

Though the boy made no reply, William realized that he was demanding to be worshiped himself. He hitched up the legs of his pants and knelt on the lowest step of the clinic's entrance.

The boy held out the radio control device, except that it had become a caduceus.

William put his hand on the caduceus, and prayed aloud: "Thou, Mercury, art my god. I place my being in thy care. Now I lay my soul in pawn. This upon thy staff I swear." As he renewed the pledge he'd first sworn so long before, Rottencore slid down from the child's shoulder, coiling round his pale, bare arm and about the caduceus, to brush the back of William's hand. The snake's chill length looped once more round William's wrist, effectually handcuffing him to the child. It lifted its head to grin at him again, exposing its hypodermiclike fangs. Then, with the deft precision of the nurse who had found the same vein only minutes earlier to administer a sedative (the second within two hours), Rottencore bit into the softest part of his forearm, drawing blood with a regular suctioning peristalsis from the median cephalic vein.

—*Not too greedy, Rottencore. We don't want him to go into shock.* With his free hand the boy stroked the pulsing body of the snake. His hand was larger than it had been only moments before, and William's correspondingly smaller. It wasn't blood that Rottencore was drawing from his veins but the form and stature of his body.

—*Yes, it's as I was saying, Billy, the gods are neither young nor old, and we appeal, like Disney cartoons, to children of all ages. Indeed, when we would speak with a grown-up, like yourself, it's usually necessary to make some alteration in the consciousness we would address. As Jesus remarks in Matthew, chapter eighteen, verse three, "Unless you become as little children, you shall not enter into the kingdom of heaven." And again, it is written—Ezekiel, chapter nine, verses five and six—"Go through the city and smite: let not your eye spare, neither have pity. Slay utterly young and old, both maids, and little children, and women: but come not near any man upon whom is the mark; and begin at my sanctuary."* As he quoted the verses of Holy Writ, his voice took on the familiar redneck twang of Brother Orson. His mimicry captured both the man's sanctimony and his belligerence. Then the mask was dropped, and Mercury spoke in his usual smooth, musical baritone.—*What do you say, Billy: let's enter the kingdom of heaven, shall we? Let's smite a few maids and little children?*

The god (who had grown to the stature of a youth in his early teens) reached forward to grasp Rottencore's head and, not without some resistance on the part of the snake, to extract its fangs from the flesh of Billy's forearm.

—*You're turning to marble, you see.* He ran his finger along the vein from which the snake had been drawing blood.—*Soon you'll be stone from the tip of your nose to your pituitary, stone through and through. But still as human as I am.*

"Are gods human, then?"

—*You can see for yourself that we are. Oh, the Jews objected to letting it be known how much the Creators share with their Creation. (Indeed, the scandal goes deeper, for who did the creating, and who was created? The jury's still out on that.) And the early Christians were no better. How does John end his first epistle? "Little children, keep yourselves from idols. Amen." It wasn't till nearly the year one thousand before decent statuary began to appear again with any regularity.*

Billy looked up at the god with puzzled respect. He couldn't understand anything he was saying. What was the jury he was talking about? How had Mercury grown so big so quickly? And how had Billy become so small, a boy again, no bigger than he'd been when he was five?

Mercury regarded his massive marble hands with a complacent smile.—*That? A simple matter of transfusion, together with the repetition, three times, of the scriptural phrase "Little children," and the work was done. But come, hop on my shoulder, and I'll take you to Olympus. We don't have that long before your sedative wears off, and I've an omen to show you.*

Obediently, Billy let himself be lifted to the god's shoulder. Then Mercury opened the door to Medical Defense Systems and they went inside.

The lobby clock said it was 6:04. A maintenance worker in blue coveralls was waltzing a whining polishing machine across the terra-cotta tiles of the floor. He didn't look up as Mercury and Billy passed before him and went inside an elevator. The elevator doors closed, and when they opened again they were on the ninth floor, where the administrative director, Valerie Bright, was sitting at one of the work stations, squinting at the monitor through her large glasses and typing in short, decisive bursts. The early sunlight, slivered by the venetian blinds, made bands of brightness on the dark silk of her jacket.

The god set Billy down like a giant paperweight on the desk beside Ms. Bright, who glanced up with a look of annoyance and then resumed her work at the keyboard.

Billy felt slighted. Even though he might appear to be five years old and wasn't wearing any clothes, he was, nevertheless, her boss, she should treat him with a bit more respect. He considered pissing on her keyboard: *that* would get her attention. Then he realized that the god must be playing another one of his tricks on him. He twisted his torso round (it was slow work, since he had turned to stone) and regarded Mercury with an impish smile.

"This isn't really happening, is it?"

—It is and it isn't. In fact, if you were in your office now, it would appear just as you see it. The janitor would be in the lobby, polishing the floor. This woman would be busy with the same task. But you *are not really here. At the moment you are somewhere else, under sedation, and that has had the effect of bringing us into a more tender rapport.*

As Mercury placed a hand on his shoulder, Billy felt a sickening warmth diffuse through his body, a conviction of certain harm to come, such as a child feels when a doctor assures him that what he's about to do is not going to hurt, all the while the doctor is intending to perform surgery.

He cast about for some delaying tactic, a question that would fend off the knife's approach.

"What is she doing?" he asked the god. "Why is she at the office so early?"

—Why don't you ask her yourself?

"Can she hear me?"

—*She can and she can't. But whatever question you put to her she must answer truthfully, for she is under my compulsion—just as you are.*

Billy turned his eyes toward Ms. Bright, and asked her, "What are you doing?"

She removed her glasses and grimaced and spun round in her office chair to look at the naked marble boy on the desk. "I'm transferring funds," she told him, "from MDS's unnumbered Swiss account to my own. *This* time I don't intend to leave the sinking ship without something to show for it."

"This time?"

"I worked seven years for the McKinleys, fiddling and finagling, and when the Son of Man Foundation went down, I didn't even have pension rights. So when I started here, I made damned good and sure that wouldn't happen again. This time I've been provided for. I figure, with Dr. Frankenstein in E & D, I've got at least forty-eight hours, providing I can keep that old fart Winckelmeyer out of my hair. And *he's* still waiting bail, and there hasn't been even a phone call yet from Frankenstein. So far so good. Knock on wood." Ms. Bright looked around for anything that might be made of wood, but she was not at her own desk, and there wasn't so much as a walnut nameplate.

Billy was furious. "You mean to say you're stealing Dr. Michaels's money? My money?"

"It's my money now, kiddo. Screw Dr. Michaels." Ms. Bright turned back to the monitor that connected her with her broker's office in Zurich.

Billy couldn't believe what he'd heard. Ms. Bright was supposed to be a born-again Christian businesswoman. She was always going to fellowship breakfasts and pinning cheerful Christian thoughts on the bulletin board. And here she was calmly embezzling company funds. He couldn't move, he couldn't even speak. But he still could do what any other naked five-year-old marble statue could. He pissed on Ms. Bright's busily typing, beautifully manicured hands, a steady stream of hot yellow urine that vanished in steam as it struck the keys of the keyboard. Ms. Bright didn't even deign to look up. She'd been released from the god's compulsion, and none of this had ever happened, except in the mind of the sedated man strapped to the stretcher in the vast Admissions Wing of Como Hospital, the man pissing in the pants of his Giorgio Armani suit and moaning in his sleep.

68

The first thing he was aware of was the bad smell. Then he could feel a generalized pain throughout his body, an aching within and a soreness over all his skin. He wanted to return to sleep, to feel nothing, to be no one, but now there were noises as well as smells and aches, voices and footsteps on the stairs, and then the void before him brightened as the overhead light came on, and the mattress shifted beneath him as someone sat on the bed. He braced his mind against the shock of the light as fingers peeled his eyelids back from his eyes. The brightness speared right to the middle of his brain, erasing every other sensation.

Then his mother's voice said, "All right, you can come in."

He did not want his eyes to focus, to have the bleary shapes resolved into known forms, but the process was as much out of his own control as the opening of his eyes, and there blazing beneath the ceiling bulb were two faces—one that of his mother, too familiar to register as more significant than the buzzing of a fly, but the other face, the man's, was unfamiliar and somehow unsettling.

"Ned?" Receiving no response, the stranger turned his face sideways and asked of his mother, "Can he hear us?"

"Who can say. The sounds may register, but whether our words make any sense to him . . . I doubt it. There's no way to tell."

"Jesus."

"His irises will dilate or contract according to the level of light in the room. All the processes that are autonomic: breathing, peristalsis. Even the occasional blinking of the eyes. But they're like windshield wipers, it's not something his mind controls."

"He looks so young. But he must be . . . thirty-six?"

"Thirty-seven. After about the age of twenty-two, when I made myself stop overfeeding him, he seemed to stop aging altogether. I used to kid myself he looked like you, but really I don't suppose he looks like anyone. If you never smile or frown, your face doesn't develop an identity."

"The secret of eternal youth." The stranger picked up his hand and turned it around, palm upward, as though reading his fortune. "Is he a lot of trouble—feeding, cleaning up?"

"It used to be, but I've got it down to a science now. It doesn't seem possible to get rid of the smell, though. It must have penetrated through the whole house by now, but I don't usually notice it, and Mother hasn't been able to smell anything for years. And we don't have many visitors. Except for William, now and then. He'll still come and spend the whole evening here with just Ned and Mother."

"No kidding. What's it like, having a celebrity in the family?"

"I can't think of William as a celebrity. I mean, he's not that different from other doctors in the same income bracket. They're all rolling in money, and they all think they're the center of creation, and William's no different. But I guess it still seems a little strange to be his employee. I'm sure the only reason he set up the Memorial Clinic was to give me my own little kingdom. He can be very generous."

"I'm glad to hear it."

"Also, to be fair, I suppose he does have a real concern for people with Colmar's syndrome. He lived here all these years in the same house with Ned. It must have got to him."

The buzzer sounded, and his mother went to the phone on the wall and listened, nodding and purring assurances. "Mother's in a fret," she explained. "I've got to go down and smooth her feathers for a moment. Would you mind staying with Ned a little while?"

"Your mother never was that happy to see me."

"She's not used to having visitors in the house. Especially overnight visitors."

"Is that an invitation?"

"Unless you've already arranged something else."

"I'm a homeless person."

The buzzer buzzed again.

"Duty calls," his mother said, but she still hesitated at the door. "Lance, it really is wonderful to see you."

When she had left the room, the stranger was still holding his hand. Now he began to experiment with it, lifting it, lowering it, shaking it by the wrist to make the fingers waggle. All these motions were accompanied by the familiar bone-deep pain he experienced during each day's patterning exercises.

The man put his hand beneath his chin and tilted his head back to look him in the eyes. Where the man's fingers pressed against the flesh of his face he could feel a kind of burning. The burning became more intense until it seemed his head had been put inside a furnace.

And then, where the web had been weakened, it was rent. The light lanced through his eyes to pierce the long-sealed ducts of the lachrymal glands. Tears began to issue from the gland, each one a blissful remission of the pain and the burning, each exerting a further minuscule pressure on the web.

The web was vast. Each bane and each blessing that had been created by the power of the caduceus was a filament in its immense architecture. But the center of the web was here in Ned Hill's inert and pain-wracked body, the first to be blighted by William's curse. Here was the knot that secured the integrity of the entire fabric, and now that knot had slipped.

The fabric was unraveling.

69

For a fleeting instant, as he woke, William could remember the dream, though only in a shattered form: the snake's hypodermic fang entering his arm, the polisher gliding across the lobby's floor (which seemed, even as the memory faded, as real as if he'd been there in person), and a general sense of grievance against Ms. Bright. But the gist of the dream escaped him, whatever the god might have said, whatever of warning or portent it might contain.

He was staring up into the springs of a metal cot. There was a stabbing pain in his lower gut. But he could not touch the spot, his hands were strapped to his side. His feet, as well. He could lift his head just enough to see the canvas restraints that bound him. But he could see nothing of the larger space beyond the narrow confines of the cot, for curtains were drawn on either side, through which a fluorescent brightness penetrated to create a diffuse institutional twilight, unchanging by night or day. Even with so little evidence, he knew, from the smells and a low thrumming of respiratory ills, coughs and wheezes and moans of self-communing misery, he knew where he must be: the ward of a public hospital where those suspected of having ARVIDS were tested and—the great majority—dispatched to the camps.

He tried to call out, but he was unable to raise his voice above a hoarse rasp. Even that effort hurt his throat. He waited, as captives must, thinking the thoughts of captivity: futile anger, impotent rage, fantasies of revenge. But he did not pray or try to strike a bargain with the forces that had betrayed him to this fate, for helpless as he found himself, he did not, in an essential way, doubt his power. Someone would come, he would explain who he was, he would submit to the blood test (his blood had been tested at weekly intervals, as was everyone's who worked at MDS; he'd nothing to worry about on that score), and then he would be released. What had happened was an accident, a slip on the ice. One moment one is walking along the sidewalk, the next one is on one's back, short of breath and sore, amazed but still structurally sound.

The one thing that nagged at him was the pain in his lower right abdomen. His problem calling out was no puzzle. The last thing he remembered inside the little shed at the PHA checkpoint was the woman guard getting her knee in his back and wrapping her arm around his neck, forcing him to his knees. In the process she must have hurt his larynx. But why the pain in his gut? She must have kicked him when he was on the floor, unconscious. Thinking about it, imagining the kick, triggered an anger that let him forget the pain. He promised himself he would track her down and see that she paid a suitable price for what she'd done, something to pain *her* gut. Appendicitis? Yes, that was precisely where she'd kicked him. Appendicitis it would be.

—*Appendicitis*. It was the god's voice, distant and muffled, as though he stood some distance away from the cot in which William lay restrained. A kind of shimmering appeared on the curtains veiling the ward from his view, like a TV tuned to an inert channel, a scattering of pale violet blips that did not resolve into coherent forms.—*You had appendicitis once, but you wouldn't remember it. You thought it only a stomachache, and you had the good sense to use the caduceus at once. That was the first time you used it, in fact, after poor Ned had had his accident.*

"I don't remember."

—*Who remembers every cough and cold and stomachache they've ever had?*

The suspicion formed, as beads of sweat, before his mind had framed the words. "Why are you telling me this? Why are you here at all: I'm wide awake, I'm not doing drugs."

—*I've come to say good-bye while there's still an opportunity. I've become quite fond of you, William, in a peculiar way. We gods do have our vulnerabilities, though not in the same sense you mortals do.*

"No! Please! If I've done something wrong—"

The god's laughter pierced his flesh like a blast of winter wind through a thin cotton shirt.

—*Wrong! Can you suppose I concern myself with right and wrong? Have I ever urged such considerations on you? Health and unhealth, life and death, these are my antinomies. And they've been yours. You mustn't think, because I'm leaving you, that you have fallen in my estimation. That has never been the way of it. When the god withdraws his aegis, then must the hero come into his own.*

"I'm going to die then?"

—*Had you ever supposed otherwise? All mortals die, and William Michaels is mortal. You can draw your own conclusion from that. What I hope, William, is that you will die well, not in abjection but bravely and with a little style.*

"Then don't let me die here!"

—*You have my word for that: you won't die here.*

"I mean, in quarantine, a prisoner."

—*I wasn't quibbling, I knew what you meant, and my promise is for that. You'll die just where you wish—at home, in bed.*

"Thank you." He managed a rueful laugh.

—*And so farewell.*

The flickering faded from the curtain. It was too late to offer his own good-bye. The god had departed.

70

Mrs. Obstschmecker was in such a state she didn't know what to do. She was sure that having Lance Hill in the house spelled trouble, she knew it like she knew two plus two. But would her daughter listen to her? No, not a word. Madge even swore he'd done some kind of miracle for Ned, started him to crying. Mrs. Obstschmecker couldn't see anything very wonderful in that, especially since ever afterward Ned hadn't stopped crying except when he was asleep. His tears meant about as much as the water dripping from a leaky faucet. The boy's plumbing was broken, simple as that, but Madge insisted it was a sign Ned was going to get completely better, and now there was another one of her cases at the clinic who was the same age as Ned and he had actually started to be able to move his lips and curl his fingers, so that made Madge even more certain about Ned. She couldn't talk about anything else. She was upstairs all the time with that Lance Hill, from the moment she got home from work to the moment she went back to the clinic in the morning. She even had her dinners upstairs, and when Mrs. Obstschmecker dared to complain about having to eat nothing but microwave dinners, Madge just laughed and told her she had only herself to blame if she was too proud to sit down at the same table with Lance. She could hear them up there laughing and moving furniture around, and not a word about how long the man was going to go on staying with them. Officially his room was down in the basement, in the room Henry had fixed up for a playroom for the kids before Ned got sick, but he was almost never down there, he was upstairs with Madge all through the night so far as Mrs. Obstschmecker could tell, and in the daytime he was all over the house, in and out of the kitchen, up and down the stairs, as though the house were his.

It wasn't pride that made Mrs. Obstschmecker leary of sitting down to dinner with Lance Hill or having any more to do with him than was strictly necessary. It was a concern for her health. You could tell just by looking at him that the man was sick, and if that wasn't enough you could hear him in the bathroom throwing up into the toilet, not to mention his coughing in the morning, which he said was a smoker's cough, though he never smoked. Thank heaven for that at least. She'd said to Madge, what if it was the plague? It was the same symptoms they warned you to look for on TV. Madge just told her to mind her own business. She wouldn't discuss it, and when, in desperation, Mrs. Obstschmecker had threatened to call the Public Health hotline, Madge said, "You do that and you'll have the lot of us sent to a quarantine camp."

And that was probably true. The Public Health officials denied all the time that they put everyone who was living with someone who had the plague into the camps along with the sick person. Mrs. Obstschmecker as a general rule believed what the authorities told her, but in this case you had to wonder. Madge said there were two houses within just a block along Ludens that were boarded up with black-and-yellow striped tape that meant the PHA had been there, and that was just one street. What happened to the other people living in a house, the ones who weren't sick, when it was sealed up by the PHA? Alternative housing, that's what the newscasters said, and they could show pictures on TV to prove it. But still, you had to wonder.

So she hadn't carried out her threat to report Lance to the Public Health Authority, and she probably wouldn't even if the man died of the plague right here in the house. She didn't know what they'd do with the body, probably bury it in the basement or stick it into the deep freeze, if the deep freeze still worked. That's what you were always hearing other people had done. That was safer than trying to dump a dead body on an empty street, since a lot of people got caught when they tried to do that. What a world it was where you could sit at your own kitchen table drinking hot milk and eating strawberry jam on toasted raisin bread and think about things like that!

Looking at the almost empty jar of strawberry jam gave Mrs. Obstschmecker a clever idea. It used to be, back in the days before Mr. Obstschmecker had died and she had been busier in the kitchen, that Mrs.

Obstschmecker had made her own jam and applesauce and canned tomatoes and pickles and such, and the bulk of her home canning had been stored on shelves in the basement. There almost certainly was nothing left of those efforts but the empty jars, but Lance Hill wouldn't know that, so if he should happen to come down to the basement while she was there (which wasn't likely, since he usually slept till well past eleven), it wouldn't seem as though she'd gone down there to snoop in his room— which she was perfectly entitled to do in her own house, you couldn't even call it snooping. No, she'd gone downstairs to look for a jar of strawberry jam.

The bulb at the top of the steps had burnt out (Madge was terrible about replacing bulbs), and when Mrs. Obstschmecker had got to the bottom of the steps, there wasn't even a dead bulb in the main basement overhead socket. For a moment, in her exasperation, she considered tramping all the way back up the stairs to get the flashlight, but just coming down the steps had left her a little winded. To be able to manage the steps at all at age ninety-two was remarkable enough, if you thought about it. Anyhow there was enough light to find her way around.

In the room where Lance had put his things Mrs. Obstschmecker was astonished to discover the brass standing lamp that used to be by the chair in her own bedroom before Madge had remodeled everything. With a working three-way bulb in it! And here was the couch that had been up on the sun deck till the springs busted out through the bottom. And sheets and two blankets draped over the armrest. Still unfolded: Obviously Lance was sleeping upstairs, and probably right in the same bed with Madge.

When Mrs. Obstschmecker had hinted at this suspicion to her daughter, Madge had shot right back by asking her if she and Lance weren't still married in the eyes of Holy Mother Church, an expression Madge used only when she was trying to be sarcastic. Even so, Mrs. Obstschmecker hadn't known what to answer. In fact, even though he'd left the States in his twenties and was now of mature years, even though he'd deserted the army and had admitted to being a sexual deviate and had got AIDS back in the eighties, despite all those things, it was true, Lance *was* Madge's husband and therefore entitled to sleep with her any time he liked, which Mrs. Obstschmecker had always found a hard pill to swallow when Mr. Obstschmecker had told her that was the Church's teaching and her confessor had said he was right. "That is the cross," Father Windakiewiczowa had told her, "that the wife must bear."

Lance's one little suitcase was unlocked, but there was nothing very interesting in it, just shirts and ties and papers and underwear that hadn't been properly laundered for some time. Men's underwear was a problem never discussed on the ads on TV. She used to have to soak Mr. Obstschmecker's shorts for an hour before washing in order to get rid of the stains from where he hadn't wiped himself properly. There were more crosses wives had to bear than Father Windakiewiczowa ever dreamed of.

The papers didn't look that interesting. All official-looking documents. No letters, no pictures, just one old grubby paperback titled *Astrology for Leos*. But then, inside the breast pocket of the jacket he'd left hanging on the hook behind the door, Mrs. Obstschmecker made a discovery that justified the effort of coming down to the basement. A gun. Not a very big gun, but definitely a real gun that would fire real bullets. Mrs. Obstschmecker had never had a gun in her hand before. It was an odd feeling. She almost could have wished the gun belonged to her. She *almost* considered taking it. But of course Lance would have known whom to blame. She returned it to the pocket of his suit with a cluck of disappointment.

And just in the knick of time, too, for the next moment she could hear footsteps coming down the stairs, and she barely had time to step outside the room before Lance appeared, wearing the peach-colored cotton bathrobe that Madge had spent eighty-five dollars for at Dayton's.

"Well, well, Grandma O.!" he said, with a big smirk. "I didn't think you could handle the stairs."

"I don't know why not."

"That's what you said yesterday when Madge wanted you to come up and see Ned."

"I can handle the stairs if I make an effort."

"I see."

She knew what he was thinking, he was thinking she'd come down here to snoop in his room. So she played her trump: "I came down here to get a fresh jar of strawberry jam. We're almost out of jam."

She headed toward the farther, darker end of the basement, which meant having to go past the deep freeze. As she did, she could hear it rumbling to itself. So it *did* still work! But why was it on? There certainly was plenty of room in the freezer that was part of the icebox in the kitchen. Madge wouldn't have had to bring anything down here. Unless there were things in the freezer she didn't want her mother to know about. Ice cream?

"Can I help you get the jam?" he asked in a way that seemed like he was really asking something else. It dawned on her that it might have been Lance, not Madge, who'd turned on the freezer.

She said, "Yes, I'd appreciate that," and she led him to the shelves that

Mr. Obstschmecker had built so long ago (it must have been before the war) and pointed to the topmost shelf, where there were rows of dusty pint-size Mason jars. "Up there, I think."

Lance went and got the stepladder from beside the broken washing machine and brought it back and climbed up to the top step. "It's so dark. I can't see very well."

"That's why I went into the playroom and turned the light on there," Mrs. Obstschmecker declared, with a sense of having perfected her alibi.

"Well, I can't see any jars that aren't empty. But there's this." He came down off the stepladder and showed her a letter.

"What's that?"

Lance blew dust off the envelope, and squinted. "It says, 'For Billy.'"

"Oh yes." Mrs. Obstschmecker nodded her head as though she'd just remembered something. "*I* put that there a long time ago. Let me see."

He handed her the envelope. "Yes, of course," she said. She recognized the jaggedy handwriting at once as Henry's. "You see—it's my handwriting. My goodness, what a long time ago I must have left that there!"

He looked at her skeptically but made no direct challenge. "What about the strawberry jam?"

"Just look around, it'll be on one of those shelves. I'd better go back upstairs."

She managed the steps faster going up than she had coming down, she was that eager to get to her room and open the letter. She couldn't imagine what Henry would have written in a letter to Billy or how the letter had ended up where it was, but she was sure its contents would be interesting.

Once in her room, she switched on the electronic lock that bolted the door shut. Then she took the letter into the bathroom and wiped off the dust with a Kleenex. She wiggled a fingernail under the flap of the envelope but the glue held fast. "Darn *it!*" she fretted, but she did not give in to impatience. She'd dealt with this same situation before, and she knew that if she took the time to steam open the envelope, no one would ever be the wiser, if and when she had to pass the letter along. So she hid the letter at the bottom of the lingerie drawer until such time as she would be sure to have the kitchen to herself.

No sooner had she closed the dresser drawer than the telephone rang. She picked it up without waiting to hear who it was on the answering machine.

As usual, it was someone asking for Madge.

"I'm afraid my daughter is not here now. You can probably reach her at the clinic."

"Is this Mrs. Obstschmecker?"

"Yes, it is," she answered, surprised at even that degree of recognition.

"This is Judith Winckelmeyer."

It took a moment for the name to register, and then she said, "Judith Winckelmeyer! For goodness' sakes. It's been years since I've heard your voice. Where are you?"

"I'm in Minneapolis, at the bus station."

"I didn't know you were planning a trip here! You know, I just had the nicest time with that boy of yours. He drove me out to visit Mr. Obstschmecker at Veterans' Cemetery, and to Mass beforehand, and all the way there I kept thinking how much he looked like my husband. I don't believe you ever met Mr. Obstschmecker. He would have been before your time."

"You wouldn't know where I could find William, would you?"

"Well, if he's not at home, I suppose he must be at work."

"I've tried phoning both places, and I simply don't get an answer. I don't want to take a taxi all the way out to Willowville if there's no one there."

"Of course not."

"So I called you on the chance that William or Judge or Lisa might have stopped by."

"No. But you wouldn't believe who *is* here: Lance Hill!"

"Who?"

"Madge's first husband. Ned's father. He used to be called Lance, but now he says he's Launce, because he's been living in Canada such a long time. And now he's living in our basement. Isn't that something?"

"Do you have a number where I could call Madge?"

Mrs. Obstschmecker read off the number, which was written on a piece of adhesive tape taped to the phone.

Judith thanked her and hung up. She hadn't paid attention to a single word Mrs. Obstschmecker had said. She hadn't even asked a polite how-are-you. Where did young people learn their manners?

71

Since the last time she'd come here, in '93, when she'd brought John (at age eleven he wasn't "Judge") to visit William and his grandfather, downtown Minneapolis had become a nightmare. But that was true of almost any downtown area nowadays. First the recession and then the plague, and Hennepin Avenue was as dead as Nineveh. There were no shoppers and little to shop for. Except for the bus depot and a Salvation Army thrift shop, the street-level stores were either boarded up or gaped at the desolated streets through broken windows. One such shop, the Shoe Tree, with a sign in its single intact window saying LAST DAYS—BIG BARGAINS, had become a kind of dovecote, all full of coos and flutterings when Judith stopped in the doorway to admire the effect. In its own way it was as romantic as a ruined chapel.

A few blocks east of Hennepin there still were functioning office buildings and a few restaurants and shops that connected to them along the second-story skywalks, but even here the city gave the impression of a genuine ghost town, at least at street level and at 11 a.m. In an odd way, Judith felt personally responsible for what she saw, for it hadn't been that long ago that she'd been a believer in deep ecology and in the absolute necessity of trimming the human race back to a sustainable, preindustrial-era size before people simply poisoned the planet with their waste products, all the pollutants and gases and radioactive sludge that were laying the foundations for an otherwise unavoidable ecological catastrophe. In a sense, these desolated streets were what she had been wishing for, since you couldn't reduce the size of the human race so drastically without dooming a lot of prime real estate to abandonment—and, more to the point, sentencing millions of people to death. In her deep ecology days she'd never worried much about the means that would be required to put man and nature back in the right proportions, probably because she hadn't believed it would ever happen. Now it was happening all around her. The figures on ARVIDS were appalling, and there didn't seem to be any upward limit to the harm it might still do. In some areas, nearly ten percent of the population had been killed, and there was no end in sight. During the Black Death of 1350, half the population of Europe died;

according to some authorities, three-quarters. For years that plague had raged, and then, for no known reason, it had stopped. It was not a comforting precedent.

She turned left on Fifth toward the Nicollet Mall, where there were still a few pedestrians and almost as many PHA officers. One of the officers headed toward Judith the moment he spotted her and asked to see her green card. She'd had three different blood tests on the bus trip up from Florida, all duly noted on her card, but even so the PHA officer acted as though she were an illegal immigrant caught trying to cross the Rio Grande. Despite the fact that ARVIDS seemed to be distributed uniformly through the country, strangers were treated everywhere with suspicion and hostility. The problem was that in a city of any size, everyone is a stranger to all but a small circle of neighbors and co-workers, so everyone in the big cities went around feeling suspicious of everyone else.

Dayton's, for a wonder, was still open for business, and opposite Dayton's, in the middle of the mall, was an unattended canvas-roofed kiosk with a sign that said, THE CHAMBER OF COMMERCE WELCOMES YOU TO MINNEAPOLIS. FREE MAPS AND INFORMATION. An arrow pointed to the maps that weren't there. All along the mall the Muzak was playing an all-string version of a Beach Boys song.

Next to the information kiosk was a Sprint booth, and it occurred to Judith that Lisa or William might have left a message with her housemates in Florida explaining the situation. Everyone in the Twin Cities seemed to have disappeared. She had called William at home and only got an answering machine. She'd tried to reach John on his private line, but no one answered. At MDS there was a recorded message saying that the central switchboard was being reprogrammed and anyone calling MDS should wait until Friday to call back. She'd tried calling her father at home and got another answering machine. She'd called Madge and got her mother, and when she'd tried to reach Madge at the clinic she'd got a "please-call-back-later" receptionist.

She entered the booth, took her receiver from her purse (there was no such thing anymore as a public telephone, only cable access), plugged it in, and punched in her ID number, and then 111, which put her through automatically to her own number in Florida.

Griel answered, and said yes, there had been a message from her father, who'd called from a PHA detention center in a state of outrage. Apparently both he and William had been arrested at a highway checkpoint, and he couldn't be released until someone came to where he was being held and vouched for his being who his ID said he was. He'd waited a whole day for one of the directors from MDS to come and sign him out, but the woman had apparently vanished from the earth. There was more, but he hadn't been able to tell Griel the whole story, because the PHA had only let him talk for two minutes.

Judith dialed the number of the detention center at once, and spent fifteen minutes confirming the fact that Ben Winckelmeyer was indeed still there. For more information she would have to come to the detention center in person.

Which she did. The taxi ride cost her a mind-boggling forty dollars, paid in advance, and even at that rate the driver refused to wait outside. He was probably right in predicting that it would take at least a couple of hours to process all the red tape it would take to get Ben checked out.

The detention center had been a Holiday Inn in an earlier incarnation, and the only indication that it was so no longer was a high, wraparound cyclone fence topped with razor wire and the letters on the marquee identifying it as MINN. STATE POLICE HEALTH INVEST. UNIT 17.

The policewoman at the reception desk was much more human than the people she'd had to deal with on the phone. She only had to show her green card and answer three questions on an ID check and she was shown to the room where Ben had been put. Her armed escort could not have been much older than fifteen and full of the special kind of self-importance that comes to those who exercise authority at a precocious age.

When the young guard unlocked and opened the door, a mingled stench of Lysol and vomit whooshed forth. Ben was standing up, his back to the wall, looking like he was waiting to be shot. His face seemed finally to have caught up with his true chronological age after all these years of looking perpetually, pudgily fifty. He was an old man now.

"Judith," he said, "thank heaven."

She kissed him on both cheeks. "Are you okay?" she whispered.

His smile was almost recognizable. "I think I'll have to take the Fifth Amendment on that."

"What happened? Is William here with you? I don't know any more than what I learned from Griel."

"It's a long story. Maybe we should wait till we've got our exit visas. As to William, I've no idea where he is. He was still at the checkpoint getting a blood test when they took me here. I've tried calling him at home. No one answers. I've tried to talk to someone at the checkpoint, but it's like arranging an audience with the pope."

"And the MDS switchboard isn't working."

Ben looked grim. "I know. And I think I know why. But that's something else we'd better save till later."

Later was not long in coming. Ben's own BMW had already been retrieved from its garage and was waiting, with the keys in the ignition, by the time the paperwork was completed. Off her own bat, just to be helpful, the policewoman at the reception desk made a determined effort to learn from the PHA what had become of William. The PHA people swore that no one by the name of Michaels had been dispatched to Detention & Evaluation or to any local hospital. They were able to provide the name of the officer who'd been in charge of the checkpoint on Monday afternoon—Sgt. Janet Beale—but she had failed to report to work since that time. Presumably, William had been released after his blood test showed he was clean. Otherwise, the PHA people insisted, there would be something in the records at the checkpoint—as, for instance, there was for Ben and the chauffeur and even the limo.

"You'll probably find him at home," the policewoman suggested with an unconvincing smile. "Many people become very upset when they're stopped at a checkpoint. And with the window of his car shot out, well, who could blame him if he's not feeling all that sociable? There's days I don't pick up the phone for a lot less reason than he's got."

"You're probably right," Ben agreed. He'd have agreed to anything at that point he was so anxious to get away.

And then they were out on the expressway, and moving at what seemed to Judith a criminal speed. "Father!" she shouted, bracing her feet against the floorboard. "Watch out for that *van!!*"

Ben neither slowed down nor speeded up, and the van that had tried to pull in front of the BMW swerved back to its position in the slower-moving right lane.

"I'm sorry," Judith said. "I'm just not used to being in a car. In Florida I ride the bus or I walk. Mostly I walk."

"You left your luggage at the Greyhound station?" Ben asked, as they neared the downtown exit.

"Yes, but there's no need to pick it up now. Getting home is the first priority."

"My first priority is finding out what's become of William. Do you mind if we detour by his place first?"

"As you like. Though my concern is more for John than William. If John's found some way to remove his parole band so he could leave town without triggering any alarms—"

"That's not too likely. And you'd better remember to call him Judge. He's sensitive about that."

"Judge, yes, of course, I'll remember. But with so little time left before he turns eighteen, a couple weeks, it would be so foolish to violate parole."

"Ten to one the reason he wasn't answering the phone is that he was communing with Brother Orson. Was his answering machine on?"

"All it said was leave your message at the beep."

"He's probably just avoiding you. He's at the age when he prefers to be left alone."

"He was always at that age, Father. Always."

Ben chuckled, but said nothing. He didn't have to. Judith knew he was thinking "Like mother, like son." And it wasn't really fair. As a girl and a teenager, she'd been prickly in many ways, but never systematically hostile. She hadn't seen her father and Sondra as the Enemy. Her mother, off in Florida, that was another matter. She *had* been the Enemy, until, in the last few years, Alzheimer's disease had made her a mere object of pity.

Judith sighed, realizing just how much she did have in common with John. With Judge, she corrected herself. She must remember to think of him by that ridiculous name.

As they came in sight of the exit to Willowville, she finally broke the ice and said, "If you'd rather not tell me about what happened . . ." It was all the cue Ben needed, and the story was not long in telling, how they'd been pulled over at the checkpoint, the stray bullet, the shattered windshield, how William had insisted on leaving the limo to look at the girl who'd been shot by the PHA officer, and how they'd been separated, Ben and the chauffeur being hauled off to the detention center while William was still inside the little shed where they did the blood testing.

"The worst of it was afterward, when I was waiting for Ms. Bright, and she didn't show. I got so fraught. It was getting to be one a.m., two a.m., and I was locked in that nasty little room—you smelled what it was like—and I could feel my heart . . . fluttering. That's not the word, but I don't know how else to describe it. I felt like I'd been sent back to Stillwater. Except the quarantine camps would be even worse than that. Finally I bribed that kid who let you into the room to get me some Seconals and I was able to sleep. I slept till noon, and then I had to wait hours to use the phone. And when I couldn't get through to *anyone* I really started to panic. I'm still panicking."

"You *sound* as rational as ever," Judith reassured him.

"I know. There's a part of me that just wants Ben Winckelmeyer to continue on a business-as-usual basis, and then there's the other part of me that's in charge of my basal metabolism and not my thought processes, and that part of me is still going Bong! Bong! Remember that smoke alarm that went off every time you started to fry a lamb chop? That's what I feel like right now. Inside me that alarm is screaming 'Lamb chops! Lamb chops!' "

Judith laughed aloud. "Oh God, I'd forgotten that alarm. And it only ever went off for lamb chops, nothing else. The house could have burned down, it would be mute, but just try and fry a lamb chop!" She leaned sideways as far as her seat belt allowed and was able, by stretching her neck, to plant a kiss on Ben's cheek.

"My goodness," he said, switching effortlessly to a tone of mellow reminiscence, "how long has it been. It's good to see you. You've got so big."

"My bottom, I know. If my thirteen-year-old anorexic self could see me now. But a big ass is actually supposed to be a good thing, especially for women, as against a big gut. It means you're less at risk for some dread disease or other. Father, isn't that motorcycle going to—No, I'm sorry, highways simply do this to me."

When the motorcycle had weaved on ahead through the traffic far enough so she could take her eyes off it, she asked, "How is Judge?"

"Bizarre. I like the boy, mind you. He's actually more interesting for being so peculiar. Though it's hard, at times, to think of him as my own lineal descendant."

"One of the women who lives with us—Griel, the one you talked with on the phone—she swears there's a real person behind Brother Orson's cartoon face. She says she's met people who've talked to him in the flesh. But that's not what the news is saying, is it? Griel has also met people who claim to have been taken up in flying saucers. Do *you* think there's an actual Brother Orson?"

Ben hooted. "You might as well ask me, do I believe in Santa Claus? Yes, Virginia, of course I do."

"You and William!"

There was an awkward pause between them. Judith had never openly acknowledged to Ben—to anyone, for that matter—that William was her son's natural father. Yet she knew that Ben had long ago figured it out for himself, and they'd come to an unspoken understanding on the subject just as they had about her being a lesbian.

So there was no need now to spell out what she'd meant by her unconsidered "You and William!" William's steadfast faith in Santa at the age of six and Judge's dauntless faith in Brother Orson now seemed to have issued from the same stubborn root, from some genetic disposition to belief in its purest form.

Yet she couldn't reconcile herself to the boy's invincible wrongheadedness. "Does he *know* what's been happening in the news?" she demanded of Ben. "Has he watched the coverage of the trial in Florida? Has he heard the witnesses? It's not their enemies now who are saying Orson is a fabrication, it's the people who've been running the organization for years."

"Remember how long some people went on believing in Nixon? In Reagan? In Guru Ma? The worse the charges, the tighter the noose, the more a loyalist can pride himself on his loyalty."

"But eventually . . . ?"

"I agree: eventually Judge will be disillusioned. If he isn't already. He's not as willing to get into an argument on the subject as he would have been a year ago, even six months. Maybe he's stopped believing but is just too proud to admit he lived such a long time in Fantasyland."

"What does William make of it all?"

"He takes it in stride pretty much. Refuses to argue about it with Judge. I think he may even admire his stubbornness. The chip-off-the-old-block effect."

So there it was, out in the open after all these years, the truth she had no wish to discuss.

"If there's a gene for stubbornness," she said, "he might as easily have gotten it from me, don't you suppose?"

Ben glanced sideways with an amused smile. "Oh, I'll grant you that."

"It doesn't seem ever to have upset you, the thought, or the suspicion . . ." She could not, even now, say it in so many words.

"I think it might have, if I'd figured it out soon enough. That is, before Judge was born. But I was in prison then, and prison was like a toothache. You can't think of anything else. You must have gone through hell, though."

"I worried. And I prayed a lot."

"And then your prayers were answered."

"In the sense that he didn't have Bradley-Chambers syndrome, yes."

"But you knew that was a possibility."

Judith nodded.

"And you never considered getting an abortion."

"Of course not."

Ben shook his head. "You are," he marveled, "an amazing offspring."

Ben fell silent after that, and Judith slouched back against the leather seat cushion, relieved to be let off the hook, and turned her attention to the scenes of Willowville unscrolling through the windows of the car. At least half the lawns were enclosed by metal fences of the kind erected around the detention center, as though a man's home these days were not so much his castle as his dungeon. The lawns were still well kept up, and you could see sprinklers operating, a luxury that Florida had had to re-strict years ago. Otherwise, it was the Willowville she remembered. Even the fact that the only people you could see were people in cars had been true in the Willowville of yore.

While they were still a long way from William's neighborhood at the northern edge of Willowville, Ben slowed the car to a crawl and pulled over to the side of the street. They coasted to a stop beside a red, white, and blue mailbox.

"Father?" she asked. "Are you all right?"

He smiled the way he did when he was getting ready to deliver a zinger, but then he didn't deliver it.

"Could you . . . help me . . . release the . . ." His fingers fumbled at the safety belt release.

She helped him out of his safety belt, then loosened his tie.

"It started to go dark there for a while," he explained without her asking.

"Would you like me to go telephone for help?" she asked.

He shook his head. "Just give me a minute or so. A hospital sends out an ambulance these days, there's always someone from PHA with them. This time we'd both end up in detention. Or worse. I'd ask you to drive us, but I really don't think I could get up and out of the car and over to your side. These damned bucket seats, I can't just slide over. I think the best thing right now is a little nap."

He laid his head back awkwardly on the seat's headrest and closed his eyes. Judith held his right hand and watched his life quietly ebb away, like the sun sinking through the limbs of trees at a far horizon. It was the kind of death you pray for, a divine Mickey Finn, no pain, no warning, just the simplest closing of the door. She envied him and felt blessed.

72

At the moment of Ben Winckelmeyer's death, a shudder passed through the web. Those filaments nearest the center, already under the strain imposed by the earlier snapping of its first-woven thread, registered the effect most forcibly.

The elms along Calumet Avenue and in Brosner Park, on which Billy Michaels had so long ago exercised the power of the caduceus, felt a sudden sickening incapability at their phloem's soft core, and all through the night that followed, as the affected sap spread through their limbs and leaves, the elms succumbed to the deaths deferred by the caduceus's potency. By morning their yellow leaves littered the streets and lawns.

There was a tingling in the scalp of Mrs. Obstschmecker as dark, wiry hairs formed within the follicles that had lain fallow so many years, and as she slept, the old woman's right hand crept out from its cocoon of bedclothes to scratch at her bristly scalp.

In his bedroom upstairs, Ned knew a more painful quickening as his tongue, so long inert, pressed against the roof of his mouth, hungry not for food—for he heeded the operation of his digestive tract no more than the beating of his heart—hungry, rather, for speech. His jaw clenched; the left zygomatic muscles tensed, tugging at the flesh of his upper lip. Then the muscles all went slack, like a weight lifter's arms as he collapses onto the bench after his utmost exertion.

In the next room his mother slept, and she, too, dreamed, her tongue pressed against her soft palate, remembering a thirst it had not known for many years, craving a single drop of chilled wine, a sip of orange juice laced with vodka, a long, cold draft of beer—booze in whatever form, barrels of it! Nothing less could fill the void that years of abstinence had hollowed out in her. She woke and went downstairs to the kitchen and filled a tumbler with diet cola, and then, barefoot, she went into the backyard, where the lawn chairs had been left spread out, and sat and marveled at the yellow leaves drifting down through the windless June air.

Many blocks away, on Luckner Boulevard, in bed 38 of the Henry Michaels Memorial Clinic, Robert Corning stared at his fingers with fascination, as they clenched and relaxed, clenched and relaxed in complete obedience to the dictates of his will. Robert had felt the shudder that had passed through the web more keenly than anyone. When Ben Winckelmeyer had died, he'd felt a jolt of adrenal panic, as though, an infant again, he'd heard his mother cry out to him: "Bubby! Bubby! Be careful!"

And in the 4-H Pavilion of the former State Fairgrounds William Michaels palpated the rigid area of his abdomen. There was direct tenderness, but it was not acute, and (fortunately) no rebound tenderness. Another diagnostic test for suspected appendicitis involved the patient lying on his left side and stretching the psoas muscle, but that was not a maneuver William could attempt by himself.

A voice from the darkness whispered: "You up there, in the top bunk. What time is it?" When he felt a prodding through the thin mattress of the bunk, he realized that the question was directed at him.

"I don't know," he replied. "I have no watch. It was stolen."

"There's a clock over the main door. If you sit up, you can see it."

The effort of bending forward at the waist produced a flash of exquisite pain. He drew a sharp breath and gripped the rough edge of the wooden partition reflexively. A splinter pierced the side of his thumb. As though he'd opened the door of a furnace, he felt the heat of his anger suffuse his whole body. While that door remained open he could not focus his mind on any particulars, there was only raw white rage blotting out everything else. Each new annoyance, each least reminder of his helplessness and pain, triggered another blast of wrath.

It had been just the same when they'd made him strip off his soiled clothes that afternoon in the tent erected just inside the fairground entrance. The PHA workers behind their Plexiglas partitions had paid no heed to any protests from the arriving detainees. They went through the motions of accepting, tagging, and boxing the old clothes and issuing the white cotton hospital uniforms with a maddening bland indifference to the distress of the people filing by. They did their work like cashiers at a supermarket, and most of the detainees being processed seemed to accept the situation with an unquestioning sheeplike docility. No doubt, they had known they had ARVIDS for some time and had foreseen being sent into quarantine. When William had protested and tried to bring his case to the attention of someone qualified to deal with it, he had been treated with routine brutality, as though he were just another overwrought and potentially dangerous detainee who required the simple remedy the PHA guards were always equipped to dispense—sedation. He had only the foggiest of memories of being forcibly undressed and wrestled into these concentration camp pajamas, ill-fitting and stiff with starch. Later, here in the 4-H Pavilion, someone had told him that most of the PHA personnel inside the camp spoke little or no English, so complaining was useless. Illegal aliens were given a choice between deportation and working in the quarantine camps. Most chose deportation.

"Hey, asshole! What the fuck *time* is it?"

William scanned the shadowy geometries of the pavilion—the sloping roof and bare rafters, the labyrinthine zigzags of the wooden partitions, all lit by one distant 40-watt bulb. He could see no clock, so he said it was four twenty-five, which seemed to content the man in the bunk below him.

At ten the guards would unlock the main door and issue meal chits. Then those who hadn't been detailed to clean up would have the liberty of most parts of the camp. Yesterday, still woozy from the sedative, he'd waited hours in order to use one of the reversed-charge telephones in Pioneer Hall. Staring at the plaques of mounted walleyes on the dark log walls, probing with his fingertips at the tender spot on his abdomen. Each person was allowed to make one call, and if there was no answer or the charge was refused, you had to go to the back of the line and start the long wait all over. He'd made three calls: to Lisa, which got answered by the answering machine; to his private line at MDS, which no one picked up; and finally (unable to remember Ms. Bright's private number) to the general MDS number, where the operator refused to accept the twenty-five-cent charge. At that point Pioneer Hall closed down and William had had to return to the dormitory in the 4-H Pavilion before the seven o'clock curfew went into effect.

He could not believe that he'd been reduced to such a zero, that with all the power he knew he had he could not do such a simple thing as to secure his own release from the hell into which he'd stumbled. This entire system was in a sense his own creation. So any rage he might feel was, in the same sense, his just dessert. But that made no difference. There was nothing he cared about now but saving his own skin. And he didn't know how.

73

According to the clock on the tower of the Hanging Gardens Town Hall it was four twenty-five, but Judge wasn't sure the clock was accurate or even functional. Since arriving in Wyomia, he'd learned that you couldn't necessarily trust appearances or believe what people told you. At the inn where he was staying, for instance, there had been a big vase of roses in the lobby, but when he'd typed out the command SNIFF ROSES they smelled like rotting meat. Judge had always been a little suspicious of flowers, so he wasn't surprised. But there were probably lots of things here in Wyomia just as false and deceitful that he accepted at face value. As Brother Orson never ceased to point out, the mouth of the wicked man is full of deceit and fraud. He lurks in the alleys of the villages, and in the secret places he murders the innocent.

So Judge knew he had to watch his step or he would end up like one of the bodies hanging from the trees in the gardens of Hanging Gardens, some of which were still alive and writhing in pain though most were dead and rotting. Sometimes it was the simplest things that could trip you up. You'd forget to eat for a few hours and then faint from hunger. You'd go too long without sleep and become groggy and careless. And not just in gametime but in realtime. Wyomia was like one of those drugs they lectured about in Phys Ed classes, the kind like crack that just takes over your whole life and you forget everything else. Now, forty-eight hours after he'd hacked his way into the program (he'd found the disc in a locked file of backups in the top drawer of William's desk), the edge between gametime and realtime had become so blurry that he had to set the laptop's internal timer to buzz at four-hour intervals so he would remember to visit the bathroom and go down to the kitchen and nuke a pizza or a can of soup. He'd also taken a couple of long naps on the couch here in his father's study, but when he did, he left the game on the screen out of fear that a SAVE command might be boobytrapped and that he'd have to start from square one the next time he booted up the disc.

Wyomia was a scary place, a country with more cemeteries than cities, and even those cities mostly deserted or else inhabited by demons and witches and other minions of evil. Dead people did most of the work, though you couldn't tell they were dead just by looking at them. You needed a special kind of glasses available only here in Hanging Gardens. (He'd learned this from a talking raven called Karn, who'd told him that once he had the Spectacles of True Vision, Judge would understand the secret meaning of everything around him—and what was around him was William Michael's soul enchanted into a landscape.) Exploring the simulated environs of Wyomia was better than being able to read his father's diary; it was like walking around inside his dreams. But to know the meaning of those dreams he needed the glasses.

And there, around the corner from the Town Hall, on a street of sleazy shops, was an optometrist's office, with a pair of gigantic spectacles hanging over the door as a shop sign. On the door was a brass plate with the optometrist's name, Dr. Neudista. Judge knocked. The door swung open. He entered.

—*Hello*, said Dr. Neudista. *How can I help you?* He was a short, bald old man with skin the color of white candlewax and lips as red as strawberry jam.

ASK FOR SPECTACLES OF TRUE VISION, Judge typed.

—*Do you want wire frames or plastic frames?*

HOW MUCH ARE THOSE? he asked, using the mouse to point to a pair of glasses displayed on a severed head on the counter.

When the optometrist turned round to see which glasses he'd pointed to, Judge took a straight-edge razor from the satchel he had been carrying all about Wyomia. It was filled with a jumble of medical paraphernalia he'd acquired in playing the game: knives, scalpels, forceps, tweezers, rope, glue, blowtorches, antibiotics, and placebos.

KILL DR. NEUDISTA, he typed.

—*Oh, I wouldn't do that*, Dr. Neudista said, without turning around. *Kill me, and you'll never know what any of this means. That's what my name is a pun on, didn't you notice that? Herman Neudista.*

"You're a nudist, is that what you mean?"

—*Only when I take my clothes off. Here.* He handed Judge the glasses the head had been modeling and held up a mirror. *See how you look in these.*

Judge stared at the mirror in dismay. He'd become a demon with short pointy horns and his whole face the dull, scaly red of an old tattoo. He lifted the glasses up from the bridge of his nose and saw his usual face in the mirror, but when he lowered them he became a red devil again.

But what was more dismaying—when he looked away from the mirror, the old optometrist's face had changed into Brother Orson's. And he had horns like Judge's, and his skin was red, and he'd taken off all his clothes.

—*I wondered when you'd recognize me*, Brother Orson said with a chuckle.

"How can you be here? In Wyomia?"

—*Why not in Wyomia? Do you suppose your father owns the entire country? No, it's yours as much as his. Don't you remember when you were just a toddler in little bib overalls with Smurfs on them? William would come down to Florida for long visits in the summer and on spring breaks, and he'd have his computer with him, and instead of telling you bedtime stories, you'd see them on the computer screen. That's when you first got to know Wyomia. That's why it all seems so familiar now. You've been here before, many times.*

"And *you* were here, too?"

—*In one form or another, yes. Don't you remember?*

"I remember an apple that was lying in the grass."

—*Like this one?* Brother Orson held up a perfect picture-book apple of uniform unmottled red.

"It was a poison apple. And you sliced it in two with your fingernail."

Brother Orson touched the skin of the apple with a taloned finger, and it split open to expose rotted pulp teeming with black specks.—*See the legions serving Herman*, he hissed. *See a million microscopic vermin!*

Judge squinted at the specks in the apple and saw that they were an army of infinitesimally small, infinitely evil insects.

—*What we have here's a mutant gene*, Brother Orson explained, or rather, recited, for his explanation took the form of rhyming verse:

> *So small it slips through every screen.*
> *Stained by it, your vital juice*
> *Ripens to illness, pain, a noose*

Of varied, slowly strangling ills,
A plague that almost always kills.
All this is bound within my curse
Till I have thrown it in reverse.

At first Judge did not pay much attention to Brother Orson's words from an ingrained suspicion of anything that sounded like poetry. Poetry was a form of secular humanist propaganda that he'd been force-fed at school and more hateful than other forms because of the way it would stick in your head like the ads on TV. But then it dawned on Judge what the words were about.

"That sounds like ARVIDS," he said to Brother Orson.

—Indeed. And these little critters are its seedlings.

The insects made a shrilling sound, as though agreeing.

—Vermin is not quite accurate. Properly speaking, these are mycoplasmas, the smallest, simplest free-living organisms.

"Uh-huh," Judge said. His aversion to scientific gobbledygook was more pronounced than his aversion to poetry. One of the things he liked about Brother Orson was that he never made you feel like you were in school being lectured at. Until now.

—You're not interested? Brother Orson asked, reading his mind.

"I'm just not that good at science."

—But aren't you curious to know the secrets of your father's success?

"I suppose. But I don't see what that's got to do with these microplastics."

—A long time ago, when the white man was taking charge of America, he found that he could kill many more red Indians by giving them blankets than by shooting them, if the blankets were infected with smallpox germs for which red Indians had no natural immunity. Whole nations were exterminated.

"Uh-huh," said Judge, who hated history probably more than any other required subject. History teachers were always trying to make you feel guilty about something—slavery or women not being able to vote or giving smallpox to Indians. And then, again, it dawned on him what Brother Orson was getting at.

"You mean William did something like that with ARVIDS?"

—No one has ever understood the etiology of infections associated with Mycoplasma incognitus. *It can affect many tissues. It cannot be isolated in blood samples; the test for ARVIDS is rather for the by-products of the infection in its terminal stages.*

Now he was sounding like a Public Health Authority lecturer at school assembly, when everyone in the auditorium has to recite what the letters in ARVIDS stand for: Acute Random-Vector Immune Disorder Syndrome. Like the words were supposed to be some kind of charm to keep you from coming down with it. Whereas Judge knew ARVIDS was God's judgment on sin, pure and simple, the sword in his right hand.

—*There are weapons more powerful than the sword.*

Judge glanced over his shoulder uneasily at the fire irons standing sentinel beside the fireplace. "I guess you mean the pen," he said evasively.

—*No, not the pen. Not the poker, either. The caduceus. Do you know what that is?*

"Sure, it's that twisty thing over the doorway at MDS."

—*Your father has a caduceus.*

"Uh-huh."

—*All that he's achieved as a doctor has been through its power. It was by using the caduceus that he created ARVIDS. It has also been the source of your own unmerited good health, and all your family's: your brothers, your mother, old Mrs. Obstschmecker, whomever your father has chosen to benefit.*

"How come I've never seen it?"

—*He keeps it secret. Wouldn't you?*

"You mean hidden away."

—*Hidden from most eyes . . . but with the Spectacles of True Vision—*

A buzzer rang.

—*Excuse me a moment*, Brother Orson said, and disappeared through the back door of the shop.

As soon as he was gone, Judge realized that the head on the counter was Lisa's. There was still blood oozing through her hair where he'd struck her with the pointed hook of the poker.

Lisa regarded him balefully. "I always did think you were a nasty little shit."

"Yeah, well. I never liked you much either."

The buzzer rang again.

"It isn't the phone this time, you know," said Lisa's severed head. "It's someone at the *door*, you born-again redneck moron."

"Uh-huh," said Judge, still without quite taking in what she was saying, since he'd turned his attention to the actual corpse on the leather sofa off to the side of the fireplace. He realized that sooner or later he was going to have to deal with the problem it represented. At some point corpses started to smell and get maggoty. He'd also have to clean up the blood, though he wasn't sure there was any way to get the stains out of the carpet.

He'd better start now, he decided. Reluctantly he typed SAVE, and the image of the severed head on the counter of Dr. Neudista's shop shrank down to a white dot and disappeared, which was just what he wished would happen to the body on the couch. But Lisa's dead body was here in realtime, and so was the person downstairs at the front door who would not stop ringing the bell.

74

Judith had very nearly despaired of anyone's hearing the bell and was considering simply walking away from her problems—leaving the body in the car and returning to the bus depot and taking the bus back to Florida. But finally, after what must have been ten minutes of ringing, Judge came to the door.

"Oh, it's you," he said, peering out suspiciously through the one-inch crack allowed by the door chain. "I was wondering when you'd get here."

"I've been ringing the doorbell for ten minutes."

"Sorry, I had earphones on. Just a minute." He closed the door, took off the chain, and opened it only a little wider, still barring entry.

Even with everything else she had to feel distressed about, the first sight of him was a shock. His had become one of those faces that attract the morbider sort of photographer, a face that registers at a glance as demented or, at the very least, disturbed. And then, on the heels of that distress, guilt—the guilt of knowing she must be responsible in some way for what she saw. This was her son. Her words, her cooking, her shifting moods and abiding presence had been the die that had formed his character and modeled his face. Even the name he'd taken for himself—Judge— seemed to point the same moral. Every child is time's truest judgment on its parents, but even as a child Judge had seemed to gloat at the judgment he represented. And she had always refused to believe that he was just what she deserved.

"You all right? Why's Ben sitting there in the car by himself?"

"Because he's dead. He died while we were driving here."

"No shit."

There was something almost Buddhist in his lack of affect, something one might rather envy than pity. But then she was not evidencing much overt feeling herself. Nothing settles the nerves and staunches hurt like the need to cope. She'd had to drive the length and breadth of Willowville with Ben still strapped in the driver's seat, her puppet. She'd stopped at every traffic light and stop sign (her foot could barely reach the brake), scanning the cross streets at every corner, with no idea of which way to turn to reach William's house (always in the past she'd been a passive visitor, letting her hosts do the driving), certain any time Ben's head dropped forward to his chest that a passerby would notice and phone the Public Health Authority. She would pull his head back by a lock of hair and continue steering with her right hand, and no one had noticed anything, because there were no passersby except the other drivers on the street.

"He died in the driver's seat? Then how'd you get here?"

"I'm sorry, I can't explain all that now. Is William in the house?"

"No, I'm here by myself. Lisa sent the kids and their nanny on the airplane to see her folks in the East. Then she followed on a later flight. But I don't know where William's gone to. He hasn't been home for a few days now. Sometimes he stays at MDS or else at Madge's place in St. Paul. So I wasn't worried."

Judge had that shifty look he always got when he was lying, but Judith knew better than to confront him head on.

"What you figuring to do with . . . ?" Judge nodded discreetly in the direction of Ben's corpse. "Ain't we supposed to call the Public Health number any time someone dies?"

"Ben was just released from a PHA detention center. It's quite likely we'd both be put in quarantine if we went by the rules and reported his death. So what I suggest is that you open the garage door and I drive the car in there. After that, William will know the best course to take, once he gets home. Do you have *any* idea where he might be?"

"Not if he ain't where I said first—MDS or Madge's."

"When was the last time he was actually home?"

"Monday night was when he didn't get home to dinner. Since then."

"And Lisa set off?"

"Next day."

"You've been here by yourself since then?"

"Where'm I going to go with this damn thing on my ankle?" He tugged at the cloth of his jeans, lifting the frayed cuff high enough to reveal the bulge of the parole band beneath his stocking. "Anyhow, I'm not alone. I can talk to Brother Orson any time I need to, and God is always right beside me. He is my buckler and the horn of my salvation."

She almost laughed out loud, not so much at his absurdity as at her own in having come all this way in the hope of having some effect on him. In just this little time she knew (she remembered) that there was nothing she could say that he would hear. Knowing that was oddly liberating.

"Something funny?" he asked with his usual alertness to being looked at askance.

"The situation—our standing about like this, chatting, while a corpse is waiting to be disposed of. It's a little macabre, wouldn't you say?"

"Uh-huh. Well, I'll get the garage open. You can handle the car?"

"That's what I've been doing most of the afternoon."

She got back into the car and did the maneuvering needed to ease the car into the center space of the garage, next to Lisa's Volvo.

Judith turned off the ignition as the garage door rumbled closed. She repositioned her father's head against the headrest and tried, without exerting much pressure, to make his eyelids close.

"Here," Judge said, reaching in through the open window of the car. "Let me do that." She looked away, and when she looked back Ben seemed at rest.

"You want to leave him in here?" Judge asked. "Or what?"

"I think so. For now."

Judith followed Judge along a hallway hung with Lisa's bright, innocuous watercolors and prints—floral close-ups and rudimentary landscapes that wanted to be Matisses but wound up looking like greeting cards and record sleeves for easy listening music. Judith was glad that Lisa had spared them the effort of trying to be civil to each other by her early departure.

When they entered the dining room, the smell that had been only a faint sickliness in the hallway became an outright stench.

"Goodness! What in the world—?"

"I guess I should of thrown out all these flowers."

There were vases of dead and dying roses anywhere there was a level surface to put them, whole bushes torn from their beds and sagging despondently in the room's curtained twilight. The carpet was strewn with petals.

"It's the roses that smell so bad?" Judith marveled.

"When there's a whole lot of them like this it can smell pretty bad."

"It smells more like something that's gone bad in the refrigerator."

"You can go check the icebox if you want. Thing is, a smell builds up gradual and you don't notice if you're always there where the smell is. People visiting at Starke used to complain about how we all smelled, but we couldn't smell it. Didn't you have a suitcase?"

"I left it at the station."

"I thought it might be at your hotel."

"I'm not staying at a hotel, John," she said firmly. "I'm staying here."

He scowled. "Lisa didn't say anything about that to me."

"I suppose she took it for granted."

"And don't call me John! In the baptism of the Gospel my name is Judge."

"I know," she said. "One of the last things your grandfather talked about was to remind me you were touchy about your name."

"I am not *touchy!*"

This time she really couldn't help it, though she pressed her lips together and lowered her eyes to the petal-strewn carpet. The laughter welled up from inside like carbonation fizzing up from a bottle the moment it's uncapped. And not just a snort or a chortle but hard, muscular laughter.

Judge, of course, swelled up with indignation, and that was even funnier. He glowered at her as she went on laughing, but at last, defeated, he turned on his heel and left her alone in the dining room with the rotting flowers. There was the sound of loud, reproachful footsteps mounting the stairs and the slamming of a door.

At once she stopped laughing.

It seemed as though someone had entered the room at that moment, not as though someone had left it. It was her sorrow, and as soon as she had recognized it, she was able to welcome it with the first tears she'd shed since Ben had died.

75

Finally, after wasting one whole day trying to go through the official channels, William had been able to get someone to listen to him—a black teenager named Larry who was in charge of the food tent where William got his meals. Larry had been living in the camp over a year and was well enough connected with its clandestine hierarchy that he was able to send a message to a woman named Lorine, who would be able, according to Larry, to sneak William into the old Midway area, which housed the PHA offices and living quarters. From there, William would be able to phone anywhere in the Twin Cities, and if he was who he claimed he was, he'd be able to contact someone who could vouch for him.

Lorine appeared at three thirty. A squat, blond woman who must have been at least ten years his senior, Lorine still wore the traditional uniform of teenage rebellion—leather jacket, jeans, and lots of junk jewelry. She smoked nonstop, sucking at the cigarettes as though she were fighting to draw a breath of air from a faulty respirator.

William went through his story again. Lorine listened with selective inattention. She seemed to have no interest in how he'd been shanghaied into the camp or in whether or not he had ARVIDS. It didn't take medical training to see that *she* did. Her fingers had a telltale tremor every time she lifted a cigarette to her lips. Tears leaked, unheeded, from the corners of her eyes, tracing lines of melted mascara down her cheeks. And the sour smell of the disease came off her like the smell of a caged animal in the zoo. Even the stink of her Salems couldn't mask it. But strangely, on Lorine these marks of imminent death seemed less to be symptoms of disease than badges of defiance, like her leather jacket and the haze of her cigarette smoke.

Lorine was interested, essentially, in only one thing—how much William might be able to pay for his release.

"In *cash*," she emphasized. "For obvious reasons"—she had a brief fit of coughing, recovered, blinked away tears, and took a drag on her cigarette—"it's got to be cash. Gold is okay, too. Not jewelry, just the kind of gold that looks like candy bars."

"I've got money in various bank accounts. If I wrote out a check to cash . . . ?"

"Yeah, but who's going to take it into a bank? That's the problem. See, how could we trust you not to try and turn us in once you're out of here?"

"If I did that, I'd put myself in danger of being sent back here myself."

"Maybe, maybe not. If you're the big shot you say you are, and if you don't test positive, once you're out, you're out. And as soon as you're out you'll forget the reasons you had to be grateful to me and my friends. That seems to be human nature." She took in a lungful of smoke and grimaced philosophically.

"If you want money, I can get you money. I keep a reserve of cash in my safe. If I can get through to someone on the phone, I can tell them how to open it."

"Now you're cooking. How much you think is in the safe?"

"Ten thousand, maybe more."

"You'll need to come up with more than that if you want exit papers, but that ought to set the wheels in motion. No, don't tell me—I'm telepathic—you're going to say, 'That's blackmail!'"

William tried to echo her smartass tone. "No, more like ransom for a kidnapping."

She nodded approvingly. "Right. This is your own personal hostage crisis. So, since we're agreed on that, let's head to the trailer."

Lorine led him on a zigzag path through the fairgrounds, stopping along the way to confer with other unofficial figures of authority: the bouncer outside a big merry-go-round (which had become a crack house, according to someone William had stood in line with the day before in Pioneer Hall); an old woman selling frayed paperbacks and used magazines from a Pronto-Pup stand.

The sidewalks were crowded with people, mostly dressed in the pajamas supplied by the camp, but few of them were going anywhere. They stood in clusters, or sat along the curb, a few speaking, most silent, all with an air of aggrieved resignation, as though they had been waiting hours for a parade that would never appear. At intervals one of the green and white PHA service vehicles would crawl by, like a police car cruising a high-crime neighborhood.

"So, Larry says you're some kind of doctor."

William nodded. "I run a research facility."

"Researching what exactly?"

"Various aspects of immune response."

Hearing Lorine's wheezy laugh was like looking at an X-ray of her damaged lungs. "*Meaning* you specialize in ARVIDS?"

"Someone has to, if there's ever going to be a cure."

She stopped in front of a boarded-up concession booth and squinted at him through a twisting veil of cigarette smoke. "What did you say your name was?"

"Michaels."

"*William* Michaels—the guy on the news?"

"From time to time."

"You're the one who's got this plan for turning some whole county up north into another plague camp like this?" She didn't wait for confirmation. "Shit," she said, dropping her cigarette to the pavement and grinding it out. She looked at him with candid, gloating calculation.

William felt reassured. Now that he'd been recognized for who he was, it would only be a matter of time until he was released. The size of the ransom demanded was a matter of indifference to him.

Lorine developed a sense of urgency, and they headed directly to the midway with no more side stops, entering through a secondary gate, where the guards weren't uniformed in PHA green. The trailer they went to was located behind the main Ferris wheel, which was still operational, being run for the entertainment of PHA personnel and for its value as PR. From a distance, the sight of the revolving Ferris wheel gave the fairgrounds an air of business-as-usual cheeriness. It served the same purpose, though on an immensely larger scale, as the bouquet beside a sickbed.

The trailer was furnished sparely with two desks and a few office chairs. Supplies of liquor, chocolate, and cigarettes—the unofficial currency of the camp—were arrayed in cabinets with padlocked doors of steel mesh.

Lorine unlocked one of the cabinets, took out a phone, and plugged it into a wall jack. "So tell me, what do I dial?"

He gave her Ben's home number first, and when no one answered there, his number at MDS. When Ben's secretary answered, Lorine refused to relinquish control of the phone. "All she could tell me," she summarized, when she'd hung up, "was that he wasn't there now and she didn't know when he would be. So who do I call next?"

He gave her the general number for MDS and told her to try and be put through to the administrative director, Valerie Bright. After being shunted about to various extensions, Lorine hung up. "It's the same with her as with that Winckleberger guy: she's not there, and no one can say where she is or when she'll be back. Strike two."

There was no recourse but to have Lorine dial his number at home. He hadn't wanted to involve his wife in his difficulties any more than he could help. Lisa did not cope well with unexpected demands. He also did not want to give her the combination of his safe. She didn't even know there was a safe in his study.

William was already figuring whom to call next when someone answered the phone after just two rings. "Hello," Lorine said, "is this Mrs. William Michaels?" And then, after a pause, "Well, is Mrs. Michaels there? I'd like to speak to her." And then, after a longer pause, in a tone of exasperation, "Shit. Hung up."

"But *someone* was there," William insisted.

"A woman. She had the same last name as the first person you had me call."

"Winckelmeyer. Judith Winckelmeyer?"

"Right."

"Judith wouldn't just hang up, that isn't like her."

Lorine snorted derision and dug into the zippered pocket of her jacket for a pack of Salems. "You'd be surprised how many people hang up their phones when they hear where the call is coming from. I got a brother in

Edina. You think he's happy to have me call up? You think if I ask to talk with one of my nieces they are ever there? Once you're inside this fence, you are already considered dead by the people outside. And they don't like to be visited by ghosts, even over the phone. Welcome to hell, Dr. Williams."

"But Judith didn't know who was calling. Let *me* use the phone. I know she won't hang up on me."

Lorine lighted a cigarette. "Help yourself."

Just feeling the beige plastic of the receiver in his hand was like catching hold of a lifeline. He had only to dial the right seven digits and, like a lottery winner, all his problems would be over.

He dialed his home number and Judith answered at once with a questioning "Hello?"

"Judith? Judith, it's William—please don't hang up again. This is very important."

"William! I didn't hang up, the line just went dead for some reason. Where are you? Ben said you were picked up by the PHA."

"That's where I am now. At the fairgrounds. It's been a nightmare, but I can't go into it now. Is Lisa there?"

"Lisa had already left before I got here."

"Left for where?"

"To visit her brother in the Berkshires. She left on Tuesday with the boys and your au pair. I'm alone here with Judge. William, are you all right?"

The question seemed to act like a karate chop right to the root of his pain. It flared through his nervous system like magnesium, a blast of pure white agony obliterating everything else.

Lorine pried the phone from his fingers with the schooled indifference of a nurse to whom another person's pain is only a symptom to be dealt with, like fever or incontinence. "Hello, Miss Winckelberger?" she said into the phone. "Your friend is experiencing some temporary distress. The reason he called is that he wanted someone at that number to open his office safe and take some money from it. And then be ready to bring the money to . . . at this point it hasn't been decided where. So if you could get the money and wait for us to call again later . . . do you think you could do that?"

William could not hear Judith's reply, but it seemed to satisfy Lorine.

"What is the combination of the safe?" Lorine asked him.

He couldn't answer at once. The aftershock of the pain and fear that it might return made it hard to think of anything else.

"Dr. Williams?" Lorine insisted, squeezing her eyes into slits.

When he had told her the combination of the safe, he felt a strange and humbling helplessness.

"And where *is* the safe, your friend wants to know."

"In the wall to the right of my desk. Behind my medical degree."

Lorine passed on the information to Judith with her own commentary: "He says it's in the first place anyone would look, behind the degree on the wall of his office. Maybe there's even an arrow pointing to it and a sign saying, 'Safe Here.'" After a pause, she said, to herself, "I don't believe it," and then, looking up, to William, "She hung up again. You think I said something to offend her?"

But William wasn't thinking at all. The pain had returned, not at full force, only a dull pain, bearable if it didn't get worse.

Lorine dialed the number again, and reported, "Busy." She returned the receiver to its cradle. "Just out of curiosity, is that Judith someone you know real well? I mean she isn't likely to just take the money and run, is she?"

William shook his head. "I think," he said very carefully, "I should see a doctor."

Lorine laughed. "You and me both, sweetheart."

"I think this may be urgent."

"Hey, it wasn't me who hung up the phone, it was your friend Judith."

"If you could get someone to drive me to 1350 Calumet Avenue here in St. Paul. . . . It's not more than a mile from the fairgrounds."

"Why, what's there?"

The caduceus was there, where he had first hidden it, in the insulation of the attic. The caduceus had never failed to be efficacious in the past. If he could lay hold of it, he would be well, the pain would be gone. But how could he explain that to this leather-clad harpy, this would-be teenager who looked older than Madge?

All he could think to say was, "My stepmother lives there. She's a nurse, she—" He caught his breath as another magnesium flare of pain swept through his nervous system.

Lorine leaned forward, squint-eyed, her interest captured by the signs of his suffering as an iron filing might align itself inside a magnetic field. "Hey, you're not bullshitting, are you? You got some kind of problem."

"Please," he begged, with the abjection that comes as hope vanishes. "Just take me to . . . 1350 Calumet."

"Yeah, well, we'll keep dialing. But meanwhile I think you could use a little mood alteration. Something to take your mind off your immediate problems." She went to the steel-mesh cabinet from which she'd taken the telephone and returned with a box containing a hypodermic and various sized ampules. She readied his injection as skillfully as any R.N. and found the vein she was looking for after only the second try.

The morphine flowed into him like the waters of baptism, erasing the pain, filling any darkness with bright white light. His body became a dawn meadow, shimmering with a dew of pure hurtless sensation.

"That feels better?" Lorine inquired. Her husky voice seemed to have gained a clarinetlike timbre.

He nodded.

Lorine put a finger under his chin and tilted his head up so that she could look directly into his eyes. For a moment he thought she meant to kiss him, but then, reverently, she refilled the hypodermic from another ampule.

"There was a song," she remarked, "back in the sixties . . ." She paused as she felt the first rush of the drug, and resumed, "I can't remember the lyrics anymore, but I used to listen to that song all the time."

76

It was clear now that everything had been happening for a purpose: his father's phone call coming just when it did, and Judith having arrived just when she did, so she would answer the phone when William rang and he would talk to her. Judge was sure that no matter what sort of fix William was in he wouldn't have told Judge the combination of the safe, not when he knew that inside it was not only the pile of money he'd wanted Judith to bring him but—Praise God!—the anchoring device for the Parole Board's house-arrest system. He'd torn the office apart trying to find the damned thing—until he'd discovered the wall safe and realized that that was where it must be.

At which point Lisa was already dead.

He was sorry he had had to kill her, though at the time he'd felt a kind of satisfaction. Not a carnal satisfaction, but the feeling you get when the last piece of a puzzle slips into place, the righteous *thwack* of a knife as it keeps hitting the high-score areas in a target. No, he was sorry because he knew he was in deep shit and couldn't see any way out. If he went any distance from the anchoring device in the house, the Parole Board band

around his ankle would trigger an alarm and he'd be picked up and returned home. And if he'd removed the band himself with the garden
shears, the police would have been at the house in no time and found
Lisa's body. No matter what he did, he seemed headed back to prison, so
he had just sat tight and concentrated his attention on exploring Wyomia,
which turned out to have been exactly the right thing to do.

And now? Was it still the right thing to do? Wyomia was a gold mine
of information, especially once he'd gained the Spectacles of True Vision.
In some ways, in most ways, Wyomia was a more interesting place than
Willowville or Minneapolis or anywhere real. It wasn't like looking at pictures on a TV screen, it was like the world to come, the world of the last
days promised by the Gospels and by Brother Orson.

And he was there, even more vividly than when Judge had interfaced
with him through his 900 phone number. People were always trying to
explain away Brother Orson, saying he was just a computer-generated
illusion of interactivity. But nothing could explain away what Judge had
seen and heard in the last few days. He would have liked to boot up the
disc again right now, but he really had to deal with the bodies first. Especially Lisa's body, which smelled. One of the good things about living in
the last days was knowing that your own flesh would never be corrupted.
It would pass through the Rapture and be rendered incorruptible.

Judge freed up the edges of an Oriental rug from the sofa legs pinning
it to the carpet. He placed Lisa's body at one end of the rug and got her
rolled up into a fairly manageable bundle. He fastened the bundle to stay
closed with three rep ties from William's dressing room closet. When he'd
finished and dragged the bundle out into the hall, Lisa's hair was visible at
one end and the tips of her shoes at the other, but basically she looked like
a rolled-up rug.

He left Lisa at the head of the stairs and then went down to the living
room to figure out what to do with his mother. He really had not meant to
kill Judith, but she hadn't left him much choice. Once he'd refused to let
her into William's office, she'd said, "Okay," and turned away and would
have walked right out of the house. He'd had to stop her. The fact she was
his mother really didn't enter into it, though he knew if he got caught and
there were newspaper headlines, they'd make him out to be some kind of
monster for killing his mother *and* his stepmother, and they'd probably
even try to blame him for Ben's being dead, too. They'd say he was some
kind of sex maniac, and it really wasn't fair. And just try and explain to
the media that neither Lisa nor Judith was his parent in the baptism of the
Gospel. Oh, if he got caught now, there would be hell to pay.

Judith's corpse looked like she'd fallen asleep on the sofa where he'd left her. Her head lolled sideways across the upright cushion. Her left hand was wedged between her thighs, and her right hung limply from the armrest. Except that her eyes were closed, you might have supposed she was posing for a picture. Only if you looked at her neck real close could you see the marks his fingers had made when he'd strangled her.

Judge wasn't sure what to do with Judith. There was another Oriental carpet in the living room, but it was nine feet by twelve feet and not well adapted to the task. He knew, from the last time he'd taken a pizza out of it, that the freezer in the basement was too well stocked to get a body into it without taking out a lot of the food. Burying the bodies in the backyard was out of the question, even if he waited till late at night. There were just too many other houses with a view of what he'd be doing.

As Judge stood there wondering how to proceed, the doorbell rang. He felt an instant of panic, but no more than that. Unbidden, the words of the Eighteenth Psalm came to his lips: *The Lord is my rock, and my fortress, and my deliverer; my God, my strength, in whom I will trust; my buckler, and the horn of my salvation.*

He squatted down, grabbed hold of the baseboard of the sofa, and hauled it out by main strength a couple of feet from the wall. With one hand he got hold of Judith by the waistband of her slacks and slid his other hand under her knees. Then, much as he might have executed a clean-and-jerk, he flipped Judith's body up over the back of the couch and let it drop to the floor.

He pushed the couch back to the wall, or as near as it would go. He regarded the effect from a distance, and he figured it would pass muster. Then he went to the monitor in the vestibule to see who was at the door.

It was the black priest who'd preached the fine sermon about the Lord's Prayer at Our Lady of Mercy Church and then gone out with him and old Mrs. Obstschmecker to visit the cemetery. Father Lyman Sinclair.

Judge was delighted.

He unbolted the door and opened it and held out his hand to be shaken. "Well, as I live and breathe! You said you was going to come and pay me a visit and here you are!"

The priest smiled. "Is this a convenient time? I'm not intruding?"

"I can't think of anyone I'd rather see at this moment than yourself, Ly-man Sin-clair. (You will remember that you said I didn't have to call you Father.) Come inside! Come inside!"

77

Father Lyman Sinclair knew he was being a snoop, but that did not make him feel sinful, since where was the commandment that said thou shalt not snoop? Partly he'd been drawn here by ordinary celebrity curiosity, the same that could fill roadsides with a million unbelievers every time the pope stepped into a limo. Judge Winckelmeyer's father was many notches lower on the scale of newsworthiness than the Holy Father, and lower than most movie stars, but he was at least the equal of the governor or even a news anchorman. He was also the only famous person Lyman had gone to school with, and since Lyman himself had become famous in a local way, there was a class reunion aspect to the visit. Even the school bully (and that surely had been Lyman's role) develops a kind of sentimental interest after enough time has passed.

Beyond that, however, was a bond of guilt that ran so deep in Lyman's soul that it seemed sometimes that Billy Michaels was his brother, an Abel left alive after a botched murder. When he'd heard, the day after the trick he'd played on Billy, how Mr. Michaels had been killed in a car accident when he was driving Billy to the hospital, Lyman had gone straight to Father Youngermann at the rectory of Our Lady of Mercy and made his confession. The first real confession in his life. But Lyman had never felt forgiven, not entirely, and the sense of his sinfulness had eaten at him year after year until at last it had turned him into a priest. *O felix culpa*, perhaps, but even so he was sure that the ledgers of heaven had yet to be balanced between himself and the boy who'd become Dr. William Michaels.

So here he was at the man's home in Willowville, seated on his living room couch, yielding to the tug of all those years of curiosity and guilt. It might not be the scene of the crime he was returning to, but it felt like it.

But that was only a part of his curiosity. He was fascinated no less by Judge Winckelmeyer, Dr. Michaels's loutish stepson, and though he knew it was a morbid fascination, he could not resist the impulse, when his parochial duties had called him to Anoka, to turn off U.S. 10 at the Willowville exit. Here, in an interior that might have served as a cover for one of the magazines that cater to the houseproud—all lush fabrics and fine-grained woods—the boy seemed even stranger, more ungainly, than he had at the church or the cemetery. Nothing of this house's genteel style had rubbed off on him. He looked like a plumber who'd come to fix a plugged drain, with the latex-pale skin some white men have that makes them look half dead and that even in his worst moments of envy or self-pity in seminary days Lyman would never have wished for in exchange for his own deep cocoa-brown.

The boy's eyes were what most fascinated Lyman. The eyes of fanaticism, of perfect faith, of lunacy. His own faith had never been so pure, nor had he ever seen quite the same telltale gleam in the eyes of other Catholics, except perhaps for some of the nuns, the ones he remembered from childhood. He envied such purity of heart and singleness of vision, but he feared it a little, too, and as usual when fear is complicated with desire, it had become a temptation, and he had yielded to it and come here.

"I'll bet I know what you're thinking. You're wondering why there's such a smell in here. It's the roses. On Monday my stepmother filled up all those pots she's got on all the tables and then she went off east to see her brother, and I've been here since then more or less by myself. I didn't think to get rid of the damn things till this afternoon, and that's why there's the smell."

"The church can get to smelling the same way—after a funeral."

Judge jutted his head forward, squinting.

"Just a joke," Lyman soothed. One had to remember that people with great faith were liable to have zero sense of humor.

Judge nodded and seemed to relax. He was seated on the edge of a wingback chair, his elbows braced against his knees, his thick fingers tightly interlocked in a double-fist. "I didn't notice it myself," he went on, "till my real mother pointed it out to me. She's come here to visit. But she is not here now. I told you about her."

"I remember you said your mother was a nun."

"Mm-hm, that's her. You'd probably like her. Or maybe you wouldn't: she's a heretic."

"Yes, you mentioned that, as well, when we were driving to the cemetery. I probably would like her. Some of my best friends are heretics."

"That's probably another joke, huh? Myself, I cannot see how you Catholics know what to believe when one bunch of you believes one thing and another bunch believes something else, and the newspapers say that some big percent of both sides don't put any store by what the priests on either side say and just go their own way."

"We're a bit like families that way, I suppose. Outsiders only hear the noise we make quarreling. The love is quiet."

"I've got to disagree with you there. With God there can't be no room to quarrel. He says do this, you better do it. *Thy will be done*. It was you preached that sermon. Though when you hit that line, you kind of skittered off, as I recall. You just said we got to all love everybody else, and left it at that."

"I didn't invent that idea myself, you know. That's in the Gospel, too."

"But loving's got to be the easy part. You won't get no one to disagree about love. It's when God's got other ideas that *Thy will be done* can get tricky."

"Other ideas than love?" Lyman asked in a defensive tone. "Such as?"

"Such as when he told Abraham to take his baby boy Isaac up on top of the mountain and kill him. I don't see what love had to do with that."

"Truly, faith was more the issue in that case. But Abraham didn't have to kill Isaac in the end. A ram was substituted."

"Mm-hm. But the reason we're supposed to think Abraham was so special was because he would've done it if God hadn't changed his mind at the last minute. Right? And then what about Jephthah? Jephthah went ahead and did what Abraham was let off the hook from having to do. He killed his only begotten. Course, it was his daughter he killed, not a son, but nowadays that's not supposed to make a difference."

"I know the story of Jephthah," Lyman said, in a tone of annoyance. The story of Jephthah was, in his opinion, one of the Old Testament's major warts. Feminists loved to use it as ammunition to prove that Jehovah was not much better, from an ethical point of view, than Baal or Dagon or the other major contenders of that era. Yes, he knew the story very well, and he knew there was only one loophole: "But nowhere in the story does it say that God *told* Jephthah to do what he did. It was his own dumb idea to make the promise he did."

"Well, if it was such a dumb idea, why does the Bible say, chapter eleven, verse twenty-nine, *Then the Spirit of the Lord came upon Jephthah*, and then, the very next thing, verse thirty, *Jephthah vowed a vow unto the Lord, and said, If thou shalt without fail deliver the children of Ammon into mine hands, then it shall be, that whatsoever cometh forth of the doors of my house to meet me, when I return in peace from the children of Ammon, shall surely be the Lord's, and I will offer it up for a burnt offering*. Seems pretty clear from that the Lord was inspiring Jephthah to vow that vow. And when it was his daughter stepped through the door, don't you think the Lord must of had a hand in that, too? The Lord was *testing* Jephthah by making him burn to death the person he loved the most. That's got to be the meaning of the story. And once he done what he vowed, then God made him one of the judges of Israel, like Samson. *And Jephthah judged Israel six years:* chapter twelve, verse seven. It's in the book."

"What is your point? Does Brother Orson think we should reinstitute human sacrifice?"

"It ain't *my* point, and it's not Brother Orson's point. It's God's. God can ask us to do some damned strange things. Like suppose there had to be nuke-ular war to keep the Com-munists from taking over the whole world, and we'd bring on nuke-ular winter if we did that. I guess that might be some kind of human sacrifice, but we'd have to do it."

"Actually, Christ had different ideas about how to deal with one's enemies. That's why we speak of an Old Testament and a New Testament."

"What Brother Orson says, and what I believe, is there is just one God and he's eternal. I am that I am! And if he says you got to kill the next person comes through the front door, why then, that's what you got to do. No ifs, ands, or buts. But I'm forgetting my duties as a host. Would you like something to drink? I can offer milk or O-Jay or something from my father's liquor cabinet."

"Some orange juice perhaps. I still have a long drive home."

Judge got to his feet and headed for the farther end of the living room, where it merged with a dining room of equal extent. "It's too bad my father isn't here right now," he said, pausing in the archway between the two rooms. "I remember your saying how you went to school together."

Judge went through the arch, then turned left, out of sight, presumably toward a source of orange juice. When he'd gone, Lyman sniffed at the stink that hung in the air of the room. It went beyond the cloying scent of decaying flowers. It was more like meat that had begun to turn.

There was a rustling sound that seemed to come from behind the couch. A pet of some sort, Lyman supposed. Since the couch had been pulled several inches away from the wall, it would have been an easy matter to crane his neck and look over the back of the couch, but just as he was about to do so, Judge returned with two glasses of orange juice.

He was still harping on Jephthah. "What I don't understand about you Cath-olics"—he handed Lyman a glass tinkling with ice cubes—"is what you think the Bible *is*. If it's God's word, then isn't the whole thing God's word? Including the story of Jephthah? What do you think God *means* by that story?"

"St. Mark answers that question. Christ spoke to the multitude in parables. *And without a parable spake he not unto them.* Only alone with his disciples did he expound his full meaning. I'd say that the God who gave us the Old Testament was often speaking in parables, too. The story of

Jephthah is a myth, like the story of Agamemnon and Iphigenia. They're very similar stories. A father heading into battle makes an oath to kill his daughter, and does so. The main difference is Agamemnon kills his daughter before the war, and Jephthah waits till afterward."

Judge made a hoot of derision. "Aga-memnon? Effa-genia? Those are Greek names, ain't they? Brother Orson says all that Greek stuff is seckular humanist bullshit. Like that Oedipus we had to read about at school. Killed his father and married his mother, and then this psycho-analyst Sigmund Freud comes along and says we all of us are just aching to do the same thing. I knew that's what Jews think, but I'm surprised to hear it from a Catholic priest."

Momentarily, Lyman was stopped in his tracks. Could the son of a doctor, a prominent scientist, really be such a redneck ignoramus as this? He was tempted to call Judge's bluff. But the gleam in the boy's eye had grown brighter while they'd been talking, and Lyman doubted that was something that could be faked. Somehow, just by living in Florida and watching untold hours of evangelical TV cartoons, the boy had soaked up the essence of fundamentalist dementia. So, it wouldn't do just to say, "Bullshit!" and take his leave. That might do for a liar; a madman deserved more courtesy.

It was the orange juice that gave him his cue. Ever since his four-year stint of missionary duty in Calcutta, he'd associated the color of orange juice with the garish robes of the priestly caste and with the garishness of Hinduism generally.

"Oh, Catholicism would have many surprises for you, and the religious world beyond Catholicism would have still more. It did for me. After my seminary years in Rome, I did mission work in Calcutta, and I found out what idolatry is at first hand. Americans pick up the term from reading the Bible, but the actuality of idolatry would boggle even your mind, my boy. The most popular god of their vast pantheon is called Ganesh, who looks like a man except that he has the head of an elephant. How he came to look that way takes us right back to Jephthah, and to Oedipus. Originally Ganesh looked like any other god, that's to say, human. But one day his father, Shiva, came home after a long absence and discovered a young man with his wife Parvati in her bedroom, and having a hot temper he cut off the young man's head. Only afterwards did he realize it was Ganesh, and so to keep Ganesh alive he cut off the head of an elephant that was passing by just then and fastened it to the dead boy's neck, in which form Ganesh has been worshiped for centuries."

Judge looked at Lyman with genuine amazement. "But, that's impossible. You can't put an elephant's head on a human being!"

"We don't think so. But there have been billions of Indians who believe in Ganesh just as fervently as you believe in Brother Orson."

"What's your point? Are you trying to say Brother Orson is some kind of pagan idol?"

"No. My point is about the nature of idolatry. That its nature is to ascribe human attributes to God, and so every culture is liable to end up with myths that look alike, because human nature, as Freud pointed out, and St. Augustine pointed out much earlier, is the same in India as in Greece or North Africa or Minneapolis. Freud speaks of the Oedipus complex, Augustine calls it original sin."

"And I call that bullshit!" Judge's pallid face was flushed with anger. "Elephants! Aga-*mem*-non! Jesus Chrahst Almahty!" He got to his feet, and stood with his eyes fixed on Lyman as though he were considering hurling his glass of orange juice at him.

At that moment, in answer to the prayer Lyman had not yet thought to make, the phone rang.

Immediately Judge switched into his mode of high courtesy. "If you will excuse me just a moment, sir, I must answer the telephone." He strode to the far end of the room and promised, as he went out the door, "I will try not to be long."

Lyman set down his sweating glass of orange juice on a rosewood end table, careless of the stain it might make. He intended to be out of the house and on the road before Judge had finished on the phone.

But as he stood up, there was another sound from behind the couch, faint as the rustling he'd heard a moment earlier, but not such a sound as any pet might make. It was a woman's voice, which whispered a single word, "Please . . ."

He knelt on the edge of the seat and bent over to look into the shadowy recess behind the couch. A woman's body was wedged into the narrow space, one arm twisted over her head and pressing the side of her face into the flowery upholstery.

Their eyes met.

"Don't say anything," she whispered. "He may hear. Just go . . ."

"Did he—"

"Now! He's very . . . dangerous. Go to the police."

"And leave you here, with him?"

"I'm safe if he thinks I'm dead." She smiled a smile of desperate entreaty. "Please . . ."

"You're his mother, aren't you."

In answer she only closed her eyes.

Lyman got to his feet, but before he was halfway to the door, Judge appeared and, with the quick perception of paranoia, understood the priest's intention. He grabbed a large ceramic vase from one of the rosewood tables and hurled it at Lyman, aiming low. The bowl struck his knees and shattered.

Lyman retreated back into the living room, and Judge positioned himself some feet in front of the door.

"There's a body behind that couch," Lyman said. "A dead woman."

Judge looked about for another missile.

"That's your mother, isn't it?" Lyman took refuge behind the wingback chair, and the second vase struck the chair's arm without shattering.

"I am sorry," Judge said in a normal conversational tone. "I didn't mean things to work out this way. She just appeared, like you did. I suppose in a way it must be a sign."

Lyman did not think he would be a match against the boy in a physical struggle. His only hope was escape, but the boy stood between him and the only way out of the room. Except the large picture window that faced the couch. If he broke the window and vaulted through it . . .

He took a firm hold on the back of the wingback chair, lofted it, and had begun to swing it round toward the glass when Judge's knife struck him in the back. The chair crashed into the coffee table in front of the couch, sending up a spray of orange juice, shattering the rosewood.

Lyman, on his knees, felt the knife being drawn from his flesh, and a final flash of astonishment as the blade slid between his ribs and pierced his heart.

78

"Do you realize," Madge marveled, "how long it's been since I've had a drink? Since I've been *drunk!*" She held up the stemmed wineglass and gave a little spin to the liquor store's most expensive French wine so that its swirling vein-red contours caught the last brightnesses of the solstice sunset and threw them back like a little liquid chandelier. Lovely. "More than two decades," she answered herself with a sigh, "and closer to three."

"That's a lot of water," Launce agreed, "that never went under the bridge."

Madge laughed immoderately and went on to marvel at her own laughter. "And jokes! I used to joke all the time. Though Henry was the real stand-up comic. He could tell jokes all night long, one after another without repeating himself once. God, I don't think I could remember one of those jokes now."

"Oh, I remember one he must've told. It was a real popular joke in the sixties. The one about the three Jews pissing in the snow in Wisconsin was how I first heard it. Another time it was three Norwegian farmers. Remember?" Lance leaned forward to empty the last of the third twenty-four-dollar bottle into their glasses, filling his own right to the brim, then lifting the filled glass to his lips without a drop spilled.

"I think so. The third one spells out the president's full name—is that the joke?"

"That's the joke. He writes 'Lyndon Baines Johnson—President of the United States of America' in foot-high letters."

Madge felt a glow of nostalgia that was also, without any contradiction, the glow of the burgundy as it smoothed its way down her throat. "I can remember Henry telling that one. We were in a bar on Snelling over toward Marshall that isn't there anymore, and there were a bunch of us all at one table. But I can't remember why it was funny."

"What's funny is that the third guy, the Jew or the farmer, the one who writes so much, has to have someone else to hold his pecker to do it."

Madge considered this for a while and then had to ask, "Why?"

"Because he says he can piss all right but he doesn't know how to spell."

Madge spluttered wine joyfully all over her lemon-yellow blouse. The joy of the joke and of the blouse's ruin were a single pleasure, which was one with the burning of the wine that had gone up her nose.

She had forgotten what it was like to be so thoroughly sloshed, the way the edges disappeared from things and at the same time their clarity deepened. The wonderful insights she'd probably forget by tomorrow. The recklessness! For what could be more reckless than having sex with someone who had ARVIDS, which Lance almost certainly did, though they'd avoided discussing it. They'd been as awkward and greedy as teenagers. Lovely.

But loveliest of all the way the sunlight gilded everything with its own beauty, the leaves on the trees and their shadows on the white siding of the house. The ant crawling along the wooden armrest of the lawn chair. The leaves that had fallen mysteriously at midsummer from the elm above them and which now decorated the unmown grass at geometric intervals. Even the blotches of the wine on the yellow of her blouse were like the blood-red speckles on the pale petals of a flower she could see in her mind's eye though she couldn't think of its name. Cineraria?

She laughed—not a laugh that would spill more wine but a laugh that felt like her own body's form of sunlight, a glow deep inside.

"It wasn't *that* funny," Launce said, leaning back in the aluminum lawn chair and looking up into the leaves of the tree.

"No, I was thinking how we aren't sinners."

"Aren't we? I thought we gave it a pretty good shot."

"No, we're still husband and wife. The Church doesn't recognize divorce. So if we make love it's not a sin. We're entitled."

"Ah, but the Church *also* doesn't recognize oral sex."

"Even if you're married?"

"Nope. Father What's-His-Name made that real clear. So we're sinners, after all. If that's what you want."

"Well, it would make *Mother* feel better, I'm sure. She just about blew a gasket when she saw me kissing you on the stairs."

"I'm amazed she's got any gaskets left to blow."

"Don't look now, but I think she's watching us through the blinds. See, where there's that little crack?"

Launce lifted his glass to salute the crack in the venetian blinds, which instantly winked shut. "That was her all right."

Madge giggled. "She was in such a *state* this morning when I came down to make breakfast."

"It was more like noon when you made breakfast. That's probably why she was in a state."

"No, it wasn't that. It was her hair."

"What's wrong with her hair?"

"It's growing back. Her real hair, that is. What you've seen is just her wig. She had an accident at a beauty parlor years ago, and all her hair fell out, and now it's growing back. She says the itching drives her crazy. Also it's coming back the wrong color. Carroty red. She's in a tizzy."

Madge sipped the St. Emilion, and this time it had the taste of philosophy. "You know, it's strange. It seems the best way to get anything done is to stop trying."

"How do you mean?" he asked, and the wonderful thing was he wasn't just being polite, he was genuinely interested in what she had to say. Madge couldn't remember the last time anyone had paid her that particular compliment.

Out of sheer gratitude, she tried not to be vague. "For instance. At the clinic. Yesterday, and again today, I get these reports. Patients are actually getting well. One in particular, Corning, bed 38. One aide says she actually saw him smiling. Of course, you never know, sometimes you see what you hope to see. I can't tell you how many times I could have sworn I thought I saw Ned start to say something to me. And now, the way he's been crying . . . Of course, that's possible without any kind of miracle—a speck of dust gets under his eyelid. . . . But God, just think, if he *should* snap out of it after all this time. He'd be an eleven-year-old in the body of a thirty-seven-year-old man."

Launce laughed sharply. "That's better than being what I am—a thirty-seven-year-old man inside of *this* body."

Madge smoothed his feathers: "Would you rather have the mind of an *old* person? Like Mother? Old people get set in their ways, they get to be like robots. Or like when they warned you as a kid how if you made a face it would freeze into that expression." She crossed her eyes and stuck her tongue out of the corner of her mouth to show what she meant—

And at just that moment around the corner of the house came Judge Winckelmeyer, who reacted to her mugging with the most delightful double take.

Madge burst out laughing and lofted her glass and called out, "Judge! Come join us. We're having a picnic."

"I didn't think you drank," he said in a reproving tone.

"I didn't. I couldn't. But Launce brought home a bottle, and all of a sudden I knew I could. And I can! Isn't that wonderful?"

"Well, no, I wouldn't say so."

"Oh, you would if you had some of this. Twenty-four dollars a bottle, you're sure you're not tempted? Just so you'll know what kind of temptation you've been resisting all your life?"

The boy stood, confounded and blushing, on the narrow concrete path that bisected the lawn. He was dressed in his usual killjoy uniform of dark suit, white shirt, and black tie.

"Madge," Launce said in a stage whisper, "don't be a tease."

"Launce is right, I'm being a tease. There's some Coke in the icebox if you'd like a Coke."

"Thank you very kindly but no."

"Why don't you introduce us?" Launce hinted.

"Of course, where are my manners. Launce, this is Judge Winckelmeyer. He's the son of Judith Winckelmeyer, who is William's stepsister in Florida, but now you're officially Judge Michaels, yes? William adopted him when he came here, what was it, two years ago?"

Judge nodded. "I was paroled into his custody."

"And this is Launce Hill. Launce is Ned's father."

"I'm pleased to make your acquaintance, sir." He stepped across the grass and leaned forward so Launce could shake his hand without rising from his lawn chair. "I was just about to ask if I might go upstairs and say hello to Ned." He turned to Madge. "With your permission, ma'am?"

"Of course, Judge, any time, that's very thoughtful of you. Did you come here with Lisa? Or William? Are they in the house?"

"No, ma'am. I'm here by myself. But I expect my father to be arriving later. I said I'd meet him here."

"That's nice." She sighed resignedly. "I suppose I should be getting up. It'll be dark soon. It's amazing we haven't already been bitten to death by mosquitoes."

"Don't stir yourself on my account. I noticed that the screen door was open and I know where Ned's room is. After I've seen him, I will say hello to your mother, if she is feeling like a visitor."

"Well then perhaps we'll enjoy the breeze here a little longer."

When Judge had gone out of sight around the side of the house, and they'd heard the screen door bang closed, Launce remarked, "That's one weird kid."

"I was thinking myself he seemed a little strange tonight, but I suppose that's how he usually comes across. Mother likes him."

"It figures."

Madge gave the wine in her glass one final swirl of admiration and drank it down. At just that moment, the lights went on behind the venetian blinds in her mother's room.

"You remember in the sixties when we'd go to Lake Calhoun in the summer after work?"

"And rent a canoe. Oh yes, I do."

"Do they still rent canoes there?"

"I have no idea."

"Wouldn't that be fun? Get another bottle—"

"We couldn't, not with that boy in the house, and William on his way over."

"Why not? The kid's not going to steal anything, or murder your mother, more's the pity."

"Launce!"

"What's the use of getting this drunk if it doesn't give us the excuse we need to do what we'd like to do?"

This seemed so unassailably logical that Madge could think of no reply. "You mean just *drive* there?"

"If you think you're too drunk to drive, we could take the bus, like we used to."

Madge took umbrage. "I'm not *that* drunk."

Launce struggled to his feet. "Think about it. Meanwhile, if you want to plump for another bottle of *vin extraordinaire*, I'll walk over to the liquor store on Pillsbury."

"You know where my purse is."

Launce nodded and went into the house.

The leaves of the elm made a hushing sound, and an unseen car on Calumet whooshed by in front of the house. Bats flittered out from the eaves and past the higher branches of the elm, and at that distance (and at this degree of mellowness) even the bats seemed beautiful.

Then she noticed something odd: the light was on in the attic. It was a dim 40-watt bulb near the head of the stairs, at the other end of the attic from this one dormer window that faced on the backyard, so it made a barely perceptible glow. It would have looked well as the backdrop for the cover of a Nancy Drew mystery: *The Light in the Attic Window.* The bulb must have been burning since the last time she'd been up there. When? Weeks ago, at least. But more likely it was Launce who'd been poking around in the attic and forgotten to turn out the light. Whatever the explanation, her concern for energy conservation was not so strong as to propel her into the house and up to the attic to save .005¢ on the electric bill.

Such a beautiful evening. But could she really be thinking of driving off drunk to Lake Calhoun, just as though she and Launce were teenagers again—with Elvis on the radio and Lake Street bumper to bumper with great gas-guzzling cars the names of which she couldn't even remember anymore. But she *could* remember the feeling of sweet release stepping outside the house—this same house, more oppressive now than then— and the wind that flowed in through the open window, fluttering her hair across her face.

Even if they couldn't still rent a canoe, what did it matter? The lake would still be there, and they could lie in the grass and look across the water and for two or three hours nothing else would exist. They'd be back in the eternity of their youth. She should say yes for Launce's sake if not for her own.

So when he returned with the store's last two bottles of the miraculous wine she didn't take any more convincing. He said, "Well, what do you say?" and she said, "What the hell," and went into the house to get the car keys and left a note on the kitchen table: "We're going for a drive. Back later. Madge." It was the same note she might have written and left under the same salt shaker forty years ago with exactly the same delicious feeling of guilt.

79

Lorine smoked while her dinner flowed through the translucent IV tubes and into the hidden plumbing of her own body. There were so few foods she could count on being able to digest, and those few so bland, that she'd really come to prefer this more direct approach to the problem of nutrition.

Doc MacDonald, meanwhile, was looking at the naked and unconscious body of his medical colleague, where it was spread out on the examining table of surgery. He palpated the man's lower abdomen, eliciting a low, dreaming groan. "Well, I'd have to go along with his own diagnosis."

"Appendicitis?"

He nodded, though, doctorlike, he had to find a longer way to say it: "Acute septic inflammation. No telling how long he's got."

"Until what?"

"Until it bursts. Then it's too late. The poison fills the peritoneal cavity."

"So he's got to be operated on, is that what you're saying?"

"Outside of this place, he would long since have been sent for surgery. But here . . . " Doc MacDonald shrugged. "What would be the point?"

"We only need to keep him alive a day or two. Till we can arrange for the transfer. If he pops off after that, so much the better. I'm not speaking for myself, you understand. I am passing along the wishes of top management. The Commandant."

"If wishes were horses . . ."

"This is not something you've ever done?"

"I am an orthopedist, not a surgeon. I deal with bones, not guts."

"But you're always going on about how you were in that field hospital in Viet Nam."

"They didn't have us doing appendectomies."

"But you must've dealt with spilled guts. It's supposed to be a pretty simple operation."

"Lorine, my dear, these days I have difficulty tying my shoelaces." By way of illustrating his motor control problems, he removed the thermometer from the armpit of the unconscious man and tried to hold it steady as he took a reading.

Lorine ignored his bid for sympathy. "What does it say?"

He frowned. "It's up over a hundred and three." He put a finger to the man's neck, measuring the pulse against his wristwatch. "Ninety-five," he announced at length, with a grave shaking of his head.

"Listen," Lorine insisted, deftly removing the IV needle from her arm. "We both have a nice deal here, right? We've got perks and privileges that neither of us would care to jeopardize. So if you perform an appendectomy that is less than state of the art, who's to know? You think there's going to be some medical board of inquiry? If the guy doesn't recover, that could even be a plus for us, 'cause there'll be no chance of his lodging a formal complaint and trying to get an investigation started. So why don't we just do the best job we can? Details you don't think you can handle, I'll do myself. I am not at all squeamish. Just give me directions. I've always thought surgery was one of those things, like skydiving or eating oysters, that everyone should do at least once in her life. So I consider this my big opportunity. What do you say?"

Doc MacDonald shrugged. "I'll need a couple bottles."

"Chivas Regal okay?"

"That would be fine."

"I'll go get 'em. Meanwhile, you prep him. That's the right word— 'prep'?"

"Lorine, you're going to leave this camp a registered nurse."

"A nurse? Hey, Doc, women today have got higher expectations than that. I'm going for an M.D." She laughed huskily and pointed to the patient on the table. "That one!"

80

Judge had put off corruption, taken on incorruption, and was feeling terrific as a result. It was like having X-ray eyes, like being consumed in the fires of Pentecost. He could see things the way they really were, the way they had been and had to be. All at once and all together, broken into pieces, like a monitor with many windows, and each window streaming with light. As though everything in the world were lit up from inside like a light bulb. And if he looked *into* the light and held his gaze steady, Brother Orson would be there with the Angel Lazarus, but now the two of them were one, and that one was God, just as, in his heart, Judge had always supposed. Till now Brother Orson, like Jesus, had had to sidestep questions about who he was and where he came from, but now he stood revealed.

So when he read the note Madge had left under the salt shaker on the kitchen table, he was not upset, though for a moment he was surprised, since he had supposed that she had been set down for a sacrifice, like Lisa and Judith and the priest. Why else had a salt shaker been placed on her letter? For it is written—Ezekiel, chapter 43, verses 23 and 24—*Thou shalt offer a young bullock without blemish, and a ram out of the flock without blemish. And thou shalt offer them before the LORD, and the priests shall cast salt upon them, and they shall offer them up for a burnt offering unto the LORD.* All that was clear, but it was just as clear that the Lord did not intend Madge and the man she'd had with her to be part of the sacrifice. At least not now.

What he must do now was to search through this house and find the caduceus that Brother Orson had said had been hidden here for years and years. Though where exactly he would not say; only—*Seek and you will find.* The logical places to look were the basement and the attic, since those were the places where something would be likely to stay hidden for the longest time.

The bulb at the top of the steps going down to the basement was burnt out, and even with his new powers of vision Judge had to feel his way by fingertip down the steps and along the rough cinder-block walls. The only light in the entire cellar was a pinpoint of red at waist level, dimmer than a bathroom nightlight. It turned out to be the light on a deep freeze.

He opened the deep freeze and was able to make out the rough outlines of other features of the basement from the light spilling out from its white interior. At the far end of the room was a wall of shelves with a ladder beside it. Something inside him told him to go climb up the ladder and look on the shelves, but when he did all he found was empty jars intended for canning. Even so, he couldn't shake the certainty that there was something here he was meant to have. Not the caduceus. Something . . . else. Its absence mocked him. He threw one of the bottles at the concrete wall for the satisfaction of hearing it smash. But if he'd broken every bottle on every shelf it would have only honed his frustration to a sharper edge.

He descended the ladder, feeling balked and cheated, and returned to the side of the deep freeze. He'd almost lowered its bulky lid without noticing, or taking in, the nature of the freezer's contents—a single package bundled in a supermarket bag, its white plastic mottled with what Judge was suddenly sure was blood. And in the package, when most of the plastic had been peeled away, a man's head. A bloated frozen tongue protruded from the distended jaw, and the eyeballs had become glassy and crackled like ice cubes. Judge felt a momentary pang of proprietary resentment, such as a hunter hidden in a blind might feel hearing another hunter's discharge only a short distance away. But then he realized that however this head had come to be here it was intended as a sign, a sign prefigured (he realized) by the priest's pagan parable of the elephant-headed Hindu god Ganesh. The thick, purple tongue—could it but move again—had some purpose to communicate, like the impaled head that had spoken to him on the counter of the optometrist's shop. Another prefiguration. In what he did God left no room for accidents.

He decided that the head had to be thawed and took it up to the kitchen and punched instructions THAW—MEAT—8 pounds—onto the keypad of the microwave. With its cheek on the turntable, the frozen head barely fit inside. Then, remembering Madge's invitation earlier, Judge helped himself to a can of Coke from the icebox and settled down in front of the microwave and watched the head revolve on the turntable for the time it took to finish off the Coke. He remembered how, when he was little, he'd sat spellbound in front of his mother's 33⅓-rpm phonograph, watching the music as he listened to it.

As he sipped his Coke and watched the man's frozen features turning a brighter and brighter pink, he felt a kind of reverence such as (he supposed) people of a more conventional religious temperament must feel when they're at church, looking at the flickering candles and smelling the incense.

Then a voice spoke to him, saying—*Thrust in thy sharp sickle, and gather the clusters of the vine of the earth, for her grapes are fully ripe*, just as the angel cries out in John's Revelation, and when the vine of the earth had been cast into the great winepress of the wrath of God, blood had spurted from the winepress—*even*, John writes, *unto the horse bridles, by the space of a thousand and six hundred furlongs*. There'd been a time when many of these details had been confusing to Judge, and when he'd asked Brother Orson about them, his answers had seemed obscure or evasive.

But now all that was changed. Brother Orson was beside him. It was his voice that had spoken aloud, repeating the words of the angel; his hand that had pulled the tab from the can of Coke, and now when the phone rang, it was the voice of Brother Orson that answered, and said—*Yes?*

It was the woman whose call he'd been waiting for, the one who'd phoned earlier to Willowville. She was very brusque and businesslike, and Judge was the same. He said he had the money, and he promised to bring it, at eleven o'clock, to the point they'd agreed on at the edge of Brosner Park.

He felt uneasy about leaving the house, not knowing when Madge might return with the old man she said was Ned's father. She would undoubtedly be upset if she noticed what was in the microwave. But it was too soon to take it out, for it was far from being thawed through. Finally he figured that the Lord could be trusted to guide Madge to do the right thing just as he was guiding Judge.

For all that he felt the hand of the Lord on his shoulder, and Brother Orson's footsteps beside him, Judge realized, when he went out to the Cadillac he'd left parked on Ludens at the side of the house, that he'd left the engine running and the keys in the ignition. It was natural enough, with all that had happened, to feel nervous, but he really couldn't afford to be so careless.

He drove east on Ludens, hung a right onto Brosner, and drove the six blocks to the park at the sedate pace of a jogger. The breeze had quickened to a light wind, and as he came to the park and the larger sky that the trees had blocked from view became visible, he could see clouds being swept across the moon, risen now to its meridian.

In Eternity, soon, there would be no clouds, nor even a moon, changing its shape from night to night, and the sun would be fixed in the sky as it was above Jericho, impaled by Joshua's horn.

At the hour appointed a large black van pulled up in front of the Cadillac, and two men, in jeans and T-shirts, came around to the rear of the van and opened the door and shone a flashlight across a figure lying on a mattress. Then a woman in a leather jacket came to the window of the Cadillac and asked Judge for the money. Judge watched her while she fanned through each rubber-banded sheaf of bills, checking the denominations. A smoking cigarette hung from the side of her painted mouth. Judge felt disgusted and tried not to breathe through his nose, so he wouldn't smell her cigarette.

"Okay," she said, with a nod to the two men waiting beside the van. Tugging at the corners of the blanket on which he lay, they pulled the man partway out the rear end of the van until one of them was able to bend over and get a grip on his legs. Then they carried him to the passenger side of the Cadillac, where Judge had already pushed the door open.

Judge regarded his father with subdued, anticipatory triumph, but that feeling was complicated by a natural revulsion at the way he looked and smelled. His head lolling back against the seat's headrest with a low, wordless moan. His two front teeth missing, which made Judge remember the times in Florida, long ago, when William would pry the flipper from the roof of his mouth and pretend to be an old bum. Now he really had become that old bum.

"You got to be careful how you handle him," the woman with the cigarette cautioned. "He's still pretty sensitive down here." She rubbed the lower part of her leather jacket.

"You don't have to worry," Judge assured her. "I will take proper care of him."

"You've got a southern accent," she observed.

"Yes, I'm from the South. Florida."

She smiled, and touched his cheek with one of her long painted fingernails. "Cute," she said. "Real cute. Just my luck we should meet like this."

Judge was at a loss for words.

"Well," she said, still in the same suggestive tone, "see you around." She winked at Judge, and then returned to the van. The two men with her had already crawled inside and pulled the rear door shut behind them. The taillights lit up bright orange, and the van drove ahead to the stoplight at Calumet and turned south along the park.

"Are you okay?" Judge asked, without looking at his father.

"I will be . . . soon." William's voice was the barest whisper.

Judge waited to start the engine in case he meant to say more, but when there was no more forthcoming, he turned the key in the ignition and headed back toward the old house on the corner of Calumet and Ludens.

81

Each familiar sight along the length of Calumet was an assurance that the nightmare was over. He would be safe where he was going. Whatever butcheries had been committed in the name of surgery would heal as soon as he had again possessed himself of the caduceus.

The car hit a red light at the corner of Calumet and Hubbard. All of the small shops had gone out of business, including the Rexall drugstore, where on the coldest winter days he'd stopped on the way home from school to get warm. The empty windows of the onetime drugstore seemed for a moment to epitomize all that was tragic and fatal in human existence.

Then the light changed, and the car moved ahead, and the meaning of the scenes sliding by became jumbled and unclear. The drugs he'd been given before the woman cut him open were still in his system, dulling the pain but also making it difficult to form clear thoughts. His sense of time was all distorted. The car seemed to be moving at the speed of a person walking along the sidewalk.

A few houses ahead he saw a hedge, its tiny leaves jittering in the wind, a sickly, glittery yellow under the sodium street lamps, and he remembered passing before this same hedge, running home after the accident with the kite, bleeding then too, and how the woman who'd been trimming the hedge had called out to him, "Little boy!" and then "Young man!" He could remember the exact X of the open clippers in her hands, the screechy timbre of her voice, the bloodstains down the front of his shirt.

He could feel the wet warmth of the blood soaking his underpants. It seemed a shameful thing, like incontinence, and the thought of asking Judith or Madge to clean his private parts was even more unbearable. But such a simple action—leaning forward, reaching down—was beyond his capabilities now. Even to be sitting upright in the car in his condition was ill-advised. He should be on his back so the weight of his bowels would not be pressing down against the crude sutures stitching the incision closed.

The car came to a stop at Davis, only two blocks from home, and two kids on a single bicycle crossed the street in front of them. From an open window came the sound of rock music, simplified by distance (or the morphine) to a simple compound beat, systole and diastole.

"Listen! You can hear the devil," Judge commented, "dancing in hell."

The light changed and the car lurched forward. The silhouette of the Obstschmecker house hove into view, lights aglow in every window, a haven of welcome.

As the car turned the corner and rolled to a stop at the curb, William had his first intimation that everything was not as it should be. When Judge got out of the car and walked round to open the right-hand door, no one came out of the lighted house. Surely they would have been waiting for Judge's return, there would be some show of concern, of curiosity. "Where . . ." He hadn't strength to say more than that single word, but Judge understood.

"I should of said before that Madge ain't home. She'd already gone out for the night with a friend of hers when I called. The old lady had to let me in."

Judge slid his right arm under William's knees and his left arm under the shoulders and lifted his father, with a grunt of effort, from the car. Then he toed the car door shut and carried his sagging burden across the lawn toward the front porch. William felt each footstep Judge took as a shudder in his body's core. When Judge stumbled, mounting the porch steps, there seemed a kind of inevitability to it.

For some time after this, William was in a state of confusion. He did not lose consciousness; rather, he lost control of its direction, so that at first, lying on the wooden boards of the porch, his attention was fixed on the overhead light bulb as fat June bugs circled it and battered themselves against it. Then he was again being carried upstairs, and he remembered the remark a medical lecturer at the U had made concerning hospital care, that it is a ritual of infantilization: the bland foods, being bathed by other hands, the regulated bedtime, the steady erosion of one's personal authority. And here he was, in his son's arms as once he'd been in his father's, being carried up the same staircase, and placed in the same bed he'd slept in as a child. There could be a strange comfort, the lecturer had argued, in being treated so, but William couldn't remember the reason he'd put forward. It had something to do with fear.

He remembered why he had demanded to be brought to this house. He must have the caduceus, which was hidden in the attic. But he could not go there himself, nor could he ask to be carried up another flight of stairs and left alone there, even if he'd have had the strength to uncover the caduceus himself, which was doubtful. Yet for some reason he did not want Judge to look for it for him. Better to ask Judith.

He cleared his throat, and Judge bent down over him, and he was able to ask, "Is your mother here?"

Judge shook his head, offering no explanation.

"Or Lisa?"

Again he shook his head.

There was no help for it. "There is something in the attic I must ask you to get for me."

Judge nodded.

"A kind of good luck charm. A superstition. But if I could have it now, I'd feel much better."

"What does it look like, and where should I look?"

"It's a kind of stick with, uh, a dead bird tied to it."

"Where exactly in the attic?"

"Under the loose insulation . . . in the floor."

"What part of the floor?"

He hesitated, for answering the question seemed tantamount to a confession. But what choice was there? "Just above Ned's room, I think. About where his bed would be."

"I'll get it right now."

The moment Judge left the room, William felt he should be called back and told not to summon any kind of medical assistance. There was no doctor he knew whom he could trust not to insist on his being taken to a hospital, and there were PHA personnel screening every admissions room. But there seemed no need to caution Judge. Somehow he had understood without having to be told.

Tentatively, as much from weakness as from self-solicitude, William fumbled at the buttons of his bloodstained pajama top. When the last one had been undone, he discovered to his horror that the fall on the porch steps had caused the threads of the suture to rip through the soft dermal tissues through which they'd been inexpertly sewn, and the long incision in his abdomen gaped wide, exposing pink coils of intestines. He felt like one of the fabled victims of the guillotine—aware, however briefly, as the executioner holds his head aloft, that he has been decapitated. A doctor would have to be called in now, whatever the consequences. The caduceus could not perform surgery.

"That don't look too good," Judge said in level tones. He stood in the doorway, holding the caduceus raised before him, as one might hold the stem of a wineglass.

William lifted a blood-smeared hand to accept the precious talisman, but when Judge did not proffer it, the remaining strength ebbed from the muscles of his arm, and his hand collapsed to the bedspread.

"I know what this is," Judge said. "It's one of those things like you had the sculpture made at MDS, a caduceus. And I know *lots* of what you've done with it. I even know how to use it myself. Brother Orson explained how you got to spell out what you want it to do so that it rhymes."

"Please, Judge . . . I need it."

"Oh, you will get what you need. But this"—he twirled the caduceus wineglass-fashion—"this ain't yours anymore. It's mine now, and the first thing I aim to do with it is touch it to this big toe of yours." He tapped William's toe with the caduceus. "Till I tell you otherwise, you'll just lie there paralyzed."

Judge stood back to see what effect he had produced. William glared back defiantly. But no, it was rather a glare of helplessness, the canceled stare of a person stopped cold at the moment he realizes every exit has been sealed.

"Shit," Judge marveled. "You really can't move, can you? Even if I was to . . ." He advanced to the side of the bed and dipped the caduceus down to prod the intestines coiling from the surgical wound. "Do this?" He waited for an answer, and added, as afterthought, "You *can* answer questions when I ask. Only you can't lie to me. In fact, you *got* to answer truthfully."

Whether Judge had intended the rhyme or it was fortuitous, it was there, and William replied, truthfully, "No, I cannot move, no matter what you do."

Judge smiled and placed the caduceus on the bedspread a scant inch from William's paralyzed fingertips. He stepped back from the bed, confident of his power. "You can't even reach ahead that bitty bit and grab hold of it. Can you?"

He exerted his entire will, effectlessly. "I can't."

"You're like old Ned was all that time laying there in his bed. Helpless. And anything I do . . . anything the Lord may require of his servant . . . you'll just have to sit there and take it. I could cut off your pecker and you'd just have to smile."

Judge hooked his forefinger under a loop of the extruded intestine and tugged at it gently. It seemed to obey his bidding like a living thing, a large pink snake sliding out of the dark hole in which it lived.

"You're like old Jehoram who had a daughter of Ahab to wife. You know what happened to Jehoram?"

"No."

"The Lord smote him in his bowels and they fell out. Second Chronicles, chapter twenty-one. Only difference is he couldn't get crem-ated. Whereas with you the Lord will smell a sweet savor and his nostrils will be pleased. I see the flames of the burnt offering already right now. Don't you?"

"I see only what's here."

"The flames are all around us, everywhere, bright as him standing there by your bed. You see *him*, don't you?"

"There's only you beside this bed."

"Then he has struck you blind! But blindness cannot save you. Your crimes are set down on Brother Orson's scorecard. And you will testify and bear witness to them. I know some of it already. I know you used this stick here a long time ago against your brother in the other room. And you probably used it on me and all the rest of your family to keep us so healthy we don't any of us even get a cold. And when you want to use it to make patients get well, you do that too. Am I right?"

"Yes."

"But the plague—thousands and thousands of people you'll never even see—maybe millions before it's all over—I can't understand why you would do that. Unless you thought you was acting for the Lord. I might do that, I might have to someday as part of a larger judgment against the iniquities and sins of the world. Because I am an instrument of the Lord. But you? Why did you want to make a plague?"

"So I could become rich, and for the power."

"Power?"

"The power of life and death. Finally that is the hinge of all power, but it is most nakedly the power a doctor possesses. Except that medicine is so iffy. With the best of care patients may die. But with the caduceus I was like God."

"I can understand you'd want to be able to cure people. But why hurt people you don't know? Why a plague?"

"The caduceus can be used to cure only in proportion as it has already been used to afflict. Say I'd set out to be the next Dr. Salk and had developed a wonder drug that cured Alzheimer's disease. I would have been able to reduce the suffering of my patients only by enlarging suffering in some other sphere. I might have set up, in a limited way, on that basis, becoming a cancer quack in Mexico, or some kind of faith healer. But I didn't want to become a one-man Lourdes. I had no wish to be a celebrity, my every action scrutinized. I wanted another kind of power, the kind I got by running, and owning, MDS."

"So how did you get the money to build MDS? That was before ARVIDS."

"The caduceus was effective against AIDS, but the cost of each cure was exorbitant. A matter, literally, of having to kill Peter to save Paul. But even a glimmer of hope in those days could bring enormous research grants, and Ben Winckelmeyer could write better grant applications than anyone in the business. I killed enough Peters and saved enough Pauls to suggest promising avenues for research. And the research that was funded was the genuine article. Likewise the vaccine."

"So why did you start *another* plague?"

"In a way it was like planting a garden. I would reap only what I'd sown, and so would always possess a surplus of healing capability."

"You thought this all out in advance?"

"I figured out the final details at just the age you are now, when I gave a grocer who'd annoyed me a sty, and later removed it. The important thing was to figure out a vector for the disease that could never be traced back to me, and it never has been."

"And what was it, your 'vector'?"

"American Pride."

Judge took this to be a taunt and in reprisal pulled out another loop of intestine from the open wound. "You got to tell the *truth!*" he insisted.

William could make no reply, for no question had been put to him. But Judge was not familiar with the computerlike literalness of the caduceus's operation. He felt that William was defying him. He grabbed up a handful of guts and shook them in front of William's face. "Answer my question, damn it, or I'll tear *all* this shit out of you. What was the fucking vector?"

"A bull that was exhibited at the state fair, part Charolais, part beefalo, and registered under the name of American Pride. He was two years old that summer, and his sperm was said to be worth its weight in plutonium. I decided to make American Pride—or rather, his offspring—the bearer of my plague. The wording of the curse was framed to make its dissemination both widespread and untraceable. I also built in a timedelay factor of ten years so that by the time the shit finally did hit the fan, I would be in a plausible position to 'discover' a cure."

Judge let the guts in his hand fall to William's side. "And that curse? How did it go?"

William recited the words:

> "Let the meaty steers you breed
> At the end of ten full years
> Infect with plague, infest with fears
> One-half percent of those they feed.
> Once this contagion has occurred
> May it only be wholly cured
> By my hand, my work, my word
> Upon receipt of the fee agreed.
> Now to your task, and breed, bull, breed!"

There he stopped, unable to say more. It was like finding himself at the end of a plank with only the sea and the sharks below. Judge, he was sure, would soon kill him, led by the wiles of his Brother Orson, who was surely the god of the caduceus in another of his disguises. William felt himself to be a fool for never having suspected.

There was still so much he wanted to explain—not really to his mad son but to some imagined jury of his peers. Chiefly he wanted to insist that he was, despite the uses to which he'd put his powers, a basically good person. Not a saint, by any means, but a man with a sound conscience and decent instincts. When he listened to Mozart or Mahler or Bach, he understood what their music was saying. At the sad moments in movies he cried. His soul had not withered or atrophied through the exercise of his power. What he had done through the caduceus was something that had taken place in a separate moral realm. It was as though he'd been a pilot assigned to bomb a country whose language he could not speak, whose ruins he would never visit. It all seemed so clear to him, so expressible—if only he had not been made mute by the caduceus's power.

Off in another room a bell began ringing and didn't stop.

"Shit," said Judge, using the bedspread to wipe the blood from his hands. "It's the smoke alarm. I forgot all about the microwave."

82

It was as though a chain had been removed, an immense chain of weighty links wound round so tightly and completely that chain and flesh had come to seem one, as sometimes a tree's bark fuses with the chain meant to support a hammock. But at the moment Judge took the caduceus from its hiding place the chain was shattered and Ned Hill was free. He raised his hand, obedient to his will, and made the living fingers flex almost into a fist.

He turned his head toward the door of his room, which stood slightly ajar. He felt as though he were operating an enormous and untrustworthy piece of machinery, a derrick that has stood rusting out of doors for years. Some of the muscles in his neck seemed too weak to support the unsteady mass of the cranium, much less to control its complex motions. But it was wonderful that the machinery worked at all, for which the credit was surely owed to Madge's patient patterning exercises.

Raising his torso to a sitting position proved to be almost beyond his powers, since it was the muscles of his abdomen and lower back that had been exercised the least. At last, by raising his knee up and letting it fall sideways across the other leg, he got into a sideways position in the bed from which he could use his arms' larger strength to tug at the sheets and prod and leverage himself into an upright position.

Then he planted his feet on the carpet by the bed and, keeping a careful grip on the maple spindles of the backboard, he stood up. He took a tentative, shuffling step forward, toward the door, not daring to flex his knees for fear the whole contraption of bone and muscle would collapse into a helpless heap. His feet were baffling in the constant adjustments and readjustments they required. He wondered how people think of anything else when they were walking than simply how it was done, and then he remembered, dimly, that when he'd been alive and a schoolboy at OLM, there'd been a joke more or less to that effect.

And he smiled, not so much at the joke as at the memory of a world where jokes might be made.

It was then that the smoke alarm went off in the kitchen, followed a moment later by a confident clattering down the stairs, great thudding hoofbeats that Ned somehow knew posed a danger to his own safety and to a purpose still unformed.

But if unformed, quite clear even so. Each step he took now, each small shift of weight, seemed to be guided toward that necessary and inevitable goal. The silent opening of the door, his passage across the corridor and entry into his brother's room. It more surprised Ned to find Billy grown into a man than to see that he was partially disemboweled, even though in a rational way he knew that they had both become adults. But that was by the mere passage of time, while the disembowelment was an act of fate, something ordained and large with justice. Ned did not *reason* so, but he felt its necessity with a penetrating gratitude. He even found the strength to reach down and take the gluey warmth of the uncoiled intestine in his hand. As he did so more of it unraveled from the bleeding abdominal cavity.

His brother did not stir. It seemed fitting to Ned that if he were now released from his long paralysis that the agent of his torments should take his place. It is every prisoner's most fervent prayer to witness such a moral symmetry, to hold a knife to the throat of the guard he most detests and trace a line of blood across the flesh.

Then he saw, just inches from his brother's fingertips, the cause of all these events, the caduceus he'd made himself from a twisted stick and the withered corpse of a sparrow and a bit of twine. His for the taking. Grasp it firmly, and with the whisper of the wish he would be strong again, nor need he fear (as he knew he must) whoever it was who'd gone hurtling down the stairs.

Yet he saw as well that if he did take up the caduceus and use it, it would be as though he'd become just the thing he hated, as though he'd caught hold of an endless bowel spilling out of an eternal wound and could not release it. He would be glued to its evil until it became part of him, intrinsic and invisible.

He did not take the caduceus, but instead, with wonderful dexterity, slipped his brother's sticky intestines into his own unresisting fingers.

He left that room and returned to his own just in time to escape the attention of the young man now returning to William's bedside—bearing (Ned only had a glimpse of it) a large roast of meat steaming on a platter.

But the glimpse was enough: Ned knew now clearly what he must do. He must burn down the house with William—and the caduceus—in it.

Which meant that he must make his way downstairs. There had always been a box of matches on the mantel above the fireplace.

The stairs posed a greater physical challenge than he'd foreseen. To throw his foot into the void before him and expect his knee not to collapse at the moment of impact on the tread below seemed a feat as much beyond his present powers as walking a tightrope. After some long time poised on the brink of this impossibility, he came to the same solution every arthritic octogenarian reaches. He turned round and, with the banister's help, got down the stairs backwards, as down a ladder.

There was an arrangement of dried flowers in the fireplace, and no longer any box of matches on the mantel above.

On the kitchen table he found the smoke detector, its battery ripped out to silence it. The air reeked of burnt meat. For a little while he regarded a large dark boxlike appliance on the Formica counter, which seemed, from the mess all about it and crusted to it, to have been used to cook the meat. A kind of miniature oven.

The stove was electric, and nowhere could he find matches, but this posed less of a problem than the staircase. He found a jar of cooking oil in the cupboard (it was as much weight as he could manage with both hands) and with it doused a broom, which he found, just where it should be, in the broom closet. He depressed the HI button for the front right burner on the stove and waited till the coils were glowing red. The broom straw ignited almost as soon as he touched it to the burner.

He torched the kitchen curtains first, and then methodically he went about the dining room and living room, setting fire to whatever looked like ready tinder: the lace covering on the dining table, the dried flowers in the fireplace, the curtains (but they refused to catch). The flames leapt up eagerly at first, but then they seemed to possess no power of contagion, dying away without setting anything more substantial on fire. The room was full of smoke, but his torch was extinguished and the only flames were a faint blue flickering across the top of the dining room table.

"Madge!" screeched a familiar voice. "Madge, are you out there? I think something must be on fire. Madge! Can you hear me over this microphone? Madge, damn it, answer me! I'm sure there's smoke in the air. And I know I heard the alarm go off. Madge, how do I get this so-called security system to open my door? Madge!"

Then, just when he supposed his efforts at arson had failed, the back of the upholstered platform rocker burst into flame, and a moment later the lampshade above it was burning, and then a hanging plant.

"Madge!" Grandma O.'s voice was choked. "I *know* there's a fire—and the phone is *dead!* Madge!"

Ned returned to the kitchen and took up the heavy bottle of Wesson Oil. He poured some into a cup and set the cup atop the stove and tipped it over so the oil flowed toward the red-hot coils. Without waiting for that oil to catch, he took the bottle into the living room and doused the carpet all about the burning platform rocker and made a trail, from there to the couch.

He mounted, with effort, the four lowest steps of the staircase and splashed oil from the bottle (which was much lighter now) onto the banister and the runner and the wall alongside the stairs.

Then he tried to leave by the front door, but he did not know the combination, any more than Mrs. Obstschmecker, that had to be punched into the keypad of the security system. He'd scarcely had time to register dismay before the smoke got to him.

83

The clouds had thickened across the sky so that the moon appeared only in glimpses, and it seemed, because of the erratic motion of the rented canoe, to peek out from a different quarter of the sky each time Launce looked up from the task of paddling. He'd remembered canoeing as effortless, a kind of slow luge that required only the feathering of the paddle to point it in the right direction. *This* canoe took all the strength he could muster, and Madge's efforts at the front of the boat were so mismatched to his own that they were constantly veering off in an unintended direction. Finally he had to ask for mercy. His shoulders just couldn't take any more.

"Were the canoes always as big as this?" Madge wondered as she tucked her paddle under the seat.

"And was the lake so dark?"

"It's the clouds, I suppose. I'm so *thirsty.* And I feel like I'm burning alive. My back is all pins and needles. I didn't think we were out in the sun that long."

(It was at just that moment that the smoldering platform rocker burst into flame.)

"You want me to open the last bottle?"

"More than anything in this world."

Launce laid his paddle down on the ribs of the canoe's bottom and twisted around to reach for the bag from the liquor store. He split the red aluminum foil seal and peeled it from the top of the bottle. It was slow work, and the effort of inserting the corkscrew of his Swiss army knife into the bottle's cork proved even more taxing.

"Want me to do it?" Madge asked, trying not to show her impatience.

"No, that's okay."

But it wasn't okay, the cork wouldn't budge (nor would the door of the Obstschmecker house, which Ned at that moment found himself unable to open)—not when he held the bottle under his left arm and tugged at the corkscrew with his right hand, and not when he braced the bottle between his thighs. The only result of his efforts was a sudden urgency to get to a toilet.

"Really," Madge insisted, "let me do it." She reached forward and took bottle and corkscrew from Launce.

Her first effort was no more successful than his. "It's really in there."

She tried again with the bottle between her legs. "It doesn't *budge*."

She stood up.

"Madge," Launce said cautioningly.

"Don't worry, I'm steady. I just need to get the leverage."

At just the moment Ned died, asphyxiated on the floor of the burning house, the cork came out of the bottle. Madge went over one side of the canoe, and Launce over the other. She'd vowed to herself, long ago, that she would do everything she could to outlive Ned. Though she would never know it, she'd been faithful to her vow.

She was able, by clinging to the side of the capsized canoe, to polish off half the bottle, before her strength finally gave out. She enjoyed every blessed drop.

84

The fires of Pentecost were burning all around him, a curtain of bright orange flames, spiritual fires by the light of which Judge could see the glory promised to those like himself who were washed in the blood of the Lamb. He was standing smack dab in the middle of the Valley of Death, with fire to the right of him and fire to the left, but he feared no evil because the Lord God was there beside him and inside him. He was seized in his Rapture and squeezed in his hand, till he had to shout aloud from the joy of it, "Praise God! Glory hallelujah!" And still the flames grew brighter and leapt higher, climbing the trellised roses of the wallpaper and writhing about entrails that spilled over the edge of the altar prepared by the power of Judge's faith and the wrath of Almighty God. A sweet smoke rose from the sacrifice, as from a bed of spices or a barbecue.

And then the lips of the charred head parted and the mouth gaped wide like a second smaller wound within the larger wound where Judge had crammed it into the gutted belly of the sin-offering, like a battery inside a flashlight's cavity, and the lips spoke to him in the language of Pentecost, which he alone could understand.

—*You are mine*.

"All yours," Judge agreed. "Hallelujah!" Though there was in that hallelujah a faint uncertainty, a wavering, a diminishment of rapture, for even as he looked at it, the blackened face of the sacrifice shifted and changed, to become the face so well-known to him from all their hours of communion together, yet not Brother Orson's either wholly, but also his own.

—*Mine entirely*, the severed head insisted, with a wink of its blistered eyelid over the hollow socket.

It was as though he were looking at his own corrupted flesh, as though the promise so long and so certainly promised him had been withdrawn and in its place only a plate of worms and maggots.

And in that moment he knew the flames of the fire about him were not the flames of Pentecost, not of the spirit only, but a physical fire that was licking at the walls around him and searing his own flesh.

—*You need not feel the flames*, the face before him promised. *All their heat will be as a cool lotion to your skin if you will only take up the caduceus and worship me. But quickly, you have only a little time before the caduceus itself is consumed.*

Judge took up the caduceus from where it lay on the smoldering bed.

—*Repeat after me: Thou, Mercury, art my god. I place my being in thy care.*

Judge shook his head.

—*You must say the words. I cannot help you otherwise.*

"You are *not* my god!" Judge protested fiercely. "My god is the god who delivered Shadrach, Meshach, and Abednego from the burning fiery furnace, and he'll deliver me now. 'Cause I *believe* in him, and that's his promise to those who do."

—*You have never believed in anyone but me, you deluded ignorant redneck asshole, and I'm the only hope you have left. Not for eternity. Only for this moment's anesthetic. Now kneel and adore me. Or, if you prefer, die in agony.*

The fire was all around him, inescapable. There was a terrible smell of burning meat, as the flames reached his father's corpse and began to crisp its skin.

Judge knelt and closed his eyes and repeated the words of his damnation. "Thou, Mercury, art my god. I place my being in thy care."

—*Now I lay my soul in pawn.*

"Now I lay my soul in pawn."

—*This upon thy staff I swear.*

It was too much, he would not do it. Though all his life had been a lie and this false god the very core of that lie, he would not commit this last abject abomination. He thrust the caduceus into the flames rising from the bed and held it there until it had been consumed, a burnt offering such as the law demands.

EPILOGUE

"Ms. Winckelmeyer?" the doctor's receptionist called out, looking up from her switchboard toward the ceiling, as though she would not venture to guess which of the three people in the waiting room, Judith, Henry, or her lawyer, might be the Ms. Winckelmeyer in question.

Judith stood up, and the lawyer leaned forward in his chair by way of indicating his willingness to accompany her into the doctor's office. She signaled by a curt shake of her head that that wouldn't be necessary.

"I won't be gone long," she assured Henry, who did not look up from the puzzle cube in his hands.

The assurance might well have been more for her own sake than the boy's. The last time she'd been here at Willowville Memorial Hospital, she'd been kept incommunicado for two days and in quarantine for another week, not exactly the treatment one expects after almost being murdered. Her lawyer had assured her that even if the hospital had acted at the behest of the police, she had good grounds for a suit. But Judith did not have a litigious nature, and indeed was secretly grateful for having been spared the very worst of the news for so long. Had she known, in the days immediately afterwards, the extent of the horrors that had taken place, she might well not have been able to recover so quickly from her own traumas.

However, it helped to have the hospital's director think that she had such legal leverage, since it had allowed *her* to postpone the date of this meeting these many months and to set the agenda for what she would and would not discuss. If there were matters that she must be informed of, as the director insisted there were, and if these could not be imparted in a letter or over the phone, she was willing to receive that information, but she felt no answering obligation to satisfy his curiosity.

In any case, she had no idea why Judge had done what he had done. It was not even certain *that* he had done it, at least not with regard to setting the house on fire. At first the police had thought the fire had been set by Ned, until it was pointed out that he had been in a state of coma since childhood. There had been so many horrors, and some of them so inexplicable (the decapitated head that had been identified as that of a northern Minnesota farmer, one Ray Bonner), that at last the prosecutors had given up trying to reconstruct the precise order in which Judge's horrors had been perpetrated. As to his motives, what possible motive but total lunacy could there ever be for such actions?

The director's office bore a generic resemblance to all such, with decor that served no practical purpose but ritual expense: walls of never-to-be-read leather-bound books; a single abstract oil, crisp-edged organic forms in soothing earth tones; three framed diplomas (in case anyone doubted the man's bona fides); and a concealed bar that had already been swung into sight by way of declaring the director's, and the hospital's, willingness to forget and be forgotten.

Dr. Sackuvich introduced himself and offered his formal regrets for Judith's treatment by the hospital, speaking with a constraint and stiffness that Judith found more congenial than the smoother maneuvers of a PR expert. He was a short, balding, middle-aged man who tried to remedy his general dowdiness with a bold mustache.

After the formalities Dr. Sackuvich asked after the children, and Judith explained, somewhat reluctantly (for she didn't see how they were his concern), that Jason Schechner had agreed to adopt the boy named after him. The other twin, Henry, had been staying with Judith at her deceased father's home in Willowville, and would accompany her when she returned, sometime in October, to Florida.

"And you feel that their separation at this time . . . ?"

"They would certainly have stayed together if that had seemed the better course." She did not elaborate.

"Yes, I'm sure you would not have . . . I didn't mean to, um, poke my nose in. And of course they've been well provided for. The late Dr. Michaels was unusually, um, well, that's none of my business. The reason I insisted on seeing you, Ms. Winckelmeyer, has to do with a letter that was found in the Obstschmecker home after the events of June 17. It had been written quite some time ago, and addressed to Dr. Michaels (though he would not have been a doctor when the letter was written). We believe— that is, the police believe—that it was kept in the possession of Dr. Michaels's grandmother, for it was discovered in a dresser in the one room of the house that was not destroyed by the fire. It was the police who found it, and who opened it." Dr. Sackuvich looked down at his desktop and cleared his throat. "But because of the nature of its contents, they thought it better that I be the one . . ."

"I take it that there's some reason why I should be acquainted with what is in that letter?"

Dr. Sackuvich nodded. "Yes, you should as Henry's adoptive mother, and the other boy's new parents should as well. I'm sorry I couldn't contact you until Mr. Schechner had returned to Cambridge. But the police wouldn't allow us to discuss this matter until a medical determination had been made in the disposition of your son's case. Your older son, that is—Judge."

Judith bit her lip. "I thought we had agreed, Doctor, that I would not be discussing my son's *case*, as you put it."

"Indeed. Well. Here is a Xerox of that letter. The police have the original, but they say the paper is too crumbly to bear much handling. Perhaps you should read the letter now, and then if you . . . have any questions . . ."

Judith took the four pages of the Xeroxed letter and read the message that, twenty-three years earlier, Henry Michaels had written to his son.

April 3, 1976

Dear Billy,

I hope you never have to read this letter. I wish even more I didn't have to write it. If you are reading it now, it'll probably mean that I'm dead, and that I've been dead for quite a while, since what I guess this is is a suicide note. Maybe I'll be stronger than I feel right now, maybe this will turn out to be a false alarm, I hope so. I love you, that's the basic thing, and if I kill myself, that's my own problem. I do love you though, Billy, you've got to believe that.

One way or another, dead or alive, what I've got to tell you is bad news. For both of us. It seems that I've got a fifty-fifty chance of having about the worst goddamn disease in all creation—and if I've got it, then there's an additional fifty-fifty chance that you do too. It's called Huntington's chorea. Chorea means having spastic-type fits, and the fits can be extreme, I've done research and seen pictures, and I don't want to go into the details here, but believe me it's awful, and the spastic fits aren't the worst of it. The *best* you can hope for is that you get locked up in the loony bin before you do something that gets your picture in the paper. There have been a lot of cases where that's happened, where someone just snaps and goes on a killing spree, someone who'd always been sane till that moment. And the damnedest part of it is there's no way the doctors can tell you *beforehand* if you've got Huntington's chorea or not.

It's in the genes, and you get it from one or the other of your parents. If one of them has it, then your own odds are fifty-fifty like I said. *But*—since it usually doesn't hit you till you're around forty or fifty or even later, you don't necessarily find out that you're at risk till you've already had kids of your own. My own dad died before it got to him, killed in Germany in the war, and I only found out that I'm a candidate two weeks ago from my sister-in-law Luisa. My brother Ed and I were never that close, he went into the Marines when I was still a kid after a big argument with my mother, which never got made up. We met a couple times later on but didn't get on any better as grown-ups than as kids. Anyhow, when Ed came down with this disease and was hospitalized, they knew from the way that genes work that I have got a fifty-fifty chance of inheriting it, too. Those may be good odds for poker but not for staking your life on. I always thought that if I became blind or had something equally awful happen to me, I would take the easy way out, but this was a situation I never made any contingency plans for. I haven't told Madge yet, and don't intend to, since we've already agreed we don't want any more kids.

But if I do kill myself, I don't want to put you in the position my dad put me and my brother in. He knew it was in his family, Luisa's looked into it and found out he had an aunt and an uncle who got put into asylums when he was a kid, and his dad—my granddad—went off the deep end when my dad was in high school. So my dad knew, and kept it a secret. The thing is, if I'd known, I don't think I'd have become a father. That's a terrible thing for a man to say to his own son, but think about it. Because you're in the same situation, or you will be when you get this letter. Maybe by then genetic research will have progressed to the point where there's a diagnostic test, but I'm not sure if there were such a test that I'd want to take it. If I knew for certain that one day I would inevitably come down with it, then I don't think I'd hesitate at all, I'd just pull the plug. This way I at least have that fifty-fifty chance, and if time goes by and it looks like my flip of the coin was lucky, then that will make your odds look better. So maybe for your sake I'll try and hang on, and if I do, then I guess I'll be explaining all this in person.

Anyhow, sometime or other you've got to be told, because one day soon—assuming you get this when you turn eighteen—you'll be thinking of having kids. And maybe you should think twice. I wish I could think of a positive note to end this letter on, but there isn't any pony in this shitpile, kid. I'm sorry.

 I luv ya!

Dad

 After Judith had finished reading the letter, she pretended for a while longer still to be reading it in order to avoid having to speak with Dr. Sackuvich.

At last he took the initiative. "I would have spared you having to read that until some later time, but the police insisted that both yourself and the Schechners, as the two boys' new parents, be informed as soon as possible."

"Because you think they're also . . . at risk?"

"Definitely, yes, they are at risk."

"But if the information in the letter is correct . . ."

"Essentially, it is, yes. Quite a good account for a layman to have written. Ordinarily it would not be appropriate to become . . . unduly alarmed. Both Dr. Michaels and his father, the writer of the letter, died without having shown any sign of the disease. However . . ." The doctor swiveled his chair sideways to avoid Judith's questioning gaze. "Let me be blunt, Ms. Winckelmeyer. Your son Judge's, um . . . breakdown—please hear me out, I realize this is a painful subject. Such bizarre behavior is an almost classic manifestation of a variety of Huntington's chorea that strikes in adolescence rather than later in life. In such cases dementia can be sudden and acute. And violent."

Dr. Sackuvich forced himself to look directly at Judith. "I hate to have to ask you this, Ms. Winckelmeyer, and it need not become a part of the official record, but was William Michaels the father of your son?"

"It would be pointless for me to deny it, wouldn't it?"

"I'm not asking this question from mere curiosity, Ms. Winckelmeyer, I hope you understand that. But this is a matter that has an important bearing on the future lives of Dr. Michaels's sons."

"Their chances, then, are . . . ?"

"As the letter states: fifty-fifty."

Judith closed her eyes and tried to pray, but there were no prayers left. Her heart was like the ruins of that burned house, fenced round, with nothing left for flames to consume.

"I'm sorry to have had to tell you this. But I must add, for what little it's worth, that the situation today with regard to medical knowledge is not quite what it was when Dr. Michaels's father wrote that letter. There has been no *cure* for Huntington's chorea, and no immediate prospect of one, but the genetic mechanism by which it is transmitted is now better understood, and there are diagnostic tests available that can indicate with fair certainty whether an individual at risk does or does not bear the gene for the disease."

"Do you mean that those two boys, now, at their age, could know with certainty that some day—But that's worse! That's a nightmare!"

"In some ways, yes, I have to agree. Medicine did not create Huntington's chorea, Ms. Winckelmeyer; it can only investigate it. We draw the map, you might say."

"I won't allow it!"

Dr. Sackuvich nodded solemnly. "No doubt it would be premature to administer such tests at this point. But when Dr. Michaels's sons are older, they *should* be told. At what age precisely is for you and Mr. and Mrs. Schechner to determine amongst yourselves. Then each boy can decide whether he wishes to be tested."

Judith stood up. "Doctor, if you don't mind, I'd really rather not continue this discussion."

"As you choose, Ms. Winckelmeyer," the doctor said without any change in his businesslike demeanor. "Thank you for having come in. I'll see that your lawyer receives the appropriate papers for you to sign. Again, you have my apologies for having imposed on you at a time of such stress."

Judith murmured an apology for her outburst, though she might more candidly have thanked the doctor for having relieved her of the immense burden of the guilt she'd felt as the mother of the monster who committed such unthinkable crimes. The gene had come from William, and so the fault was in no way hers, neither as his biological mother nor for having failed in his upbringing. With such an assurance, she might begin to feel a sorrow that was not mere bitterness and enfeeblement.

While the doctor hesitated whether to offer his hand for a parting handshake, Judith hurried back into the waiting room and there evaded her lawyer's questions by telling him that Dr. Sackuvich was waiting to discuss the papers that had to be signed. Then she excused herself and took Henry by the hand and led him out of the hospital and to the car in the parking lot.

"Did the doctor say you were better?" Henry asked, as he was buckled into the seat.

"Yes, he did. I'm fit as a fiddle."

"Can we go see the house now?"

"Oh, Henry, you don't want to do that. There's nothing to see. The part that didn't burn down has been torn down. There's nothing but a hole in the ground."

"You said!" With the marvelous facility for tears some six-year-olds still possess, Henry began to cry.

"When did I say that?"

"When Jason got to go to the funeral and I had to stay home. You said you'd drive me to see where the fire was before we went away to Florida."

"But it's at least an hour's drive from here."

"You promised!"

She had, in fact, made such a promise, and it would not be an auspicious way to begin their life together if she were to reneg in a matter of such symbolic significance. Besides, she was curious herself to see the result of the fire.

During the drive she played a cassette of Couperin's *Leçons de Tenebre* that must have been the last piece of music Ben had listened to in the car. Henry continued to work the puzzle cube with what seemed an abnormal attention span for a six-year-old. For the rest of their lives together, she realized, she would be assessing everything he did in terms of normality and abnormality, sane and insane.

The Couperin and the September weather helped settle her nerves, and by the time they'd reached the corner of Calumet and Ludens (with only one wrong turn, as they exited the thruway), Judith was feeling much steadier on her pins.

An eight-foot-high cyclone fence had been constructed around the property, and the demolition work on the charred shell of the house had been completed, leaving only the gaping L-shaped cavity of the basement and the stumps of the fireplace and of the backyard elm, also a victim of the fire. Already the front lawn, never well cared for, was thick with waist-high weeds.

"If the fence wasn't there, we could go over and look right inside the basement," Henry noted respectfully.

"Yes, but the fence is there. So we can't."

"How long did it take for the fire to burn down the house?"

"I don't know, but probably not very long or the people wouldn't have been caught inside."

"I'll bet there was a big explosion, like when a bomb goes off. Jason says if you turn on the stove but don't light it, the house fills up with the gas, and then if someone lights just one match, *boom!*"

Henry seemed to take such satisfaction from this explanation that she did not undermine it by pointing out that the stove in the Obstschmecker kitchen had been electric. Her own imaginings of what had happened that day were no more informed, finally, than his.

"Jason says they all must've gone to sleep first, from breathing in the smoke, and they never felt themselves being burned. That's what Uncle Jason told him. But I think he just said that to keep Jason from crying all the time."

"It's impossible to say exactly what happened, Henry. If Jason wants to think that, there's no point arguing with him."

"It was Jason who *started* the argument. I'm glad it's him who's going to live with Mr. Schechner and not me. He treats you like you're a baby." Henry glanced sideways to see if this had registered, as it was intended, as a declaration of loyalty to Judith.

She knew that this would be the proper moment to give the boy a hug, a kiss, some better assurance than words that he was loved and protected. But the knowledge was mere administrative reflex from years of social work and crisis management. It sprang from no deeper source. In any case she didn't have the energy to deal with the seat belts. It was all she could do to shift from park and steer the car along Ludens. At Brouwer she turned right and drove the six blocks to Brosner Park. There she parked again.

"Would you like to play in the park for a bit?" she suggested to Henry. "I just want to sit and think for a while before we drive back to Willowville. Okay?"

"Okay," he agreed sullenly.

He popped open his seat belt and took up his knapsack with the puzzle cube and a follow-the-dots book and other time-passing toys. "How long?" he asked, standing outside the car.

"Five minutes?"

He looked at his wristwatch. It was not quite three thirty. "Okay, I'll be back in five minutes."

He set off into the park, steering clear of the area around the swings and teeter-totters, which were securely in the possession of a bunch of older black kids. He looked around for somewhere shady to sit, where he could just go on twisting the puzzle cube till he got at least two sides to be the same color, but all the trees seemed to have disappeared.

Then the far-off sound of a chain saw explained what had happened to the trees. They were being cut down! At the other end of the park was a green truck with a ladder on it, like a fire engine, and a man on the ladder was sawing off the branches of one of the few trees that was still left.

Ordinarily Henry would have gone over to watch such a process, but that would have meant walking through the playground area with all the black kids. So instead he went in the other direction, up the hill to where the lopped-off limbs of three other trees had already been piled into big stacks. The tree trunks were still in place, like arms reaching up and the fingers of their hands cut off at the knuckle. Henry considered climbing up one of the stacks of wood, but without Jason or someone daring him to, there didn't seem to be much point.

Then something on the ground beside the nearest woodpile caught his attention. A stick. There were a lot of sticks all round the woodpile, of course, but somehow this one seemed different. Partly it must have been its twisty shape. Partly something else he couldn't figure out.

He picked it up and looked at it more closely. It was about as long as a ruler and almost as straight, and right where his finger would have felt the trigger if it were a ray gun was a knob.

Someday (although Henry had never told this to anyone yet, not even to Jason), when he grew up, he was going to be a fighter pilot in the air force. He'd fly a jet with four laser cannons.

Like this one: he pretended the stick was his cannon and the knob its trigger. Then he aimed it, with one hundred percent accuracy, at another fighter jet (actually at a robin that had alighted on top of the woodpile) and pulled the trigger, and made a machine-gun sound and told the robin it was dead.

A NOTE ABOUT THE AUTHOR

Thomas M. Disch was born in Des Moines, Iowa, in 1940 and grew up in Minnesota. He was educated at New York University and currently lives in New York City.

A NOTE ON THE TYPE

This book was set in a digitized version of Janson, a redrawing of type cast from matrices long thought to have been made by the Dutchman Anton Janson, who was a practicing type founder in Leipzig during the years 1668–87. However, it has been conclusively demonstrated that these types are actually the work of Nicholas Kis (1650–1702), a Hungarian, who most probably learned his trade from the master Dutch type founder Dirk Voskens. The type is an excellent example of the influential and sturdy Dutch types that prevailed in England up to the time William Caslon developed his own incomparable designs from them.

Composed by Graphic Composition, Inc., Athens, Georgia
Printed and bound by R. R. Donnelley & Sons,
Harrisburg, Virginia
Typography and binding design
by Virginia Tan